"If a reader is a fan of the J.R. Ward and Lara Adrian series,
and is jonesing for something similar,
this may fit the bill."
—*Dear Author*

"This is Kaylea Cross's first crack at paranormal romance,
and she hit a home run…. Not only was the writing
near flawless, but the suspense around the lore and the
new twist on the supernatural element at work here was
a breath of fresh air…. I think fans of Kresley Cole's
Immortals After Dark series will love this book."
—*Paranormal Wastelands Crazy Book Reviews*

"Even if paranormal romance is not your typical genre,
I suggest trying *Darkest Caress* out. This book has romance,
suspense, passion, friendship, evil, grief and love in it. It was
a tough book to put down, since it had me
on the edge from the beginning until the end."
—*Magical Musings*

Praise for Kaylea Cross

"The battle scenes were very exciting…
vivid and fascinating. I felt immersed in the action."
—*Dear Author* on *Deadly Descent*

"Great action scenes… If you are a fan of military
or suspense romance I definitely recommend."
—*Smexy Books Romance Reviews* on *Deadly Descent*

"A few of the things I love the most about Cross'
writing is that she does such an amazing and incredible job
of describing everything that is going on."
—*The Bookpushers*

Also available from Kaylea Cross and Carina Press

Deadly Descent
Tactical Strike

Coming soon from Kaylea Cross and Carina Press

Lethal Pursuit

DARKEST
CARESS

KAYLEA CROSS

CARINA
PRESS™

Recycling programs for this product may not exist in your area.

CARINA PRESS™

ISBN-13: 978-0-373-00210-8

DARKEST CARESS

Copyright © 2012 by Kaylea Cross

www.CarinaPress.com

Printed in U.S.A.

Dear Reader,

I hate flying, so never in my *wildest* imaginings did I ever think I'd wind up visiting the Baltic states. But that's exactly what I did in the fall of 2010. (See? Never say never.)

While in Lithuania touring the Curonian Spit and the spectacular seaside town of Nida, I got hooked on the ancient folklore of the area. During a tour of the Hill of Witches, I swore I felt magic tremble in the air. That's when the idea for this story first whispered to me.

Standing on that ancient, pagan site of worship amidst the folklore sculptures, I listened raptly as our guide regaled us with tales of witches and devils, mythological creatures and the powerful sea goddess Neringa, who threw sand from her apron to form the Curonian Spit and its huge sand dunes to protect local fishermen from the fury of the Baltic Sea. Though I normally write military romantic suspense, I just couldn't ignore the story line for this book.

With a little encouragement I sat down to write *Darkest Caress*, and wove the ancient legends I'd heard about into my modern-day story. I hope you enjoy it!

Happy reading,

Kaylea Cross

For Cousin Mike, the best travel partner of all time. I will always cherish my memories of our trip to the Baltics, especially that anti-cyclone in Lithuania. Good thing that cross was strong enough to hold you!

For my Dad, who shoved me outside my comfort zone and made me expand my horizons.

Last but not least, to Katie and Rhonda for believing in this story. And in me.

DARKEST
CARESS

KAYLEA CROSS

is an award-winning author of military romantic suspense. Her books have won a Heart of Excellence Award and a Laurel Wreath Award, and have twice been shortlisted for an EPIC Award. A Registered Massage Therapist, Kaylea is an avid gardener, artist, Civil War buff, special ops aficionado, belly dancer and former nationally carded softball pitcher. She lives in Vancouver, British Columbia, with her husband and two little men.

Her books always feature alpha military heroes, and showcase the incredible capabilities of our men and women in uniform. She loves researching so much that despite her fear of flying, she even braved a few helicopter rides so she could interview the pilots and experience flying in a helo firsthand. To get through it, the whole time she secretly imagined she was a spec ops soldier heading into enemy territory.

Visit www.kayleacross.com to find out more about Kaylea and her books.

CHAPTER ONE

FIRST TIME IN weeks she'd seen that creep, and still she came down with a migraine.

Liv Farrell downed two extra-strength Excedrin then checked her rearview mirror again. The road behind her was empty, but she couldn't shake the thought that he might have followed her.

Stop. You're being paranoid. And you have more important things to worry about right now.

She squinted as she pulled into the mansion's long driveway, but those damned sparks started to dance before her eyes. She loved her youngest piano student, but the same couldn't be said of the girl's father. After he'd been sexually inappropriate with her one time too many, she'd threatened to stop teaching the girl unless the mother brought her to and from her lessons. The arrangement had worked fine, until tonight.

Now, because of him, Liv had the mother of all headaches to deal with while she faced what might be the most important property showing of her realty career.

A blast of muggy, sea-tinged air hit her face when she climbed out of her car. She winced. Not even the sight of the gorgeous stone mansion could dim the pounding in her head. Swallowing hard against the slicing pain, she fought back the wave of nausea that threatened to bring up what little dinner she'd forced down her throat. More than anything she just wanted to go home and curl up in the dark with an ice pack on the back of her neck, but this was one appointment she couldn't reschedule.

As she neared the walkway to the front door, a blessedly cool breeze whipped up from the ocean at the foot of the bluff. She gazed up at the sprawling house before her with a strange sense of familiarity. Of all the high-end properties on her list, this was her favorite by far. Set on seven acres of park-like grounds, the three-story limestone mansion looked like it belonged outside of Paris, with its graceful slate roofline and twin *vers-de-gris* cupolas. The deceased's executor had finally cleared the legal hurdles and made the decision to list the property last night, so it wasn't even officially listed yet. She had no idea how this prospective buyer had found out about it.

On her way to the front door the heady scent of roses mixed with the rich perfume of the stargazer lilies, punctuating the thick border on either side of the path. Ordinarily she loved flowers, but right now the smell made her stomach roll.

When she stepped inside the house, the clean scent of lemon oil soap greeted her, along with a breath of cool air from the air conditioning. Sighing in relief, she set her briefcase down and took a moment to look around the huge vaulted mahogany ceilings of the foyer and family room before her gaze strayed to the west facing windows on the far wall. The view beyond was enough to take her breath away, but there was something about this house that called to her. Something that had resonated inside her when she'd driven past it the first time a few months ago, long before it landed on her list.

Too bad she didn't have the tens of millions to buy it. And then another million a year to maintain it and pay the taxes.

Whoever he was, the man coming to meet her must have more money than he knew what to do with. Doing a quick run through of the main floor to make sure everything was as it should be, she stopped in the kitchen and turned on some soft lights over the stainless steel range and under the moldings above the rich cream cabinets. It cast the room in a soft, inviting glow.

She glanced at her watch. A few minutes before eight. Just enough time for her to step out onto the marble balcony and admire the sunset.

The security system beeped, signaling someone had opened the front door. "Hello?" a deep, masculine voice called out.

Doing her best to conceal how much pain she was in, she tugged on the hem of her gray pencil skirt and started out of the kitchen. "Coming," she answered, but before she'd stepped into the hallway a man's silhouette appeared there, blocking her path.

Before she'd even caught a glimpse of his face, his scent hit her, a rich mix of evergreen and spice that lessened the nausea and made her pull in an appreciative breath. As he came toward her the air conditioning kicked on high. A deliciously cool wave swept through the room, bringing more of his luscious scent with it. But the polite greeting she'd prepared died on her tongue the moment he stepped out of the shadows and entered the light. They both froze.

Icy blue eyes speared hers. He was tall, over six feet, broad-shouldered. His dark brown hair was cut short, the strong planes of his face clean-shaven. He looked to be in his mid to late thirties, the swells of muscle beneath his snug black dress shirt telling her he kept in very good shape.

Shock flickered in his eyes for a split second before he masked it. Unfortunately she didn't recover as quickly. A sudden ripple of heat spread over her face, flowing down her spine like the lazy stroke of a lover's hand. Under his intent gaze, somehow the raging headache receded to a dull throb. Her heart sped up, the pulse point in her neck throbbing erratically with the force of his penetrating stare. Surprisingly, the pain didn't increase.

The man gazed back at her, unmoving, imposing as hell as he sized her up with a lingering sweep of those eerie blue eyes. Stunned by her reaction to him, she looked into those pale depths and struggled to find her voice.

"H-hi," she finally said, inwardly cursing her awkwardness as she held out her hand. "I'm Olivia Farrell."

His long fingers curled around hers in a firm grip, warm and undeniably masculine. "Daegan Blackwell."

That low voice rolled over her suddenly heightened senses, started a strange tingling in the pit of her stomach. Not sharp enough to be fear. More like insanely strong butterflies. Daegan. An ancient name. It was sexy, suiting its owner perfectly along with the faint Irish lilt she detected in his voice. A primitive shiver rippled through her, the heat of his palm lingering on hers after she pulled away.

She put a hand to her stomach and stepped back. Weird. She'd had several migraines over the past few months, but the symptoms had never gone away this fast before. "I'm so glad you could come see the property. Since we're already here, shall we start with the kitchen?"

"That's fine."

Forcing away the lingering physical awareness of him, Liv shifted into professional mode and started the tour. He followed her in unnerving silence, his eyes taking in every detail she pointed out, scanning the surroundings with a thoroughness she found intimidating. The only indication that he was listening to her was his occasional nod.

Nerves began to take hold as she neared the staircase leading to the lower floor. Did he not like the place? Or was her subconscious trying to warn her something was wrong about this whole setup?

She hesitated at the top of the staircase, her pulse drumming at her temples. She was about to go downstairs with a complete stranger who unnerved her. The can of pepper spray in her pocket seemed completely inadequate all of a sudden. And yet…she wasn't truly afraid of him. A dangerous vibe clung to him, but she sensed it wasn't directed at her. Unlike the blatant, masculine interest in his eyes. That was *definitely* aimed at her. The thought sent a primal shiver down her spine.

When she looked over her shoulder he was watching her closely. As though he could see *into* her. She blinked.

Those beautiful, cold eyes regarded her thoughtfully for a moment. "Are you not feeling well?"

She put a hand to her temple, a blush spreading across her cheeks. The bright lighting from the stairwell probably washed her out, but she hadn't realized it made her look that bad. "I'm fine, thanks. Just a headache." Actually the pain was much better than it had been. The air conditioning seemed to be taking the worst of it away, thank God.

"We can continue the tour tomorrow if you'd prefer." His voice was deep, commanding.

A pang of guilt stabbed her. "It's fine, really. But I appreciate the offer."

His gaze never wavered from hers. "You don't need to show me the lower floor if you're uncomfortable taking me downstairs. I can find my own way around."

She barely stopped her mouth from falling open. How did he know? Was she doing that poor a job of hiding it? "No, don't be silly. I'm not uncomfortable." Well, maybe a little, but she wasn't worried that he'd do anything to her. It was his magnetic presence and too-knowing eyes that bothered her.

Shaking herself, she walked down the stairs to show him the entertainment areas. A billiards room with an antique table, a fully equipped gym, a movie theater and fully stocked wine cellar. He said nothing, following a few strides behind, moving so silently she never heard his footsteps. All the while, she felt his presence like a physical touch against her back.

After climbing to the upper floor and showing him the lavish bedrooms, she led him back to the living room and forced a smile. "Well? What do you think?"

"It's nice."

Nice? She lifted an eyebrow. "You don't like it?"

He watched her carefully. "Do you?"

Was he kidding? "It's a rare, beautiful home. The finishing rivals some of the most expensive manors in Europe."

"I take it that's a yes." The barest hint of a smile curved one side of his mouth, warmed his frigid eyes a fraction.

Some of the jitters subsided and she grinned. "Yes, I like it. I love it." Spreading her arms, she gestured to the open room before them. "Just look at the solid mahogany in this room, and that view." She nodded toward the floor-to-ceiling windows framing the brilliant streaks of color lighting the sky.

Her high-heeled sandals made a light tapping sound on the cream marble floors as she made her way over to admire the breathtaking view. The sun was almost at the horizon, bathing the sky with rosy and purple hues spilling over the glittering water. In the distance, the San Juan Islands rose out of the sea like slate blue whales' backs breaching the surface of the Strait.

When she turned back to him, he smiled. It completely transformed his face, turning him from potently attractive to dangerously gorgeous. It made his crystalline eyes sparkle, showed off a hint of even, white teeth. "Maybe you should buy it then."

"If I had the money I would in a heartbeat." She folded her hands in front of her before continuing. "The price includes all the furnishings, but if they don't suit your taste I can—"

"They're fine."

Fine, he said. As in, *meh*. With effort she kept from frowning at him. "Mr. Blackwell—"

"Daegan," he corrected.

"Daegan," she amended, fighting the ridiculous flush trying to engulf her face. Using his first name seemed…intimate for some reason. "I'm curious to know how you found out about the property. It hasn't been advertised yet."

"Heard through a friend it was up for sale."

Must be a well-connected friend to get that kind of information before it was even listed. "Do you have a big family?"

Those beautiful eyes settled on hers. "If you mean a wife and kids, no."

Oh. Why did that make her heart leap? "It's a rather large house for one person."

"I'm going to need a big place." He glanced around the room, then out at the vivid sunset. "For all the… relatives coming to live with me."

Something about the way he said it struck her as cryptic, but she didn't press him for more. "I'd be happy to show you the grounds if you like. There's a hot tub out on the edge of the cliff and a beautiful formal rose garden with a fountain."

A cynical smile touched his lips. "I'm not really into gardening."

No, he wouldn't be, she mused. He seemed more like a high-powered CEO or something, though his controlled demeanor and posture spoke of something far more dangerous. Military maybe? She hated to think he might be a drug dealer or gangster of some sort. "Do you want to walk outside for a while?" Headache be damned, she needed this sale.

Again, that potent gaze held her captive. "No, I've

seen enough for tonight." He took a step toward her and she instinctively backed up, alarmed by the powerful effect he had on her. When he raised his hand she stiffened, but he only touched her throbbing temple briefly.

She was too stunned to pull away. That spicy evergreen scent intensified when his palm brushed her cheek ever so gently, his smell filling her lungs, loosening her muscles. Warmth flowed from his hand. The remaining pain in her skull instantly faded to a dull ache.

She blinked as a towering wave of sexual heat suffused her body. Before she could move, he lowered his hand and stepped back. A curious hollow sensation settled in the pit of her stomach.

His gaze was inscrutable. "Thanks for the tour, Olivia."

A hot rush of moisture collected between her thighs at the sound of her name spoken in that intoxicating voice. She flushed, horrified by the way her nipples had tightened against the cups of her bra, but couldn't think of a single thing to say. What was wrong with her? She'd never reacted to a man this way before.

His mouth curved into an amused smile, as though he knew what she was thinking. "I'll be in touch tomorrow. Have a good night."

He left her there staring after him in helpless astonishment, his scent still permeating the air around her.

THE PERFECT ENDING to a bitch of a day, Daegan thought sourly.

Staring broodingly at the ocean, he slumped into the cushioned chair on the deck and brought his scotch to his lips. The water was like glass tonight, reflecting

the perfect half moon like a mirror on its clear surface. Calm. Tranquil. The exact opposite of how he felt.

His mind was in fucking chaos, and his body wasn't
far behind.

A sudden shadow moved through the light coming
from the living room. He glanced over in time to see
Cade pull the sliding glass doors open. His cousin's
moss-green eyes twinkled in amusement as he stepped
out onto the deck. "Well? Are we proud new home-
owners, or what?"

"Or what."

One dark gold eyebrow swooped up at his grim tone.
"You didn't like the place?"

"I liked it."

"Yeah, it shows." He nodded at the partially finished
drink in Daegan's hand.

Daegan sighed and leaned his head back against
the leather. His body was edgy, restless. Aching. And
it was going to get much, much worse before the night
was over. "I told her I'd call her tomorrow. I'll put in
an offer in the morning." He was looking forward to
that about as much as sticking a knife into his eye. But
he had no choice. This was how it was meant to be, no
matter how much he rebelled against that reality.

Cade frowned. "Nice attitude. Somebody put a dent
in your Porsche on the way back or something?"

"Nope." He took another sip of his drink, wanting
to be alone.

Never one to pick up on subtle cues, Cade sat in the
chair across from him, resting his thick forearms on
his thighs. "Then what's up?"

Daegan slanted him an irritated look, swirling the ice around in his glass. "The woman."

His cousin leaned back with a big shit-eating grin on his face. "You hit on her and she turned you down?"

"No," he growled, fighting back the knot tightening around his lungs. He stared out at the ocean, envying its serenity. Starting now, his life was going to be in turmoil for the foreseeable future. All their lives were. "She's my mate." He almost strangled on the word.

Cade's jaw fell open. His eyes bulged. Daegan might have laughed at the stunned look on his cousin's face if there'd been any humor in the situation. "You're *shitting* me."

"Wish I was." God, did he ever. This was the last thing he needed. The last thing *they* needed. He took another bracing swallow of scotch, but the burn did nothing to mellow him out. At least now he knew why the pull to settle them in Vancouver had been so strong. A little warning would've been nice, though.

A shocked silence spread between them, the tension rising higher and higher in Daegan's gut while he waited for his cousin to say something.

"Did you foresee this?" Cade asked finally.

Daegan snorted. "Nope." And wasn't that ironic? He swallowed a bitter laugh with his next sip of scotch.

"What did she say?"

"Nothing." That bothered him too. He'd never expected this. Not to meet her, and certainly not for the predicament that came with her. "She doesn't know anything."

Cade gaped for a moment longer, then ran a hand over the back of his neck. As though he was the one wanting to crawl out of his skin to ease the emotions tearing through him. "Shit, man, are you sure she's… you know."

Daegan aimed a baleful glare at him. "Yeah, I'm sure." It wasn't something an Empowered male could miss. Being struck by a hormonal lightning bolt tended to get a man's attention. "For Christ's sake, Cade, look at me." He gestured to himself, his body already strung taut as a tripwire, every muscle quivering with sexual tension. Already a goddamn mess, fighting to hold it together. And it had only been two hours since he'd laid eyes on her.

"But the prophecy states—"

"I know what it says," he snapped. *The three shall become six, and together with The Lost they shall battle the Obsidian Lord for the fate of mankind.*

Whatever the fuck that really meant.

Cade watched him for a full minute, his expression full of alarm. "But it can't mean we're all gonna be mated." He sounded horrified, like the idea of it was worse than death. For Cade, it probably was. "What about Vaughn?"

"I don't know." None of it made any sense, because Vaughn would never mate again. Couldn't. But even if he could have, why would they meet their mates now, when the war was about to start anew? The premonitions had shown him that much at least. The Obsidian Lord was out there somewhere. Biding his time before he struck.

"Want more of that?" Cade finally asked, gesturing to the near empty glass.

"Yeah." While his cousin went inside to get the bottle, and probably a glass for himself, Daegan gazed out at the water, wondering what the hell to do. It was all so incredible he could only shake his head.

After almost two centuries he'd finally come face to face with his mate, and she hadn't even recognized him. Not only that, but she obviously didn't have a clue what she was. What they were, and what was coming.

Or that she held the power to destroy them all.

The knowledge made the protective male in him roar to life, filling him up in a violent surge that took his breath away. His hand shook when he raised the glass and drained it. As the liquor burned down his throat, he prayed for numbness. Shit, it was starting already. The bonding need. His heart pounded out of control from the hormones flooding his bloodstream and he could feel his eyes getting brighter. Then brighter yet, glowing until they practically lit up the darkness like pale blue lasers. His muscles trembled with the need to find her, claim her, bind her to him.

His cock went rigid as an image of her slammed into his brain. Olivia's bright hazel-green eyes gazing up at him, filled with raw need as he pressed her down into the bed in that stone mansion's master suite. His hands wound into her deep caramel waves. Her naked, curvy body writhed beneath him, raising his need to a fever pitch. Her elegant hands clutched at his shoulders, her slender fingers digging into his muscles. That soft pink mouth opened in a cry of raw ecstasy as he plunged into her warmth.

The sliding glass door opened again. Daegan looked over at Cade as a bead of sweat rolled down his temple.

"Jesus," Cade muttered, hurrying over to snatch the glass from him.

With a start, Daegan realized he'd squeezed the tumbler so hard he'd cracked it. The fracture lines spread out across the surface, catching and reflecting the unearthly blue glow of his eyes.

His cousin set it down on the granite-topped table beside them and gave him a worried look. "Do you, uh…want another one?"

Squeezing his hands into fists, Daegan closed his eyes and leaned back into the leather, fighting the urgent need enveloping him. He didn't want anyone seeing him this way. He was the leader, the strongest of them. Had to lead by example.

But even he couldn't fight biology.

"Just leave the bottle and go," he rasped.

A soft clink came as Cade set the bottle on the table. "Do you need anything?"

As a doctor, Cade had access to all kinds of meds, but nothing short of unconsciousness would help stop the Heat Cycle. Daegen wasn't that far gone. Yet. "No."

"I'll have my cell on if you need me."

Daegan nodded without opening his eyes, fighting to get control of his body and slow his breathing as Cade left. His skin felt too tight, like it might split apart from the heat and pressure inside him. Tonight marked the first of his descent into hell, but his cousin couldn't help him now. Only one person could, and she was completely unaware of what was about to hit her.

CHAPTER TWO

Barcelona, Spain

XAVIER STARED OUT the window of his hotel penthouse suite at the sparkling Med below. The endless expanse of blue was as rich as sapphires under the July sun, rolling gently against the ribbon of sandy beach. The sea was a living, breathing thing, full of endless power. He could practically feel the rhythm of the tide pulsing in his veins, filling his aging muscles with strength.

As always, the pull of Neringa's ancient magic was strong for him. Sometimes when he walked the shore he thought he heard her speaking to him in the old language, whispering above the sighing of the waves. Trying to call him back.

But for him there was no going back.

A knock at the door signaled his lunch had arrived. He crossed the room and unlocked the deadbolt before opening the door. A fiftyish woman stood there in her black and white uniform, her head downcast so she didn't have to meet his eyes. After two weeks here, very few of the staff were brave enough to make eye contact with him. But he sensed something more in her than wariness. A lingering sadness in the droop of her shoulders.

He stepped aside to let her push the trolley bearing

his meal inside, and as she passed him he caught the first raw surge of pain radiating from her. There was unease, too, but pain overpowered it. Loss. He could smell it now, an acrid sting in his nostrils. She'd lost someone close to her. Someone she'd loved with all her heart. His gaze fastened on her hungrily, his lungs expanding as his body prepared to absorb the powerful emotion.

Setting the trolley next to the dining table, the woman dared a quick glance up at his face and bobbed a curtsey. Despite himself, his heart lurched. Her skin was pale, her dark eyes holding the source of pain he wanted to drink from so badly. He needed it more than he needed the food she'd brought. But those eyes. They pierced the shell protecting the remnants of his blackened, withered soul.

With effort he clenched his jaw and turned away, blocking the intense impulse to feed. She reminded him too much of Marie. He couldn't look at her, hated his body's need to gorge on her pain. He trembled as the door closed softly behind her, his body battling for control as he let the memories of his dead mate wash over him. They raked at him with sharp claws, the jagged remains of his life that fuelled his existence and forged him into the empty thing he'd become. Into the monster he soon would be.

His phone vibrated against his hip, bringing him back to the present. "Diga."

"I think I've found a lead," a male voice said in English, his strong New York accent flavoring the words.

Xavier's hand tightened around the phone, a spark of excitement flashing through him. "What kind of lead?"

"It took some digging, but I found documents show-ing this British soldier that emigrated to Boston eleven years ago."

He frowned. "And?"

"Well the date of birth is weird," the man went on. "It has to be a mistake, because it lists him being born in eighteen-ten, and that would mean he went to Bos-ton when he was over a hundred and seventy years old, which is impossible."

Not necessarily, Xavier thought, fighting the hum of anticipation buzzing through his veins. "Go on."

"I assume the date of birth should read nineteen-ten, which would make it possible for him to have served during the war, so I kept digging like you told me."

This had better be good. They all knew better than to waste his time. The stark consequences ensured that. "Anything else?"

"Yeah. The guy crossed into Canada six months ago. Even with the date correction, he'd still be over a hundred years old. I find that very unlikely."

Xavier's heart quickened. This could potentially be the first solid lead he'd found about the Empowered in decades. "Where did he cross?"

"Near Vancouver."

Something inside him stilled. The jewel of a city was nestled right against the ocean. A necessary source of strength for their kind when they settled in any place for longer than a few months. "What's his name?"

"Daegan Blackwell. Sound familiar?"

No, but it didn't matter. "Send me everything you can find on him."

"That's just it, sir, there's nothing. And I mean *noth-*

ing. It's like he vanished into thin air the moment he crossed the Canadian border."

Is that so. A slow smile pulled at Xavier's mouth. If he was an Empowered, the man could easily have wiped the mortals' memories clean. "Did he cross alone?"

"I don't know. I couldn't find anything more."

"Get some people over there and find him. Report anything you find to me immediately." He injected a hard edge into the command, so there would be no mistaking the consequences for failure.

"Yes, sir." His voice held a distinct note of apprehension.

He felt it, Xavier realized with a start. Even an ocean away, through the phone connection he could actually *feel* the man's unease. The ravenous hunger inside him begged for the sustenance.

On the other end of the line the man kept babbling, but Xavier didn't hear a word, focused solely on the palpable fear in his voice. The complex emotions layered within it entranced him. He closed his eyes, letting the thread of apprehension slide into him, readily absorbing it into his cells.

A euphoric haze filled his brain, his skin tingling as he fed off the new power source. He could feel his cells expand, swell throughout his body. Warmth flowed through his veins. His organs filled with it, his shriveled muscles grew.

He barely heard the thud on the other end of the phone as the man lost consciousness and dropped to the floor. If Xavier didn't stop, the man would die. He didn't even try to fight the endless thirst that plagued him. The need for more power drove him, his body greedily sucking the energy from its victim. When he'd extracted every last drop possible, Xavier inhaled deeply then disconnected. His hand was completely steady as he slipped the phone back into his pocket and drew a slow, deep breath to calm his racing heart. Fresh power tingled, surging inside him. He felt stronger than ever before. Like he was twenty-five years old all over again. Damn near invincible.

His eyes. He had to check his eyes.

Rushing into the marble bathroom, he half expected them to light up the darkness. They didn't, so he flipped on the light and peered at his reflection. A shiver of anticipation sped through his muscles. His once dark brown eyes were nearly yellow in his pale, withered face, with only a trace of hazel remaining around the pupils. Soon they'd turn completely citrine. Then the final transformation would complete itself.

So close, he mused as he stroked two bony fingers over his sunken cheeks. He barely looked human anymore, but now his physical form was beginning to mirror the shattered soul within. A mirage. Physically he was more powerful than he'd ever been in his over three-hundred-year existence. His outward appearance was merely an advantage. No one would guess what he was capable of in a body that looked like a seventy-five-year-old man's.

Not long now. The hardest part was behind him. Fueling and pushing him with relentless force toward his destiny.

His lips stretched in an awed smile, the unearthly gleam in his eyes sending a shiver of excitement up his spine. Almost seventy years he'd waited. An average human lifespan spent in a hellish state of limbo, focusing and channeling his rage until he could fully claim the title of Obsidian Lord. His Dark Army grew every day. His soldiers were ready. Soon he would be too.

Then he'd end this once and for all.

Liv JERKED AWAKE when her phone rang on her nightstand. She sat up and grabbed it, dragging a hand through her mussed hair to check the clock. The glowing blue numbers read eight minutes after seven. Who the hell would call her at this time of the morning? Catherine wasn't due here until eight and wouldn't dream of calling this early unless something was wrong. She frowned at the unfamiliar number on the call display.

"Olivia Farrell." Her voice was hoarse from sleep.

"Hey. Is the estate on the bluff still available?" a strangely familiar male voice demanded.

The sharp tone jolted her. Ignoring his rudeness, she fought back the fog in her brain and tried to figure out what he was talking about. "You mean the one on—"

"The stone mansion overlooking the ocean. It isn't even listed yet, but I understand it's been shown already."

She had no idea how he knew that. None of her coworkers even knew about it. Maybe he'd asked around and one of the neighbors had seen her there last night. "Who is this?"

A startled pause met her words. "It's Aaron Moore."

Her stomach seized. She shouldn't have answered her damn phone.

When she didn't respond he huffed out an impatient breath. "Melissa's father. I picked her up from her lesson last night." He sounded offended that she hadn't recognized his voice.

"Yeah. Hi." The man gave her the creeps, and she didn't blame his ex for wanting to be rid of him. In past encounters he'd made no effort to stop himself from being inappropriate or conceal the way he stripped her with his eyes. There was something cold about them. Cruel. And the calculating gleam in his gaze set off alarm bells every time she caught him staring at her.

When she'd first met him he'd stayed for the first ten minutes or so of each lesson, managing to make her uncomfortable in her own home with that same predatory air. He'd even come right out and hit on her a couple of times, despite the way she shut him down. The man had all the makings of a deviant.

After that she'd watched his interactions with Melissa carefully, wondering if his disturbing sexual vibe was in any way directed toward his daughter. Liv had even checked with the child's mother, but as far as she could tell everything was okay on that front. She didn't like Aaron, simple as that, and trusted him even less. That monster headache after seeing him last night merely proved he was toxic to her health.

"It's still available," she told him reluctantly. "Why?"

"I want to see it tonight."

"Why do you want to see *that* property?" He might be well off, but there was no way he had that kind of money available to him.

"It's not for me, it's for the CEO of my company," he said with a hint of annoyance. Tempered, she knew, since he'd been pissed off by her rudeness last night. "He's in Tokyo right now, but when I told him it might be for sale he asked me to look at it personally for him. He's very interested."

She didn't believe him for a second, yet she couldn't discount him entirely. Was this some lame attempt to get her alone with him? "I may have someone putting in an offer today." It was stretching the truth, but she wanted to put him off. She'd told him to his face never to come to her house again, been flat out rude to drive her point home, and still he'd shown up last night. Now this weird phone call.

"I'll be there at six sharp."

His high-handedness was starting to piss her off, but she managed to keep her tone civil. Showing him the property with another agent there as backup would be safe enough. Besides, Mr. Blackwell—Daegan—she mentally corrected, hadn't exactly seemed in love with the place last night, and she might never hear from him again. "Fine. Six o'clock." But no way in hell would she meet him alone. The man made her skin crawl.

"I'll see you then."

Liv tossed her phone to the foot of her bed with a disgusted snort and flopped back against her pillows. Talk about offensive. Phoning her that early in the morning and then having the gall to speak to her like she was some sort of servant? And after she'd spent most of the night tossing and turning from weird dreams too. Disturbing ones featuring the sexy prospective buyer she'd taken through the mansion.

Probably because she'd spent over an hour before bed researching him on the Internet. All she'd found was his name listed as the CEO of Trident Group, some mysterious company she hadn't been able to learn much about. No pictures of Daegan anywhere, just some information on Trident Group's holdings and charitable donations to places like children's hospitals and orphanages. Whatever Daegan did for a living, he was a generous philanthropist. Unfortunately that only attracted her more.

At least her headache was pretty much gone, she thought with a sigh. Only a vague tension remained in her neck and temples, no doubt brought on by the idea of having to see Aaron later on. Damn, she was tired.

She frowned and rubbed at her nape, trying to remember what the dreams had been about. Erotic flashes came back to her. Nebulous images of Daegan looming above her on a wide sleigh bed draped in dark satin sheets. His naked body poised above hers, large hands pinning her wrists above her head as he pushed his rock-hard erection into her.

Let me ease you. His deep voice was as clear in her head as if he'd actually spoken to her.

Without warning an intense rush of heat pooled between her thighs, making her sex throb. She gasped and rolled to her side to try to push the images away, but the ache didn't ease. Every inch of her skin tingled. Her breasts felt swollen and sensitive, the nipples hard and tight. All in response to that seductive, Irish-tinged voice in her head. What the hell was happening?

Liv threw the light cotton sheet off her body in annoyance. She hadn't been single *that* long, but for some reason her body was suddenly desperate for sex. A cool shower was definitely in order.

When she threw her legs over the side of the bed, her ringtone went off again.

Seriously? She grabbed her phone and glared at the display, expecting to see Aaron's number come up. It wasn't his. For a second she thought about not answering it, but then sighed and took the call. "Hello?"

"Olivia, it's Daegan Blackwell."

Her heart did a slow roll in her chest. His low voice slid over her sensitized skin like a caress, making the throb between her legs worse. She pressed her thighs together to stem the relentless ache and drew her knees up, fighting to ignore her need for relief. "Good morning."

"Sorry to call so early. Did I wake you?"

"No, it's okay. I was already up." Somehow she didn't mind *him* calling so early. Not when his voice did such wicked things to her body.

"Sleep well?"

"Fine," she lied. "You?"

"No, actually."

His dry tone lit her curiosity. "I'm sorry to hear that. Were you stressing about the property? No one else has seen it yet, so you've still got time to put in an offer before the listing goes up."

He gave a short laugh. "It wasn't that. Listen, have you eaten yet?"

"No, I'm still in bed." And now she couldn't stop thinking about rolling around on it with him. Naked.

A taut silence filled the line for a moment. She thought she heard him suck in a deep breath. "Can you meet me at the house again? I'd like to take another look. I'll bring us some breakfast."

She sat up straight. Was he going to put in an offer already? Her heart beat faster. The commission on that property would pay off her line of credit and most if not all of her mortgage. "Sure, what time?"

"Can you be there in forty-five minutes?"

"Sure."

"Perfect. Any food you hate?"

"No—where are you coming from, anyway? I can grab us something."

"Downtown. And I'll take care of it." The way he said it made her body even hotter. As though the "it" he referred to was the insistent pressure building between her thighs.

Let me ease you.

A moan built in her throat at the thought of him doing just that. Liv closed her eyes and pinched the bridge of her nose. She could *not* think about him that way. God, how was she going to look the man in the eye when she saw him? "See you in a bit," she managed.

"Yes, you will."

The words caused another flare of arousal, but the instant he disconnected she felt an emotional crash. A disturbing sense of loneliness filled her.

"Okay, you're way overtired," she muttered.

No way was she making it to the gym this morning. She texted Catherine to say she couldn't make it and received the expected response less than a minute later.

Oh no, you don't. I'm already on my way over.

Well, she was in for it now.

Liv set her phone down and crossed to the bathroom, the unrelieved sexual tension in her body setting her teeth on edge. Since when did her body get so hot and bothered? She didn't appreciate her lack of control over it.

When the shower was warm enough for her to tolerate, she got in and scrubbed herself down roughly to desensitize her skin. It seemed to work because the worst of the throbbing subsided. She leaned her forehead against the slick wall with a sigh of relief then got out and toweled off.

After quickly dressing in a pale yellow sundress that showed off her summer tan, she wound her hair into a careless knot on the top of her head then grabbed her briefcase and purse. When she got to the door, her best friend Catherine was just marching up the walkway. She was clad in her usual Saturday morning battle gear of yoga pants and workout top, her wavy chestnut brown hair pulled back into a sleek ponytail.

Catherine scowled when she saw her, her dark gaze taking in Liv's appearance as she continued up the path. "Seriously? You missed Wednesday morning, too, and now you're going to make me go by myself again today?"

Liv waved her inside for a second while she grabbed a light sweater. "I'm really sorry," she answered, shutting the door behind them, "but I have another showing right now on the big property I told you about."

"I thought you showed it last night."

"I did. The guy who looked at it called this morning and wants to see the place again."

Catherine's disgruntled expression softened. "Sounds serious, if he wants to see it again so soon."

"Not sure, but I hope so."

Her friend gave a sly grin. "Bet the commission on that place would be sweet."

"God, you have no idea. And Cath, you should see this guy."

"Hot?"

"So much more than hot. He's total alpha male sex appeal."

Catherine's eyes widened. "Wow, coming from you, that's quite a compliment. Is he single? Maybe I should come with you."

"He's single, but you'll just have to take my word on how hot he is, because I have to run. Do a mile for me on the treadmill, okay? I'll make it up to you next week, I promise." Liv gave her a quick hug.

Catherine bussed her cheek with a kiss. "Not likely," she said, heading out the door."And skipping out on me's gonna cost you a bottle of my favorite red wine plus full disclosure about this meeting. I want to hear all about this guy and whether or not you get the sale."

"Okay, that's fair." After locking the door behind them she stood next to her car, waved as Catherine pulled away.

The ten-minute drive to the property was uneventful except for the beginnings of another headache building at the base of her skull. It always happened like this—once they started they came in clusters and the whole cycle took a few days to go away. But lately they'd been worse.

She rolled her head around a couple of times to ease the muscles in her neck, silently cursing Aaron Moore. Apparently her body didn't like the man any more than the rest of her did.

When she turned into the French country mansion's driveway, her mood lifted. The house was as beautiful as ever, and Daegan's black Porsche was already parked under the porte-cochère, looking like it belonged there. A ripple of excitement stole through her. It surprised her how much she was looking forward to seeing him again.

He wasn't waiting for her at the front door. She walked around the side of the house to the back lawn and froze when she found him standing with his back to her at the cliff's edge. His dark hair gleamed in the sun as he stared out at the calm water below, the muscles across his shoulders and back evident under his sapphire dress shirt.

She drew a sharp breath and caught a faint whiff of his scent carried on the breeze: cinnamon and cloves with a touch of citrus. Her heart started a painful thump against her ribs, a flare of heat hitting her between the legs.

Before she could move, he turned his head and saw her. She couldn't see his eyes beneath the dark wrap-around sunglasses, but she knew without a doubt he was looking at her. She couldn't move. Her muscles refused to obey as he came toward her, his long legs eating up the distance between them.

"Morning," he said, closing the gap.

"Hi," she answered breathlessly. Had she ever been this attracted to a man? Her body was going haywire. And she didn't even know him.

Daegan's hard expression softened as he smiled and removed his shades. The result took her breath away. She felt the impact of those pale blue eyes right into her center. Her body was hot and cold at the same time. Her core squeezed, dampened, assaulting her with memories of the naughty dreams she'd had about him.

Stop it. Stop it right now.

Liv held out a hand, determined to act like a professional no matter if the man made her body go crazy. "Welcome back."

"It's good to be back," he said, grasping her hand in a gentle grip.

Her stomach did a pleasurable flip, like she was plunging down the first drop of a rollercoaster. The pressure between her legs intensified. She snatched her hand back, set her palms against the small of her back. Okay, no more touching him. No matter how much she wanted to.

"I left the food in my car," he said, shoving his hands into his jeans pockets. The move emphasized the roped muscles in his forearms.

She could feel a blush working its way up her neck. *Stop staring.* "Sounds good, thank you." Leading him back to their cars, she was acutely aware of him behind her. Her skin tingled, the hair on her nape prickling. Was he checking out her butt?"So," she began as they reached the front of the house, "are there any questions you have about the place?"

He stepped up close beside her, gave another smile that made her heart flutter before looking up at the stonework above them. "What kind of stone is this, anyway?"

"Baltic limestone."

His head snapped around, eyes filled with shock. "What?"

"Baltic limestone," she repeated, wondering why he looked so surprised. She was good at her job, made sure she knew the details on a property like this. "As in, the Baltic Sea. Up near places like Lithuania, Latvia and Eston—"

"I know the Baltic States."

"Oh, have you traveled there?"

He nodded, still gazing at the house, a hint of awe in his expression. "Many times."

He seemed fascinated by the stone, walking over to place a hand on the exterior wall. His palm slid over the hand-chiseled surface, almost like a caress.

Her body heated another hundred degrees as she imagined that hand smoothing over her naked skin the same way, like it had in her dreams.

Liv blew out a breath. What the hell was wrong with her today? "See all the fossils in it? Sometimes there are specks of amber in it too. It's pretty when the sun shines on it. And the limestone for all the trim came from Ireland."

He looked up at the milled windowsill above him, smiled wider. "Of course it did," he murmured.

She didn't know what he meant by that, but he seemed pleased and that was all that mattered. "Are you from there?"

"Born there, yes. Didn't realize I still had an accent."

"It's faint, but beautiful," she assured him. And oh, the things it did to her inside. "Want to go in now and look at the rooms again?"

He faced her, letting his hand drop away from the stone. She noticed his fingers lingered on it a moment, as though he didn't want to stop touching it. Lucky stone.

"Think we could eat in the kitchen? I'd like to see it with the morning light streaming through the windows."

She shrugged. "Why not?"

While he got a couple bags from his Porsche, she unlocked the heavy front door and disarmed the security system. Daegan came up behind her to set a hand on the small of her back as she stepped across the threshold, and the feel of it created a curl of heat in the pit of her belly. The delectable scent of cinnamon drifted up, twining with his spicy scent. "Oh, God," she moaned. "Cinnamon buns?"

"With fresh strawberries and cappuccinos."

"I love all those things."

"Lucky guess," he said with a mysterious grin.

She was supposed to be leading him to the kitchen, but it felt more like he was escorting her. An almost protective vibe radiated from him, and she realized she liked it. If he decided not to put in an offer it would be nice if he'd stay while she showed Aaron around the place later on, because then she wouldn't have to find someone else to come with her. She could ask Catherine to come along, but though Daegan was a near stranger, his size and air of command made her feel safe.

Daegan pulled out her chair and seated her before taking his place across the antique marble table set in the breakfast nook. The show of manners seemed as natural to him as breathing, giving her the impression he hadn't done it just to impress her. She let her eyes rove over the beautiful but hard planes of his face while he unpacked the food, for a moment giving into the urge to imagine what it would be like to curl her fingers into his thick hair, pull him close for a kiss.

In the midst of filling a plate he looked up, his gaze locking with hers. "Hungry?"

"Yes. Starved." And not just for food. Her pulse thudded in her throat.

"That makes two of us," he said, sliding a paper plate toward her.

An arc of pure sexual electricity passed between them, so strong she had to swallow and force her gaze away. "Thank you for picking up breakfast."

"It's the least I could do after dragging you out of bed first thing in the morning."

"That's okay. I'm usually an early riser." *Just not when I've been having erotic dreams about you.* Eating a ripe red berry, she watched him cut a neat square of cinnamon roll with his plastic knife and fork. "So, I assume you asked me here because you're interested in the property?"

His mouth twitched in a quick smile at her directness. "I am. I was thinking of putting in an offer."

Already? "That's—"

"I don't have a lot of time, though."

"Oh, well the listing hasn't officially gone up yet, so you've definitely got some time. But there is someone else coming to see the place tonight."

He frowned, giving her the impression he didn't like the idea. "Who?"

"Someone who found out…" Her voice trailed off as a thought suddenly occurred to her. How *did* Aaron know the place was for sale? Her boss wouldn't have told him if he'd called to ask. Maybe Aaron knew she'd shown the house last night because he'd seen her here.

Maybe he'd followed her after Melissa's music lesson and she hadn't noticed.

A shiver of alarm snaked up her spine. She rubbed her fingers over her forehead, her head beginning to pound.

"Another headache?"

She nodded. "It's not too bad. Not like last night."

"Do you get them often?" A note of concern touched his voice.

More and more often, it seemed. "No, I'm fine." She didn't need to bore him with her medical history.

A warm hand cupped her cheek. She froze, jerked her gaze up to his. Daegan searched her eyes intently for a moment then brushed her hands away from her forehead to stroke his fingertips across it.

The pain eased immediately, going from a dull pounding to a faint discomfort, but his touch sent what felt like tiny sparks showering over her skin. Surreal.

He pulled away, leaving warmth in the wake of his fingers. "Better?"

Liv stared at him in shock. Twice now he'd touched her face and the headache had eased. It wasn't her mind playing tricks on her. "It's gone. How did you do that?"

"Magic." His secretive smile made something deep inside her abdomen flutter. Her nipples peaked tight and the petals of her sex swelled. She wanted to kiss him so badly she had to dig her fingers into her thighs to keep from grabbing him.

Jesus.

She jerked to her feet so fast her chair toppled over.

"Are you all right?" He'd risen from his chair and now watched her carefully.

"Yes. Sorry." God, she must look like an insane woman. Something wasn't right. She cleared her throat. "It's just…that was really weird."

"What was?" He hadn't moved, simply stood there staring at her. Like he was waiting for something.

"When you touched me. The pain disappeared, like…"

"Like?"

"Magic," she whispered, gazing helplessly into his eyes.

Another of those knee-melting smiles. "I'm glad." The sunlight streaming through the bay windows made his eyes glow with an unearthly light. She thought she detected amusement in them.

And almost a sort of longing.

Her heart squeezed. It had to be her imagination, but she would have sworn he seemed lonely. She couldn't bear the thought of him being alone. Something inside her wanted to hold him, draw him into her.

What the hell is wrong with me?

"Maybe we should talk about my offer," he said in a low voice.

"Great." She felt like she'd lost her mind. Grabbing her briefcase, she took out the necessary papers and spread them out on the table. She babbled a bit more about the house while she got everything ready, acutely aware of the way he stared at her mouth as she spoke. As though he was thinking of kissing her too. The man made it hard for her to breathe. She got out her pen, forced a smile to cover her nerves. "What figure did you have in mind?"

He stared back at her for a long moment before naming a number just ten thousand dollars under the undisclosed asking price.

Her fingers reflexively tightened around the pen.

"Think that will get me the house?" he asked with a speculative tilt of his head.

She swallowed. "I—I think that's a very good offer."

"If it's accepted, when can I get possession?"

Possession? She stared into his eyes, imagining what it would be like to be possessed by him. No doubt he'd do it spectacularly. Her inner muscles clenched in agonized denial. She struggled to answer him. "Ah, as soon as the lawyers clear everything and the paperwork is taken care of."

Daegan leaned back with a satisfied grin, the sexiest thing she'd ever laid eyes on. "Good. This place has really grown on me."

With effort she wrestled her mind out of the gutter and got busy filling in the paperwork. She sent some e-mails and made a few calls, got the offer accepted, subject to financing and inspection. When it was done she helped him tidy the table, then locked the place up, prepared to say goodbye. Though she wasn't frightened of him, she had the driving urge to put some distance between them before she did something stupid.

"I hope you don't mind me asking," she said, starting for her car, "but what do you do for a living?" The man had a serious amount of money at his disposal.

One side of his mouth turned up. "I'm a businessman. My company's name is Trident Group, but you know that already because I'll bet you Googled me last night."

Heat crept into her cheeks, but she didn't deny it. "I couldn't find out much aside from some businesses you own and the charitable donations you've made." She tilted her head, considered him for a long moment. "You don't seem like just a businessman. I got the impression you might have a military background." His bearing radiated that sort of confident, controlled power.

"I do."

"Is it recent?" He still had a razor-like edge to him beneath all the civilized manners and sex appeal.

Something moved in his eyes. A shadow. "Fairly. I've spent most of my life in the military."

"I can tell. So is part of what you do military contracting?"

He nodded, the hint of a smile softening his features. "A big part, actually."

"Do you still do it?"

"Yeah. I was in Afghanistan for a few months not too long ago."

She didn't like the thought of him doing such risky work. "I'm glad you're back safe and sound."

"Me too." Daegan surprised her by snagging one of her hands when she started to unlock her car.

She looked over her shoulder at him, the keys dangling from her hand.

"Will you have dinner with me tonight?"

The intensity in him intrigued her. An aura of strength and authority clung to him. He was so incredibly masculine, so in command. She suspected his time in the military must have been hard-core. Maybe he'd even served in Special Operations. "You don't have to take me out to dinner."

"I want to."

"Because I showed you the house?"

"No, because I want to get to know you better."

Good. She didn't want this to be about the house. And she wanted to get to know him better too. Badly. "I'd love to. I was supposed to have another showing here at six, but...just a sec."

She dug out her phone and scrolled through the call display until Aaron's number came up. Thankfully his voicemail picked up. She left a message saying the estate had already accepted an offer, so there was no need for him to see the property. If he called back she fully intending to let *that* call go to voicemail. With luck she'd never have to speak to him again.

Tossing the phone into her purse, she smiled at Daegan, her heart pounding at the thought of going on a date with him. "There. Where do you want to go?"

Instead of answering, he took her right hand, raised it to his lips. His pale eyes held hers as he bent his head, brushing a soft kiss to the back of her hand. Tingles raced up her arm, shot throughout her body. She sucked in a sharp breath.

He paused, gauging her reaction, then turned her hand over and pressed another seductive kiss to her trembling palm. His lips were soft and warm, so incredibly gentle despite his obvious strength, that hard edge to him. It made her melt. Her eyes drifted closed on a wave of pure desire as it swept over her body. Goosebumps broke out all over her skin.

His grip on her hand firmed. "Cold?"

Not cold. Try melting hot. She pressed her lips together and shook her head, fighting to regain control. God, she'd never felt anything like this. Whatever was happening between them, it went way beyond chemistry. She just hoped he felt it half as keenly as she did.

Daegan kissed her palm once more before lowering her hand, then gently released it. When she finally opened her eyes he smiled and opened her car door. "I'll pick you up at six-thirty. I'll need your address."

She hesitated for a brief moment, then gave it to him. Maybe it was crazy, but she trusted him.

As she drove away, she took one last longing glance at him in the rear view mirror. Standing in front of the house, he looked like he already owned the place. It suited him perfectly.

A huge grin spread across her face. If he could make her senses explode with a simple kiss to her hand, she couldn't wait to see what else he would do to her tonight.

"OKAY, TELL ME again so I can understand it—why Lithuania?"

Dr. Nairne Roberts smiled at her coworker then slid her laptop into her briefcase. "Research trip."

"Witch hunt, more like it," Liz grumbled, making a face. "And how will I get through my mornings without your charming Scottish accent to listen to?"

"I'm sure you'll manage."

Liz swiveled around in her chair, facing away from the spreadsheet on her computer screen, the rows of test tubes and other equipment atop the bench beside her work station. "You're seriously going to spend your two weeks' vacation in a place that just came out from behind the Iron Curtain a couple decades ago? To study folklore?"

"Aye. I've wanted to go there since I was a little girl, to find out if the stories my granddad told me were true."

Liz frowned. "Must have been one hell of a story-teller to get you interested enough to go to Lithuania."

She laughed. "You make it sound like it's a third-world country. The place I'm going to has been a popular summer resort destination for decades."

"Yeah, well I can think of a lot of resorts I'd rather visit. Mexico, Hawaii, anywhere in the Caribbean…"

Nairne shrugged, stripped off her white lab coat. "To each her own, I guess."

Liz eyed the papers Nairne gathered up, carefully organized into various folders for the long plane ride ahead. "You writing a book on all this or something? Because from the looks of it, this is hard-core research, not just a hobby."

"I'd love to write a book about it," Nairne confessed. "Not sure many people would want to buy it, though." She didn't care if people thought she was obsessed and wasting her time researching myths. This trip would satisfy a curiosity that had burned in her for as long as she could remember. "You'll hold down the fort here while I'm gone?"

Liz gave her a bland look. "Yeah, because the lab's going to suddenly explode with activity once you're gone."

"Never know," Nairne said with a shrug. "If anything comes up you can always reach me on my cell."

"Of course, because you're the only person I know who would be willing to work while on holiday." Liz shook her head then waved her away. "Go, have a good time. Research those witches and goblins—"

"Goddesses and devils."

"Sure, those too. But for God's sake, promise me you'll do something *fun* too."

"Will do." She couldn't wait to get to Nida, stand on the largest sand dunes in Europe and drink in the breeze blowing off the Baltic. Just the thought energized her. "See you later."

On her way out of the lab she checked with a few other lab techs about some of the genetics projects they were working on, then headed for the elevators. She took one to the ground floor and exited onto UBC's main mall.

The air was pleasantly warm, smelling of fresh-cut grass. The leafy oak trees bordering the Mall glowed in the summer sunshine, creating generous patches of shade for students to sit in. Being July there were fewer students around the university, mostly populated right now with full-time staff, faculty and grad students. Nairne preferred it that way. She got along with people, but she preferred her own company most of the time so she could work on her secret project without having to explain herself. She might be a geneticist by trade, but she was just as much a genealogist and historian.

The main library beckoned ahead. Nairne picked up her pace, anxious to check on her secret document one last time before she went overseas. Once inside the main stacks, she headed up to the special collections area to find Thomas, the librarian in charge of keeping the collection safe.

"Hi, Dr. Roberts," he said with a grin. "Come to say goodbye to your baby?"

"Aye, please."

He led her into a special room, seated her at a table before disappearing into the back to retrieve the document from a secure vault. "Here you are," he said, laying the scroll in front of her. She'd stumbled across it by accident in an old Edinburgh library while researching her family genealogy.

"Thanks." Nairne tugged on a pair of white cotton gloves he'd provided her. They protected more than just the parchment, however. The barrier on her skin kept her from the shock of emotion she'd felt when she'd first touched the scroll. Hatred and hope. Fear and resolve. Snatches, really, nothing she could truly decipher.

Sometimes when she touched an object she got clearer impressions. Once she'd even experienced a mother's grief when she'd held an infant's christening gown. Later she'd found out it had belonged to her great grandmother who'd lost her firstborn baby and held a posthumous baptism for the child. The same woman who, according to family legend, had "the gift" and could see things before they happened. Nairne had always wondered if her great grandmother had foreseen her baby's death.

"Decode all its little mysteries yet?" Thomas asked with a hike of his eyebrows.

"Not yet, no." But she would, eventually.

Once he left, Nairne gently unrolled the scroll. Every

time she looked at it she got a thrill. The parchment was about four feet long but in amazingly good condition, considering how old it was. Carbon dating confirmed it was from the period when the Teutonic Knights ruled the part of Lithuania she was about to visit. The scroll was written in both Gaelic an old German dialect, covered with elaborate, painstakingly hand-colored illustrations.

This single document had given her the clues necessary to finish her PhD dissertation on Baltic Lithuanian genetics, pointing to the Celtic connection she'd found in certain bloodlines.

Her gaze immediately went to the depiction of Neringa, the sea goddess. Done in golds, greens and blues, the goddess's eyes seemed to glow up at her from the parchment. A rush of excitement flashed through Nairne as she read a passage of old German she'd finally managed to translate with the help of a few linguistic experts.

AFTER THE PURGE, *three victorious Empowered Warriors shall rise from the ashes to form Neringa's Trident.*

The three shall become six, and together with The Lost they shall battle the Black Lord for the fate of mankind.

SOUNDED DIRE, whatever it referred to. Almost biblical.

Beneath the prophetic words, a demonic creature she assumed must be the Black Lord was depicted. Colored all in red, it looked like it was eating human victims' souls. Sucking the life force out of them with its open mouth. Its eyes blazed an eerie yellow, and around its body a thick line of black encircled it. Like some sort of aura.

Several other passages remained below it, still guarding their secrets within the old German and Celtic text. Intriguing allusions to people with special powers, as far as the linguistic experts could piece together. Nairne hoped they might be references to the Empowered themselves.

The tales of the Empowered told by her grandfather had fueled her imagination since childhood, sending her on her career path in genetics. Her interest in genealogy led her to trace his side of the family back to coastal Lithuania over three hundred years ago, and she was determined to dig even further. She couldn't wait to unlock every last secret hidden within the priceless scroll. Something told her she was close to finding the key.

Nairne stroked a fingertip across the parchment, right over Neringa's picture. "I'm finally coming to visit," she whispered excitedly, almost able to smell the briny scent of the Baltic in the air.

Rolling up the scroll carefully, she took it back to Thomas.

"I'll take good care of it while you're gone," he said with a fond smile.

"I've no doubt of that. Thank you." She couldn't wait to get on the plane and start the grand adventure ahead. The answers she sought were out there somewhere, just waiting to be found.

THROUGHOUT THE AFTERNOON, Aaron never returned Liv's call. She tried him repeatedly all through the day but never got an answer.

At five-thirty she gave up and called Daegan. "I have to go to the house again. The guy might still show up." She didn't want him hanging around the property without supervision. "Can you meet me there instead?" She rubbed her temples to soothe the building headache away. It didn't help the pain, but she had to go anyway. It was a point of professionalism for her.

"Sure. Everything okay?"

"Yes." *No.* She didn't want to see Aaron, but at this point she had no choice. The creep had probably chosen to ignore her message, would show up pretending he'd never received it. Her boss wouldn't be happy if she left a prospective buyer waiting at such a high-end property. "I'm really sorry."

"No, it's fine, but are you okay meeting him there alone?"

His perception was spooky. "Actually, no, I'd rather not, but the friend I asked to meet me can't make it."

A pause. "Has this guy threatened you in some way?"

She was startled by the fierce protective note in his voice. His lovely, sensual voice."No. He just makes me really uncomfortable."

"Just stay in your car until I get there."

"Really, it's okay—"

"Promise me you'll stay in your car."

His concern was palpable, increasing her anxiety. "Okay." Her heart rate increased in response.

By the time she arrived at the house a few minutes before six, the damned headache was digging its claws into her. Sharp, sickening spikes of pain drove into her skull. Her vision started to go slightly hazy, like it always did at the onset of a migraine. The aura, doctors called it.

Liv parked in front of the house, blinked a few times to help clear her eyes, but her vision didn't improve. The pain relievers she'd taken weren't helping at all. She closed her eyes and focused on taking slow, deep breaths to combat the first stirrings of nausea churning in her gut. God she hated this. The doctors had never found a reason for the headaches since they'd begun almost a year ago. The medication they'd prescribed barely touched the pain during a full-blown migraine.

The sound of tires crunching over gravel made her eyes snap open. In her rearview mirror she watched the blurry form of Aaron's white Camry pull up. Her stomach grabbed. Damn him, he *would* be early to-night when he'd never managed to bring Melissa to a lesson on time.

Now what? She didn't know how far away Dae-gan was.

Gathering her strength, she prepared to face Aaron alone.

He climbed out of the vehicle, a handsome man over six feet tall with an undeniable air of anger about him.

Her palms began to sweat. She wouldn't get out of the car. She'd just crack the window, tell him the prop-erty was sold, then leave. Before the headache com-pletely took over. Fumbling on the inside of her door, her fingers found and pressed the button to lower her window slightly. The pain swelled as he approached. Her vision became more unfocused, making every-thing around her shimmer like a colorful mirage. She grimaced, fighting through the haze of pain.

His footsteps crunched on the pea gravel. Drawing nearer. Each time his feet touched the ground it seemed to reverberate in her skull like a hammer blow.

Stop, she wanted to scream as he came closer. The pain was unbearable, swelling along with the fear. Worse with every step he took toward her. She could hear the rasp of her own breathing, loud in the car's interior. Her lips and fingers started tingling. Turning numb.

Stop.

Aaron came up to lean his palms on the roof above her door, no doubt deliberately invading her space. She felt trapped. Her throat seemed to tighten, like an invisible hand squeezed it. Depriving her of air.

"Are you getting out?"

She blinked, squinting up at him. A fuzzy outline of dark orange light danced around his body. Her stomach rolled. She heard him speaking, but couldn't answer past the pain in her head. Cold sweat broke out across her face and chest. God, she was going to be sick—

"Don't you dare ignore me, you icy bitch. Think you can treat me like shit and get away with it? *Open* the *door.*"

The sudden malevolence rolling off him made black spots swim before her eyes. That strange orange color intensified around him. She shook her head, a tight movement of denial. Something was wrong. Horribly wrong. The keys were in the ignition but there was no way she could drive like this. She couldn't see straight.

"I said open the damn door, *now.*" He gave an angry grunt and reached for her door handle. Thank God she'd locked it. His sudden rage shocked her. He yanked on it impatiently, rocking the car in his fury, and she knew he would become violent if she didn't get out. Maybe even break through her window to get to her.

The hair on her arms stood up.

He *wanted* to get to her. Wanted it badly. She could feel the cruel intent rolling off him. He wanted to hurt her. Rape her. She was alone. No one would hear her screams.

Her throat clamped tighter. The fear ate at her like acid, burning through her veins.

Evil. He was evil. She could taste it in the back of her throat. It coated the inside of her mouth with a bitter film.

Liv groped blindly for her cell phone, tucked into the side pocket of her purse, next to her on the passenger seat. Her fingers glanced off the cool plastic cover. She grasped it, drew it out with a shaking hand, tried to make out the tiny numbers on its keys.

Aaron's fist slammed down on the roof, his angry shouts hitting her skull like blows from a sledgehammer. His heavy hand thumped against her window. She braced for the sound of shattering glass. Any second now it would fracture, covering her in a hail of shards. *Hold on*, she ordered herself. *Daegan is coming. Hold on.*

Struggling to see past the pain, her thumb found the 9 on the keypad. The numbers blurred before her eyes. A sob of frustration and fear choked her, searching futilely for the 1. Damn it, she couldn't see.

She fought to breathe while the fear crashed over her like a dark wave. Aaron's angry voice grew louder, adding to the cruel spikes driving into her head. The phone slipped from her trembling fingers, crashing to the floorboard with a sickening thud. She clapped her hands to her skull, swallowed back the bile in her throat. He was going to get her. *Help me...*

"Get the hell away from her," a deep voice snarled.

Someone ripped Aaron away from her door.

Daegan, she realized with a sob. He was here.

Liv gasped in a breath as her constricted throat opened up again. Sweet, cool air rushed into her aching lungs. The headache remained a crushing vise around her head. She couldn't see. Was going to pass out. The pain was hideous, worse than it had ever been. She couldn't stand it. Just wanted it to end. Distantly she heard the sound of fists thudding against flesh, Aaron's outraged cries.

Then a sudden, deafening silence.

"Olivia?" Daegan's voice.

A moment later her door jerked open, despite that she hadn't unlocked it. Daegan cursed and reached for her. The instant he touched her, the pain seemed to lessen. His scent enveloped her, filling her burning lungs.

In the distance she faintly heard a car speeding away over the gravel. Aaron leaving. She shuddered in relief.

"Olivia, look at me, love."

The endearment, the slight Irish lilt in his voice soothed her enough to unlock her frozen muscles. She took an unsteady breath and turned her head toward him, reaching out blindly. Still on his knees, he gathered her up in his arms and lifted her out of the car, settling her onto his lap. She clung to him, fingers digging into his muscled shoulders.

"You're okay. I've got you." He held her close, his arms strong and warm around her.

Safe. She was safe now. Daegan wouldn't let anything happen to her. She shook in his embrace while the pain slowly faded to a more tolerable level. When it decreased enough for her to open her eyes, she found him staring down at her with a worried frown. His large hands cradled her head. The awful pounding subsided but a fuzzy blue aura remained around him, almost the same shade as his eyes. She blinked, but it didn't go away. There was something wrong with her.

"Breathe, love," he said softly.

She pulled in a few slow breaths, fighting back tears of pain and confusion. Her fingers dug into his hard shoulders. "Daegan...what's happening to me?"

CHAPTER THREE

THE FEAR ON Olivia's face stabbed at Daegan. His mate was huddled against him in a helpless, trembling mass, eyes squinted as though the light hurt. A primal rage ripped through him when he thought of that asshole trying to harm her. She'd been right to be afraid of the man. Whoever he was, the bastard was lucky to still be alive.

Exerting every ounce of his self-control, he forced the rage back and focused on providing safe, calming energy for Olivia. When her heart rate regulated and she seemed steadier, he sat her up, taking her pale face between his palms. The feel of her velvety skin seared him, but his concern for her overrode the continuous sexual need. "Tell me what happened," he said softly, watching her eyes.

She squinted up at him, but her pupils weren't constricted like they had been a few minutes ago. He maintained his hold, glad he seemed at least able to ease her physical pain. He'd do whatever he could to ensure the same for her emotional state.

Her dark lashes fluttered, as though her lids were too heavy to keep open. "The headache came back. Got worse when he showed up." Her voice was hoarse, the words almost a mumble. "He wanted to hurt me. I felt it. So I stayed in the car."

Daegan's muscles tensed. "Thank God you did." If he'd realized she was in physical danger by meeting the guy, he'd have risked the side effects and dematerialized to get here faster. He wanted to kick the bastard's ass all over again.

"You took my pain away again." She struggled to focus on his eyes. "How did you do that?"

For a moment he thought of telling her the truth, but she wouldn't believe him. Not yet. Maybe never. So he tucked her head into the curve of his shoulder, enjoying the feel of her cuddled against him. The pliant feel of her body assured him she felt safe in his arms and it washed over him like a balm. "I guess I have a…gift." One he'd never known he possessed until he'd touched her forehead that first time. In that instant he'd known she was his mate.

Olivia nodded as her lids closed. "I'm tired."

"I know." He breathed deeply of her scent. The fragrance was light and clean, almost like fabric softener. He wanted to bury his nose in her shiny hair and begin the bonding process, but he could never take advantage of her weakened condition and call himself a man. Impossible as it seemed, he'd have to wait, no matter that his body demanded otherwise. Right now she was in no condition to face any of it. "Come on," he said as he scooped her up and headed for his car. "Let's get you to the hospital."

Her eyes snapped open, disoriented, alarm in their hazel depths. "No, not there. I'm fine now. I just want to go home."

He hesitated. The hospital probably wouldn't help because whatever was happening to her was beyond the realm of medical science. But he could get another opinion from someone he trusted. "I'll take you home if you let my cousin come and look at you. He's a doctor."

"All right," she muttered tiredly.

By the time he bundled her into the Porsche and got her home, she was fast asleep. After parking in front of her white single-story house with its wide porch, he glanced down at her peaceful face, wondering how in hell he was going to explain everything to her. He didn't know her yet. Didn't know if she had the strength to handle it all. He'd planned to take her for dinner to spend some time together and give the relationship a chance to form, then drop her off well before the sun set, before the nightly rush of oxytocin and dopamine took effect.

But none of that was going to happen now. The eye thing was going to be a problem. He couldn't exactly wear shades around her house all night to hide the ir-refutable evidence of his Heat Cycle.

But damn, his heart swelled at the sight of her asleep against the leather seat, her lush lips parted slightly. The logical part of his brain wanted to blame it all on the increased levels of oxytocin pumping through his veins, triggered the moment he'd met Olivia. But he knew there was more to this than mere chemical re-action. He wanted to know her. Find out what made her laugh, what she liked to eat, what she liked to do. Wanted to know everything there was to know about her. She looked so feminine, so beautiful while she slept. He wanted to lean over and thread his hands into the luxurious softness of her hair, kiss her awake.

Give in to his growing hunger for her and let nature take its course.

He was out of time though. She deserved answers as much as he owed them to her. The transition was going to be hard for her. He hated that he didn't know how to make it any easier. He'd never felt this helpless, so out of control. It shook him. He, who'd fought in countless battles and faced death more times than he could remember, was afraid he'd somehow screw everything up and lose this one shot with his mate.

He couldn't fail. Their lives depended on it.

The continuation of the human *race* depended on it.

Shaking off the morbid thought, Daegan carefully lifted her from the car, took her to the door. She didn't have an alarm system, he saw, making a mental note to remedy that first thing in the morning. Focusing on the lock, he picked it with his mind, turning the mechanism to slide the deadbolt back. Once inside, he locked the door then carried her down the hall.

He smelled her room before he saw it. Her clean scent drifted from it, pulling him like a magnet. His body hardened at the thought of joining her on the queen-sized four-poster, but he shoved his raging libido into its cage and settled her on the bed. Olivia sighed in response, snuggling deeper into the covers. She was still pale, but for her flushed cheeks.

He wanted to crawl in next to her so badly his muscles clenched. Instead he made himself step out into the hall, gently shutting her door before pulling out his phone to call Cade. "I need you here," he said without preamble.

"What's up?"

He explained what had happened. "Olivia almost blacked out from the pain, and I think her eyes might be affected. I don't know if there's been a previous head injury." He refused to think it might be something more serious than a migraine.

"Shit. She all right?"

"Yeah." He paused, staring out the living room sliding doors that led to the patio and backyard. The sun was starting to set. He was almost out of time. "I think I shield her." That was exactly how it was supposed to work between mates. Each complemented the other's powers. And minimized their weaknesses. Would be interesting to find out how hers affected him. "She was exhausted, so she's asleep now." He gave Cade the address.

"Keep checking on her every ten minutes. I'm on my way."

Relieved that she'd get a thorough medical assessment, Daegan wandered through to her all-white kitchen and glanced around the tidy space. His gaze landed on the cappuccino maker on the counter. After giving her a few minutes more to rest, he found what he needed in the cupboards and figured out how to steam the milk with the machine. She'd seemed to like the foam best, he remembered, adding one sugar as she had that morning. When it was ready he put it on a tray with some fruit he found in the fridge then went back to check on her.

She didn't stir when he opened the door, but her fragrance drifted up to tease him. Her breathing was quiet and even, the sheets rising and falling over the gentle slope of her breasts. His hands tightened on the tray. He thought about how it would feel to stroke the pads of his fingers over the lush mounds. Did she like to be teased slowly, or did she prefer to be taken hard and fast? He could almost hear her breathless gasp as he imagined cupping her breasts, lowering his head to suck on her hard nipples. She'd moan and lift into him, wind her fingers through his hair to hold him there. Needing him.

His cock swelled in his jeans, throbbing for relief. With a hard swallow, he set the food on her dresser and hunkered down next to the bed. "Olivia."

She murmured and shifted, but didn't wake up.

He used the excuse to stroke a hand over the crown of her head, trail his fingers through her silky blond hair. The only part of her he'd allow himself to touch. "Olivia, wake up."

Turning onto her back, she blinked up at him sleepily. She stiffened, but he knew the second she recognized him because she relaxed and let out a deep breath. "Hi," she whispered.

"Hey." He didn't like that she was still squinting. "How do you feel?"

"Better, I think." She put a hand to her nape and rubbed, frowning.

Daegan folded his arms across his chest to keep from putting his own hand there. "My cousin's on his way over, just to make sure you don't need to go to the hospital."

She nodded slowly, watching him with a thoughtful frown. "How did you take the pain away? And don't cop out and say you have a gift. You did something to me."

"All I did was touch you."

It was obvious from the look on her face that she didn't believe him.

"I made you some coffee."

Her expression softened. "Oh. Thanks." She sat up a bit, winced. "I think I'll drink it in the family room."

He wasn't surprised she didn't want to stay with him in here. Some part of her subconscious had to sense how much he wanted her. Moving away from her bedroom was definitely the wisest course of action. He didn't know how much longer he could control his body's reaction to the Heat Cycle. "Sure."

She settled on the sofa in the room off the kitchen, curling her shapely legs beneath her. A tentative smile curved her mouth as she took the steaming mug from him. "Thanks."

"You're welcome." The banality of the conversation was starting to eat at him. The Empowered blood in him demanded he touch her, imprint himself on her in the most primitive way and worry about the rest later. But she was completely unaware of everything, even the reason why she was so attracted to him. He cleared his throat and sat on the opposite end of the sofa. Where did he even start something like this?

A knock on the front door saved him from jumping off that ledge.

"That'll be Cade," he said, getting up to answer it. He let his cousin in, relieved to have him there. "Thanks for coming."

Cade nodded. "She awake?"

"Yeah. Come on." He took him back to meet her. "This is Olivia." He watched her silently assess his cousin through squinted eyes. "Olivia, this is my cousin, Cade."

"Nice to meet you," she answered.

"Likewise, Olivia," Cade said.

She waved a hand. "Please, call me Liv. Both of you," she added, glancing at Daegan.

Cade raised his brows in question, and Daegan took a deep breath. His body was restless, edgy with the start of the nightly torment about to begin anew. He wanted to pace. Instead he made himself sit down on the end of the sofa while Cade knelt in front of Liv.

"I guess Daegan told you I'm a doctor?"

"Yes. A GP?"

"General Surgeon, actually. Army trained." He peered into her eyes. "How's the headache now?"

"Pretty much gone." Her gaze shifted to Daegan, but she didn't say anything about how he'd taken her pain away.

"Is the light hurting your eyes?" Cade asked.

"A bit, but not as much as before."

He took out a pen light, quickly checked her eyes. "Do you get migraines often?" he asked as he put it away.

She shook her head. "Just in the last few months or so. They come in clusters."

"Any symptoms on the onset?"

"I get tension in my neck and shoulders, then the pain starts up at the back of my skull and spreads up around my temples like a vise is squeezing my head. Sometimes it's so bad I get that aura thing, and my vision goes all wonky. But today's the first time my lips and fingers have gone numb."

Cade nodded and continued with his examination, feeling along the back of her neck. Daegan bit back a warning growl as he watched his cousin's fingers exploring Liv's skin. Cade flashed him an annoyed look. Daegan bit down hard and looked away, fighting his body's need to shove Cade aside and stake his claim on his mate.

When Cade sat back on his haunches, Daegan exhaled then turned back to them. Liv's hands fidgeted in her lap, nervous energy pouring off her. Because he couldn't stand by and watch her suffer even that little bit, he immediately went over to sit next to her. She relaxed visibly.

His fingers itched to curl around hers to offer comfort, but he refrained. It was all he could do to stay in the same room with her and not put his hands on her. He was afraid of what might happen if he did.

"I've had the whole battery of tests," she told Cade. "CT scans, EEGs, all that. They came back negative. The doctors don't know why I keep getting the headaches."

Cade grunted. "Besides the numbness today, did anything else unusual happen?"

Liv looked up at Daegan, then back at Cade. "I…" She swallowed. "The man I was meeting makes me nervous, and I've had headaches before whenever I've seen him."

Daegan tensed. "You've seen him before?"

She rubbed her palms over her jeans. "He sometimes brings his daughter here to her piano lessons."

So the bastard had been here, in her house. It made

his hackles go up. If he'd known that he wouldn't have settled for merely breaking his face.

"And you got another headache when you saw him tonight?" Cade asked.

She shook her head. "Before that. It started this morning when I spoke to him on the phone, then came back when I realized I had to meet him tonight. But nothing compared to when he showed up." She bit her lip. "Do you think stress might be triggering them?"

"It's possible. But back to tonight. Anything else?"

Daegan cast a curious glance at his cousin. Cade was fishing for something, like he sensed Liv was holding a critical piece back.

Liv lowered her eyes before responding. "I saw halos."

"Halos?"

She nodded. "These weird outlines of colored light around him. That's never happened before, but Aaron was livid. It was almost like I could *feel* it. He was going to hurt me if he got his hands on me."

Daegan's hands curled into fists as a pulse of rage emitted from him. Cade must have felt it because he shot him a warning look before turning his attention back to Liv. "And then?"

The look in her eyes was far away, lost in memory. "I could hardly see, but when I looked up at him there was a ring of dark orange light surrounding him. Fuzzy. Crackling like electricity." She frowned. "Then he was gone and I saw Daegan. You had one too," she said to him. "Pale blue, though. Almost the color of your eyes."

The hair on his nape stood up. Turning his head, he

shared a long look with Cade. His cousin looked every bit as stunned as Daegan felt. *Holy shit.*

"What?" Liv demanded, worry clear in her voice. "What's wrong?"

Cade's eyes bored into him like lasers. "Tell her. Tell her now."

"Tell me what?" She looked at Daegan, put a defensive hand to her throat. "What's going on?"

The fear in her voice unfroze him. He didn't want to have to tell her this way, but apparently he had no choice. "Liv, were you an orphan?"

She frowned. "Yes. My parents died when I was a kid."

"And you're an only child?"

"Yes. Daegan, what's—"

"What's your ancestry?"

She looked at him like he was crazy. "What the hell does it matter?"

"It matters," Cade said, his eyes riveted on her, body tense.

Liv curled up into a tighter ball. Daegan wished he could comfort her, but he couldn't. And after this she probably wouldn't want anything to do with him. She chewed her bottom lip. "Um, Irish mostly. Some German, I think."

"Baltic German?"

She glanced at him in surprise. "I...maybe. I'm not sure."

He knew without a doubt there was a Baltic connection. Had to be. "How old are you?"

Her chin came up. "Twenty-eight, and if one of you

doesn't explain what the hell is going on here, I swear
I'll—"

"It's okay, Liv. Please trust me." He needed to know
she believed in him, even if only on an instinctive level.

She scowled but closed her mouth, watching him.
Cade dropped onto the ottoman, then glanced over and
shook his head in disbelief. Daegan could hardly take
it all in either.

It all fit. Every last detail. They'd been waiting almost a century for a Seeker. Now she sat in front of
them, looking utterly bewildered. And she was his
mate.

A fine current of electricity raced over his skin.
When he spoke next, his voice was rough. "You asked
me how I took your pain away."

"Yes," she said softly, her fingers clenched so tightly
in her lap the knuckles were white.

He crouched at her feet then reached out to take her
hand, letting the energy flow from him. She gasped.
"Feel that?" he asked.

She nodded, her mouth pressed into a thin line.

"And this?" he asked, sliding his other hand around
the nape of her neck. Heat immediately flowed from
his palm.

Liv swallowed, her eyes full of apprehension. "It's
warm. Really warm."

"Yes. What else?"

"My vision's getting clearer," she said in a trembling
voice. Tears glazed her beautiful eyes as she stared
down at him. "How…"

He took a deep breath. "It's because I can shield
you."

"What does that mean?"

"I can take away the pain your gift causes."

"What do you mean, gift?" She looked so confused it hurt his heart.

"The auras you see. The orange one was the manifestation of violence. The light blue one around me is healing energy and means I can shield you." He swallowed as his throat tightened, but he couldn't hold the words back any longer. "And that means I'm also your mate."

The resounding silence in the room pulsed against his eardrums.

Liv stared back at him with wide eyes, her body utterly frozen, her hand slack in his. Then she batted his hands away and leaped off the couch, backing away from him as she shook her head. "I don't...You're crazy." She cast a furtive glance at Cade, as though he might laugh and tell her this was all a joke.

Her reaction didn't surprise Daegan, but it still hurt to have her pull away. Everything in him demanded he close the distance between them, gather her up in his arms. Soothe her. Arouse her. Seduce her. Make love to her until she understood they were fated to be together. His body was more than willing. His brain knew she needed more time.

It was hell.

He stayed where he was, maintaining eye contact. "You're an Empowered, Liv, and a rare one at that. A Seeker. Someone who can recognize violent intent or evil in another person." So she could help identify members of the Dark Army in the coming war. But he couldn't tell her that part now.

Rather than answer, she wrapped her arms around herself and shook her head again, her whole body rigid with denial. With outrage. "I don't know what you're *talking* about," she finally cried. Raw fear radiated from her, and he hated that he'd made her tremble.

Daegan held her gaze. "You do. Somewhere inside, part of you understands exactly what I'm telling you."

Her chin came up, her eyes blazing with anger. "You're saying I've got magical powers. That you do too."

"Yes."

A short laugh escaped her. The bitterness in it drove into him like nails. "Right. And you just happened to need a ten-million dollar house that hadn't come on the market yet because you knew it was the only way to get me to meet you. So you could make up some crazy story about me being your 'mate.'"

"No, that's not it at all—"

"You're full of shit."

Even angry, she was magnificent. Afraid and confused, yet so incredibly strong he couldn't help but admire her. "Am I?" The dominant urge to claim her snapped the rope on his patience. His voice hardened. "What about after you met me last night, Liv? Did you go home and dream about me in that bed you were just in?"

Her eyes widened, and she went pale before a bright flush of pink bloomed on her cheeks. "It's none of your business."

He could imagine the acute sexual frustration she'd woken with. Satisfaction filled him that she was already pining for him on that level. "You might have started getting these migraines a few months ago, but I'm willing to bet you've been able to pick up on people's emotional energy long before that. Maybe your whole life." He stared at her, daring her to deny it.

She didn't move. Didn't so much as blink.

"And now your upper teeth are sore, aren't they?"

He saw her tongue move beneath her upper lip, as though checking to find out. When she frowned, he knew he was right. If he told her the reason for it though, she'd most likely bolt from the house in terror. She already thought he was nuts. Likely thought she was too.

He kept pushing, determined to get through to her. "When I left you this morning you felt lonely all of a sudden, didn't you? And when I held you tonight the migraine suddenly disappeared." He raised a brow. "Am I wrong?"

She stared at him for a long moment, then gave a tiny shake of her head. A frown creased her forehead, her teeth worrying her lush lower lip.

He softened his tone, desperately wanting to hold her again. Kiss away the fear he sensed ripping through her. His muscles twitched with the need to go to her. "I know this is a shock. It was for me, too, when I transitioned. But what you're feeling is only going to become more intense. The longer you fight it, the harder it will be for you."

"What will?" Her voice was a mere breath of a sound.

He chose his next words carefully. "The dreams you had last night are nothing compared to what's coming. I know you're scared, and you have every right to be since you don't understand what you are, but you're going to have to face this whether you're ready or not. Your body won't give you a choice. If there was another way to handle all of this I would, but we're out of time." An image formed in his mind. Of her twisting beneath him in sensual agony, her cheeks wet with tears as she clawed at his naked back, begging him for release. Pleading with him to end her suffering.

Without warning the heat in him roared to life, igniting him from the inside. It exploded through his bloodstream, making him tremble and pant.

Liv gasped and shrank away from him, her face a mask of alarm. "Your eyes…"

Shit. "I know. It's all right." Already the blue was bright enough to illuminate the space between them. Soon they'd be as bright as spotlights. The fear coming off her cut him like a steel blade. "You don't need to be afraid, Liv. I won't touch you." *Not until you're ready,* he vowed silently. The need he felt was almost uncontrollable, but he wouldn't let himself act on it.

"I should go," Cade said behind him, reminding him he was still in the room. Daegan had almost forgotten he was there.

"You both should," Liv said sharply, her voice vibrating with tension.

"We'll leave," Daegan assured her, feeling torn in two. She was frightened and in shock, but if he left she'd hurt later on. Almost as much as him. He went to the phone, wrote his number down on a piece of paper. "That's my cell number. Call me if you—" He almost said 'need me' but caught himself in time. "If you want to talk about anything."

She didn't respond, merely stared at him. It was obvious she couldn't wait for him to leave.

But Daegan couldn't go without trying to reassure her one last time. "Whatever happens, just know it's going to be okay. I promise you that."

With her face drawn into lines of misery, Liv turned away.

Walking out the front door, he felt like he'd just peeled his skin away with a razor. His lungs tightened, every muscle in his body screaming in denial.

"You okay to drive?" Cade asked him once they were outside on the driveway.

"Yeah." Christ, it felt like his lungs were being crushed. With each step farther away from her the pressure increased until he thought he'd suffocate. "I gotta go." It hurt to leave, but he couldn't stay and not touch her. It would kill him. She wasn't ready to face this yet.

Besides, he had things to do. Namely, making sure that bastard who'd attacked her never came near her again. The perfect outlet for the anger and sexual frustration pounding at him.

Daegan climbed into his car and hissed in pain as he shut the door. His cock was swollen, painfully hard. When he fired up the engine his hands shook so badly he almost pulled the key out of the ignition, but he managed to put it into reverse. He had to get the hell away from here before the shakes got too bad for him to drive.

THEY WERE INSANE, Liv told herself. Both Daegan and his cousin. And she was insane for getting sucked this far into their delusions.

Magic? Right. Not in this lifetime. What the hell had possessed them to say such crazy things to her? Although she couldn't explain the way his eyes had gone all weird, or why he'd made the headache go away with a touch. And damned if the explanation of the colored halos she'd seen didn't resonate with part of her. She shivered.

But even as she thought it she rubbed a hand over her breastbone and frowned. Her heart was beating way too fast. She felt almost frantic. And she was panting like she'd just done a hundred-meter sprint, when all she'd done was pace from one side of the family room to the other.

The house was too quiet. It made the static in her head much too loud. She paced the hardwood floor while the agitation built. Being alone right now should have been comforting, but now she had no choice except to confront everything. By herself.

Was she going crazy? Much as she'd like to deny it, every single thing Daegan had said to her was true. Her upper incisors did hurt. Well, not so much the teeth, but her gums over her incisors. She tested them with her finger, trying to think of a cause. They felt inflamed and tender, like she'd jammed dental floss up too hard and cut her gums.

A knock startled her out of her reverie, making her tense. "Who is it?" She didn't want to see anyone right now. Maybe ever.

"Cade."

She groaned in annoyance. Why was he still here? "What do you want?"

"I forgot my phone."

Liv glanced around, spotted it on the ottoman. She snatched it up and stalked to the front door. Flinging it open, she shoved the phone at him just as Daegan's Porsche pulled out of her driveway.

"Thanks."

She nodded but didn't look at him, gazing instead after the car. It annoyed her that she even cared he was leaving. What did she care where he went? But when the vehicle turned the corner and disappeared from view, a sharp twinge hit her square in the chest.

She gasped, pressed a hand there. God, was she going to have a heart attack now?

"You'd better go in and sit down."

She jumped and looked over at Cade. "I'm f—" Another flash of pain almost sent her to her knees. Beneath her palms, her heart pounded frantically. But then the fear was surpassed by a loneliness so sharp it felt like a spike in her chest. Sudden tears burned her eyes. God, she felt *gutted*. Utterly devastated. Despite her efforts to stop it, her chin quivered. "What's…happening?"

"Easy." Cade gently took her by the elbow, helped her straighten before leading her back into her family room. "It's because he's gone," he explained, seating her on the couch where she immediately curled into a miserable ball. "Once the Heat Cycle begins, both mates suffer when they're apart."

She heard the words but didn't understand them. "It can't be true," she gasped, wiping at the tears flowing down her cheeks. No matter how hard she tried she couldn't get a grip on herself. "This can't be real."

"I understand how you feel."

"I n-never cry," she choked out. "I h-hate crying." Her shoulders jerked with fresh sobs, but she was too angry to be embarrassed. "W-will it g-go away?"

Cade gave her a rueful smile. "Nope. It only ends once mates have bonded."

Bonded. It sounded so deep and…permanent. How could this be happening? She didn't know him. Wasn't sure she even liked him. "B-but he's g-gone." What if he never came back? She doubled over at the thought, crying in earnest.

Cade laid a solid hand on her shoulder. She flinched, but felt only simple comfort in the contact. No heat or any weird emotional reaction. Nothing like when Daegan touched her. "He won't go far, trust me. Not when he knows you're suffering like he is."

She met Cade's bright green eyes. Daegan was hurting like this too?

"Oh, yeah."

She blinked. Could he read her mind?

He smiled, as though he knew what she was thinking. "I know none of this makes sense to you, but it will." Cade was so calm. Like he'd planned out this whole speech.

She tried to glare, but she doubted she pulled it off with the tears coming hard and fast. "Y-you forgot your ph-phone on purpose, d-didn't you?"

He grinned, affirming her suspicions. "If it's any consolation, I've known Daegan a long time. He's the best. You're lucky to have him as your mate."

Lucky? How did any of this make her lucky? "How old are y-you, anyway?" she demanded.

He stood, equal parts sympathy and amusement in his eyes as he turned to go. "Almost two hundred."

CHAPTER FOUR

AFTER ANOTHER NIGHT of endless sexual torture Daegan walked through his front door, barely keeping his eyes open. He dragged his sorry ass inside to find Cade already seated at the island, drinking coffee.

His cousin raised one golden brow at him as he stumbled into the sunny kitchen. "Rough night?"

"Fuck off."

Cade laughed and slid an empty mug across the island to him, looking fresh and relaxed after a night of sex with whichever woman he was currently screwing. Daegan never bothered trying to keep track. "Pot's fresh. Help yourself."

Daegan grunted and poured himself a cup, his body perking up at the prospect of some hot caffeine. He downed half the mug before his cell rang. He knew who it was without looking at the display. The lawyer, telling him everything was in place so they could take possession of the new house today. Thanks to some foresight and a bit of mental persuasion, the whole legal and logistical process had completed itself in a matter of hours instead of weeks. "Today's moving day," he told Cade when he hung up.

Cade set down his mug. "That fast?"

"Yep. Moving truck will be here within the hour."

He was nothing if not efficient. "I want you to set up the training area first thing."

"Okay..."

"Where's Vaughn?"

"Dunno, haven't heard from him in a few days."

Not an unusual occurrence, but Vaughn needed to be informed of what was happening. Would be nice if the guy stayed around more often. It made logistics a hell of a lot easier when they were all in the same place—one of the main reasons Daegan was moving them all into one secure location. They needed a safe home base for training and operations, and the estate on the water was ideal for their purposes. The Baltic and Irish limestone it was built of merely solidified it was where they were meant to be.

But forcing Vaughn to move in could be a problem. He was a loner and hated being around anyone else. Still hard to see him like that after all these years. Before the unthinkable had happened, he'd been the life of the party and Daegan's best friend.

He pushed the painful memories away with a sigh. As he turned away, Cade flipped on the TV, but Daegan didn't hear a thing over the static in his head.

He ran a hand through his hair, tried to gather his thoughts. His mind was in chaos, and he resented the hell out of it. The lack of sleep was definitely starting to catch up with him. He'd spent most of the night twitching and sweating in his car, down the street from Liv's place. Partly because he'd hoped she'd contact him, but mainly because he didn't want to leave her unprotected.

When it was clear Aaron wasn't going to do a repeat performance of the attack and the physical symptoms of the Heat Cycle got too bad for Daegan to handle, he'd caved and rented a cheap motel room for the remainder of the night. Luckily the man at the desk had taken his money with barely a glance at him, because no way could he have made it all the way back to West Van in that condition.

Holed up in that shabby room, for almost five hours he'd made repeated trips into the shower to take the worst of the edge off the sexual need with his fist and a bar of soap. Right up 'til sunrise he'd waited for his phone to ring, but Liv hadn't called. Hadn't even texted him. He had no idea how she'd coped with the vicious erotic torture she must have endured, but he'd been too proud to reach out again. A male could only take so much rejection from a woman, let alone his mate.

When the physical need finally became too much for her to take, she'd eventually have to come to him. And that had better happen soon, or he would lose his mind. Literally.

"Um, Dae?"

He stiffened at the warning tone in Cade's voice, his mug poised partway to his mouth. "What?"

"You'd better take a look at this."

Ah, shit. What now? He spun around to face the TV.

While his cousin turned up the volume, Daegan focused on the newscast. It featured a breaking story about a rash of deaths involving recently paroled dangerous offenders in the area. Seemingly healthy men in their thirties and forties, all convicted rapists or pedophiles. All suddenly dead. Four fatalities in the past week, to be exact, the autopsies listing massive heart attacks as the cause of death.

Cade set down the remote and let out a low whistle. The muscles in Daegan's jaw clenched so hard his teeth hurt.

The reckless *bastard*.

"Fucking Vaughn," he growled, hitting his number on speed dial. They didn't need this added risk right now.

Vaughn picked up on the second ring with a bored, "Hey." His voice was raspy, his vocal cords never having healed from the emergency tracheotomy that had saved his life the last time he'd tried to kill himself. That time his weapon of choice had been a Taliban remote-detonated IED embedded in a road outside of Kandahar in southern Afghanistan. One the suicidal maniac had watched them plant.

"I want you back here," Daegan said through gritted teeth. "Now."

The insolent bastard hung up before Daegan could say anything else. A few seconds later he heard the sound of a key scraping in the front door lock.

Daegan scowled. The bastard *would* rub it in that he could materialize to any place he wanted, unlike him and Cade. But that ability came in damn handy for Vaughn's role as Reaper.

The door swung open and Vaughn strode through it, a six-foot-four wall of muscular menace wrapped in a black leather jacket. He was more dead than alive on the inside, and it showed. The disfiguring burn scars over the left side of his face and throat made him look chilling enough, but it was the eyes that scared people shitless. Black and cold except for the disturbing shards of bright yellow embedded in the irises, they pierced right through a man.

The odd coloring was a constant warning to Daegan. It told him just how close Vaughn was to turning to the darkness. If those eyes of his ever completely turned yellow…they'd all be in a world of hurt.

The happy consequences of what happened when an Empowered male lost his bonded mate.

Looking at Vaughn, a renewed urgency to protect Liv surged through Daegan. The thought of anything happening to her knotted his guts, though they weren't bonded. Hell, they hadn't even *kissed* yet. He had no idea how Vaughn had made it alone this long without turning, though the guy made it abundantly clear he didn't want to live anymore. Unfortunately for Vaughn, his heart kept beating regardless of his constant suffering.

The Reaper wiped his big steel-toed boots on the mat twice, about as close to a show of respect as he ever gave anyone. He entered the kitchen, leaned negligently against the wall with his arms folded across his massive chest. Raising one mocking black brow, he stared at Daegan. "What's up?"

Daegan carefully set his phone down on the counter, fighting back his irritation. "Been busy?"

Vaughn shrugged.

"You know, if you're that bored I guarantee I can find more useful ways to fill your free time."

The Reaper's expression remained completely remote and unapologetic. "I gave those wastes of skin the chance to redeem themselves. They declined it."

A dull throb spread through Daegan's temples. "How many witnesses did you have to scrub afterward?"

"A few, but I was thorough," he answered, a defensive edge in his gravelly voice. "They don't remember anything."

That wasn't the point, but stripping mortals' memories was the least of their worries right now. "Ever stop to consider that offing four victims in such a short time frame might alert someone to our presence? Like, maybe a member of the Dark Army?"

Another shrug, this one bordering on belligerence. It meant *fuck you—I don't want to be here anyway.*

Daegan's temper rose to a simmer. Vaughn was a hardheaded son-of-a-bitch, but this increasing disregard for risking their exposure was a huge problem. Especially now. "You don't care? Then let me make this real clear for you. No more of that bullshit. Because as of two days ago, things are different." He held Vaughn's eerie stare, completely unafraid of him as he dropped the bomb. "I've got a mate to protect now."

Vaughn's head snapped back, his eyebrows drawing together. "*What*?" He cast a disbelieving glance at Cade, who verified the news with a nod.

Daegan understood his shock, but for him Liv's welfare trumped everything else. "She's a Seeker. I won't tolerate anything or anyone jeopardizing her safety. That includes you pulling more reckless stunts. The DA could come after us any day now. Regardless of your personal vendetta and the way you operate, my mate's safety comes first from now on. Period. Understand?"

Those empty black eyes came to life for a split second, and Daegan caught a flash of naked agony in their depths before Vaughn masked it.

Knowing he'd just hit the male's deepest wound, he quickly changed the subject. "And we're moving, so you'd better get your stuff ready."

Vaughn's face was utterly devoid of emotion. A blank screen. If Daegan hadn't been so used to that expression, it would have made his skin crawl. "When?"

"Today." Daegan reached for his coffee, slid his other hand into his front pocket. "But before we do, you and I have something to take care of."

Vaughn straightened, a hint of interest creeping into his expression. "Coven business?"

Daegan gave a hard smile. "Yeah." Coven Law. The old-school way to bring the pain. "We're going to pay a visit to the bastard who went after my mate last night."

AARON WINCED, biting back a curse as he bent over the sink to splash cool water over his ruined face. The pain in his cheekbone made it feel like his eye was going to explode. He glanced up into the mirror."Shit."

That asshole might have broken the bone. The entire right side of his face was swollen and turning a purplish-blue. All because of that snotty bitch locking herself into her car. If he'd been able to get to her before that guy had shown up, things would have turned out much differently.

Someone pounded on the front door.

Cursing, he gingerly pulled a T-shirt over his head then went to the foyer to answer it. Pulling it open, he took an involuntary step back.

The fucker who'd smashed in his face stood on his doorstep.

Aaron's heart stuttered. "What the hell do you want? Get out of here before I call the cops."

The dark-haired man blocked the door from slamming shut with his forearm.

Aaron whipped around and brought his hands up to defend himself. Crazy bastard—who knew what he was going to do? "Get out of my house." He couldn't control the wobble in his voice.

"I want to talk to you."

"Fuck you."

Before he could get to the door and jam it shut, the guy reached in and snatched him around the back of the neck. Aaron let out a sharp cry as he left the ground, hurtling headfirst through the doorway and over the front steps. He hit the grass hard, taking the impact with his ribs and the good side of his face. The hot bolt of pain in his chest was nothing compared to the searing blaze in his battered cheek. He howled in agony and scrambled to his knees, cradling the swollen half of his face in both hands.

A powerful fist grabbed him by the front of his T-shirt, hauling him six inches off the ground. His eyes popped wide as he clawed at the hand, staring down at the scary-ass dude. He was freakishly strong, holding him in the air like a rag doll despite Aaron's height and size. Those ice-blue eyes were so cold they burned.

"Christ, put me down!"

"Why did you go after Olivia?" he snarled, pale eyes narrowed to slits.

"I didn't!" Aaron kicked and struggled in that iron

grip, but to no avail. "She was supposed to show me the…house," he managed past the pressure of the twisted neckline pressing on his throat. "She wouldn't get…out of the car…"

"Because she knew you'd rape her if she did."

He blanched, then flushed. *How did*…"No—"

The man flung him down with an angry growl.

Aaron knees thudded on the dewy grass, his heart thundering against his chest. He cast a frantic glance around him. It was fucking Saturday morning in the middle of summer—why wasn't anyone else outside? No joggers, no kids outside riding their bikes, not one of his neighbors out getting their papers or washing their cars. He trained wary eyes on his attacker, hating the way his insides shriveled under that cold blue stare.

The man's whole body radiated power and menace. "Last chance, asshole."

Shrinking from the promise of hell in those eyes, Aaron shook his head in helpless denial. He wasn't going to say anything.

That hard mouth thinned in disgust. "As much as I'd love to take you out myself, Coven Law dictates you get to make the final choice about your fate."

A shiver of apprehension raced down his spine. Coven Law? Final choice about his fate? What was this crazy fucker *talking* about?

The man's jaw clenched, his eyes hardening further as he pulled out his phone. He held Aaron's stare while he hit a button, then a second later said, "Vaughn. He's all yours."

Aaron yelped and fell backward onto his ass when another man suddenly appeared on the grass next to the other one. Apart from the way he'd just poofed onto his front lawn, this dude was bigger than the last, with a scarred face and weird-ass eyes that made Aaron's bowels cramp in terror. If the first guy was lethal, this one was the angel of death.

Aaron scuttled backward like a crab, his brain shrieking in denial as the big bastard stalked toward him. A whimper clawed out of his tight throat at the promise of death he saw in those eyes. Oh shit, he was going to die. Right here and now the guy was gonna kill him, in his own front yard, and there were no witnesses around to see it.

The tips of the man's boots stopped inches from Aaron's shaking bare toes. He didn't make a move to touch him, but Aaron couldn't budge, trapped by those freaky eyes. Though he wanted to, he couldn't look away.

He stared up at the frightening man helplessly, and everything else around him faded away. He no longer heard the birds chirping and the drone of a lawnmower one block over. He couldn't feel the pain in his face or the damp grass beneath him. Everything went numb and quiet and kind of...fuzzy.

His mind went blank for a split second. Then pictures began flashing through his brain, one after the other, like a high-speed PowerPoint presentation.

His sister's sixth birthday when he'd pulled the head off her new doll and made her cry. Bullying kids during middle school. Backhanding a girlfriend across the face during their first fight. Screaming and threatening another one. Shoving his wife down the stairs the day they'd come home from their honeymoon. Years later, wrapping his hands around her throat as he pinned

her to the bedroom wall, liking the terror in her eyes
as he squeezed.

A flicker of shame curled somewhere deep inside
him, but it was quickly extinguished by another, more
disturbing image: the stricken look on his little girl's
face when she'd come around the corner and seen him
choking her mother.

His soul flinched as he physically experienced her
reaction. Fear and hurt flooded his body, turned his
knees to jelly. It clawed at him, ripping at his insides.
She was afraid of him. His own daughter.

Then, as suddenly as they'd appeared, the sensations
died away, leaving him shaken. He'd lost his daughter
that day. Revulsion rose up, so thick he almost choked
on it. God, how had he done those things?

"Look at me."

His head snapped up at the raspy command. He
squinted at the man in front of him. Judge, jury and
executioner all in one. He felt so confused, disoriented.

I see evil in you. The harsh words whispered through
his mind, dark and insidious. *I destroy evil beings.*

He recoiled from the accusation. Him, evil? No. He
couldn't be. He had a bad temper sure, but...God, that
image of him choking his wife and liking it. Getting
off on the helpless terror in her expression. The pleading in her tear-bright eyes. The hair on his arms stood
up. Maybe he *was* a monster.

The snapshot of his daughter's stricken face stayed
on his mind's screen, her terror and devastation crushing him. He used to be her hero, before he'd ruined everything. More than anything he wanted her to look up

to him. So far he'd only given her reason to hate and fear him. No more, he vowed.

"I'm not evil," he wheezed. He wasn't. Not really. He was just so angry at the world. Sick of feeling that way.

Change now, or die.

Change. Was it possible? He wanted to believe it was. Did this mean he could? He wished he could wipe the slate clean and start over fresh. His life would be so different. But the anger had always gotten in the way. He didn't know how to let it go.

Choose.

He started to shake. *Yes.* He wanted to change. Had to, for his daughter's sake. He'd lose her forever if he didn't.

Something shifted deep inside him. Like a mechanism was turning. Unlocking. A surge of hope rose in his chest as he stared into those creepy, swirling eyes.

A heartbeat later something split open under his ribs. He jumped under the sharp jolt of pain then watched transfixed as thick black vapor escaped from his nose. It rose above him to form a small cloud over his head, slowly dissipating in the clear morning air. In its wake a beautiful warmth spread through his veins. He closed his eyes as it filled him up, bringing a wondrous sense of calm. Of peace.

He breathed in deeply, gave a startled smile. He felt light. Whole.

What just happened? He'd been thinking about something. Something upsetting. He winced as a sharp pain speared through his head.

When he opened his eyes, he was kneeling on the

damp grass of his lawn. A stranger was standing on the front walk, watching him. "You okay?"

Aaron blinked at the man. Climbed to his feet. Damn, his face hurt, he realized, gingerly placing his fingertips against it. "Yes. Sorry. Can I help you?" Why was he outside on the grass in his bare feet?

The man's pale blue eyes assessed him for a moment. "Quite a shiner you've got there."

Aaron nodded, then frowned as a sudden vision came to him. Last night at that big house. He was screaming through the car window at Olivia, Melissa's piano teacher. Pounding on the glass and ripping at the door, like he was bent on breaking through it to get to her.

Guilt and remorse seared him. Christ, that hadn't actually happened, had it? He didn't remember the incident or what happened afterward, but she must have hit him to get away.

His stomach seized at the thought of what he'd done. He didn't blame her for smashing in his face. He deserved that and more for his behavior. What if she'd called the police? How was he ever going to face her again?

The stranger was still standing on the walkway. Aaron cleared his throat. "Do you need something from me?"

"Not a thing," the man replied, staring for another moment before he walked down the path to the black Porsche parked at the curb.

As it drove away, Aaron's only thought was that he needed to call his daughter, see if she'd let him take her out for breakfast. His legs weren't quite steady when he climbed to his feet, headed for the front door. He had to make things right again between them. Starting now, he was going to be the kind of man she'd be proud to call her father.

CHAPTER FIVE

XAVIER STROLLED THROUGH the rundown Barcelona neighborhood, his senses alive with all the energy spewing at him. The air was permeated with the usual suffering one would expect to find in an area like this. Poverty, and all the effects that came with it. Crime. Drugs. Alcohol. Prostitution. Abuse, both physical and sexual. Murder.

His skin tingled with excitement as he walked deeper into the slum. The emotions came at him almost too fast for him to decipher. Anger. Betrayal. Jealousy. Bitterness. Despair. Hatred. He soaked them up like a dehydrated sponge, every ounce of him absorbing the emotional toll of human suffering. He could almost feel his cells expanding with the constant supply of power.

A thirtyish prostitute gave him a sloe-eyed look as he passed, but he ignored her. She was too far gone with drugs to be of any use to him, numbed out and not registering any emotion at all. A half block down he heard a couple fighting. The man screamed obscenities while the woman cried and pleaded, her squeals turning shrill between the sounds of fists thudding into flesh. Xavier breathed in deeply and let it fuel him, drawing from the man's mindless rage and the woman's pain.

He was practically shaking with sensory overload when he neared the edge of the slum. His body hummed with raw strength. The power felt so good. Maybe if he walked this same neighborhood each day, the last change would finally come upon him. He was tired of waiting for his body to come to full strength.

Crossing the street to step over a gutter streaming with garbage and human waste, he spotted a woman in his peripheral vision. He paused, something about her making him take a closer look. Then she turned and he saw her face. He froze in startled recognition.

The woman from the hotel. The one with Marie's eyes.

She lifted her head, gazing back at him mournfully. An unwanted surge of pity welled up inside him. Whatever burdens she carried, they had all but killed her. Her back was hunched, stooped from age and a lifetime of backbreaking labor. Her dark eyes were dull. The spirit was gone, the empty shell of her body merely going through the motions of living.

Xavier knew all too well how that felt.

His feet began moving on their own. He crossed the street and followed her. She cast a nervous glance behind her then slowed, as though accepting death if he caught up to her and tried to kill her. She'd let him. Might even welcome the release from her earthly suffering. Xavier knew it to the marrow of his bones.

It disturbed him greatly. That surprised him.

Pulled toward her by some invisible force, he followed her through the crowded row of hovels constructed of cardboard and corrugated iron sheets. Mostly Rom families lived here, bedraggled gypsy refugees without the means to support themselves. Filthy, ragged children stopped what they were doing to watch him pass. The few adults he saw watched him with unease and distrust. Stained and threadbare laundry hung from the dilapidated structures, many of them half-buried in refuse. The sickly stench of rotting garbage rose up in the thick, humid air. He pulled his shirt up over his nose and mouth to block it, but it didn't help.

The woman turned and disappeared into a tiny shack. Unlike the rest of the filthy hovels lining the alley, hers was almost painfully clean. The front stoop had been swept clean and no garbage lay around it.

He stepped up to the plywood door, knocked sharply.

The woman stepped out of the shadows, her expression at once wary and resigned. But he hadn't come to harm her. As he reached into his pocket, his eyes adjusted enough to see into the tiny dwelling. His gaze fell on the young boy sitting cross-legged on the dirt floor, playing with a stick and a piece of twine. No older than eight or nine, his facial features were sharp with the terrible mark of hunger. The bones in his shoulders and face stood out too prominently.

Xavier's heart throbbed hard in his chest. He moved toward the child, a sense of anticipation shivering through him.

The old woman suddenly blocked his way, putting herself between him and the boy. Her dull eyes flared to life, radiating a fierce resolve to protect him or die trying.

Xavier held up a hand. "It's all right. I'm not here to hurt you." There was something about this boy that called to him. Some reason he'd been led here. He felt it.

The woman moved aside hesitantly, never taking her eyes off him.

Xavier stepped toward the boy, peering at his thin face. The black eyes were strange. Unfocused.

Blind, he realized with a start.

"You're not from here," the boy said, staring eerily past Xavier's right shoulder.

"No, I'm not. What's your name?"

"Miguel." The boy smiled. Didn't seem the least bit afraid of him. "Have you brought me a toy?"

"I'm afraid not, but perhaps I've brought something much better." He fingered the roll of money in his pocket.

The smile disappeared. "You don't have to pay me for what you want. I'll still give you what you came for."

Xavier's stomach tightened. Did the boy think he wanted to have sex with him? He was sick at the thought of this young boy being forced to prostitute himself to survive. Felt physically ill that anyone could touch a child that way. It was why he enjoyed draining the pedophiles before he turned them into Dark Army soldiers. They disgusted him, deserved every moment of the torture he inflicted.

Xavier swallowed past the sudden constriction in his throat. "I don't want anything from you." He shot a lethal glare over his shoulder at the old woman. How could she allow this?

A startled pause met his words. "I'm not a whore," the boy said in an offended tone.

The knot in Xavier's gut eased.

"And you do want something from me. You're the man from across the Channel."

He jerked around to stare at him in surprise. The

child couldn't possibly know he was from Britain. His Spanish was perfect, without any trace of an accent. "How do you know that?"

The boy shrugged and fiddled with the twine wrapped around his fingers. "My sense of smell's very good. I recognize your cologne. I smelled it in my dream last night."

The hair on his nape stood up, goose bumps rising across his skin. Dear God, it was the prophecy. He stared at the boy with hollow, burning eyes as everything slid into place. *The all-seeing child shall point you to the key.*

"There's a lady," the boy continued, his expression serious, "with the man you're looking for. She's his... not his wife," he added with a frown. "Something different that means the same."

"Mate," Xavier whispered.

The boy grinned, nodded. "Yes. His mate. She's the key."

Xavier began to tremble. His heart raced, forcing him to breathe in choppy bursts. "I..." He didn't know what to say.

Those black, sightless eyes seemed to focus on him for just an instant, then sought the woman, hovering nervously by the door. "I'm hungry, Grandmother. May I have something to eat?"

Xavier's heart squeezed, a foreign sensation he hadn't felt in decades. He rubbed a hand over his chest, thinking of the meager food supply these people must have. Probably some polenta, maybe some stale bread or rancid fruit. Not enough to fill in the terrible hollows beneath the boy's cheekbones. Not even enough to ease the terrible grinding he must feel in that concave stomach. He looked too much like the children Xavier seen in the concentration camps. It made him want to weep.

His hand shook as he withdrew the wad of cash from his pocket. Crouching down, he took the boy's hand and wrapped the bony little fingers around the money. Enough to feed him and his grandmother for a year. "Thank you," Xavier said hoarsely.

The boy's eyes widened, fingers investigating the roll of bills. "It was nothing."

He barely heard the grandmother's gasp of exclamation or the frantic thank yous she called after him. In a daze he walked back the way he'd come.

He finally knew what the key was. Now he just had to find her.

ALREADY IN A foul mood, Liv made a sound of disgust when she turned into the long cobblestone driveway late the next morning. A moving truck was parked out front of the mansion beside a cable company van and one from a furniture store. Daegan's Porsche was there, too, along with a new black Shelby Mustang and a Silver Range Rover.

Apparently Daegan had not only taken possession without her knowledge, but he'd pulled off the impossible and arranged an entire move in less than two days. After the emotional and physical torture she'd endured last night, she was good and pissed off. She wanted answers. Right the hell now.

Her temper did a slow burn on her way to the front door. Her eyes still felt scratchy and swollen from crying on and off all night. When her body wasn't caught in the grip of sexual frustration, that is. Despite her exhaustion today she'd done her usual Saturday morning schedule of piano lessons, then found a message on her phone from the estate's lawyer saying the paperwork had been completed and the buyer had taken possession of the property. All within a matter of hours, and all without her having any clue. Liv had no idea how Daegan had managed to pull it all off, but she intended to find out.

The deep chime of the doorbell echoed in her ears. A minute later Cade pulled the door open, holding a drill and wearing a tool belt around his waist.

"Hey," he said, looking surprised to see her. "How's it going?"

She pasted on a smile. After last night how did he *think* she was doing? "I'm dealing. I see you guys are settling in fine?" *And that you've managed to coordinate a small army to help you do it.*

"Um, yeah." He took a step back, his expression a bit wary. "I'm guessing from the look on your face that Daegan didn't tell you we got the place, huh."

"No, actually. He hasn't told me about *a lot* of things." That was all about to change, however.

He seemed to smother a grin. "Wanna come in?"

"Yeah, thanks." She glanced around the spacious living room where a crew from an electronics store was already installing a huge flat screen TV over the marble mantle. No way should all this be happening so smoothly. Anyone else would have suffered through the ordeal of trying to arrange all the various steps necessary for a move this size. Not Daegan. If she didn't know better she'd swear he'd organized everything days

ago, like he'd already known what day he'd get possession. Or maybe…maybe he'd used some sort of magic.

She almost laughed at herself for thinking that way
but let out a sigh instead, not knowing what to think
anymore. When she'd woken up this morning she'd
wondered for a moment if it had all been nothing but a
vivid, crazy, erotically charged dream. Unfortunately,
last night's bombshell of a conversation and the insistent pulsing ache between her legs the moment she
thought of Daegan said it wasn't.

The handful of orgasms she'd been forced to allow
herself throughout the hellishly long night hadn't done
anything to take the edge off. She'd awakened incredibly horny and lonely. And sad. She'd actually missed
him, and on a level that didn't make any sense. Like she
was irrevocably linked to him already in some way. It
was slowly driving her mad.

"I was just down setting up the equipment area,"
Cade said to her. "Do you want something to drink?
Fridge is stocked."

Shocking, she thought wryly. "I'm fine, thanks. Is
Daegan in?"

"He was helping me a few minutes ago. Come on
down with me."

She followed him down the curving mahogany
staircase, still trying to figure out how Daegan had
managed everything. Cade led her through the fully
equipped gym with weights and fitness machines already set up, then past a room they'd arranged with
what looked like boxing stuff. They passed through a
steel reinforced door into a brightly lit room.

She stopped cold. Stainless steel tables lined one

wall, cabinets filled with medical supplies filled another. On the opposite side of the room, tall lockers covered the length of the wall. There were no windows. The overall effect was cold and a bit creepy.

Her eyes widened. Was that an operating table in the corner? She wrapped her arms around her waist. "What *is* this place, anyway?" It looked like a damned morgue.

"Medical area. Used to be an open storage room."

She looked at him in surprise. "You're going to see patients *here*? Out of your house?"

"Uh, not exactly." Cade cleared his throat and looked around, as if trying to figure out how to explain it.

Liv frowned for a second, then put her hands on her hips. "Just—where's Daegan?"

"I'm right here."

She whipped around, completely unprepared for the shock to her heart when she saw him standing in the doorway. Despite herself, her body instantly warmed, her nipples tightening. The tips rubbed painfully against her bra, so sensitive she almost winced. "Hi," she replied. Her voice was all breathy, and it annoyed her. She was here to get answers, not get sucked further under his spell, or whatever the hell was happening to her.

"How was your night?" he asked as he crossed the room, gaze locked on hers.

"I'm guessing it was about the same as yours," she snapped. She hoped he'd been every bit as miserable as she had.

A flash of satisfaction lit his eyes. "You could've called me. I would have helped you."

Liv folded her arms across her throbbing breasts and

scowled. "Not going to happen." She refused to give in to this ridiculous physical need and the bullshit story about mates and bonding. Whatever that meant. So she was horny all the time, and worse at night. So what? She'd cope. "I can handle whatever this is on my own."

"Not for long."

Her eyes narrowed, and they stared at each other in the expanding silence. She refused to be the first to look away.

"See you," Cade suddenly blurted behind them then took off. She heard his rapid footsteps retreating down the hallway but didn't take her eyes off Daegan.

She thrust her chin out. "You've gotten a lot done since I saw you last, considering it was only last night. At *midnight*."

He tilted his head. Calm, but emanating that undeniable authority he held. "Want to talk in here, or outside so we have some privacy?"

"Fine." She tossed her hair over her shoulder and marched over to the heavy bronze French door that led out to the granite patio, then down the few steps to where the lawn began. Without waiting to see if he'd followed, she continued past the formal courtyard garden and down the slope to the rose garden.

Fragrant blooms of crimson, pale yellow and apricot nodded in the gentle breeze. Bees hummed in the summer sunshine. Below the cliff, the tide was out, leaving dozens of tidal pools shimmering among the glistening sand. A few gulls circled the shoreline, their faint cries carrying on the salty breeze.

The beautiful setting should have relaxed her, but instead she felt only a crushing sense of confusion.

Her stomach was in knots. What was she supposed to do about all this? How could she actually believe what had happened last night?

Daegan came up next to her, put his hands in his jeans pockets. "Are you all right?"

She scoffed. "What the hell do you think?"

"I think you're beautiful even though you're scared and angry."

Under the circumstances, his compliment was pathetic. "I'd be stupid not to be scared, even if it was just because of what Aaron did last night."

Daegan's eyes changed, glittering dangerously. "He won't ever bother you again. You have my word on it."

His grim expression and tone alarmed her. "Why, what did you do to him? Is he in jail?" She'd been too upset and distracted by everything else to follow up with the police.

"No, but I took care of it."

The deadly look in his eyes made the blood drain from her face. "Oh my God, you killed him?" She took a quick step back.

"No," he said quickly. "Other than a busted face he's fine. But I swear to you, he won't bother you again."

Liv blinked at him, trying to read between the lines. What had Daegan done? What else was he keeping from her about his "capabilities"?

Stop it. It's not real. It can't be real.

She felt like clapping her hands over her ears.

"You're upset," he began, searching her eyes.

"Of course I'm upset! Last night I felt like I was losing my mind. Then you go behind my back and pull I don't know how many strings to get this deal closed without me having a frigging clue. Do I even get my commission, by the way? Or did you go through my boss instead to get this deal done so fast?"

A muscle clenched in his jaw. "You'll get your commission."

The thought of all that money should have taken the edge off her temper, but it didn't. Part of her didn't even want it, on principle. "I have no idea how in hell you got the kind of funding to pay for this place up front. What is it you do exactly? Are you some kind of arms dealer or drug lord the law hasn't caught up to yet?"

"It's not like that." His jaw tightened.

She raised an accusatory brow. "No? Then how is it? Tell me—I'm dying to know. Because on top of all of this, since I met you my life has become a roller coaster and I'm perpetually horny. I have every right to be upset!"

Rather than rise to the anger in her tone, Daegan remained irritatingly calm. "I told you, I'm a business man and a military contractor. A legitimate one."

A shiver sped up her spine. He seemed sincere, but she couldn't discount the dangerous vibe that clung to him. He'd done time in the military. Was trained to kill. She swallowed. "And what about arranging all of this so fast?" She waved a hand around to encompass the estate, the move.

He exhaled slowly. "Sometimes I can predict things. I get flashes of images, things that are about to happen."

"Uh-huh," she replied. "Like when a real estate deal will close and how far in advance you have to book moving and installation services." Her tone dripped with annoyance.

"In this case, yes."

If he was playing some sort of elaborate prank on her, she'd kill him. Pure and simple."Did you do something to make all this happen? Put a spell on someone? Change the time continuum, what?"

"I can use mental persuasion on most people. Like a mental push."

"Have you done that to me?" she asked, horrified.

"No. Never, I swear."

God, she'd lost it to even be thinking those things were possible. She ran her hands over her face, trying to decide if she should seek professional help. Medication at the very least.

"You're not crazy, Liv."

She jerked her head up. "Did you just read my mind?"

"No," he said, holding up his hands. "I could see it in your face."

Yeah, well, could he see that she was an inch from bawling too? She'd be damned if she'd let *that* happen again. "Did you know we were going to meet before I showed you the property?"

"No. Meeting you was as much a surprise for me as it was for you."

"I highly doubt that." Her voice was bitter, full of anger. She despised that she couldn't help it. "I hate feeling like this—this isn't me. I'm a nice person. A calm person. I have a quiet, normal life and I like it that way." Sure, besides Catherine she didn't have a lot of friends and she got lonely sometimes, but she'd been thinking about getting a dog to fix that. "Everything was fine. Then you come along and *bang*, it's all chaos."

She shook her head, letting him see the torment inside her. "I don't know what to think, what to believe right now. I'm not even close to ready to face something like this. I can hardly process what happened last night, let alone everything else." Daegan shook his head and reached out a hand, but she flinched, jerked back. "Don't touch me. I can't think straight when you touch me."

"All right." His voice was rife with frustration but he dropped his hand.

She resented feeling so angry and out of control. Hated speaking to him that way. "My whole life I've struggled to fit in. I've never felt like I belonged anywhere, and just when I'm starting to make peace with what I have, you show up and blow it all to hell in less than a day."

"I'm sorry. I know it's been hard. But there's a reason for all those things you just described."

Cold seeped into her, despite the warmth of the sun on her bare shoulders. "Like what?"

"We don't have many close relationships, especially with mortals, because we age so much slower than they do."

Mortals. Like they—he—wasn't quite human. She lifted her chin and tightened her arms under her breasts. "I've aged at a perfectly normal rate."

"Up 'til now, yes. But it will slow down to synch with mine."

God, that was so weird. "So how old *are* you?"

He looked her dead in the eye. "Two hundred and three."

She gaped at him. After Cade's parting comment

last night that's what she suspected he'd say, but it was still hard to hear. She put a hand to her throat. "How is that even possible?"

"Our race usually lives to about four hundred or so. Sometimes longer."

Our race. Meaning she was part of this, too, whether she wanted to be or not. The words sent a shiver skittering over her skin. She rubbed her arms to warm them. "What else?"

"We tend to keep to our own kind because it protects us from suffering the constant grief we'd experience if we befriend mortals. And because it makes it easier for us to fulfill our purpose."

"And that is?" She braced herself, convinced she wasn't going to like the answer.

Daegan sighed, and for the first time she noticed the lines of fatigue around his eyes, his mouth. He must not have slept much either the past two nights. "There's so much I have to tell you. It's going to take time to sort everything out."

"No, I want to know what's happening to me. Who are you, really? *What* are you?"

"I'm an Empowered, same as you."

"But what does that mean?" She was ready to scream.

"Our ancestors have mixed Celtic and Baltic blood. Legend holds we descended from the Lithuanian sea goddess, Neringa. Have you heard of her?"

Liv shook her head.

"Folklore says Neringa was a giantess with many powers. She formed the Curonian Spit with sand thrown from her apron, to protect the fishermen of the area from the powerful storms of the Baltic."

"A giantess from a Lithuanian fairytale," she repeated blandly.

He nodded, his expression all too serious. "No one can prove she existed or that we came from her, but then, no one can disprove it, either. Every one of us who's ever existed has both Celtic and Baltic heritage, and each of us has different abilities that aren't necessarily passed on from ancestors. Cade's found that the genes required to create the Empowered can skip several generations, but I guarantee that if you could trace your family tree back far enough, you'd find stories about strange abilities some of your ancestors held."

Right now she'd give anything to know more about her family history. "And you're saying mine is to see these auras, to tell if someone is dangerous."

"No. I think your gift is to recognize specific people who are evil and pose a direct threat to us."

Her brain struggled to keep up. "Why now? How did I not know about this sooner?"

"Because the Empowered don't usually start developing their abilities until their mid-twenties."

That was true in her case. It was weird to be having this discussion, but there was no way to refute the auras she'd seen, or that Daegan had healed her. "Is that how old you were?"

"Yes."

That would have been back in the eighteen-thirties, she realized with a sickening sense of unreality. She forced down the panic trying to bubble up. "How many of you are there?" She refused to say *us*. There was still a chance he was wrong about her. A slim one maybe, but she wasn't willing to entirely give that up yet.

"Including you, there are only me, Cade and Vaughn left that we know of."

Only four known Empowered in existence. The tiny number took her off guard for a moment.

"But there are more, Liv, out there somewhere. Empowered just like you who don't realize what they are because there's been no one to guide them. We call them The Lost, and we have to find as many of them as we can. You're the first we've found since the end of the Second World War."

"What if I still don't believe it includes me?"

He raised a challenging brow. "You need more proof?"

"What if I do?" She needed something more. Something empirical to provide the logic missing from this whole equation.

"Then get Cade to collect a DNA sample," he said.

"Yeah, and what will that prove?"

"Your heritage. Your lineage. That you're linked to the rest of us through your maternal DNA."

She stared at him, wondering if the answer could really be so simple. What if it *did* prove it? Hell, at this point anything scientific was worth a shot. "Fine, I'll ask him to take a sample next time I see him." She shifted her feet. "So there's only four, plus any of these 'Lost' you might find." It didn't seem possible.

He shrugged, the motion stiff, almost defiant. "In the early days there were hundreds of us, but the Dark Army has hunted us near to extinction. We've lived off the radar ever since."

God, they'd been all but exterminated. A chill spread through her body. "Who?"

He shifted uncomfortably and jammed his hands deeper into his pockets. "Look, I don't want to scare you, but you have a right to know."

That didn't sound good, and it didn't help the churning in her stomach.

He exhaled, and she caught the regret embedded in his crystalline eyes. "There's a war coming, Liv."

Her eyes widened. "What do you mean? Here?" As in, fighting and killing? The thought horrified her.

"Between us and the Obsidian Lord's Dark Army. Your arrival as Seeker is a sign it's about to begin again."

Begin again, meaning it had happened before. The unfamiliar names he'd just used were as frightening as the rest of it. "So there's a bad guy out there somewhere with an army, and he's coming after us. You," she corrected quickly.

Daegan nodded, a muscle clenching in his jaw. "The Obsidian Lord is an Empowered male who lost his mate. Usually a former Coven Leader. When he turns to the darkness inside him he becomes the embodiment of evil, intent on destroying the Empowered to enslave human kind. The last one was killed at the end of World War II, but another will take his place soon. There's a prophecy that's been handed down verbally through the generations, telling of the final battle between us. We think this is it, we just don't know when it will start, or who he is."

Before her knees could buckle, she reached behind her and felt the hard edge of the garden bench. She dropped onto it, her body rigid. "That's why you need all that equipment in there," she said hoarsely, waving a hand toward the house. "The gym, and that…awful room with all the surgical stuff in it." She hadn't liked that place at all. The simple memory of it made her feel cold. On a shaky breath, Liv turned her gaze on him. Those tall lockers must be holding weapons. "Because you're training for battle and you know there will be casualties." The word made her gorge rise.

Daegan took a step toward her, his eyes full of torment. "Liv, just—"

"No," she said sharply, holding out a hand to ward him off. Right now the numbness was preferable to the heat his touch brought.

He stopped, released a frustrated breath.

She ignored it and continued. "So, let's just say I believe you for a minute—that means there's four of us and whatever Lost you can find against an entire army created by some evil magical person called the Obsidian Lord."

A reluctant nod, his gaze squarely on hers. "We have to find the Lost before he does."

"And I'm…I'm going to be part of this war?" Her stomach felt queasy. She was a realtor. A piano teacher. Just two days ago she'd been comfortably ensconced in a safe, sane world, savoring her peaceful evenings curled up with a book, or sharing a bottle of wine with Catherine. Now that was all over.

"In a way, yes."

She swallowed. "And will I have to fight soldiers of this Dark Army?" She didn't know the first thing about fighting. She'd never even hit anyone before. Not in her entire life. And suddenly she was expected to be a soldier?

Daegan dropped to one knee in front of her. She shrank away, but he didn't move closer or try to touch her. "You won't be in combat. I'd never let you endanger yourself that way. Ever."

Beneath the sickening realization that there might be no way out of this, she heard the words he *hadn't* said. "Wait. Meaning I won't, but you will? Is that what you're saying?"

"I'm a warrior, Liv. All Empowered males are."

"That's what you meant when you said you've been in the military for most of your life."

"Yes. We're elite soldiers. I've been training as a warrior since I was a boy, and I've fought in more wars than you can name, hunting Dark Army members and the Obsidian Lord all over the world. The last time was in Afghanistan a few months ago, when the Obsidian Lord had turned some Taliban into Dark Army members."

The staggering implications of it hit Liv like a sledgehammer. It changed her entire understanding of history in one moment. A sudden picture of him engaged in a firefight came to her mind. Explosions burst around him, bullets whizzed through the air. Hot tears burned her eyes. "You're the leader, aren't you?" She'd known it. On some level she'd known that from the first time she'd laid eyes on him. The air of command he held was absolute. Unmistakable.

A firm nod. "My official title is Coven Leader."

So he'd be at the front, right in the thick of the fighting, in whatever form it took. And he'd die in the futile effort of defending the four of them against a whole enemy army. If she was the first of the Lost they'd found in over a half century, she didn't hold out much hope they'd locate more to help even the odds. Despair rose up, thick enough to choke on. Her eyes stung, a tear rolled down her cheek. She swiped it away angrily.

"Liv…" Daegan reached for her.

She shook her head and bit her lip to keep the sob trapped in her chest. "No, don't."

"I have to," he said softly, gently brushing her tears away with his fingertips. "You're my mate. I can't stand to see you hurting and not touch you."

"How can you just accept that we're mates? You didn't even know I existed until a few days ago."

"Because I feel it in here," he said, tapping the place over his heart. "And because I understand the way it works between Empowered mates. Fighting this won't do any good."

"Well, what if I *can't* accept it?" Her shoulders jerked and she covered her face with her hands. Damn, no more crying! The last thing she wanted was to appear weak in front of this man or let him know how attached she was to him already.

The next instant, hard arms enveloped her and gathered her up against his muscled torso. Warmth immediately flowed over her, into her trembling muscles. On a ragged sigh, Liv squeezed her eyes shut and wrapped her arms around his strong back, burying her face into his shoulder. He felt so incredible. She might not be able to accept everything he'd told her, but she couldn't fight this physical part of it any longer. Didn't want to.

Nothing about this made sense, but she needed his

reassurance and the comfort only he could give. He was strong, protective. Her body melted against him.

Daegan made a rough sound and brought her even closer, tightening his arms around her. The bulge of his erection pressed against her hip. A light shudder ripped through him, making her heart squeeze to know she affected him as much as he did her.

Tingles of electricity sparkled at every point of contact between them. Her sadness dimmed as all her senses focused on the man holding her. He smelled so good, felt even better. She wished he didn't. "I'm scared," she finally admitted in a whisper.

Daegan stroked his palms over her back. "I know, love. But you've got me and the others to look after you now. I swear I'll never let anything happen to you. You're safe with me."

No, she wasn't. She felt like she was on the verge of losing herself completely. That the Olivia Farrell she'd always known no longer existed. Maybe never had.

The added threat of war sent jagged bolts of fear through her heart. "I'm scared for you too. I don't want anything to happen to you." She might not know him very well, but she liked him. Except for going behind her back with the paperwork, he'd been polite and respectful to her. Kind. He'd saved her from Aaron last night, then shielded her. Taken her home, cared for her without expecting anything in return.

And she couldn't deny the sexual pull between them. Her entire body lit up when he was near. The thought of him wounded or dying made her throat close up.

He hugged her tight. "I'm good at what I do. We all are, and we've been continually trained by the best military units in the world throughout our lives. You'll see."

But she didn't *want* to see that, or any of this. Being mated to a warrior while a futile war raged around them? Constantly wondering what was going on and terrified something would happen to him? It was too much for her brain to take in, much less process.

She was drained, yet the steady hum of sexual awareness between them wouldn't let go. Exhausted as her body was, she wanted him. Needed him on a level she couldn't begin to understand. Being in his arms like this felt exactly right. Scarily right. She wanted more. Needed to feel his naked skin against hers, to feel his weight pinning her to the bed while he filled her empty body and took away the horrible uncertainty and hunger warring inside her.

Warm fingers stroked the hair away from the side of her face. So gentle, despite the immense power in the muscles surrounding her. She turned toward his hand, leaning into his touch.

Daegan stilled, and the heat smoldering inside her began to build. Her fingers crept up his neck to slide into his hair, thick and soft against her skin.

She murmured in pleasure as the strands slid between her hands. "I can't stay away from you."

"Liv," he whispered, capturing her face between his hands to raise her head until she met his eyes. So beautiful, surrounded by the thick fringe of black lashes that made the hue even more startling. His gaze dipped down to her mouth for a moment, and she felt their touch deep in the pit of her belly.

A delicious curl of warmth spread through her abdomen. She wanted this. Wanted him.

He looked into her eyes, thumbs wiping away the last of her tears. "Come here," he murmured, leaning down to kiss her.

Liv gasped, tightening her fingers in his hair when his lips touched hers. The exquisite gentleness of the kiss turned her inside out, made her press her body harder against him. Daegan maintained his hold on her, refusing to let her deepen the kiss while he brushed his mouth over hers, nibbling lightly at the corners.

Flames licked across her skin wherever his lips touched. She whimpered and pushed up toward him, needing more, needing it harder. Her mouth opened beneath his, a quiet moan spilling free at the tender stroke of his tongue against her lips. She met it eagerly, sliding her tongue over his, exploring and pleasing herself. He tasted faintly of cinnamon, and he definitely knew how to kiss a woman. Each velvet caress of his tongue made the muscles in her core clench around the aching void of need until she wanted to crawl inside him. His hands cradled her face almost lovingly, his thumbs slowly skimming over her cheekbones while he kissed her until she was shaking.

But before she could get enough he placed a slow, lingering kiss against her parted lips then leaned back.

Liv pulled at his head and rose up blindly, reaching for him. She was so hungry for him. Wanted to rip off their clothes, to feel his naked skin against hers. Her breasts tingled, her body ached to be touched.

Daegan shook his head, gently caged her in his arms.

"Shh, I know, love. But not here," he whispered roughly against her temple, stroking her hair, her back.

Breathing fast, heart pounding, Liv struggled to control her body's reaction. She held onto his shoulders and opened her eyes, feeling like he'd left her dangling at the rim of a cliff.

"I know," he soothed when she opened her mouth to protest.

She felt like crying again. Her body was on edge, miserable. It hurt to pull away from him.

Daegan kissed her temple, her cheek. "But unless you want me to take you here and now, we'd better wait until we have some privacy." The steely erection digging into her and the gravel in his voice told her he was suffering too.

With effort, she released her hold on his shoulders to climb off his lap. Her muscles were both stiff and weak at the same time. God, she'd almost lost control.

On unsteady legs she stood, looking back up at the house. Heat suffused her face. She'd been ready to strip naked and have sex with him here in the middle of the day, right out in the open where anyone could have seen them. And she wouldn't have cared one bit. The knowledge jarred her.

"You must be tired," he said.

Tired didn't begin to cover it. "Yes."

"Get some sleep. You're welcome to stay here if you want. There're fresh sheets on the bed in the master suite."

His bed. She remembered the massive walnut sleigh bed anchored against the far wall of the room. Had even dreamed about being pinned beneath him in it.

The thought of sliding into it to wait for him made her exhausted body surge back to tingling life. "I think I'd better go home for awhile."

She didn't miss the flicker of disappointment in his eyes as he tucked a lock of hair behind her ear. "Okay. You know where I am if you need me."

A wave of lust hit her at the words, but she ruthlessly pushed it away. She stepped back and took a deep breath, her mind in turmoil. The whole "mate" thing was a mystery to her, but she didn't have the energy to ask him about it right now. There were a million other questions she wanted answered, and they would have to wait. She couldn't think around him. She needed some space.

"Bye." Before he could answer she whirled on her heel and rushed back up the grassy slope, leaving him standing at the cliff's edge.

CHAPTER SIX

CADE CAUGHT A whiff of Liv's scent a split second after she opened the exterior door to the patio. He cursed under his breath and slammed the gun cabinet door shut, trying to appear casual as her footsteps approached. Tough to do when he had to hide a stockpile of firearms and explosives, but he didn't want to scare her more by letting her see them.

The heavy steel door groaned open. Liv peered in at him. Her face was pale, her expression full of resignation. And a good deal of resentment. "Hi," she said, wrapping her arms around her waist. She glanced around the room, her posture stiff, then looked back at him. "Are you busy?"

"No, not at all." *Just inspecting all the M4s and Symtex because there's a war coming any time now.*

He could see the silent resolve in her as she held his stare. He almost smiled. She was a pretty little thing with an iron backbone. He was glad about the latter, because in the weeks and months ahead she was going to need every bit of steel he detected in that delicate spine.

"Daegan said something to me earlier." She blew out a hard breath and tossed her long hair over her shoulder. "I was going to leave, but when I was almost to my car I changed my mind. I thought maybe you could help me, being a doctor and all."

Cade leaned against the cabinet and maintained his laid-back demeanor. When she swallowed, looking at all the medical equipment, he sensed her acute discomfort and prompted her. "What can I do for you?"

Her eyes met his, direct and unflinching. He admired the show of spunk in light of all she'd faced in the past twenty-four hours. "He said you could take a DNA sample. That it might show if I'm really…" *One of you.* She didn't say it, but he knew that's what she was thinking.

Cade hid his surprise, wondering how much Daegan had told her. "Sure, I can do that if you want."

"Will it prove anything?"

He nodded. "It will show your ancestral lineage and where they came from. What population group they belonged to. But it's the maternal mitochondrial DNA that's most important. That's where the Empowered bloodline originated and is passed down from."

Her brow wrinkled. "Oh. So if I've got the right bloodline you think that's sufficient proof?"

He already knew she was one of them. This sample was merely about helping her come to grips with it. "Together with the intense attraction between you and Daegan plus your ability to see emotional auras, yes."

She nodded and shifted her feet, glanced away. But when she looked back up at him, her eyes were full of resolve. "Okay, let's do it. I want to find out one way or the other."

He led her over to a stainless steel chair next to a matching small table. "You squeamish about needles?"

"No." She rubbed her arms, glanced around again. "But I'm getting more that way about this room."

Cade smiled to put her more at ease. He wondered about her reaction. It went beyond mere dislike. He sensed a deeper reason behind it. "Yeah, it's pretty sterile."

Liv shook her head. "No, it's not that. Well, that's part of it I guess. There's something about this place that gives me the creeps. Maybe it's all the surgical stuff being in the same room with the weapons."

He barely kept his mouth from falling open. "Daegan told you?" While she was still struggling to come to terms with what she was?

She shrugged, continued rubbing her arms. He could see the goose bumps on her bare skin. Unease rolled off her, so thick he could almost taste it. "I know there's going to be a war against the Obsidian Lord's Dark Army. And I know all three of you are going to be fighting in it. Apparently I am too," she finished dully.

Holy shit. No wonder she was so pale. It took him a moment to respond. "Well. Guess it's best that it's all out in the open, but damn, you're taking all this pretty well." Better than he had when he'd transitioned.

Another shrug, but this one was tight with strain. "Only because I haven't decided yet if I've gone nuts."

He grinned. "No worries there. You're running on all cylinders."

A reluctant smile tugged at the corners of her mouth. "No offense, but I'll feel a bit more convinced of that when we get the results of the DNA test." She sat in the chair. "Where do you send them, anyway? Is there some lab out there that knows about you guys?"

"Not the way you mean, no. Mortals don't know about us, and that's the way it stays for our protection."

"Even if I told the best friend I have, she'd never believe me."

He grabbed some supplies from the well-organized cabinets. A rubber tourniquet, alcohol wipe, syringe, a sterile swab in a sealed test tube. More test tubes for the blood samples. "If someone does discover us, we wipe their memories clean."

"Is that what Daegan did to Aaron?"

Cade whipped his head around, his hand frozen around the test tubes. "What?"

A hint of alarm crept into her eyes. "Daegan said Aaron would never bother me again, but promised he didn't kill him. When you said that about wiping memories, I assumed that's what he'd meant."

It was possible, but Cade doubted that's what had happened. No way would Daegan let the man who'd tried to attack his mate get off so easily. And certainly not if he'd taken Vaughn with him. "Have you met Vaughn yet, by the way?" His tone sounded casual enough.

"No, and don't change the subject, thanks."

If Aaron was still breathing, it meant he'd seen the error of his ways and had a sudden, irreversible change of heart. Cade relaxed. "Daegan's right. You've got nothing to worry about." He sat down beside her and got everything ready. "Let's do the swab first." After taking it out of the tube, he handed it to her. "Rub it against the inside of your cheek for a few seconds."

She did, handing it back.

Once that was sealed he labeled it and reached for the blood kit. "Let me see your veins."

Liv held out her forearms to expose the cubital fos-

sas, while Cade examined them quickly. "This one,"
he said, touching her right arm. Her skin was cool, her
growing phobia of the room evident. He stroked the alcohol wipe over the median cubital vein, tying the rubber tourniquet around her upper arm. "Make a fist."
He capped the syringe onto the first tube, took hold of
her arm. "Want to look away?"

"No, I'm okay."

He poked the needle into her skin and drew the first
sample. Her pulse remained steady, her posture stiff.

"So where are you sending this?" she asked again.

He bit back a smile at the suspicious edge in her
voice. No doubt she wondered if he was going to fab-
ricate the whole thing. "There's a genetics lab at UBC
that I've worked with before. Apparently they just
picked up an expert in Northern European genealogy,
including the British Isles and the Baltic region. I'll
send them to her."

"Daegan mentioned the Empowered have those combined lineages," she said as he filled a second tube.

"That's right." He withdrew the needle, pressed a
cotton ball to the puncture site. "Want to see something really cool?"

"I...sure." She sounded less than enthusiastic.

"Lower your arm." When she did, he removed the
cotton ball. The blood oozed sluggishly out of the tiny
hole, already clotting, but he wanted to show her this.

For an instant he thought about raising her arm and
flicking his tongue over the mark, but Daegan would
kick his ass for it...right after he ripped Cade's head
from his shoulders and yanked out his heart. No male
ever tasted another mate's blood. Not unless he had a

death wish. Instead, Cade licked the end of a sterile swab then touched it to the puncture site.

Liv blinked, leaned closer when he withdrew the swab. While he disposed of it, she held up her arm, staring at the inside of her elbow. "It's not bleeding." She squinted and leaned in farther, until her nose almost touched her arm. "There's not even a mark." Her brows lowered as she glanced up at him. "What did you do?"

He smiled. "We have clotting agents in our saliva," he answered simply, not telling her the reason for it. She had enough to cope with, and that information should definitely come from Daegan. Preferably *before* the bonding happened. "Pretty cool, huh?"

She rubbed the inside of her elbow, frowning at him. "I guess. So can I do that too?"

"Not quite yet. As soon as the uh, bonding's completed you will, though."

"Yeah, let's not get ahead of ourselves," she said with a scowl.

Cade didn't bother telling her it was already a foregone conclusion. He set everything down then pulled out his phone. After he dialed the number he set it on the table, putting it on speaker so she could hear everything and know this wasn't some elaborate scheme he'd cooked up to trick her.

"UBC Health Sciences."

"Genealogical research, please." He waited a few moments to be connected, then when the woman answered said, "This is Dr. Mackintosh."

"Dr. Mackintosh! What can we do for you?"

"I've got another sample I'm sending you for analysis."

"Okay. The usual detailed work-up?"

"Yeah, but I want your Northern European expert to look at it."

"Oh. Nairne's overseas right now, but she's due back at the end of the week. Can she look at it then?"

Nairne. Uncommon name. Old Scottish. The mention of it did something funny to his insides. Sent a tingle through his bloodstream. He pushed the weird reaction aside. "I'd prefer she look at it ASAP. Where is she?"

"Lithuania, I think."

That piqued his curiosity. "Where, exactly?"

"Someplace next to Kaliningrad that's on a spit or something."

Every muscle in his body tightened. "The Curonian Spit?"

"That's it! Yeah, she went there to do more research. Something to do with legends and witches or whatever." The woman laughed. "Nairne's a little different. You know how history buffs are."

Across the table, Liv's eyes had gone wide. She watched him with an unblinking stare while he fought to control his sudden spike in anxiety.

Jesus. Had the genealogical expert gone over there to trace the lineages back and compare them with the legend of Neringa and the Hill of Witches? Did she somehow know about the Empowered? Cade's stomach clenched. Daegan would have to know about this. They might have to track her down, scrub her memory to safeguard their existence.

Cade rubbed the back of his neck to dispel the odd

tingling in his nape, cleared his throat. "Can you send her the report there?"

"I'm sure that would be fine. May I have her contact you?"

"Sure, she can reach me on my cell. I'll courier the sample to you today." He hung up and masked his sudden tension by arching a teasing brow at Liv. "Satisfied?"

She nodded grudgingly. "Yeah." Her tone was almost disappointed. "Weird coincidence though, don't you think? About that doctor being over there to do research?"

"Very." Weird didn't begin to cover it. This might be a serious security breach.

Liv cleared her throat, looking uncertain. "So I guess that's it?"

"'Fraid so. I'll get these packed up and shipped off."

"Thanks." Liv stood, rubbing her fingers over the healed puncture wound in her arm. "And you'll let me know what the outcome is?"

Like he'd keep something that important from her and the others? "Of course."

"Okay." She looked tired now. Tired and out of sorts. "Sorry to be blunt, but…do you have a mate?"

He almost laughed at the idea. "No, and I'm not expecting to find one anytime soon." He didn't do long-term relationships. Short and sweet—very sweet, he thought with a grin—was more his style. Monogamy wasn't a natural thing for him. He wasn't sure he'd ever be able to settle down with one mate, no matter what that fucking prophecy might say.

Liv stared at him. "And this *thing* between me and

Daegan," she began, waving a hand in the air. "Is it...
permanent?" The last word came out almost strangled.

Cade bit back a grin. "With most mates it is."

Her expression brightened. "Most?" She seemed
so hopeful that she and Daegan didn't fall into that
group. Because she didn't know the consequences to
the alternative.

"Like, ninety-nine point nine nine nine percent."

"Great." She huffed out a breath and walked to the
door with a sour expression on her face. "Thanks Cade,
you've been a big help."

"Anytime." When the steel door shut behind her with
a clang, Cade smothered a chuckle and shook his head.
For now he'd keep his eye on the geneticist and watch
the show unfolding around him. He didn't know how
much longer this little drama between Liv and Daegan
would play out, but it couldn't last.

Still, it was a damned amusing to watch his hard-ass
leader struggle futilely against his instinct to bond to
his mate. Poor bastard didn't stand a chance.

"Sir, I think we've found something important."

At the urgency in his operative's voice, Xavier sat
up on the balcony's chaise lounge and set down his
wineglass. "What is it?"

"A bunch of parolees in the Vancouver area, all
dying of heart attacks within a few days of each other.
Including one of our guys."

He was on his feet without consciously moving,
striding into the suite's living room. A Dark Army
member, recently paroled and now dead of cardiac ar-
rest. Interesting, especially when one considered the

time and place. "Did you find Blackwell yet?" His heart pumped fast and hard.

"Not exactly."

His hand tightened around the phone. "There must be something else. Some clue for you to follow." He'd gone over the chance meeting with the blind boy a hundred times. It had to mean they were on the verge of finding him.

"We're trying, sir."

"Try harder," he growled. "He'll have money. Lots of it, left over from the old Coven." God only knew how much it was worth now, having been invested into secure companies and bonds for all these years. "If he's been in the area that long it means he's planning to set up base there for the foreseeable future." And if that was true, it meant there were others with him. Or that more were coming. He struggled to breathe through the sudden spike of adrenaline in his bloodstream. "He'll need a big house, and it'll have to be right near the water. Start with expensive waterfront properties sold in the last few months."

The man made a scoffing sound. "Do you know how many properties there are like that in Vancouver? Let alone Vancouver Island or all the Gulf Islands? He could be anywhere."

"No," Xavier snapped, "he won't be. He'll have to be somewhere in the city or on its outskirts. Nowhere too isolated, and someplace they can blend in easier."

"They?" The man's voice sharpened, a hint of fear creeping in. "There's more than one?"

"Without a doubt." The question was, how many

Empowered were left? And how many were about to go into their transition?

Xavier tightened his jaw, the frustration eating him alive. He wanted to get on a plane and fly over there himself. But he couldn't. He wasn't ready, wouldn't be until he reached full strength. God, when would that be? "Get on it. Bring in more DA recruits and put everyone on it. I need to know what we're up against." He hung up before the man could answer, too annoyed to bother feeding from the useless amount of nervous energy the man had emitted.

He ran a hand over his well-trimmed goatee then went back onto the deck to stare at the rolling waves. The dark prophecy must be about to come true. Blackwell would be the new Coven Leader. If he was settling, his mate must be nearby.

The war was imminent now. Blackwell's mate was the final key. As Obsidian Lord, Xavier had to take away the Empowered mate before they bonded.

He disregarded the part of the dark prophecy stating he should take her for his own. It said he'd find peace again in the world he would rule after all the Empowered were disposed of. That the female would supposedly guarantee his rise to ultimate power and make him whole again.

The repugnant idea filled him with a dangerous, smoldering anger. There would never be another female for him, let alone a mate. Not after Marie. The shattered remnants of his heart remained true to the prescribed nature of the Empowered male he'd been decades ago. Their kind mated once and once only.

Becoming Obsidian Lord might technically change

that, but he refused to even think of claiming another female. He'd settle for taking the Coven Leader's mate and using her as bait. Or he'd kill her instead, thus guaranteeing the slow death of her Empowered mate.

A satisfied smile twisted his lips. If anything could make him whole again, that would. He'd enjoy knowing the Coven Leader was suffering through the same hell as he had all these years, then witness the annihilation of the Empowered bloodline. Maybe that's what the dark prophecy meant. The Empowered didn't even know the document existed, hidden in the place where Marie had suffered her untimely death.

The Obsidian Lord shall confront the Empowered who embodies the reflection of what he once was.

Fucking riddles, he thought, rubbing his tired, burning eyes. Always more riddles. He didn't pretend to fully understand the dark prophecy. He could only trust it would reveal its true meaning in time. For now, he would follow his own theory.

He was meant to confront this Coven Leader *after* his mate was taken from him. Xavier would start at the top with Blackwell, wiping out the others beneath him. Once they found Blackwell, he would lead them directly to the female. It would happen any day now, he sensed it.

Xavier smiled and raised his glass to the sky in a silent toast. *Let the war begin.*

CHAPTER SEVEN

WHEN THE PHYSICAL symptoms of the Heat Cycle started up again after sunset, Daegan wanted to crawl out of his own skin to escape his body. Tonight was worse than before. Having tasted a hint of Liv's hunger earlier, his body would never be satisfied with anything but sinking his cock deep inside her and pounding away until she screamed in release. His aching erection surged at the thought of what she'd feel like, smell like. Sound like as she came.

He let out a frustrated growl, dug the heels of his hands into his eyes, the bright blue glow seeping out from beneath his palms. Working out in the gym wouldn't help. Jacking off in the shower wouldn't help. Alcohol wouldn't touch this raging need. The only thing that might work was a cocktail of meds Cade could mix up for him. He dismissed the thought as soon as it formed, vowing to use that shit only as a last resort. As much as he hated the idea of using them, it might just come down to that.

She didn't know how it was between mates. He didn't know how much longer he could keep from claiming her. This was so fucking complicated, and he couldn't see any way to make it better.

His phone shrilled from his nightstand. To his overstimulated senses, it sounded like a siren going off. With a groan, Daegan rolled over and grabbed it.

When he saw her number, he sat bolt upright in bed, fought to calm his racing heart. "Liv?"

Silence.

His muscles were tight as cables. "Liv, what's wrong?" His heart tripped. Was she all right? Aaron wouldn't have gone after her again. He'd made absolutely sure of it before.

Then he heard breathing on the other end. Shallow. Rapid.

His body tightened in anticipation. Was she finally reaching out for him? "Liv, say something."

"Daegan," she gasped. "I—I can't take it. I…" Her voice trailed off, so full of agonized need it burned him.

Without being conscious of moving he was already off the bed, heading to his closet for a shirt. His heart pounded so hard against his ribcage he felt the reverberations throughout his entire body. "It's okay, Liv. I'm coming to you." His cock was hard as a steel spike against his underwear as he pulled his jeans on. He flinched when he pulled up the zipper.

"Please help."

He closed his eyes in pain for a moment. Knowing she was alone and hurting for him tied him in knots. "I will, love. Just hold on. I'll be there in a few minutes."

"Okay." He thought he heard the edge of tears in her voice.

He raced down the stairs and grabbed his shoes, frantic to get to her.

Cade came out of the living room carrying an empty

plate, stopping dead when he saw him. His mouth fell open, his eyes widening. "You all right?"

"Gotta go," he blurted. "Don't call me unless one of you's dying." Without further explanation he rushed past his gaping cousin and jumped into the Porsche. The engine came to life with a throaty roar. He shoved the stick into first and shot down the driveway.

The wrought iron gate seemed to take hours to open enough for him to drive through. The instant the tires hit asphalt, he hit the throttle and opened it up. His eyes glowed so brilliantly they were almost as intense as the car's high beams lighting up the road in front of him. His mate needed him. Had called him to her. Finally.

Reaching Liv's darkened house, he parked at the curb and ran up the front porch. "Liv?" He waited a moment.

No answer.

Cursing, he opened the lock with his mind and stepped across the threshold. The instant he did, her clean, fresh fragrance hit him like a body blow. Along with a powerful dose of pheromones she emitted.

He sucked in a sharp breath while his heart tried to pound its way out of his chest. Down the hallway, the faintest line of light came from beneath her bedroom door. "Liv?"

"In...here," she answered faintly.

Daegan pushed it open and froze at the sight before him. On the floor beside her bed, Liv stared back at him with glazed eyes. Even from that distance he could see she was shaking, how flushed her face was. A pillow was wedged high between her updrawn knees, her hands dug into the rug on either side of her. Staring at him, she began squirming in place, her expression twisting in misery. "Oh, God, not again—"

"Baby..." He almost tripped over his own feet getting his shoes off, then went over to crouch in front of her. Raising one hand, he smoothed it over her hair, wanting to touch her everywhere at once but holding himself back. "I'm here."

Rather than reach for him, she shocked him by wrenching away and crawling for the bathroom. He stayed where he was, frozen, while she disappeared, slamming the door behind her. A second later he heard the sound of the lock sliding into place.

The ensuing silence nearly suffocated him. He couldn't believe it. Even that far gone with the effects of the Heat Cycle, she'd still run from him. Had locked the door against him as though it could keep him away. Stop what was happening.

Too late. Too late for any of that now.

Crossing to the bathroom door, Daegan closed his eyes and rested his forehead against the cool wood. "Liv, open the door."

"N-no."

He pressed his palm against the hard surface. "I know you're afraid, but I need you to trust me."

A despondent moan answered him.

The muscles in his jaw clenched as he imagined her rolling on the floor, trying in vain to ease the insatiable need inside her. "Liv."

"No!" Another pitiful moan. "God, I can't *take* this."

The protective male in him howled in agony. It took everything in him not to kick in the door and grab her, take her right there on the bathroom floor to put an end to the torture. He refused to invade her space further by mentally picking the lock. "Liv, don't do this. Let me in."

"Just…go."

"Open the door. Please." It cost him to lower himself to begging, but he'd do it for her.

Just when he thought he was going to have to break in, he heard the muffled sounds of movement. The lock turned then the door opened a few inches. Liv scuttled back against the tiled wall, staring at him through tear-glazed eyes. "I don't want this. I don't even *know* you," she accused, a hitch in her voice.

The words knocked the air out of his lungs. His reaction was completely instinctive, and didn't make any logical sense. The specter from his past wrapped a ghostly hand around his throat and squeezed. He understood she was scared and confused, but hearing his mate reject him so adamantly was like a kick to the gut. Whether she wanted to face this or not, they were meant to be together. He had to prove it to her.

"You know me more than you think," he said quietly. "You know I'd never hurt you, that I'll always take care of you." He crouched down again, holding her gaze. "I'll protect you with my life." Edging closer as though approaching a frightened animal, he carefully stroked a tendril of honey-colored hair away from her cheek.

In answer, Liv grabbed hold of his wrist, moaning through gritted teeth as her body undulated in an uncontrollable wave. When it faded and she opened her eyes at last, her lips quivered. "So I don't have any choice in this at all?"

Her words hit him hard, waking the secret fear sleeping deep inside his subconscious. He was dying to hold her. Comfort her any way she'd let him. "I won't touch you without your consent. And the bonding between mates is always a choice." He meant the actual moment of marking, but didn't tell her that. It would kill him if she didn't want to bond with him when the time came, but he couldn't think about that now. Every fiber in his being wanted to slide something between her clenched thighs—his hand, his tongue, his cock—to stop her suffering.

She studied him for a long moment, her body vibrating with unrelieved tension. "Is that the truth?"

He nodded. "I would never lie to you."

She shuddered, pressed her lips together as another wave took her. When it finished she was gasping, her eyes glittering feverishly. Her expression was almost feral. The blood pounded in his veins.

He held out a hand, praying she'd take it. "Olivia. Let me ease you."

She stilled at his words, a shocked expression transforming her face. "You said that to me before," she croaked. "In my dreams."

So she'd foreseen this. Had known on some level that this would happen between them. He understood this was hard for her to accept, but what more proof did she need that they belonged together? God, he needed to touch her, wrap himself around her.

His outstretched fingers twitched, waiting for her decision. He held his breath, willed her to take that final step she was so afraid of.

Come to me, love. Reach out and take my hand. Trust me that much.

Her arm lifted, hesitantly reached toward his. Her breath hitched. There was such hope in her eyes, mixed with heartbreaking uncertainty.

Just as their fingers touched she groaned and curled into a tight ball as another wave took her. Helpless against the powerful torrent of hormones flooding her body.

Daegan couldn't stand it any longer. She'd given her unspoken consent. He wouldn't stand by and watch her suffer like this for another second. He slid his arms around her, hauled her up.

The moment he touched her everything slowed. His body calmed. His racing heart decelerated. Cuddling her close, he carried her over to the queen four-poster and laid her in the center of it. When he released her she arched up, writhing against the sheets, heat pouring off her.

He came down on the bed next to her then took her hot face between his hands, trying to calm her, soothe her. Her hands curled around his biceps like claws, her fingers digging deep into his flesh. An answering rush of hunger roared through him. His upper gums throbbed, a warning he was close to holding her down and sinking his sharpening incisors into her skin as he took her.

He fought back the dark tide of need, shuddering with the effort. He didn't want to take her like this, not when she was mindless and out of control, unaware of what was happening. This had to matter as much to her as it did to him, or it would never work between them. "Shhh. Look at me and breathe, love."

Panting, making little mewling sounds deep in her

throat, she managed to open her eyes and focus on him. "Daegan."

"Yes," he breathed against her wrist, loving the sound of his name on her lips. "It's going to be fine. I'm going to take care of you." For the rest of his life, if she'd let him. He'd begin earning her trust right now, show her he would take care of her, especially when she was vulnerable.

Liv nodded and lifted her arms, wound them around his neck tightly.

He exhaled, closing his eyes. It felt so good to have her reach for him, hold him. His mate. The woman he was meant to spend the rest of his existence with. She'd been entrusted to him and only him. The knowledge shook him. He could almost feel the empty part of himself filling up, knitting with the rest of him.

"Touch me," she begged, moving against him in an erotic wave.

Fuck, yes.

Her firm breasts rubbed against his chest, threatening to break his control. With unsteady fingers he tipped her chin up then brought his mouth down on hers. Liv groaned and curled her tongue around his, wrapping her arms and legs around him, pulling him into her. Her hands slid over his back to the hem of his T-shirt, dragging it up with an impatient tug. He broke the kiss just long enough to help her peel the thing over his head and fling it over his shoulder, then leaned down to meet her eager mouth.

Liv purred as her soft hands stroked over his naked chest, making his heart pound until he felt dizzy. She kneaded at his muscles like a kitten testing its claws, the feminine appreciation on her face making his cock swell painfully.

"Hurry," she breathed, ripping at the fragile strap of her lacy black camisole. The fabric tore in her haste to pull it off. She didn't seem to notice as she grabbed his hand, bringing it to the soft curve of her breast.

Daegan sucked in a sharp breath, clamping down on his baser need to rip off the pajama bottoms and slide into her warmth. Licking into her mouth one last time, he pulled back enough to see her. The pale globes of her breasts quivered with each of her shallow breaths. The tips were hard points of deep pink. The breath got stuck in his lungs for a moment. His fingers contracted slightly around the warm mound of flesh, squeezing gently before he trailed a thumb over the straining nipple.

She jerked like she'd been electrocuted and let out a keening cry, her legs scissoring around his hips. "Daegan, *help* me."

Swallowing a curse, he managed to snag her flailing wrists in one hand, using the other to pull the bottoms over her hips and down her long legs. He tossed them on the foot of the bed. His nostrils flared at the musky-sweet scent of her arousal. He stared at the neatly trimmed strip of dark-bronze hair between her thighs.

When she moved restlessly again, her legs parted enough to reveal the tender pink flesh within. He groaned at the sight of those glistening folds, wanting to lower his head and lap her up. The need to taste her was overwhelming. He wanted to slide his tongue into her most sensitive flesh, pleasure her until she screamed.

"It's getting worse—do something," she panted, her head tossing on the pillow. Her glossy hair spilled over it in wild disarray, her plump lips swollen and flushed from his kisses.

Daegan smoothed a steadying palm over the velvety skin of her belly. The taut muscles there quivered beneath his hand. When he looked up, her eyes were heavy-lidded with arousal, mouth parted as she sucked in little gasps. Her entire body vibrated beneath him, desperate for relief.

For a moment he savored the sight of her like that, knowing he'd remember it for the rest of his life. Hoping she would too. Then he swung a thigh over top of hers, pinning her down. "I've got you," he said in a dark voice he barely recognized as his own. "I'm going to help you through this." His blood raced through his veins, the need pulsing through him. He wanted to take her. Mark her. But there was so much he wanted to give her first. He wanted this whole experience of their first time indelibly etched into her memory forever.

Liv bit her lip when he stroked his free hand over the side of her face, down her throat to her chest. He trailed his hand over the curve of one breast, bent to kiss her there. His lips muffled her rising moan when he grasped the turgid nipple between his thumb and forefinger, rolling with gentle pressure. She struggled against his grip but he held her down and followed the path his hand had taken with his mouth. His palm moved lower, over her smooth belly to find the strip of hair covering her sex.

Liv made a choked sound and tensed, quaking in his grip.

Daegan whispered soothing words against her soft skin, glancing down at his hand between her legs before licking one distended nipple.

"Oh, God," she wailed, arching up as she grabbed handfuls of his hair.

Ah, love. Immediately he closed his lips around the tender peak and sucked, giving her more. Relishing her uninhibited response.

She made a choked sound, clutching him tighter.

He wished he could take more time with her, but he didn't want her to endure this any longer. "Easy," he whispered against her nipple, sucking with light pressure. Below, his fingers gently grazed over her swollen labia.

Liv bucked and called his name. Daegan steeled himself then drew a deep breath, kept her pinned down. Aware of his enhanced strength, he was careful not to bruise her delicate skin when he brought both her arms over her head. His fingers manacled her wrists in a firm grip and pressed them into the mattress, silently telling her he was in control. Giving her permission to abandon any remaining inhibitions she had. Demanding she give in to her need.

She was hot and wet where he touched her sex, more than ready for him. Gritting his teeth, he slid a finger into her body, slowly, firmly. Slick, soft heat engulfed him. Liv gave a throttled cry and clenched around his finger while he bit back a groan, dying to push his cock into her. *Not yet,* he told himself. Not yet. She needed

this release first. Needed to be able to trust him to relieve her while she was helpless like this.

Preparing to stroke his thumb over her swollen clitoris once, he focused on her face, memorizing every
single detail. She stared up into his face, waiting, her
gorgeous hazel eyes alight with passion. Holding her
beneath him, he slid his thumb slid upward to gently
graze the tender nub.

The instant he touched her there, Liv threw her head
back and groaned, her expression full of sensual agony.
Her inner muscles clamped around his finger rhythmi-
cally as she rode him, taking her pleasure. The cries
that tore from her throat were desperate, full of relief.

Holding her in place, he maintained gentle pressure
on her clit while she rode the waves of release. When
she groaned and fell back against the mattress, only
then did he remove his hand. Christ, she was beautiful. It shook him. His heart knocked crazily against
his ribs as he released her wrists and gazed down at
her flushed face.

Releasing a breathy sigh, Liv opened those stunning
eyes to gaze up at him. Her body was calm, a sated,
almost dreamy expression on her face, her hands open
and relaxed above her head. Then she smiled tiredly
and reached up to cradle the side of his face with her
palm. "Thank you," she whispered.

Daegan had no words, so he slid his hands into her
tangled hair and kissed her. His body hurt for relief,
but seeing her like this was more than worth the pain.
He nibbled gently at her lips, tugged the lower one
with his teeth. In answer she hummed and stroked her

hands lightly over his back, tracing the muscles on either side of his spine.

She kissed him with a languid passion that made his head spin while she caressed his tongue, sighing longingly into his mouth. His fingers tightened in her hair as he moved atop her, settling the bulge in his jeans against her damp mound. She opened for him, winding her legs around his waist. Her implicit trust almost made him lose it.

Inhaling harshly, he lifted his head and shook it, fighting back the tide of sexual hunger roaring inside him. He couldn't get enough of her. Didn't know if he'd be able to contain the lust clawing at him if he took things any further.

After a moment Liv tensed beneath him, her eyes widening. His heart twisted at the edge of fear he saw buried in them. "It's happening again," she said shakily.

"I know. It's okay."

"Is it always like this?"

"Like what?" He smoothed her hair back.

"This intense."

Her words made his skin prickle with alarm. "For some it is." And then they could only hope to hell the match was a good one. Because if it wasn't...

Don't. Don't even go there.

Liv shifted beneath him, seeming more relaxed with him than she'd been earlier. "Why?"

"It helps the couple bond faster. Forces them into intimacy so they get comfortable with each other. Begin to trust each other." At least, that was how it was supposed to work in theory. Unfortunately things didn't always go that way in reality.

Shaking off the ugly memories trying to take over, he held her gaze, allowing himself one more firm stroke against her luscious body. Pleasure tore through him like claws, his cock full to bursting.

She pulled in a sharp breath, closed her eyes as the hunger built again. In seconds she was moaning and writhing against his erection. Her hands flailed on his shoulders, moving down to clutch frantically at his hips. He could feel the pressure of her nails through the denim still covering him. Her movements grew wilder, her whole body twisting against the sheets.

With a low growl, Daegan sat up on his knees and grabbed her pajama bottoms from the foot of the bed.

She glanced up at him in surprise when he then snagged both her wrists, brought them back over her head. "What are you doing?"

"Do you trust me?"

She stared at him a moment, then nodded. "Yes."

His upper gums throbbed mercilessly, and he was careful not to show his teeth when he smiled. If she thrashed around like before she might hurt herself. Besides, he wanted both his hands free for what he was about to do. Because he needed this like he needed air to breathe. "Hold still."

LIV SHOOK ALL over while Daegan held her wrists and tied them to one of the posts with her pajama bottoms. The intense look on his face would have scared her to death, had she not been completely certain he would never harm her. His expression said he wanted to devour her. The tight ache between her legs grew to a fever pitch as he tugged the knot in place, securing her hands above her head. Rendering her completely helpless to his strength and the raw lust she read in his glowing blue eyes.

A primal shiver ripped through her.

He bent to kiss her. "So beautiful," he murmured against her lips.

Liv lifted her head for more but he moved downward, his tongue laving briefly over a spot at the side of her throat that made her bow up and whimper. Every nerve ending suddenly sizzled to life. Her hands tugged uselessly against the bond, wanting to hold him there. Wanting him to do it harder. "Daegan…"

"Mmm," he responded, licking and nibbling there. She jerked when she felt something sharp scrape her, couldn't hold back her startled gasp. More. Whatever he was doing to her neck, she wanted more of it.

Daegan nuzzled her for a moment as if he loved it, too, then seemed to fight with himself before moving lower. She moaned in disappointment and lifted into him, trying to urge him back up to her neck. Instead she felt the warmth of his hands bracketing her ribcage, sliding up to cradle her swollen, aching breasts. His wide palms cupped them together while his eyes consumed her. Another rush of moisture slipped from between her legs.

A soft sigh escaped her when he bent his dark head, caressing the sensitive mounds gently with his clean-shaven cheeks. Her nipples throbbed under his stare, unbearably sensitive. She arched her back, begging silently. He didn't move.

"More," she whispered, wishing she could tangle her hands in his thick hair and hold him to her.

As if he'd been waiting for her permission, Daegan let out a deep purr and lowered his head. With reverence he began making love to the tender points. Liv groaned in helpless ecstasy, twisting in his grip, but he held her steady while he pleasured her. Her inner muscles clamped in frustration, her body pulsing with the need to come again. He stayed where he was, teasing until she couldn't hold back the cries.

He lifted smoldering eyes to hers, releasing one breast to slide his hand to her hip. Liv wiggled and opened her thighs wider, craving his touch there.

"I need to taste you." His low voice was like another caress. Deep, full of need.

Liv bit her lip then nodded, closing her eyes as she braced for it. She was too far gone with arousal to care about modesty or embarrassment now. All she cared about was him easing the desperate tension in her body. The thought of him going down on her made the fire inside burn even hotter. He was her wildest, most wicked fantasy come to life, but if she was on fire he had to be too. "Want to touch you."

"No." Warm kisses trailed down the center of her body. Across her stomach to her navel. His hot tongue delved into it, making her gasp and squirm. Then his strong hands closed around her hips, holding her down tightly. "Don't move." It came out more a growl than a whisper.

The deep command made her quiver. She squeezed her eyes shut and gripped the post above her hands, every muscle drawn tight in anticipation of the first touch of his mouth. Her sex was drenched, a sob forming in her chest.

His hands tightened around her hips at the same instant his hot breath touched the top of her mound. She made a choked sound and turned her head aside, the need painful and sharp. Daegan inhaled deeply, growled low in his throat as though he loved the scent of her arousal. Liv felt the flush in her face grow hotter. She trembled in his grip, waiting. Praying he'd make the burning pressure inside her go away.

He dipped his head then his soft, warm tongue caressed her most sensitive flesh.

Her whole body jerked. A high sound tore out of her as she raised her hips, frantic for more. Daegan held her steady, taking her apart with slow, tender strokes of his tongue. He cherished each fold, every millimeter of her most intimate flesh before closing his lips around her pulsing clitoris. The air whooshed out of her lungs as he began sucking tenderly, lightly flicking his tongue against her.

Over the roaring in her ears, she distantly heard her own wild cries, the soft, wet sounds his mouth made against her. She writhed beneath his loving tongue, ready to shatter. Then he pushed two fingers into her body with firm pressure and pulled them almost all the way out. Again. Again.

The specific friction ignited the charge deep inside her. A crescendo of pleasure peaked then shattered. The tender motions of his mouth never stopped while she screamed and bucked through the agonizing waves of release.

She fell back against the damp sheets, utterly exhausted. Daegan moaned and licked her one last time, a slow, lingering stroke that made her tired muscles

clench. Removing his fingers from her body, he slid
his arms around her waist and buried his face into her
belly like he never wanted to let her go.

Her heart turned over in her chest, a lump filling her
throat. She tugged against the knot holding her captive.
"Untie my hands," she said unsteadily. "Let me touch
you. You're hurting." The ache inside her had receded
for now, but she still felt empty. She wanted him to fill
her, drive her over that high peak again while she held
him close and reveled in his power and tenderness.

Daegan reached up to undo the knot holding her
wrists. When she slid her arms around him he burrowed close for a moment, nuzzling that sensitive spot
on the side of her neck.

Cradling him, Liv sighed and tipped her head back
to give him more access. "There," she whispered.
"Right there…"

Beneath her hands, Daegan's muscles twitched. He
snarled softly then pulled out of her embrace. She made
a sound of protest and resisted, but he rolled her onto
her side, pulling her back into the curve of his body.
His massive erection pressed hard against her buttocks.

She wriggled in his grasp. "Daegan—"

"No." His deep voice was rough as he stilled her
movements with an iron hold.

"What's wrong?"

"Nothing." His arm tightened around her ribs. She
could feel the tension in him, the pent-up sexual energy he was fighting to control.

"I want to touch you."

"Don't. Just lie still." His voice was rough with lust.

Liv frowned and relaxed against him, wondering

why he was struggling against this so hard. He was protecting her from something, she was sure of it. But surely he wasn't worried about hurting her? "Why won't you finish it? I want to feel you inside me."

A light shudder sped through him, the hand wrapped around her ribs tightening. "You need to sleep."

She *was* tired. But not tired enough to ignore the hard length pressed against her buttocks. "I want to please you." It made her hot all over again to think of it.

Daegan pressed his face against her hair, his unrelieved hunger clear in the residual tension in his muscles. "You already have, *mo ghrá*. But I need you to sleep now." He placed a firm kiss on the crown of her head. "Trust me, you'll thank me later."

She didn't understand the strange words he'd used, but his tone made it clear they were an endearment. It soothed her. With a sigh she closed her eyes, letting the delicious, heavy languor steal through her body. She was safe, warm, and her body seemed to finally be sated. It was strange, but she *did* trust him.

Confident that he'd take care of her, Liv allowed the dark wave of sleep to pull her under.

RICK BENNETT PARKED his Harley in front of the bar then headed inside to meet his contact. The dark place smelled of stale beer, already full with the regular Friday night crowd. Mostly other bikers, a few wannabes. He spotted his contact in a booth at the back and nodded to the clean-cut, well-dressed man. Guy stuck out like a sore thumb in a place like this.

"You got something for me?" he asked, sliding into the vinyl booth.

The man's hard black stare bored into his, as though sizing him up. "You're Iceberg?"

Rick lifted a mocking brow, making it clear he wasn't the least bit intimidated. "Yep. Why, you disappointed?" Maybe the guy had assumed someone with his rep would be taller. More muscular. But standing five-foot-nine had never been a handicap in Rick's work. He could pull a trigger just as well as a six-foot-four bruiser, only he was one-hundred percent accurate. A skill he'd acquired over a decade ago as an army sniper.

"The OL wants you to take care of this personally."

Rick hid his instinctive reaction to that name. The Obsidian Lord was the only man he was afraid of, and for good reason. Any man who could bend someone as hard as Rick to his will was deserving of a twisted kind of respect. And a shitload of fear. He was glad the bastard was currently on the other side of the world, no doubt preying on other hard-ass criminals who wouldn't have a clue until it was too late. The same had happened to him. It was the biggest regret in Rick's life of violent crime.

"That's because he knows I'm the best he's got." He figured that was still true, though there was no way to tell how many others the OL had turned into Dark Army members. Had to be in the hundreds by now.

The man grunted, passing a manila folder across the scarred table. Rick opened it to find various property listings. They all had waterfront views, each of them worth at least ten million, easy.

"I've narrowed down the search to these nine possibilities. You need to check them all out and find this guy." He slid an old photograph across the table. It showed a dark-haired, pale-eyed WWII vet in British putties. "Name's Daegan Blackwell. We think he's the new Coven Leader."

Rick handed it back, already thinking of ways to perform the hit. "You want it to look like an accident?"

"We don't care how you do it, but he's not your target. There's going to be a woman with him."

He frowned. "The target's a woman?"

The man lifted one haughty dark brow. "Yeah. That a problem?"

"No." He'd killed women before. Didn't like doing it, but sometimes it was necessary. "What'd she do?"

The guy shrugged. "Nothing. But she's his mate. You take her out, he'll die too."

"I'm supposed to off this chick because she's his mate? Why don't I just take out the Coven Leader and call it a day?" Would certainly make things a lot faster than waiting for the effects of being without a mate to take hold.

The man huffed out an irritated sigh. "Because that's the way the OL wants it. Apparently it makes the Coven Leader's death more satisfying for him."

A whisper of unease began to creep in. "If he wants the Coven Leader, killing her doesn't make any sense. If I snatched her, at least that would guarantee the Leader coming after her. We could get him and the others in one operation." Wasn't that the point of all this? Rick's plan was a much better strategy, even though the Empowered were damn hard to kill.

"That's not how he wants it done. He wants the female taken out." His contact's smile was thin, taunting. "If you're getting cold feet, say so now. He won't tolerate failure."

Rick clenched his hands into fists, bared his teeth. The fucker deserved to be shot through the forehead for talking to him like that. "I'm not getting cold feet. Just tell me what she looks like and I'm outta here."

"We don't know, but Blackwell will be sticking to her like Velcro. Shouldn't be hard to ID her."

"That it?"

The man nodded, held out Blackwell's picture. "Better take this."

"Don't need it. I've got a photographic memory and a mind like a steel vault. I never forget *anything.*" He made sure the veiled threat was obvious, smiled inwardly when the man's expression tightened in apprehension. *That's right, asshole. I can get to you anywhere, anytime, and kill you without you even knowing I'm there.* Maybe he'd off this guy once the job was done. The thought cheered him up considerably.

The man shifted in his seat, breaking eye contact. "I'll call you—"

"No, you won't. That's now how I operate. I say when, and I call the shots from here on out." Rick took the folder, slid out of the booth. "I'll contact you once I find them," he said over his shoulder as he walked away. He shoved the door open and stepped out into the muggy night air.

Tucking the paperwork into his leather jacket, he fired up his bike then headed back to the clubhouse. His gang brothers didn't know the kind of deep shit he was in, but they could at least help him find Blackwell and the woman.

He had to do this, he reminded himself as he sped south toward the highway. He had no choice. Killing the woman was his only shot at getting free of the Obsidian Lord, because the bastard owned him body and soul.

CHAPTER EIGHT

DAEGAN KNEW THE instant the need awoke Liv. One moment she was sleeping peacefully, and the next she jerked in his arms and sucked in a sharp breath. He could already feel the unnatural heat coming from her skin when she turned her head to look at him.

"Daegan?" she mumbled sleepily.

"I'm here." Steeling himself, he stroked his palm over her silky shoulder, down her arm. This wasn't working, and he was hard as a spike against his fly. Even though he'd known it would only prolong the inevitable, part of him had still hoped he could relieve her intense need without actually bonding to her.

It looked like that wasn't going to be an option. God help them both.

Liv shivered and rolled to face him. Her arms wound around his back, breasts pressing against his naked chest. She made a soft sound, rubbing her hard nipples against him. In the faint light coming through her bedroom window, he could see the feverish glint in her eyes. Sweet Jesus. He didn't know if he had the strength to hold back this time.

"It's not going away," she whispered, arching into him. "Why isn't it going away?"

His hands were unsteady when he threaded them into her thick hair. "Because you're still in your Heat

Cycle, and the hormones are in the highest concentration during the night." He withheld the rest, though he felt like a shit for hiding even a little of the truth from her. But she couldn't handle it right now, and he'd be damned if he'd take advantage of her weakened state.

"How long does it last?"

"Depends."

"Is there a way to make it stop?"

He hesitated. This was dangerous territory, but he'd promised he'd never lie to her. Withholding information was one thing, but outright lying wasn't okay. Either he stuck to that now or his words wouldn't mean shit to her later on. "Yes." Only he prayed to God it wouldn't come to that.

"Make it stop," she begged, her voice a mere whisper, laced with exhaustion.

Squeezing his eyes shut, Daegan bent his head, begging for strength. His body was primed to explode. He wanted to fuck her hard until he couldn't hold on anymore, bind her to him in the most elemental way possible. But he wouldn't bond with her like this. He'd never force his mate into the same situation that had killed his mother. He'd vowed it to himself the day he'd buried her broken body in that lonely grave back in Ireland almost two centuries ago.

Shoving aside the ugly memory, he focused on the needs of his mate. His control was already tested to the limit with Olivia. Once he was inside her he didn't know if he could hold back. Sure as shit he wasn't going to be gentle about taking her. Already he could feel his incisors starting to sharpen against his inner lip. The driving urge to bond with her overrode everything else. If he fucked her he wasn't sure he could stop himself from sinking his teeth into her skin and marking her forever. She was his, dammit, and he wanted the world to know it. But first he wanted everything she had to give.

Liv hummed in encouragement and rubbed against him, pushing his arousal to a dangerous level. Daegan pulled her close, kissed her deep and hard. A mate's claim, an unspoken demand.

"I want you inside me." She wrapped one leg around his hip as she nibbled on his bottom lip, bringing the damp folds of her sex against his pulsing erection.

Daegan clenched his jaw and bit back a snarl. As much as he'd love it, his cock inside her wasn't what she really needed. But he'd do that if there was still a chance of breaking her Heat Cycle some other way than marking her. *Please God, let this work.*

Fighting for control, he pulled out of her embrace to collect himself as he grabbed his jeans. He took a condom from his wallet, put it on, steeling himself for the most brutal test of his self-control. When he stretched out atop her, Liv made a frustrated sound and twined around him, bringing his aching cock flush against her slick folds. He hissed in a breath, shook his head sharply. She was too beautiful, too sexy. And this was dangerous as hell.

"Hold still."

She did, her fingers digging deeper into his back.

He moved into position, levering up on his arms to see her face, wanting to see every expression that flickered through her eyes. Setting his jaw, he pushed the tip of his erection into her. Her body closed tight around him, encasing him in smooth heat.

Liv gasped and held her breath, watching his eyes.

Fighting the need to plunge in and jackhammer his hips until he came, he eased into her delectable body inch by agonizing inch.

With a throaty moan she arched her back and wrapped her legs around his hips. When he was all the way in her lashes fluttered, finally resting against her flushed cheekbones. A soft sigh escaped her. Her body stretched around him so perfectly, hugging every last millimeter of him in a tight grip.

Sweat broke out over his forehead. *Hang on. Hang on.*

She moved before he was ready for it.

Her hands clutched at his back as her hips pistoned in a hard, quick stroke. An erotic gasp spilled from her lips. Daegan squeezed his eyes shut. His body was on the verge of exploding but he instinctively thrust harder, deeper, taking control of the rhythm. Fast, sharp strokes that buried him as deep as he could go. Beneath him, Liv lifted into his movements with a feral cry. He could feel how close she was to coming. Could hear it in her quick, shallow breaths and sounds of enjoyment.

Helpless in the grasp of the most intense pleasure he'd ever known, Daegan dropped his head and began nuzzling the side of her neck. She let out a sob, moving restlessly under him, arching her head back. Both her hands slid into his hair, fisted tightly, holding his mouth against the fragile skin of her throat.

"Liv," he groaned, trying to hold back. She had no idea what she was doing to him. What her body was demanding. The edges of his top incisors were sharp against his lower lip. He wanted to bite her. Needed to.

Daegan captured her head between his hands and got lost in the haze of sensation as he moved within her, kissing the side of her neck. He licked the smooth flesh beneath his mouth, reveling in her wild response.

"Mmm, *there*," she insisted hoarsely, rubbing against his lips.

He dragged the sharp edge of his teeth along her skin, both a warning and an erotic punishment. She jerked in his arms.

Daegan shuddered but kept pumping into her, dangerously close to orgasm. The pressure in his groin built until he thought he'd explode. He had to pull away from her neck. Right now, before it was too late.

But Liv held him fast, desperately seeking something from him that she didn't understand. Something he needed to give her more than he needed to breathe. She tightened around him, gasping with pleasure, her hips rocking against his. Her moans became louder, rougher.

Daegan pressed soft kisses to her cheeks, her lips. A low sound of torment ripped free from her despite his efforts. He smelled the salt of her tears as it mixed with their combined scents. It pierced him. He couldn't leave her like this. Couldn't bear to let her keep suffering when he had the power to stop it.

You can't. Don't do it, his conscience warned.

I have to. She's mine.

He fought the driving urge back, every muscle trembling with the effort. But his control began to slip. The animal inside him snapped at the bonds holding it captive. Hungry for freedom.

Liv was still frantic beneath him, straining for a release she couldn't reach. He stroked inside her again and the sensual agony on her face destroyed him. After two more thrusts the orgasm slammed into him like a tidal wave. It took him under and blotted out everything else, wiping out coherent thought, leaving nothing but instinct in its wake. The ravenous beast inside him roared in victory, snapping the chains holding back its need to mark her.

LOST IN SENSATION, Liv was dimly aware of the way Daegan's muscles corded as he found his release, his strangled roar of ecstasy against her neck.

Triumph soared within her as she held him to her, but her body remained trapped on the brutal edge of orgasm. His luscious scent infused the room, enveloping her senses. Yet the powerful climax she sensed building eluded her. No matter how high he took her, her body wouldn't let go. She shook in his arms, needing something more, ready to scream, to shatter.

His arms tightened around her. Holding the endless rhythm he'd started, Daegan lapped a spot on the side of her neck that made her see stars, nibbled tenderly for a moment. He was still rock-hard inside her, stroking the delicate nerve endings that made her shiver and writhe. His angle and pace were perfect. At the end of every in-stroke his body caressed the pulsing knot of her clitoris. She strained to meet his thrusts, tightening around the hard length that stretched her inner walls so deliciously. The ecstasy intensified until she wanted to shriek. *Oh God, so close.*

He sucked gently at her skin for a moment, but then started to lift his head. *No!* Liv moaned in protest, dug her fingers into his scalp. *There*, she silently begged him. *More.*

He groaned, shook his head like a man in torment. Tugged harder against her grip. He was shaking in her embrace. Straining to hold back. She didn't want him to.

"Yes," she whispered, eyes squeezed shut. He was erotic perfection against her sensitized skin, filling her so exquisitely. So heartbreakingly tender and unselfish with her despite his size, his obvious hunger. But she needed something more now. Something darker. More possessive. "Harder," she urged breathlessly.

In answer he bent his head to nip at her neck. Something sharp scraped over her. The slight sting sent a ripple of heat over her skin. He drove into her body in a slow, firm stroke and rubbed his pelvis against her to caress her clitoris as he bit down a little harder. Her inner muscles clenched around him, making her whimper brokenly.

On a ragged groan he licked her neck, as though savoring the taste of her skin. She shuddered. The need was too much. A raging fire in her veins.

"*Daegan...*"

He shook his head again, harder this time, then pulled away. "No. I can't. You don't understand." His voice was rough, ragged. Almost pleading.

Liv only heard the unspoken pain in his words and held on tighter, bringing his mouth against her flesh again. Whatever he was holding back from, she sensed they both needed it.

"Stop," he panted, trembling in her hold even as his teeth grazed her skin.

Sensing his weakening resolve, Liv arched her neck and rubbed against his mouth. A rough growl shot out of him. Goose bumps erupted all over her body, but she didn't let up. Rough sex wasn't normally her thing, but she wanted it from Daegan right now. Whatever this was, he needed it as much as she did. His unsteady breaths were hot against her skin.

"Yes," she whispered.

Without warning his hands gripped her head tight, twisted it to the side. She gasped as a ribbon of fear slithered through the arousal. Her throat was exposed to his mouth, his grip implacable. Her heart thudded hard against her chest wall as she hung there, waiting. A low, primal snarl ripped out of him and he bit down. Hard.

Her body exploded. The sudden stab of pain in the side of her throat was instantly dimmed by the rush of pleasure. In the space of a heartbeat the intense sting of his teeth faded to a burn, then disappeared under the brutal orgasm. She cried out as the climax ripped through her in an endless torrent of sensation, leaving her limp and gasping for breath.

When it ended she could barely breathe. Daegan had her pinned against the mattress, her head still trapped between his strong hands as he tenderly sucked at the spot he'd bitten. Soothing the sting away. His tongue flicked at her ever so softly, sending delicious aftershocks rippling through her exhausted body.

Liv melted into a boneless puddle and tipped her

head back, enjoying the pleasurable little waves that shuddered through her each time he drew on her skin. She ran her fingers through his thick hair while he stayed like that, a feeling of complete contentment washing over her.

A minute later he gently nuzzled the side of her neck, pressing a lingering kiss there before raising his head. His eyes glittered like aquamarines in the dimness. She smiled and stretched beneath him, loving the feel of his warm weight atop her. She felt like a sleepy cat ready to nap in a sunny window.

Only he didn't smile back. His unreadable expression made her feel strangely bereft, like he was shutting her out though he was still buried deep inside her. *Oh, no you don't. Not with me.*

Lifting her head from the pillow, she kissed him. Her tongue entered his mouth to caress his and she caught the faint coppery tang of blood. She pulled back, frowning. God, was that his blood or hers? Had he actually pierced her skin? No, he couldn't have. He hadn't been that rough.

She peered up at him, wondering if he'd bitten his lip. "Are you bleeding?"

His jaw flexed as he shook his head.

She flicked her tongue over her lower lip again, certain she'd tasted blood. Something wasn't right. Despite his orgasm, he wasn't relaxed at all. His big body was almost vibrating against her. Muscles tensed to the point of snapping. And he was still fully erect inside her. "Are you okay?" she whispered.

Jaw clenched, he stared back and nodded.

His silence was starting to unnerve her. Worried, Liv cupped his stubbled cheek with one hand, smoothed the other over the taut muscles along his spine. The need to soothe him was overwhelming. "You don't feel all right." She was sure he'd come earlier. Was he ready for more already? She'd love to make him come again.

Before she could ask, he eased back and withdrew from her body. His face twisted with a grimace of what looked like pain as he pulled out of her.

His sudden withdrawal made her feel empty and alone. Wanting to soothe him, craving his warmth and weight again, Liv sat up and tried to draw him back. "Daegan, let me—"

"Don't." He shrugged out of her grasp, caught her chin in one hand. His gentle grip belied his tight expression, the raging, primitive heat in his eyes.

He'd made it clear he didn't want her touching him anymore, but she desperately needed to. His reaction confused and hurt her. "What's wrong? You're still hurting."

Rather than answer, he shook his head and kissed her gently to stop her questions. The tenderness of it tied her in knots. Why was he withdrawing from her like this?

Easing away, he pressed her shoulders back against the pillow, held her stare as he framed her face between his palms. His eyes were a beautiful, glowing blue. Hypnotic. But the guilt in them made her nape prickle. "I'm sorry," he whispered. "Sleep, *mo ghrá.*"

The words had barely registered before the black curtain of sleep crashed down and obliterated everything.

XAVIER'S EYES SNAPPED open in the darkness. He jerked upright in bed with a gasp tearing from his sunken chest. The dream. He'd *seen* them. Heard them.

The Coven Leader had marked the female. Time was running out.

His breath sawed in and out of his lungs in shallow rasps as he groped for his phone on the night table, located the number he was looking for. "Have you found them?" he demanded when Rick picked up. He couldn't get his pulse under control.

"I told you I'd contact you once I did." The man's tone was cold, hard.

Xavier wanted to reach through the phone line and punish him for his insolence. If Rick thought he was in hell now, he was sadly mistaken. Xavier held the power to make his every waking moment its own separate agony if he chose. He reined in the urge with effort, forcing himself to breathe, to calm his racing heart and thoughts. The man was more useful to him at full strength. "How many properties have you searched?"

"All but three. All dead ends."

"I know what she looks like."

A pause. "How do you know that?"

Xavier's hand tightened around the phone. "Don't *ever* question my abilities."

Rick let out a rough sound of irritation. "What. Does. She. *Look*. Like?"

The need to punish him surged higher, filling Xavier's mind, his lungs. Power surged through his body, making every inch of his skin tingle. *No,* he told himself. That kind of punishment would not work on this man. The Iceberg would never be motivated by pain.

Only by the crippling, visceral fear of knowing his mortal soul hung in the balance, dependent on him carrying out the orders given.

Xavier took a slow, deep breath and called up the memory of the woman's face. "An oval-shaped face," he began, "with a fair complexion. Shoulder-length light brown hair with a bit of wave to it. Her eyes are green-hazel." He swallowed past the sudden tightness in his throat. "And she's got a mating mark on the left side of her neck."

Rick sucked in a breath. "If he's marked her, then they've already bonded."

"No," he growled, every fiber in his being denying the charge. "I would've felt it. He's marked her but she hasn't marked him and I don't know why. There's still time." But it was slipping away fast. No male could withstand going without his mate's mark when he'd already bonded to her. Rick probably had only hours to find her before she naturally completed the bond.

"Why would she not mark him?" Rick asked suspiciously.

"I don't know, but he's not with her. I feel it."

Rick snorted. "If what you say about Empowered males is true, he'd never leave her after marking her."

"He's not *with* her, I tell you."

"So then he's going to be even more vulnerable. I should go after him instead and end this whole thing right now."

"*No.*" His muscles shook, his heart racing with the helpless sense of urgency. He was trapped here. Couldn't go anywhere. Couldn't search out the woman himself. "The woman. Just her." She was the key. The key to everything. The boy from the prophecy had said so.

A pause. "Any idea where I can find her?" The words were laced with sarcasm.

"I thought you had three more properties to check."

"Yeah, so? They could all be dead ends too. And if he's not with her, that's not going to help."

His head came up. "Do you have pictures of the real estate agents for the remaining listings?"

"Yeah, but just three of them. I'm sending the pictures now."

"Wait." He rushed into the adjoining room and opened his laptop to retrieve his e-mails. He scrolled through the files. Nothing in the first one seemed familiar. Nor in the second.

On the third, he glimpsed the image of the female realtor the estate was listed with. Oval face. Light brown hair. Hazel-green eyes.

For a moment he felt dizzy. The blood rushed in his ears as he sucked in a sharp breath. "It's her."

CHAPTER NINE

Nida, Lithuania

NAIRNE'S THIGHS BURNED pleasantly as she climbed the last few yards to the top of the dune. At the very pinnacle she turned to face the view, let out a delighted gasp. The seaside resort town of Nida lay before her, nestled against the Curonian Lagoon. Families dotted the promenade and curving beach. The wind pressed at her back, tugging tendrils of dark hair from her ponytail as it blew off the Baltic Sea on the other side of the narrow sand spit.

She took a deep breath of the salty air then closed her eyes, tilting her face to the sun. A wide smile stretched her mouth. She'd always wanted to come here. Finally standing on the dune overlooking Nida was a dream come true.

Something about this place had always called to her. It had magic in it that went beyond the pagan tradition or folklore she'd been relentlessly researching. She could almost feel it tingle over her skin as she basked in the warm summer sunshine.

After enjoying the view for a few more minutes, Nairne tucked the image of the perfect summer day away in her head then started back down the dune. This time she climbed down the Baltic side, heading toward the sea. Whitecaps rolled on the sparkling water as far as the eye could see. Waves curled, crashing onto the sandy shore, sending ribbons of foam scattering up the beach. This side of the Spit wasn't as crowded, and Nairne was glad. At the water's edge she walked along the wet sand, looking for treasures. It had stormed the night before so she found pieces of blue and green sea glass embedded in the sand. A few yards up the beach, she spotted something even better.

A glistening honey-colored lump lay on the sand. She rushed up and grabbed the sliver-dollar-sized chunk, studied it carefully. The piece of Baltic amber caught the sun's rays, almost seemed to glow in her palm. It was red amber, fossilized tree sap from a forest that had burned long ago.

Jurate's tears. From the mermaid sea goddess whose father had destroyed her amber palace when she fell in love with a human fisherman. Legend said it was why amber continued to wash up on the beach here after a storm.

Nairne slowed her breathing and focused on what she held. Nothing happened. No flashes, no fragmented images came to mind. She opened her eyes, unsure whether to feel disappointed or not.

Nairne tucked her new treasure into her windbreaker pocket then continued up the beach when her cell phone rang. It was her office.

"We've got another DNA sample here that you'll be interested in," her colleague informed her.

Nairne plugged her other ear with a finger and hurried away from the water, up the sloping sand back toward a path that skirted the foot of the dune. "Go ahead."

"It's like the others you've compiled in the database. Looks like strong Celtic and Northern European descent. Maternal DNA closely resembles some of the others you've earmarked."

The battering wind faded the moment she stepped behind a small dune. "Great. I'll look at that as soon as I'm back."

"Wait, there's more."

Nairne paused at the urgency in the woman's voice. "All right."

"This is from Dr. Mackintosh, and he wants you to analyze it personally right away. He's particularly interested in any Baltic heritage links."

Was he? So, she shared a common interest with the handsome doctor she'd heard her colleagues go on about since she'd started at the lab a few weeks back. It seemed like every female in the office fancied him. Apparently the man was something to look at. Most of her office was desperately in lust with him. Nairne had never met him and had no interest to. Right now her work was the driving force in her world.

She tucked an errant lock of hair behind her ear. "Aye, best e-mail the files to me then and I'll get to it as soon as I can."

"I already did. They should be sitting in your inbox."

Nairne sighed. Looked like her summer holiday was going to be interrupted. Ending the call, she strode up the footpath toward Nida and the pretty little boutique hotel she'd be staying at for the next week. A hum of excitement raced through her blood. What would the new DNA sample show? Would it be close to what she'd been searching for? A link to her own bloodline, and maybe to her family lineage. To her great grandmother's ancestors. There had to be others like her and Nairne somewhere. Others with secret abilities like the ones she'd read about in the ancient scroll.

LIV SIGHED AND stretched in her bed, her body deliciously sated and sore. Bright morning light streamed through her bedroom window, engulfing her in a warm yellow glow. Daegan's scent remained strong in the room but when she turned over he wasn't there.

She sat up. The ensuite bathroom door was open, the room empty.

"Daegan?" When he didn't answer she frowned then grabbed her robe from the closet. Pulling it on, she headed out into the kitchen. She didn't smell any coffee brewing or bread toasting. "Daegan?" she called louder, feeling the stirrings of panic.

The kitchen was empty and spotless. Nothing had been moved since she'd cleaned it last night.

She walked to the sliding glass doors that led into the backyard. He wasn't there either. Had he gone out somewhere?

Maybe he's not coming back.

The thought was like an arrow to the heart. She sat down stiffly on the sofa, wrapping the warm folds of her robe around her. Though she refused to allow herself to get dramatic about him sneaking out on her, she couldn't help the hollow feeling in her gut. Last night had been the most intense, incredible experience of her life. She'd never felt so close to anyone, had never opened her heart like that. Would he really just walk away without so much as an explanation? After he'd been so considerate and amazing?

He'd held her like she was precious. Soothed her, given her breathless orgasms despite his own obvious need. When he'd finally made love to her properly he'd been right there with her, sharing the gift of his hunger and pleasure. And when he'd finally given her the rough edge she'd craved, nipping her hard on the neck—

Liv gasped and touched her fingers to the tender spot on the side of her throat. Jesus, he'd bitten her. Hard, then kind of nursed at her neck afterward. Almost like he'd been...drinking from her.

No way.

She jumped up and ran to the bathroom. Flipping on the lights, she looked in the mirror, craning her neck to the side.

"Shit!" Her eyes widened when she saw the quarter-sized mark where he'd been sucking. At first glance it looked like a hickey, a faint bruise surrounded the dark circular mark. She leaned closer, her eyes refusing to believe what they were seeing. It looked like a faded tattoo. A round, almost Celtic-looking design of some sort. A knot, maybe.

She rubbed at it, winced. Whatever it was, it was damn sore, and it wasn't coming off.

Maybe all it needed was a good scrubbing, she thought, trying to figure out how Daegan had put it there. Liv grabbed a washcloth and soap then scrubbed at it for a minute before checking again. No good. Still there.

The cloth fell into the sink with a fleshy plop. Water

dripped in a monotonous, hollow echo that seemed to fill the bathroom.

Jesus, he'd marked her. Literally marked her somehow, then taken off without a word like she meant nothing more to him than a meaningless woman he'd picked up at a bar.

Liv stared at the tattoo and swallowed hard. What the hell was it? What did it mean? Her body might have stopped clamoring for another orgasm but the reason for the mark was pretty self-evident. He'd done it to make the sexual need go away. Was she bonded to him now?

She didn't know quite what she'd envisioned about what bonding meant or how it would feel, but it hadn't been this aching emptiness. Like he'd abandoned her.

And even if they weren't bonded, he still had a lot of explaining to do. Whether he wanted to or not, the cowardly bastard.

Liv marched into her room and fished her cell from the pile of clothes she'd dumped on the floor in her haste to get undressed last night. Battling her growing anger, she found his number, dialed it. How dare he take off on her after half-convincing her they were mates and finally spending the night in her bed.

"Daegan," she said in a crisp voice when his voicemail picked up, "I don't know where you are but you need to call me *right now*. You left something on me and I want to know what it is. I think I deserve that much." With a frustrated sigh she tossed the phone onto her bed and stood there, not knowing what to do. She was too worked up to go back to sleep. Plus her pillow and sheets smelled like him anyway. But the thought of washing them made her chest ache.

An awful sinking feeling took hold. He couldn't be gone forever. The tender spot on her neck had to mean there was something more between them than just a sizzling one-night stand.

FIGHTING A YAWN when the front doorbell pealed, Cade set down a box of special ammunition he'd been checking. It was only seven in the morning on a Sunday, so he had no idea who it could be. Definitely not the woman he'd left sleeping in her apartment downtown an hour ago. He'd scrubbed her memory before slipping out the door like the sorry excuse for a male he was.

The doorbell rang again.

"Coming," he called. Damn, someone was impatient this morning. He jogged up the stairs, down the hall to the door, surprised to find Olivia on the front step when he opened it. "Hey, good morning."

"Morning," she mumbled, looking past him to gaze around the foyer. Her voice was rough and her eyes seemed a bit red, like she'd been crying or something. "Is Daegan here?"

"Uh…not sure." He'd only gotten home half an hour ago, but Daegan's Porsche hadn't been parked out front. Cade let her inside and shut the door. "Haven't seen him since last night. I thought he was with you."

"He was." Her gaze went to the main staircase leading to the upper floor. "Is he in his room, maybe?"

"Maybe." Though if Daegan had been "with" her the way Cade imagined, it didn't make sense that he'd taken off on her, considering they were supposed to be mates. Slinking out a woman's place on the morning after was *his* M.O., not Daegan's.

Liv walked past him, disappeared up the main staircase. A few seconds later he heard her knocking on the master bedroom door, then her footsteps coming back down the stairs. Her jaw was set when she came into view. "He wasn't there. The room's empty and the bed's still made."

Cade tucked his hands into his back pockets, masking his growing concern. "Maybe he had something to take care of." Though what the hell could be more important to Daegan than bonding with his mate?

She lowered her head. "Maybe, but he won't return my calls."

What the hell? "Liv, what happened?"

"I don't know. He stayed the night with me," she said, her cheeks turning slightly pink, "but when I woke up he was gone." He started to ask something else, but her eyes flashed with anger as she pulled her hair away from her neck. "This was on my neck when I woke up. What is it?"

Cade's eyes widened when he saw the fresh mating mark on her pale skin.

"Come on, Cade, I know you know what it is. So explain it to me before I snap."

A prickle of alarm spread through him. Males were ultra-possessive of their bonded mates and didn't leave them unprotected without a good reason. They'd *never* leave them so soon after the marking, unless it was an emergency. And they certainly didn't leave them alone and confused without understanding what had happened between them. Cade cleared his throat, chose his words with care. "Uh, does he have one too?"

She frowned. "What? I don't know. How would I, when I haven't seen him since last night?"

Ah, Christ. "So you didn't mark him?"

She looked even more confused and Cades' heart sank.

He tried a different angle. "Do you feel...connected to him right now? More than before?"

Her chin lifted, a sheen of tears glittering in her eyes. "I don't feel anything right now except pissed off and used."

Cade fought back a wince of empathy and barely kept from scrubbing a hand over his face. This was bad. Very bad."It's his mating mark, Liv. It means he's bonded to you."

"He bit me," she accused.

Cade nodded, feeling damn uncomfortable. This conversation should definitely be between her and Daegan, not him.

"It hurt for a second, but his mouth seemed to stay there for quite a while," she added, a fierce blush swallowing her face. "Did he feed off me? Drink my blood or something?"

"*No.* God, no. We're not vampires." *Jesus Christ, Daegan, you've fucked this up so badly already.* "His teeth punctured your skin, but that's all. No drinking, I swear. Once he marked you, a symbol appeared at the site, bearing his initial." Peering harder, he made out the intricate D amongst the Celtic knot.

"So he was basically marking his property," she said dully, making Cade fight back a grimace. Liv shook her head. "I can't believe he'd do this to me and then just take off without saying anything."

Neither could Cade. Where the hell had he gone in *that* kind of shape? A bonded male wandering around without his mate claiming him in turn?

Wherever he was, Daegan was suffering a kind of sexual frustration beyond anything Cade cared to imagine. Poor bastard must be in agony, and feeling violent enough to tear someone's head off. Worse, he'd become increasingly unstable until Liv marked him, finishing the bonding.

Cade's heart sped up as he ran through the possible ramifications of that. "Did you check outside everywhere?"

"Good idea." She stalked past him to yank open the door.

He flinched when it slammed shut behind her, then whipped out his phone. Running through the house to check all the rooms, he waited for Daegan to answer his cell but kept getting the voice message. On the third attempt down in the empty gym, he lost his patience. "It's me," he snapped. "Where the fuck are you? Call me ASAP before I start doing the search and rescue routine, or I swear to God I'll kick your sorry ass when I find you." He might kick it anyway next time they met, just for scaring the shit out of him like this.

Cade sighed. He had no choice but to call Vaughn in now. He could dematerialize and cover more ground than Cade could.

Muttering to himself, he hit speed dial, putting the phone to his ear as he jogged up the stairs. At the top landing he passed the picture windows looking toward the front grounds and outbuildings. Liv was walking away from him at a good clip, almost to the caretaker's house. "Shit," he muttered, shoving his phone into his pocket. He wrenched open the French door and shouted her name. She didn't stop.

Cursing under his breath, he ran out in his bare feet to stop her from meeting Vaughn without Daegan there to shield her.

LIV WAS GOOD and furious by the time she reached the caretaker's house. Daegan was nowhere to be found, so if he wasn't in here she was out of places to look on the property.

Tamping down her anger and growing humiliation, she rapped on the door, also solid bronze like the main house. Her muscles knotted when heavy footsteps approached the door. What was she going to say to him? Her stupid eyes began to sting.

"Liv, wait!" Cade called out behind her.

She ignored him, prepared to confront Daegan and give him a piece of her mind.

The door swung open. A huge man filled the jambs. Liv gasped as a searing agony engulfed her skull. She grabbed her head and backed up a step, squinting through the haze of pain.

The man stared down at her out of cold, dark eyes flecked with eerie bits of yellow. His face was terribly scarred down the left side. The skin was swirled, like it had been melted. As she peered up at him a shimmering aura formed around his body. Vivid, angry oranges and yellows. All outlined in a thin band of pitch black.

Her knees buckled, hit the hard flagstone. She barely

felt the bruising force over the stabbing in her skull. Violence. This man pulsed with violence. Rage. Pain. He was lethal to the core. She had to get away. Warn Cade.

Her limbs refused to move. Her vision dimmed.

Running footsteps over the pea gravel suddenly stopped, then Cade knelt before her. Warm hands settled on her shoulders. "Liv? It's okay, look at me."

She fought to raise her head and focus on him. Every cell in her body screamed at her to get away from the huge man in the doorway. Surely Cade saw him. "Danger," she gasped out, struggling to her hands and knees. "Run."

Cade firmed his grip, his hands warm and solid. "No, it's all right."

She shook her head, unable to speak. The man in the doorway was a killer. They had to run.

Above the sickening pressure in her skull, she heard Cade curse then mutter something. The scary man answered in a deep, raspy voice. His frightening energy pulsed at her in waves, battering her overloaded nervous system.

"Step back and give her some air," Cade ordered.

In her fuzzy peripheral vision, Liv saw the stranger move back and disappear into the shadows of the caretaker's house. The ferocious pain lessened immediately. She sucked in a quick breath and blinked fast, fighting to regain control. Cold sweat prickled her skin. Her vision cleared somewhat and she was able to get to her feet with Cade's help.

When she was certain she wouldn't fall or black out, she peered after the stranger, afraid to take her eyes off the doorway in case he came after them. "Who was that?" she whispered, squinting into the shadows he'd melted into.

"Vaughn," Cade answered, his grip steady and reassuring around her upper arms.

Liv suppressed a shiver. "*That's* Vaughn?" He was an Empowered?

"Yeah. You okay now?"

She wasn't sure. That guy was a friend of Daegan and Cade's? "Yes." Stiffening her spine, she pulled away from Cade, trying to ignore the warning thump of her heart. "Is he dangerous?"

"Not to us. Not yet, anyway."

Those disturbing eyes…She rubbed her arms, fighting back another shiver. "His aura was really violent." God, he had death written all over him.

"I'm not surprised."

She looked at Cade. "How—I mean, what does he do?"

"I'm a Reaper," a deep voice rasped.

Liv jumped and faced the doorway. Vaughn stood on the threshold with his arms folded across his wide, muscled chest. His eyes were cold enough to burn despite the yellow shards in the irises, his blank expression chilling her. She flushed. The pain was still there, a dull throb in her temples, but the debilitating agony was gone. The bands of color that had surrounded him were gone. Was he masking his power somehow? Obviously he didn't want to harm her, and Cade would never put her in danger so she must be safe enough.

Swallowing, she stepped forward and made herself raise an unsteady hand. "I'm Olivia."

He made no move to take her hand or touch her

in any way, just kept his arms folded and pierced her
with those mottled eyes. "So you're Daegan's mate.
A Seeker."

His tone had an edge of derision to it. She lowered
her hand, feeling strangely rebuffed. Maybe he was offended by the way she'd reacted to the sight of him. Not
that she blamed him, but she sensed apologizing would
only make things worse. "I...maybe. I'm not sure."

"He's marked you," he said, glancing at the design
on her neck. "So where is he?"

She opened her mouth to answer but Cade beat her
to it. "We don't know, but we were hoping you might."

Vaughn shook his head, never taking his eyes off
Liv. His black brows pulled together, his visage becoming even harsher. "He left you?"

The flush in her cheeks deepened. What could she
say to that? Humiliation crawled through her. "Looks
that way."

She thought she caught a flare of shock in his strange
eyes before he looked at Cade.

"He's not here," Cade said. "Liv hasn't seen him
since this morning and he won't answer his damn
phone."

The growing concern in his tone made Liv's stomach knot. Was Daegan in some sort of danger? Is that
why he'd left her so suddenly?

"I'll find him," Vaughn said as he turned away. He
disappeared around the corner then came back a moment later wearing a black leather jacket and wrap-
around sunglasses. "Call me if you hear anything."

Before she could blink or ask why everyone was so

worried, Vaughn disappeared. Literally. One second he was standing in front of her, and the next—poof.

Liv stumbled back, coming up against Cade's hard frame. Startled, she looked up at him over her shoulder. "What did… He just…" She fought the urge to rub her eyes.

"It's what he does." Cade shrugged and set his arm around her shoulders. "Better now?"

She stared into the empty doorway, trying to come to grips with what she'd just seen. The man had freaking vanished into thin air. Some of the blood drained from her hot face, leaving her woozy.

"C'mon," Cade said with a hint of a chuckle. "Time to go back to the house with me."

Liv walked a few steps with him before putting on the brakes. "No, I'm going home."

"You sure? I'd feel better if you stuck around. Daegan's bound to come back here sooner or later."

"I have to go home." She had students coming later. Besides, she needed to think. Needed some time to be alone and lick her wounds. See if she could digest everything that had happened.

Or maybe she'd call a psychiatrist and schedule an urgent appointment.

"I'll drive you," Cade said, already striding toward her car.

She caught his arm to stop him. "No, I'm fine. But thanks."

He studied her face with a physician's critical eye. "You sure you're okay to drive? Must have been a hell of a shock to meet Vaughn like that and then see him dematerialize."

You could say that. "Can you and Daegan do that too?"

"Wish we could, but no. If we tried we'd be wiped out for a long time and probably wouldn't get very far anyway. Like maybe to the end of the driveway," he said with a grin.

The beginnings of a tension headache started at the base of her skull. Different from the debilitating headaches she'd had lately, but unpleasant nonetheless. "Good to know," she murmured, wondering what else they were keeping from her. "If you see Daegan, will you tell him I was here?"

"Of course." He walked her to her car, opened the door for her. "He'll contact you. He'll have to, so it's only a matter of time."

She frowned. "What happens if he doesn't? Maybe he changed his mind about me." Maybe he regretted being with her last night.

Or meeting me period.

"No," Cade said adamantly. "It doesn't work like that."

"Maybe this time it does."

"You don't understand."

"Then help me to," she snapped, at her wit's end.

Cade sighed, dragged a hand through his short blond hair. "A bonded male can't function without his mate claiming him in turn. Not for very long, anyhow."

She raised her brows in question.

"I mean, he can't go on without you marking him."

Her eyes widened as realization dawned. "I was supposed to last night, wasn't I? That's why my gums have been tender." She touched her tongue to the bum above her upper incisors. The flesh was still sore. But she hadn't had an urge to bite him last night. Did that mean something was missing between them? "Will my front teeth turn pointy?"

"Sort of. The bottom edges will temporarily become thinner, sharper. Just until you mark him."

His vague tone told her there was more to this than he was revealing. She knew it in her gut. "What happens if I don't?"

Cade's vivid green eyes hardened, taking on an angry glint. Anger directed at her, she realized. His square jaw set for a moment before he answered. "Then he'll die."

"He'll *die*?" He had to be joking.

But Cade's expression was all too serious as he nodded.

"What? Why?"

"Because if you don't claim him he'll turn into what we're hunting."

The blood drained from her face. "The Obsidian Lord."

Cade nodded grimly and her stomach dropped, thinking about the conversation she'd had with Daegan. The Obsidian Lord was often a former Coven Leader.

The knowledge echoed in her brain. Dear God, if she didn't bond with Daegan he'd become a monster. "So you're saying the *human* part of him would die, not that he'll literally die."

"No. I mean if he turns, Vaughn and I will have to put him down."

Put him down. Like an animal turned rabid.

Liv wrapped her arms around her waist as her stomach twisted. The thought of Daegan becoming the embodiment of evil then being killed by his friends was too appalling to think about. Whatever misgivings she had about him and this entire situation, he didn't deserve a fate like that. She'd seen the tenderness in him. Had felt it in his touch, in his kisses, the way he'd made love to her. And yet, rather than explain everything and ask her to bond with him in turn, he'd chosen to disappear. Why would he do that when the consequences were so dire? As Coven Leader, it seemed completely irresponsible of him. If she was his mate, how could he do this to her? It threatened the fragile trust she'd placed in him.

Cade watched her, and she could see the unease in his eyes. Fear for his leader, his cousin. The only real family he had left. "I know this has all been really sudden, but will you claim him, Liv?"

Her decision affected his future, too, possibly his existence. She looked away from that searching gaze, refusing to let him see the sudden tears burning her eyes. In such a short amount of time, she was inexplicably attached to Daegan. Against all odds, when she was with him it felt right. Like they were two pieces of a puzzle. She might not know him well yet, but deep down she believed he cared, that he'd take care of her. Those were promising traits, weren't they? He wouldn't abandon her without good reason. The consequences were too dire. But she deserved answers nonetheless.

An overpowering surge of protectiveness rose within her. No matter what, she wouldn't stand by and let him destroy himself. If he regretted the bond and wanted a way out, she'd give it to him. "I'll do what I can. But he's got to come to me himself. If he wants to be my mate he has to start acting like one."

If and when he made contact with her, he had a lot to answer for.

CHAPTER TEN

WHAT THE HELL?

Rick swore and pulled the Pathfinder onto the shoulder to let the light traffic pass by him. He glared at the brass address numbers on the eight-foot red brick wall surrounding the property then threw the truck into reverse. The engine protested his heavy foot with a loud whine as he shot backward. The wall ended abruptly next to one made of ornate wrought iron. But the address on that one was just as baffling. How the hell could an entire house be missing? He was looking at the damn address on the listing, and it should have been between the other two.

Whipping out his phone, he dialed the last person on earth he wanted to talk to. He didn't much care if he woke the bastard up, either.

"Diga," the elderly voice answered on the second ring.

Apparently the OL was an early riser. But of course he would be, Rick reasoned. Only way he could maximize the number of miserable souls he preyed on. "I can't find the damn house." His only leverage right now was that he hadn't given the property listings to the OL. Only he and the DA contact from the bar knew which properties he was searching.

"Excuse me?"

Rick gritted his teeth. "I found the house next to it and the one on the other side, but not the one we're looking for. There's nothing here. It's like it doesn't exist."

"They've masked it."

He frowned at the excitement in the man's voice. "What?"

"The Coven Leader, and any followers with him. They've put a masking spell on the property to shield it." His voice was ripe with conviction. "Can you see an opening between the other two properties? A path or a break in the fence?"

"No, there's nothing." He wasn't a fucking idiot.

"It's there. Find it."

Knowing it would piss him off, Rick hung up on him. He tossed the phone onto the passenger seat and got out, slamming the door shut. He pulled a pen and paper out of his jacket pocket, pretended to write notes as he examined the fence line so he wouldn't look overly suspicious.

The brick wall was solid under his hands, even where it met the cold wrought iron of the next fence. If the Empowered had put a spell on their digs to conceal them, they'd done a damn good job of it. For real, it looked like the place didn't exist. How had they managed it? Made him wonder again what he was up against.

He tried for the better part of an hour to find the chink in the defenses, even hiking down the bank to check the ocean-view side, but at last gave up and stalked back to the truck. He supposed he could hang around for a while in case anyone came in or out through some sort of magical gap in the wall.

Screw that. He had better things to do.

He threw the vehicle into drive and pulled onto the road, the tires kicking up bits of gravel as he did. This whole strategy was stupid, and he was starving. Intending to head to the Road House for a plate of bacon and eggs, he was almost to the bottom of the hill when he saw a car pull out from where he'd just been. Could be coincidence.

Or it might be the break he'd been waiting for.

He stomped on the brake, wheeling the truck around. The tires squealed as he skidded and finished the U-turn.

The engine raced as he climbed the hill, gaining on the silver BMW until he was riding its bumper. The driver hit the brakes a couple times in obvious irritation and waved a slender arm out the window for him to pass.

A woman.

Rick waited for the car coming in the opposite lane to pass then pulled out, speeding up until he was even with the front windows. The female driver threw him a nasty glare and shook her head. His heart went into overdrive.

Shoulder length light brown hair. An oval face now burned into his memory.

Olivia Farrell, the supposed mate of the new Coven Leader.

A car sped around the corner, coming at him head on. Swearing, he hit the gas and pulled in front of the BMW. The traffic thickened, ramping up his frustra-

tion. Too many witnesses around for him to run her off
the road and grab her. He'd have to circle back, sneak
back to follow her home and go from there.

LIV GLARED AT the Pathfinder as it finally pulled ahead
of her and sped off. She hadn't gotten a good look at
the driver, but she'd barely refrained from holding up
her middle finger in the hopes he'd see it in his rearview. Whoever it was, he had serious road rage issues
and it wasn't helping the throbbing headache leftover
from her little encounter with Vaughn, which was suddenly much worse. Would the pain be gone already if
Daegan had been with her?

"Idiot," she muttered to the back of the Pathfinder,
then grabbed her sunglasses to shield her overly sensitive eyes from the sun's glare. Thankfully the other
driver took off and disappeared from view.

By the time she arrived home, all she wanted to do
was crawl into bed and sleep. But it wasn't to be. A
white van sat in her driveway, marked with the logo of
a security company. Unless she'd suffered a stroke during the last migraine and lost her memory, she hadn't
hired a security company work on her place.

Frowning, she parked next to it and climbed out of
her car. As she shut the door she caught a glimpse of a
vehicle down the street—a dark green Pathfinder like
the one that had irritated her earlier. It might have been
her imagination, but it seemed to slow for a moment
before continuing past her street.

Shaking her head, wincing at the heightened throb
of pain, Liv trudged up to the front door. Someone

was in there, she could hear them talking along with the whine of a drill.

What the...

She unlocked the door then pushed it open, holding her cell phone ready in case she needed to call 911. "Hello?"

A moment later a thin middle-aged man appeared around the corner, smiled at her. "Miss Farrell?"

"Yes, hi."

He shook her hand. "I'm Pat. We're just about done here."

"Done what?" She looked past him down the hall toward the kitchen where the drilling sounds were coming from.

Pat gave her an odd look. "Your alarm system. Just putting the finishing touches in now, like the panic button for your bedroom."

What the hell was he talking about? "I think there's been a mistake. I didn't order—"

"No mistake. It's all taken care of." He reached into his back pocket to withdraw a folded receipt. "Mr. Blackwell's already paid for everything."

"Really. And when did he do that?" One hand curled into a fist.

Pat shrugged. "While ago. He came to check everything, just left a few minutes before you got here."

Her chest tightened. He'd done all of this without asking permission first, then taken off before she arrived? While she'd been forced to get answers about the mating and bonding process from his cousin? She drew a deep breath. For all she knew, Daegan had planned this all in advance, along with his move.

"Excuse me," she said, walking through the house to the sliding doors in the kitchen. Barely glancing at the two men installing a keypad next to the doors, she stepped out onto the brick patio and flopped down in a lounge chair. The overhead sun was hot, but her skin felt chilled.

She couldn't believe Daegan would do this without at least talking to her first. If he thought she needed an alarm system so desperately, he must think she was in danger. So why would he disappear on her like this?

Sighing, wishing the pounding in her head would go away, she dialed his number. It went straight to voice-mail and she didn't bother leaving a message. Just as well, since she couldn't think of anything nice to say. He might care about her on some level and worry about her safety, but right now it seemed he didn't care enough to stick around and make this whole mess any easier on her.

Maybe he didn't want to be her mate after all. The thought caused an involuntary twinge of pain in her chest.

Her phone chimed with an incoming text. Not from Daegan, but Catherine.

Haven't heard from u in a while. U OK? How'd the meeting go?

Liv sighed, a wave of guilt washing over her. God knew she could use a sympathetic ear right now. She desperately wanted to call Catherine to vent, but she didn't know how much to divulge about what was happening. It would sound crazy no matter how she explained it, though if anyone would believe her story, Catherine would.

Need to talk, she responded. *Will call u soon.*

As soon as she figured out what the hell to say.

She was still on the chair, almost lulled into a doze by the warmth of the sun and the drone of a distant lawnmower, when one of the workers came out the French door to the patio.

"Your piano student's here."

DAEGAN'S HAND SHOOK as he slid the key into the lock. He let himself in through the gym door downstairs, shutting it silently behind him. The room was dark and empty, but his hellishly glowing eyes lit it up like the sun at dawn.

His muscles trembled with the strain of holding in his agitation. When his gaze landed on the chin-up bar mounted overhead, he almost groaned in relief. He walked straight to it, shrugged off his leather jacket and was in the process of jumping up to grab the grips when the lights suddenly came on.

Blinking in the glare, he barely had time to focus on Cade's face as he stormed toward him. He braced at his cousin's furious expression. "Cade," he began in a warning tone. He was not in the mood to be messed with.

But Cade grabbed him by the collar with both fists and yanked him off the ground. Shaking him like a rag doll. "What the fuck is wrong with you?" he snarled through gritted teeth.

Daegan's temper took a dangerous leap. He struggled to contain it, to breathe while his cousin held him off the floor and reamed him out like a teenager who'd broken curfew.

"What's that? Can't hear you," Cade taunted, his nose an inch from Daegan's.

"Put me down," he ground out, "before I break your fucking wrist."

With a snort of disgust Cade dropped him, but didn't step back. "What the hell, Dae? Liv was here this morning looking for you, wondering what the hell had happened. You left her with the mating mark and fuck all else. She didn't even know what you'd done to her. Are you telling me she doesn't matter to you? That you can't feel what she's going through?"

Oh, she mattered. And he felt her pain all too clearly. Now that he was bonded to her he'd sense any strong emotions she emitted. He'd been bombarded with her hurt and bewilderment all day long, had barely withheld from giving in to the need to go to her. As it was, he'd spent most of the day watching over her from afar, parked down the street from her house like a damn stalker. He'd left only when the techs confirmed her security system was set up and armed. Then he'd scrubbed every single one of them for good measure.

"Well?"

Daegan clenched his hands into fists. "Back off," he warned icily.

"No way. Not until you tell me what the hell's going on."

His irrational anger was amplified by the sexual frustration and Liv's current state of confusion. Unfortunately the nearest outlet for it was the man blocking his way to the chin-up bar and weights. "Back. Off. *Now*." The last word echoed in the stillness between them, heavy with the threat of violence.

Cade's clear green eyes narrowed, but he wisely took a step back. "Start talking, or I'll get Vaughn involved."

"Aw, fuck." Daegan dug the heels of his hands into his eyes, dragged in a deep breath. He might want a fight, but the last thing he needed right now was to take a pummeling from the both of them. Misery might love company, but they couldn't turn on each other, especially now. His body had already undergone enough punishment without that. "I can't."

Cade folded his arms and stood his ground. "You marked her."

He nodded. "I marked her." And he'd loved every fucking second of it, even if it made him a selfish piece of shit. The taste of her, the feel of her body clenching around him, the husky sound of her cries as she'd come. His cock was still hard enough to pound nails. Merely thinking about it was torture. "And then I had to leave."

"Yeah? If it was that easy to walk away, you must not give a shit about her, huh."

"Fuck you," he snarled. "If anyone's got the 'screw 'em and leave 'em' thing down pat, it's you." The moment the accusation left his lips he regretted the low blow. But it was too late to take it back.

Cade paled for a moment. Then his mouth twisted in an ugly sneer. "Well at least you finally found the balls to say it out loud."

The raw self-loathing in his cousin's tone made Daegan want to hit something. Whatever Cade's problems were, he didn't deserve to have them thrown in his face like that. Least of all by him. Daegan needed to get himself back under control before he did irreparable damage. The urge to lash out with his fists was so strong he could barely control it. He closed his eyes and concentrated on his breathing, slowing everything down.

"Deep breaths aren't gonna help, and you know it."

Shut up, he wanted to yell. He clenched his jaw instead.

"You stubborn bastard," Cade spat, tone laced with disgust. "If her suffering isn't enough to make you end this, maybe you should look in the mirror."

Daegan opened his eyes, glared right back. "For what?"

"Your eyes are already starting to turn, asshole."

For a moment he was too stunned to move. His rigid muscles offered no resistance as Cade grabbed him by the shoulder and hauled him over to the nearest bathroom. When he flipped on the light, Daegan felt the blood drain from his face as he stared into the mirror.

A thin line of yellow outlined the edge of his pupils, almost neon against the electric blue. He looked away, sick with shame.

Cade let him go. "You know how dangerous this is. If you turn we can't help you, and Liv will suffer alone for the rest of her life. Then there's the pesky little matter of the ensuing war we've been gearing up for, and you not being here to lead us. You know what we'll have to do if you turn. Do you really want Vaughn and I to have to live with that?"

The words were like barbed wire, burying into his flesh. He was their leader. The one they should be able to look to for strength and guidance.

Cade's tone softened. "So if you won't do it for your

sake or hers, do it for ours. We don't stand a chance without you, and you know that."

Daegan dragged a hand over his face then turned off the bathroom lights. Seeing that ring of yellow in his eyes made him sick to his stomach. But what choice did he have about Liv right now? Some of the anger and aggression drained out of him. "The bonding has to be done of her own free will. Without that it means nothing. She's already been through too much. Two days ago she didn't even know the Empowered existed, let alone that she's one of us. I'm not going to force her into anything else until she's ready."

"For God's sake, she doesn't even know what you did to her or what it means. She shouldn't have had to find out about it from me. You owe her an explanation."

"I *know*." That didn't mean he knew how he was going to handle it. God, this mess would never have happened in the old days. Before they'd been driven to the brink of extinction there would have been someone in her family, in the community, to teach her about the Empowered and all the nuances of their lives. She would have been prepared for him and their relationship on some level at least. But to be blindsided this way and given no choice about her future? He could never live with that. Not after the suffering he'd witnessed as a child. "I won't force her further into this." No matter the consequences.

"You already have."

The hard words sent a fresh wave of guilt through his strung out system. Cade was right. The cold reality couldn't be ignored. There was no way out for either of them now. He'd taken away Liv's choice the moment he'd marked her. Not intentionally, but the damage was done. He'd wanted to bond with her, and it had been the only way to stop the torment of her Heat Cycle. His good intentions to pull away before he marked her had gone to shit when she'd held him to her throat and begged for more. If he'd stayed any longer she would have marked him in turn on pure instinct, without realizing the enormity of the act.

All he could give her now was the most time possible to make the final decision on her own.

He dragged a hand through his hair. This was so fucking complicated. "Shit."

His cousin's gaze narrowed as he studied his face. "This is because of your parents."

Daegan inhaled, the muscles in his neck tight enough to snap. "You know what happened."

"Yeah, but you're not your father."

No, and thank God for that. "I won't do to Liv what he did to my mother."

"Are you listening to yourself? What the hell kind of logic is that?"

Daegan shook his head, adamant. Cade would never understand. He'd had a picture perfect family. He didn't know how bad it had been for Daegan and his mother. No one did."Liv needs time," he said finally.

Cade shook his head. "She doesn't *have* time, and neither do you. What she needs is you, idiot. So if you don't get your head out of your ass ASAP, I'm going to have to take matters into my own hands."

Every cell in Daegan's body reacted to the thinly veiled threat. The bonded male in him growled in warning. "Meaning?" If Cade laid a hand on Liv in anything other than a brotherly manner, Daegan would tear him apart, cousin or not.

Cade shrugged, turned away as he headed for the door. "It means I won't sit back and watch you serve up your own death sentence."

The thud of the steel door reverberated through the hollowness in his chest.

Dammit. He had to fix this somehow. Liv had every right to hate him, but he couldn't allow her to think he didn't care. She might not realize it, but she mattered to him on a scale she wouldn't even begin to comprehend. As of last night, she held his life in her hands.

"Hell." The alarm system wasn't nearly sufficient protection for her, but he didn't know how else to keep her safe for the time being without staying there in person. Besides, being together was a risk in itself. Anyone coming after him might target her as well, though aside from that Aaron asshole he didn't think anyone had seen them together. While he wanted to give her more time to adjust, he was afraid she might only have another few days at most to make her decision.

He'd seen flickers of shadows closing in. The threat of danger lurking. From past experience, he'd learned not to ignore his visions. The hard way.

Death didn't always come at the hands of the enemy. Sometimes it was wrought by a person's own hand after suffering a lifetime of unspeakable misery from a cruel and vindictive mate.

He shoved the painful memories aside, filled with a renewed conviction that he was doing the right thing. Whatever happened from here, Liv would have the choice his mother never had.

With his muscles twitching from an overload of stress and frustration, Daegan stalked over to one of the gun cabinets along the wall of the equipment room, opened it. Cade had taken care of everything, he saw with satisfaction. All the weapons were cleaned, the amber-embedded rounds loaded into the clips. Their custom-made K-bar knives were sharpened to a deadly edge and slipped into their sheaths. Only the handles were visible, with intricately carved amber cartouches in the centers. Ready and waiting to send any Dark Army members to hell where they belonged.

"It has to be enough," he muttered. Yet looking at the small arsenal before him, he couldn't suppress another prickle of unease about his decision to allow Liv to stay in her own home.

In all honesty it would be safer for everyone if she stayed at the mansion. The hell of it was, he could never keep his distance from her if she did. And that left him pretty much fucked either way.

CHAPTER ELEVEN

Nida, Lithuania

A LITTLE BELL tinkled above the door when Nairne entered the bookshop. The elderly woman behind the desk looked up from her work and smiled. Returning the smile, Nairne used her limited Lithuanian to request the book the woman had set aside for her weeks ago.

The woman's face lit up. "You are the one searching for tales about the Empowered?"

"Yes." She wanted to see it in person before buying it, to make sure it was as old as the shopkeeper claimed.

When the lady disappeared into the back Nairne tried to tamp down her excitement. But when she reappeared with a slim, leather-bound book, Nairne's heart started hammering. It looked old, possibly from the eighteenth century. She couldn't wait to examine it further.

A gnarled, bony finger tapped the front cover. "German."

"Yes, that's fine."

"Old German. You read this?"

"Some." But she had help if she needed it.

With a satisfied smile, the woman passed her the blue leather book, babbling something too fast for Nairne to catch. Not that she was trying very hard.

Her attention was riveted by the book in her hands. The pages were thin and yellowed with age, but the printing was in perfect condition. One chapter title in particular caught her eye. The Legend of the Prophecy. Her breath caught. Was this it? Proof that the Empowered were real, that she was a possible descendant? It would explain the gift she and her great grandmother seemed to have.

Someone touched her arm. Startled, she looked up.

The woman smiled, said something else Nairne didn't understand, then gestured behind her to the door leading to another room. "My grandson. Vasilli!" she called toward the back.

A moment later a tall, twentyish-looking man stepped into the main room. Dressed in jeans and a polo shirt, his chest and shoulders were thick with muscle. His head was shaved, his face smooth. He carried an air of military bearing in his posture, his confident stare. He looked completely out of place in the old bookshop.

Nairne instinctively clutched the book tighter, resisting the urge to retreat a step. Nothing about him seemed outwardly threatening, yet something warned her to keep her distance from him. She didn't like the way his eyes locked on her. Hard eyes that missed nothing.

He glanced down at her hands, wrapped around the cool leather binding, then back up. His gaze traveled over her face a bit too carefully for her liking. As though he was memorizing it, cataloguing every detail. Her heart rate increased under the weight of that stare.

"Ah, you've come for the book. You like reading about fairy tales?" he asked in heavily accented English. "I bet I know some you've never heard."

Uncomfortable, Nairne looked away and dug her wallet out of her coat pocket. "How much do I owe you?" she asked the woman.

The lady named a price and insisted on being paid in cash. Nairne gave it to her, suddenly glad she wasn't paying with her credit card. If the nephew was interested enough in her, he could have used it to dig into her personal information.

Stop it. You're being stupid. No one cares about what you're doing except for you. And it's just a book, not a national treasure.

"I have told Vasilli all about the Empowered," the old woman said in slow, careful Lithuanian, appearing eager to offer more help. "He can translate the stories into English for you."

"Oh, that's very kind, but—"

"I'd be more than happy to talk with you further," he added. "I don't often come across a foreigner so interested in our folklore." His words and tone weren't inappropriate, but there was an undercurrent to them she couldn't put her finger on. Something disturbing that made internal warning bells go off in her head.

"Thank you, but I've got to run."

His stare never wavered from her. "Where are you staying? It's a small town. I can meet you at your hotel or somewhere else tonight if you want to hear some of the stories I've learned. I'm sure a well-educated woman like you would find them fascinating. Most people who come here don't pay any attention to the old legends, let alone have the capability to read old German."

Nairne kept her smile neutral. "That's too bad. I appreciate the offer, but I have to work tonight."

An interested gleam entered his eyes. "Researching something?"

She frowned as a tremor of unease snaked down her spine. This guy was really starting to creep her out. It was almost as if he knew about what she was working on. Which was crazy.

She tucked her wallet back into her pocket then offered a polite smile at the woman, making certain she avoided eye contact with the grandson. "Just satisfying my curiosity about some things I've heard. Thank you for your time." The bell tinkled overhead again as she stepped outside, a cool breeze teasing her cheeks.

Putting on her sunglasses, she cast a covert glance back inside. The man was still at the counter, watching her with an almost predatory interest. Despite the warm day, Nairne suppressed a shiver as she turned to walk back toward her hotel. She'd intended to find a sunny spot on the beach and read, but something told her that guy might follow her. Was she just being paranoid? Possibly. She wouldn't be the first academic to be accused of guarding her research to the point of paranoia. As a matter of habit she never told people what she was working on.

Nairne shook her head and picked up her pace, eager to get back to her room so she could dive into her new resource. She was close to finding something. Something big. Her analysis on the DNA sample information from the lab was almost complete. The woman Dr. Mackintosh had tested, whoever she was, bore a strikingly similar genetic pattern to her own. And his,

since she'd found his results amongst the files, along
with some fascinating information on his family tree.
Their ancestry was the same, comprised entirely of
Baltic German and Celtic roots, and Nairne was close
to finding out if their family trees intersected back in
the 1700s. While she couldn't be certain, Nairne was
willing to bet the similarities didn't stop there.

Once she got back to Vancouver, she intended to
contact Dr. Mackintosh and find out who the woman
was. Nairne wanted to meet her. Maybe she was the
key to unlocking the secrets Nairne had uncovered with
the parchment. Only she and a handful of others even
knew it existed. Now more than ever, she believed she
was on the cusp of a breakthrough in her research. All
the evidence supported her theory that the Empowered
existed, that she might be one of them—in a diluted
form anyway.

A tingle ran up her spine. The book in her hands
might be exactly what she'd been looking for these
past two years.

"GREAT JOB." LIV smiled down at her youngest student
as the last note faded, then ruffled her short hair affec-
tionately. "I can tell you've been doing extra practice."

Melissa nodded and smiled shyly, her eyes alight
with pride. Something Liv had never seen in those
brown depths before. No doubt due to her sorry excuse for a father, who Liv hoped she'd never lay eyes
on again.

The girl started to close the piano lid, but Liv
stopped her. "No, I think I'll play for a little bit to-

night." God knew she needed the distraction music always offered her.

Melissa swung down from the bench. "Can I listen until my mom gets here?"

"Sure."

Letting out a long exhalation, Liv let some of the residual tension out of her shoulders and set her fingers on the cool surface of the keys. As her hands stroked over them, the music began to flow. One of her favorite pieces. Haunting. Beautiful. An old Gaelic song about a man with eyes as blue as the Irish Sea and hair black as a raven's wing.

Like Daegan. His name was Gaelic for black-haired. She'd looked it up.

As she played, in her mind's eyes she pictured him walking along the cliff over a stormy sea while the waves crashed against the rocks below. Watchful, alert. Waiting for something. Longing for it.

She desperately wanted to be what he searched for.

A sharp rap at the door interrupted her thoughts.

While she swung around on the seat, Melissa jumped up and went to the door. Liv got up to pluck the girl's coat from the rack as the door swung open.

Melissa's face brightened with joy when she saw who stood there. "Daddy!"

Liv's suddenly nerveless fingers froze around the jacket while the blood drained from her face. *Aaron.* She smothered a gasp and jerked back a step, waiting for the inevitable wave of pain to engulf her. It didn't happen.

"Hi, sweetheart." Aaron went down on one knee to hug his daughter. The affection seemed genuine, not illicit in the least, despite her earlier concerns. Both of those things surprised her.

Aaron squeezed Melissa, then looked up to offered Liv a sheepish smile. That's when she saw the bruised and swollen side of his face. Jesus, had Daegan done that? It looked bad, like he might have a broken cheekbone. Not that she cared. He deserved it.

"Hi," he said.

No pain. No swirling bands of color around him. And that contrite expression on his face seemed all too genuine.

"Hi." The muscles in her face felt stiff. Part of her attention strayed to the panic button on the keypad next to the doorframe. If he made one move toward her she'd hit it.

But he merely stood and lifted Melissa in his arms, settling her on his back piggy-back fashion. "I, uh... wanted to apologize."

She stared at him, hardly able to believe what she was seeing. Hearing.

"I'm sorry if I ever did anything that might have upset or um, scared you."

Liv barely kept her jaw from falling open. What the hell was this? The guy obviously had psychiatric problems. There was no other explanation for his polar personality shifts. She eyed Melissa in concern.

But the girl beamed down at her from her perch, her little face lit with happiness. A daughter's pride for her father shone in her eyes. "Daddy came to my house this morning and promised to take me for an ice cream if I did well at my lesson."

Okay, now she was worried. Aaron had gone to his

ex's house? As far as Liv knew they weren't even on speaking terms, and the wife had a restraining order preventing him from setting foot on her property.

Aaron raised a brow at Liv. "So, how did she do?"

The man hadn't been much of a father to Melissa thus far. She had no idea what Daegan had done to him, but Liv would love to believe Aaron had finally decided to make an effort with his daughter. Melissa seemed thrilled by his sudden change of heart. Liv wouldn't be the one to extinguish that light burning in the little girl's eyes.

Finding her voice, she forced herself to reach out and offer the jacket, along with a stiff smile. "She was perfect. Better than ever."

Aaron smiled up at Melissa. "That's my girl."

"Bye, Miss Farrell." Melissa waved from atop her father's shoulders as he walked down the path to the car waiting at the curb.

Shutting the door behind them, Liv turned to lean her back against it, exhaling deeply. Rubbing a hand over her forehead, she took a couple more slow breaths. Besides breaking his face, what had Daegan done to the guy? He'd sworn Aaron would never bother her again, but to Liv it seemed like he'd undergone a complete personality transformation. Or was it merely another ploy to draw her in and make her let her guard down?

Not that it mattered. She didn't intend to let the man anywhere near her ever again. Standing on her front doorstep was still too close for her liking, so she might have to recommend another teacher to Melissa. She'd be sad to lose her favorite student, but her safety was more important to her than an extra few hundred dollars each month.

Her cell phone shrilled from the bedroom. Dashing down the hall, she picked it up, checked the display. Her heart squeezed when she saw Daegan's number. She set her jaw and put a hand on her hip as she answered it. This had better be good. "Hello?" Her tone made it clear she wasn't very happy with him.

"Hi." At least he sounded miserable. That made her feel marginally better.

"Where are you?" She didn't bother to hide her hurt or anger in her voice.

"Home. You okay? I thought I felt..."

"What?"

"I thought maybe you were scared a minute ago."

He'd felt her reaction to Aaron? Was that even possible? "Aaron showed up to pick up his daughter from her lesson."

Tension crackled across the line. "Did he do anything?"

"No, and I didn't have a headache like I did the other night, either. What did you do to him?"

"I punched him in the face and threatened to kill him if he ever hurt or scared you again. Then Vaughn stepped in and rehabilitated him."

"What? How?"

"I'll explain it later. I just wanted to make sure you were okay." He cleared his throat. "And I wanted to hear your voice."

She sat down on her bed, lonelier than ever. Just hearing his voice made her heart beat faster. "So why did you leave this morning, and why the hell have you been avoiding my calls?"

His deep sigh was full of regret. "A lot of reasons. The most important being that I have to keep you safe."

"Yeah. So you had an alarm system installed without asking me, then took off before I got back."

"Liv, this is really complicated."

"Because you're *making* it that way. How is being apart supposed to protect me, let alone convince me I want to be bonded to you?"

Daegan let out something close to a growl. "I hate it, too, but there was no other way for me to give you time."

"Time for what?"

"To think about everything, adjust to it all."

She pinched the bridge of her nose. "Daegan, I don't know *what* to think right now. How could you just leave me after last night? After marking me without even saying anything? I had to find out from Cade."

"I know, and I'm sorry." Another pause. "Leaving you was the hardest thing I've ever done."

Maybe it was stupid, but she believed him. "So what does this all mean now? That you're bonded to me but I'm not bonded to you?"

"Basically."

Nice. Even when he should be groveling he gave her half answers.

Leaning back against the pillows, she fought the sting of tears. The bedding still held his scent. She remembered the feel of his weight atop her, his body filling hers, cherishing and pleasuring while he'd watched her with those burning blue eyes. Her neck bore the mating mark, but it might just as well have been the other way around, considering how much she'd come to care about him already. Her body still ached to be with him, despite the way he'd left. "And now you're in danger because of it."

"I'll be fine."

She jerked upright. "Don't you lie to me. Not ever."

She couldn't be sure, but she thought she heard him curse under his breath.

"Cade told me what could happen. Why didn't you just stay and explain everything yourself?"

"Because if I had, your body would have made the bonding decision for you. You'd have marked me without thinking twice, no matter what the consequences."

"And what are the consequences?" She couldn't bear the thought of anything happening to him.

He gave a long, hard sigh. "When a couple bonds, they're emotionally linked for life. It's more than marriage, Liv. They might separate or even divorce down the line, but they'll always be tied to one another emotionally. For better or for worse. Only with us, it's for centuries, not decades. I wanted you to be fully aware of the risks before you make your choice. And I was hoping to give you time to get to know me better. I know this has all happened too fast for you."

She swallowed the bitter laugh that tried to crawl up her throat. "And how am I going to do that, Daegan? After last night, trust me when I say you know me better than anyone else ever has." Damn him for thinking he was being noble by giving her space. "So what now? Are we going to get to know each other better over the phone until you've decided I've had enough time? I don't think that's fair."

"I don't know how else to give you time. I can't see you right now. It's too dangerous. I wouldn't last two seconds around you without being all over you, and then your instincts would take over."

His words sent an answering rush of heat through her body. She'd never been with a lover half as considerate and skilled as him. "Maybe I want that." At least she'd get to know him better *that* way. If that were all she could have for the time being, she'd take it.

"God, don't say that right now." She could picture him running a hand through his thick black hair in agitation. "I'm trying to *protect* you, love."

The endearment made her throat ache. "From myself."

"From you, from me. From anyone who might be trying to come after me."

She gripped the phone tighter as her muscles tensed. "Has something happened?"

"No, and if anything had I'd have moved you in here with the rest of us. I'm just taking precautions."

She shook her head. "I don't understand how you can think being apart is going to help. How much time are you planning to give me before I can see you again? A day? A month?"

"You make it sound like I'm trying to punish you."

"That's what it feels like."

"*No.*" She heard rustling on the other end, then a door opening and a second later the distant cries of eagles drifted through the line. He must have stepped outside onto the balcony off the master suite. She imagined him standing there with the sun setting over the water, the crimson and coral light washing over his face. "I just…I need you to have the choice to say no if this isn't what you want."

Liv sensed something else beneath the words. Some ancient fear he wasn't admitting to. "Maybe this isn't what *you* want," she countered. "Maybe you regret being with me and you don't want me as a mate, but it's too late for you. Maybe you want me to say no so we can end it."

"God, no, not at all."

She got up and went to stand by her window. Thought about leaving the room so she wouldn't be tormented by his masculine scent. "Then tell me what the hell is really going on here."

Another sigh, this one full of resignation. "Something happened, a long time ago."

Her stomach plummeted, like the floor had suddenly disappeared from beneath her feet. Somehow she managed to get the words out of her tight throat. "You've been mated before?"

"No," he said instantly. "Never. But I—" He made a frustrated sound. "I don't even know how to explain this so you'll understand."

"Start at the beginning then." She wanted to understand. Needed to figure out how to help him.

"It was my parents. They came together pretty much like we have, in the beginning."

Liv tensed, anticipating what he would say next. When he didn't continue, she filled the silence for him. "And then it turned ugly."

"Ugly." He laughed, a short, harsh sound that filled

her with dread. He was quiet for a moment before continuing, as though battling the memories. "In that time divorce wasn't heard of. For reasons I'll never understand, she stayed with him, no matter how many times he beat her black and blue or came home with prostitutes just to humiliate her."

Liv's eyes narrowed. What a despicable asshole. She couldn't believe Daegan had grown up with a father like that.

Daegan's voice was weary, sad. "They hated everything about each other but they were trapped together because of the emotional and physical bonding link. I was too young to understand what they were or what I would become, but I still remember how miserable and broken my mother was. She cried all the time. I could hear her through the wall between our bedrooms at night when she thought I was sleeping. There was no escape for either of them, so they slowly destroyed each other. And when that wasn't enough they did their best to destroy me too."

Jesus. Her free hand clenched into a fist. "They hit you?"

"Mostly my da, especially when he'd been drinking."

Her stomach twisted. Her childhood had been hard because of losing her parents, but her grandparents had treated her well while they'd raised her. At least she'd had people to love and care for her when she was young. Daegan's tragic upbringing broke her heart.

Liv closed her eyes, aching for the frightened little boy he must have been. She wished she was with him right now. She'd have given anything to wrap her arms around him, to draw the pain away. His words cut her. "What happened?"

"One night he beat her so badly she was bedridden for a week."

Liv's skin crawled. "God, Daegan—"

"The day she was well enough to get up I was just coming home from school. I saw her walking toward the cliffs and followed her."

Her hand flew to her mouth, eyes squeezing tight as she connected the dots.

"I called to her but she didn't stop. Just walked right to the edge and stared down at the rocks for a moment. The look on her face...I'll never forget it as long as I live. It was relief. Pure, simple relief." His voice was raw, hoarse. "She looked back at me and smiled a little. Then jumped."

Liv bit her lip, trying to imagine how Daegan could have endured such a childhood. "I'm so sorry."

He made a gruff sound. "Some fishermen found her body and brought her back to the village. Took me two days to dig her grave. My father never came back. He never even came to her funeral."

He'd dug the grave? "How old were you?"

"Nine."

She put a hand to her mouth. Nine years old and he'd had to cope with all that on his own.

"My da died a few months later. Stabbed to death over a gambling debt."

Good, she thought with a rush of anger. She hoped he'd slowly bled to death. Tamping down her emotions, Liv reached out to her mate. She ached to soothe him, bring them closer. They might not have had much time together, but if he gave them a chance she knew without a doubt they'd never end up like his parents. "Daegan."

"Yeah?"

"I wish I was there right now to hug you."

He made a gruff sound, almost as though he was embarrassed. "Thanks, but I'm fine."

No, he wasn't. His parents' relationship had scarred him so badly that he'd chosen to isolate himself from her even after marking her. At huge risk to himself and the others.

"Can you see what I mean now? If you bond with me I don't ever want you to regret your choice. It's not too late for you to back out."

But it was. Far too late. She was already falling for him, would always be a part of him. "I appreciate what you're trying to do, Daegan, but I'm a big girl. I won't be forced into anything I don't want."

"Dammit, you're not listening to me." His voice rang with frustration. "The pull is too strong—you felt it last night, remember? You can't fight biology. I'm living proof."

"We're nothing like your parents. I already know you'd never treat me like that, just like I know I would never hurt you that way." How was she going to get through to him? "I'm strong-willed and I can make my own decisions. And right now I want to be with you. I *miss* you." The blurted words left her feeling vulnerable, but they were the truth.

He didn't answer.

She waited another few moments, then fought back a sigh. "So are you coming over or not?"

"I told you, I can't—"

"Then goodbye."

"No, Liv—wait!"

She hung up and stalked to her closet to snag a sweater. *Misguided, noble idiot,* she fumed. If he wouldn't come to her, then she would go to him.

And then she'd knock some sense into that thick head, whether he was ready to face her or not.

THE SOUND OF Xavier's voice coming through the phone irritated Rick on so many levels. He tried to make himself care about what the old man was saying, but couldn't. He had way more important things on his mind right now as he watched the tidy white one-story house down the street from the comfort of the Pathfinder.

"A woman in Nida is asking a lot of questions about the Empowered," the OL continued. "Vasilli did a background check and found out she's an historian working at UBC."

Rick covered a yawn and glanced at the clock on the dashboard. Ten to nine. Another few minutes and the sun would be down. Then someone in a big mansion on the ocean was going to be in sad shape without his mate, weakened by the effects of the Heat Cycle. It would make him an easier target, and he'd die faster once Rick killed the woman. The perfect time to grab her, if that damn old couple living next to her would ever finish weeding the garden beds out front. He could take care of them easily enough, but he didn't need to draw any unwanted attention before he could get Olivia. "So?"

"So, she's connected with the others," Xavier snapped.

He ignored the irritation in the OL's voice. "Even if she is, she's on the other side of the Atlantic. What do you want me to do about it?"

"I want you to find out more about her and the connection. I need to be kept informed about what's going on. If this woman knows anything important she could be useful to me."

He rolled his eyes. "Again, what the fuck am I supposed to—" His words evaporated as the delectable Miss Farrell suddenly walked out her front door. "I'm out."

He hung up as Olivia locked the door and glanced in his direction. He was parked near the end of her street behind a motor home. Had she seen him? She was smart. Maybe he should have switched to a different vehicle.

She glanced in the other direction before climbing into her car. He let out a relieved breath. The sleek silver sedan backed out of the driveway then headed east out of the subdivision.

Rick started the Pathfinder's engine and followed at a safe distance. "Where are you headed, darlin'?" he murmured as he merged onto the freeway a few hundred yards behind her. Plenty of traffic between them to camouflage his presence. They drove south for a few minutes before she took the Crescent Beach exit.

With a surge of excitement, he realized she was headed toward the water. Was she going to see the Coven Leader? Without a doubt she'd be able to get into the property. He could take her and the leader out in one op, then hopefully any others living there.

Something even better hit him.

What if she never made it there?

Rick's heart began to beat faster as he formulated a better plan. As far as weapons went, he had a few options tucked away in the glove box and beneath the seat.

A pistol. A rifle. A syringe filled with a powerful sedative. A black matte finished hunting knife.

The Obsidian Lord was a fucked-up old geezer that didn't know the first thing about executing a hit. He didn't see the larger picture. This whole problem between him and the Empowered started and finished with the Coven Leader. Why not take him out now and end the war before it began? Yeah, the woman he wanted made an easier target.

But she would make even better bait.

A slow smile curved his mouth as he kept pace with her along the darkening street, back just far enough to remain out of sight. He'd pick his moment when there were no witnesses around, make his move, then take control of his destiny for the first time in two years. Once he had the woman it was only a matter of time before her mate came after her. And Rick knew exactly where he'd take her.

With the OL safely ensconced over in Spain, this was Rick's show. He'd do this *his* way and make damn sure he killed the Coven Leader on this op.

Then he'd have more than enough leverage to free himself of the Obsidian Lord's evil grasp the next time they met.

CHAPTER TWELVE

Her phone went straight to voicemail again.

"Shit!" Daegan ran his hand through his hair, fighting the urge to hurl his phone across the room. She wouldn't answer his calls. He was strung out as it was. The last thing he needed right now was worrying about Liv's safety. He'd already raced to her house and back but no sign of her, no way to know where she'd gone. He hoped she was on her way over and he'd just missed her, otherwise he'd lose his mind. Maybe she'd taken a different route? Or maybe she'd gone out with a friend to vent. The sense of helplessness damn near tied him in knots.

Fuming inside, he headed for the main staircase. The magnificently finished mahogany walls were filled with oil seascapes he'd collected over the years, but he barely noticed them. In his mind, all he could see was his mother's swollen, tearstained face the night his father had nearly killed her with his enraged beating.

He'd been hiding in his room, too afraid to come out in case his father came back to take out his hatred on him. When the grandfather clock in the main foyer echoed through the darkened house at two o'clock that morning, he'd crept into his mother's bedroom.

His heart clenched when she turned her head to look at him. The single candle burning on the nightstand next to the bed illuminated one glistening blue eye, the other already swollen shut. Her thin body jerked with the last traces of her heart-wrenching sobs, her lips battered and bleeding. The front of her white lace bodice was spattered with her blood. Daegan's stomach twisted as he forced himself to go to her side. But this time his mother didn't reach for him for comfort or try to ease his fear. Her one functioning eye was glazed with the kind of pain that went far beyond any physical suffering.

"I wish I'd never bonded with him," she murmured. "I was so stupid. I didn't even know him. Didn't know what kind of a monster he was." Her chest jerked as she began to cry again, soft, plaintive whimpers that cut him inside. She pressed her lacerated lips together, bringing a fresh trickle of blood as her face twisted in a grimace of agony. Crying out, her bruised face blanched as she put a hand to her belly. As though she was trying stop the pain of whatever internal damage his father had finally inflicted with his big fists and heavy boots.

He stood there watching helplessly until the housekeeper came in and ushered him out into the hall. Standing in the shadows as the woman closed the door, his mother's mournful voice carried out to him. "I wish I'd had a choice. Why didn't I have a choice?"

They were the last words she'd ever said to him.

That had been nearly two centuries ago, Daegan reminded himself as he stepped onto the main floor. Somehow he had to get past that memory, because too much hung in the balance for him to risk losing Liv. He wasn't his father. He would cut off his own arm before ever raising a hand to his mate. Still, that nagging voice in his head wouldn't let up. Liv deserved to choose him of her own free will. He had to give her whatever time he could.

If his body held out that long. The frustration eating at him was quickly turning into an impotent rage. He had to find a way to stay in control. Already his muscles quivered with the need to lash out at something, someone. He hoped everyone steered clear of him until he figured out how to handle this.

Feeling torn in two, Daegan stalked into the kitchen but drew up short. Vaughn stood at the massive granite island, spreading peanut butter on celery sticks. Battling to hold back his aggression, Daegan paused just inside the doorway, stuffed his hands into his pockets. "Hey."

Vaughn flicked a disinterested glance in his direction but didn't make eye contact. "Hey."

In light of his current predicament with Liv, Vaughn's remoteness bothered him more than usual. "Got any more of those?"

Vaughn shrugged without looking up. "Sure."

When Daegan stepped up to the island and reached for one, Vaughn drew back to avoid any chance of an accidental touch between them. He did it with everyone, but in his current state it angered Daegan even more. "I wasn't going to touch you," he growled.

Vaughn didn't react to the words or the heated tone. His remote expression and eye-contact avoidance made Daegan feel like he wasn't even standing there.

Fighting back a scowl, he grabbed a celery stick and took a bite. It tasted like cardboard, but he hadn't eaten in…damn, he couldn't remember the last time he'd eaten. He had to fuel his body, keep his strength up. Whatever shit was going on in his personal life, he was still Coven Leader.

Where the hell was she?

While he crunched on the celery, his mind whirled with his current options. His mate was in pain, vulnerable without him. Away from her house, the threat of danger multiplied dramatically. There wasn't a specific threat to her safety, but his instincts screamed at him to get in his car and keep searching for her. Drag her back here for as long as it took to work things out, even if he had to tie them both to opposite ends of the house to keep their hands off each other.

Yeah, like some rope's going to keep you away from her.

Reaching for another snack, he caught Vaughn looking at his neck. No doubt checking for the mating mark that wasn't there. Daegan bit back the sharp retort on his tongue.

Vaughn swallowed his mouthful, keeping his eyes on the plate between them. "What are you doing here?"

Damned if I know. "It's complicated."

"Cade with her?"

"No, he's out." He barely refrained from snarling it, but Vaughn understood what it meant. The thought of any single male being alone with her right now made his hackles rise, let alone Cade with his prodigious sexual appetites. "And I don't know where the hell she is."

"You mask her place?"

Daegan hesitated. He'd contemplated it, but the spell wouldn't have been as strong without at least one of the others to help him. The one on the mansion and its grounds had been cast with all three of them, making it practically unbreakable. He'd decided against it because without Liv's consent it was too much of an invasion of her personal rights. If he'd masked it, no one but an Empowered would be able to find her place. Not her friends, not the mail man. Not even her neighbors, who would think they'd gone nuts when they woke up to find the white single story house missing and the house next to it their new neighbor. The only reason Liv could see the entrance to mansion property was because of her Empowered blood.

Yeah, but if her neighbors couldn't find her, no Dark Army members would be able to either, his conscience reminded him.

He cleared his throat. "I had an alarm system installed." His answer sounded defensive and stupid, even to him, but it was all he had.

Vaughn raised his head sharply, those tormented eyes boring into his from across the island. They simmered with anger and a shitload of resentment. "Are you kidding me?"

Daegan's jaw tensed. "It's good enough for now." At least, it had been until half an hour ago. "And it's only temporary." *Until I figure out what the hell I'm gonna do.*

Vaughn shook his dark head, his expression turning bitter. "You fucking idiot."

The disdain in his voice made Daegan stiffen and wrap his hands around the edge of the granite to keep from lunging at him. *No one* spoke to him that way, especially not one of his own men.

He fought back the sudden rise in his temper. "Excuse me?"

Breaking character, Vaughn planted his hands on the island and leaned forward, close enough that their noses almost touched. "You want this?" he demanded, yellow-flecked eyes so cold they burned. "*Look* at me. You want to end up like this too?"

Staring into the other male's eyes, Daegan couldn't look away. His were already beginning to turn. If Liv didn't mark him, how long would it be before he wound up as dead as Vaughn? Would he turn into a monster before he became suicidal and threatened the existence of their kind?

And if anything happened to Liv…

Shaken, he broke eye contact and took a step back. He didn't know how to respond to the accusation on Vaughn's face. The male would have done anything to save his mate and avoid his empty existence. But here Daegan was, acting too chicken shit to do what was necessary to protect them all.

Vaughn eased back then looked down at his plate. "Go." Just one word, spoken in that chilling rasp of his.

Any other time Daegan would have taken exception at being told what to do, especially by someone under his command. But looking into Vaughn's scarred face, he could still see the hell in the other male's eyes. An unspeakable pain that came from losing half of his soul when his mate died a hideous death at the hands of some Dark Army members dressed in Soviet uniforms, back in Klaipeda all those years ago.

A death Vaughn felt he should have prevented. Would have, if he'd been with her. But he hadn't gotten there in time. Instead he'd found her naked, semen-splattered body long after her suffering had ended.

Daegan couldn't risk anything like that happening to Liv. He wouldn't leave her unprotected again.

Even as he thought it, a ripple of unease ran down his spine. He had to find her, take her somewhere safe, regardless of how close to the edge of his control he was. Looking away from Vaughn's ruined face, he headed for the foyer. He wouldn't ask the Reaper for help yet, since Daegan didn't know where to begin searching for Liv. Besides, he had to take care of this himself. "I'll check in later."

His mate needed him. He was going to her no matter what it cost him.

LIV IGNORED HER ringing cell phone and turned up the car radio a little louder. She knew it was Daeagn calling, probably to dissuade her from coming to see him. Not happening. Since talking to him was clearly a complete waste of time right now, she hadn't bothered to put on her hands-free device. Her phone shrilled again from her purse on the passenger seat but she refused to answer it. She'd see him soon enough anyhow. Let him stew for the next fifteen minutes until she got there. He deserved it.

She was still angry and hurt, but more than that she ached inside. The pull toward him was stronger than anything she'd ever experienced, though it wasn't just physical. She wanted to be with him, figure out who he was, what made him laugh, what his interests were. Find out everything about him and the Empowered. There was a chance they could make this work if they were both prepared to put in the effort required. She was willing to give it a try.

Her headlights cut a bright swath across the quiet stretch of road that wound along the bluff overlooking Mud bay. With the convertible's top down, the warm, salt-scented air rushed past, bringing hints of freshly cut grass and warm pavement. The beach would be beautiful right now. Maybe she could convince Daegan to take a walk with her, see if she could relax him while they talked.

A car appeared behind her around the last bend. She didn't think much of it until it began closing in on her. It came up fast, its headlights growing brighter and larger in her rearview mirror. A glance down at the speedometer assured her she was already going above the speed limit. The road had a double solid line, but would the driver pass her anyway? She hoped so. Otherwise she was in for a painfully long drive along this quiet road.

When the vehicle came up close enough for her to see it clearly, her heart jumped. A Pathfinder. Dark color. Unease snaked through her. Too much coincidence that she'd have a run-in with another Pathfinder today. Could it be the same driver from this morning?

She pressed harder on the accelerator. The engine revved as the car picked up speed, smoothly opening up a gap between them. Even if the vehicle wasn't following her, she still wanted to get away from it. The road was dark and winding with no place to pull over and the next turnoff was still a few kilometers away.

She checked her mirror again. Despite her speed, the Pathfinder kept pace with her, pulled up right on her back bumper. An ominous headache began to tighten around her skull. Though she couldn't see the driver, this time she understood what it meant.

Oh, God—no.

She wasn't going to stop. There was no place to go but forward. The road was too tight to attempt a U-turn and next intersecting road was still so far away. Her suddenly cold hands clenched around the steering wheel as she sped up more. The needle on the speedometer climbed steadily, every incremental rise making her situation even more dangerous.

The Pathfinder stayed right on her tail.

"Get away from me!" she yelled. Her heart slammed against her ribs as the engine revved, smoothly accelerating with a rush of power. She had no choice but to keep racing down the darkened road, get to the next turn and pray she didn't lose control before then.

The headache intensified in silent warning.

Danger. Get away.

She needed help, *now*. Reaching out blindly with one hand, she groped for her purse on the passenger seat to grab her phone.

Her fingers had just found the strap of her purse when the Pathfinder rammed into the back bumper. Metal crunched. The back of her skull hit the headrest as she jerked forward against the seatbelt. A torrent of fear crashed through her. "Shit!"

Liv took her foot off the gas, jerking the wheel to correct it as her car veered toward the rough shoulder. Cold fear filled her. Was this guy trying to *kill* her? The instant she regained control she stepped on the gas, but the SUV rammed her again.

The sharp impact sent her car swerving hard to the

right. A scream locked in her throat as the tires skidded, out of control. The vehicle spun hard, heading toward the shoulder and the steep embankment on the other side of it. Her hands tightened like claws around the steering wheel, her foot stomping down on the brake.

An awful screeching sound shattered the air as the tires squealed. Then the sedan sideswiped something— a tree—and plunged down a slope. Her foot pinned the brake to the floorboard. No use.

Her car hurtled down the hill into the forest. She drew a breath to scream but it was torn out of her when she plowed into a stand of trees. The airbag punched her in the face, knocking her head back. Her vision spotted.

In the sudden silence, all she could hear was her own sawing breaths, the pounding of her heart. Liv forced her eyes open, struggling to see through the blaze of pain in her head.

She was pinned in her seat, wedged between the airbag and the damaged door frame. The entire left side of it had crumpled during the impact, making it impossible for her to get out through the back of the open convertible. She had to get out through a door.

Her hands fumbled with the seatbelt buckle. With each movement the migraine increased, sharp, cruel spikes that blurred her vision. Hitting that airbag had probably saved her life, but her face was already swelling. A trickle of blood dripped down her chin from her split lower lip, her ears ringing.

That crazy asshole had just run her off the road. Could have killed her.

Was he still coming after her?

The thought galvanized her into action. She grasped

the door handle and yanked. The door didn't budge. It was either too badly twisted or pinned against something outside. Shaking, she wriggled down in her seat then crawled across the console into the passenger seat to try that door. It moved a few inches but didn't open enough for her to get out.

Liv gritted her teeth and twisted around to kick it with both feet. The metal groaned in protest as it gave way, inch by inch. As soon as she had enough room to get through, she squeezed her way out of the vehicle, fell to the ground on her hands and knees.

The earth was slightly damp beneath her palms, smelled of the forest. Liv craned her head back. Above her, the towering evergreen trees seemed to sway in her blurry vision. She risked a quick glance over her shoulder to see if anyone had followed her. Didn't see anything.

My purse, she thought hazily. She needed to get her phone. With one hand she reached in, found the bag lying in the passenger side foot well. She fished her cell out but didn't stop to dial. *Run.* Liv pushed to her feet and staggered a few steps away from the wreck.

A twig snapped behind her.

She whirled around, setting a hand on a tree trunk to steady herself while the world spun crazily. Blinking in the glare of her headlights, she scanned the area. Nothing but shadows. The pain in her head didn't let up, telling her everything she needed to know. She had to get the hell away from here. Had to get back up to the road if she was going to have any chance of finding help.

But she wasn't going back the way she'd come. The Pathfinder's driver might be back there, waiting for her.

She headed up the slope instead. The throbbing in her head intensified with each uneven step and her mind began to grow fuzzy. She shook her head to clear it, but the pain became worse.

Another branch broke behind her.

Run.

She couldn't. The vise around her skull tightened until she could barely move. Her legs gave out from beneath her. Her knees hit the ground hard.

Shaking, panting, Liv forced herself to crawl. She could see the edge of the road now, just there beyond the screen of trees. Right there, only a few dozen yards away. Someone would see her. Had to.

Measured footsteps sounded behind her. Coming closer.

Whoever it was wasn't coming to help her.

Swallowing a scream, she scrambled on, forcing her shaky limbs to propel her forward. She clawed at the ground, dragging her forward with her phone still clutched tightly in one fist. She managed to bring up the display. Find the 9 then press it.

A deep, menacing chuckle broke the stillness. The pure malice in it sent shivers down her spine.

No! She crawled faster, too afraid to look behind her. *Have to get to the road. Have to.*

A scream built in her lungs. She could practically feel him behind her, the cruel hands grabbing for her.

With a final burst of strength she shoved to her feet and staggered a few running steps. Her thumb pressed the 1.

Her assailant laughed again. As though her desperate attempt at escape amused him.

While pressing the number 1 again, her trembling legs gave way. She fell face-first onto the fir needle-covered ground, still holding her phone. A booted foot caught her in the ribs and flipped her over.

"Get away from me!" she shrieked, lashing out blindly with her hands and feet. She had to hit send. That was the only way to get help. Her thumb found it, pressed.

The man kicked her wrist, sending the phone flying. Before she could lunge for it he caught her easily, pinning her wrists to the ground as he straddled her. In the faint glare of the distant headlights she squinted up into his clean-shaven face. A gasp tore out of her aching lungs.

Writhing around his body like a huge snake, his aura pulsed in waves of pure, pitch black.

Her vision spotted, stomach pitching violently under the agonizing burst in her head. It was numbing, debilitating. Squeezing her eyes shut under the onslaught, she grabbed her head and wrenched to the side, gagging. Her weakened legs kicked uselessly against his while she tore at his wrists.

"Shut up and keep still," he snarled, his hot breath washing over her cheek.

The terrible pressure in her skull continued to grow until she couldn't take it anymore. Overload hit. Her body convulsed in a series of hard, sharp jerks. Waves of them, like someone had electrocuted her. She barely felt him roll her over and tape her hands together behind her. When he rolled her onto her back she could hardly see.

Liv strained to see his face, fighting to stay above

the pain and loosen the tape around her wrists. "Let me go!" Her voice was a weak, desperate rasp. The nausea roiled in her stomach, filling her throat and making it hard to breathe. He would kill her. She saw it in his face. Felt it in his intent.

Daegan! her mind screamed. He was the only one who could save her, but now he'd never know what had happened to her.

The man grabbed a handful of hair with one hand to hold her still then slapped a piece of wide tape across her mouth. Blind terror sliced through her.

Daegan!

Above her, the man smiled. In that last moment before the blackness took her, she saw the unrepentant malevolence shining in his empty gray eyes.

CHAPTER THIRTEEN

DAEGAN HAD NO clue how he was going to fix this without his cock winding up buried deep inside Liv, but he had to give it a shot.

The moment he stepped outside into the fresh evening air, his lungs seemed to expand. It was like his body understood he was going to Liv and was as relieved as him.

Two steps away from his Porsche, Daegan stopped dead. The keys jangled in his hand as an overwhelming feeling of fear swept over him. His heart began to race. Cold sweat bloomed on his forehead. All the symptoms of a full-blown panic attack. Over this? Couldn't be. He hadn't had one since he was a kid.

But no matter how hard he tried to ignore the feeling, it intensified.

For fuck's sake, pull yourself together.

Thank God no one was around to see him bent over, pulling in slow, deliberate breaths to calm his heart rate. It didn't help. His heart continued to pound until his guts twisted.

What the *hell*? This was crazy. He'd faced enemy machine gun fire and Dark Army members in hand-to-hand combat with barely a rise in his pulse, and here he was, panic-stricken at the thought of confronting Liv?

But the emotion wasn't coming from him, he slowly

realized. It was coming from someone else, being transmitted to him. And it wasn't a mild sort of fear. It was powerful, vivid, the kind that paralyzed a man and made his flesh prickle.

It was coming from his mate.

Terror coiled inside him, turning his tight muscles to lead.

Then he heard her voice, loud as a scream, crystal clear in his head.

Daegan!

The raw panic in her voice buckled his legs. His knees hit the gravel driveway, the keys falling from his nerveless fingers.

"Liv," he rasped, fighting to quell the rising panic inside him. What the hell had happened? Something was wrong. Terribly wrong.

His heart beat a staccato rhythm as he struggled to his feet and dug out his phone. While his guts clenched he dialed her number with an unsteady hand, moving back toward the house. It seemed to take forever for the call to connect, then it finally began to ring. He tensed as the seconds ticked by.

Come on, pick up.

Four rings.

Five.

The sixth one echoed hollowly in his ears before her voicemail picked up.

Her panic was tangible, putting pressure on his lungs like his chest was slowly being crushed. *Fuck!*

Ignoring his weakened state, Daegan ran for the front door, wrenched it open. It slammed against the foyer wall as he flew through it and headed for the staircase to the lower floor. His feet skidded on the wooden steps. He hit the bottom in a crouch. The equipment room. He needed his weapons.

In the midst of yanking open one of the gun lockers, he sensed Vaughn entering the room.

"What's wrong?"

"Someone took Liv," he managed without looking back, blindly grabbing ammunition from the shelf, tossing it onto the steel table nearby. Everything was happening too slowly. He wanted to scream in frustration.

"Where?"

"Don't know." Vaughn would never be able to find her, only Daegan could because of his connection with her. And that ripped him to pieces. His bond with her made it impossible to stay cool and collected. All his years of military experience meant shit right now. How was he going to find her? Help her?

Vaughn went into another locker then shoved a ballistic vest at him. "Here. Put this on."

God, he couldn't slow his breathing down. Felt like he was going to hyperventilate. Throwing off his jacket, he pulled the vest over his head and quickly fastened the Velcro straps. When he looked back at the table, Vaughn was ready with a pistol in a thigh holster and an amber-embedded blade tucked into a sheath.

"Thanks," he muttered distractedly, reaching for it. But Vaughn surprised him by shooing his hands away, bending down to strap the gun to Daegan's thigh. Grabbing a rifle, Daegan didn't protest because he was too freaked out about what had happened to Liv. He had to get to her. Every second counted.

And when he found the person responsible he'd take him apart.

"We'll bring more firepower to you," Vaughn said as he straightened.

Daegan was already headed for the door. "Get Cade. I'll call you once I'm in position."

"You'd better."

The emotional echo continued to roll through him in a blinding haze of fear. Then, just as suddenly as it began, it stopped.

Daegan froze near the bottom step, sucked in a breath as his adrenaline levels plummeted. He swayed on his feet. For a moment he convinced himself he had to be wrong. That his own fear had somehow blocked his emotional link with her. But no, there was nothing. Nothing but silence from her.

His blood ran cold as a sickening thought took hold. Jesus, she couldn't be dead.

"What?"

Daegan whirled to face Vaughn while his blood pressure nosedived. The Reaper's scarred face was a study of concern. Likely because he'd never seen Daegan so close to coming unglued in the one hundred-plus years they'd known each other. "She's gone." He could barely get the words out of his constricted throat. Refused to accept what it probably meant.

Vaughn blanched. "You mean…"

"I can't feel her anymore," he blurted. It scared the living shit out of him. If she was dead, he couldn't deal with it. Just couldn't.

She'd been entrusted to him. His first responsibility

was to protect her. Take care of her. And now someone
had attacked her. Maybe even—

"Maybe she's unconscious."

Daegan couldn't look at him. His stomach lurched,
bile rising up his throat, hot and acidic. He wanted to
howl like a wounded animal, tear the place apart. He
didn't know where she was or how to locate her. The
terrible helplessness washed through him, filling him
until he thought he'd explode. There was nothing he
could do now except wait. And pray.

*Don't do this to me, Liv. Help me find you. Please
come back to me.*

PULLING THE UNFINISHED bedroom door shut behind him,
Rick looked at the four men seated around the plywood
table. All Dark Army members, all ready for a show-
down with the Coven Leader. He couldn't be far away.
No way would he leave his mate unprotected.

Rick couldn't believe she'd been such an easy target. If not for the Celtic design on her neck, he might
have believed the Obsidian Lord was wrong about the
bonding. It made no sense.

"What's the plan?" one of the others asked.

"She's still out." Her pulse was steady though, and
her pupils responded evenly when he'd checked them
with a pen light. She'd scared him when she'd gone
into convulsions. For a minute there he thought she'd
been having a stroke. It was possible she'd hit her head
on something during the crash, but he didn't think that
was the reason. She'd been conscious and scared out her
mind when she'd tried to run from him, so those con-

vulsions had to be some sort of a reaction to him. He swore she'd recognized him. Or at least, what he was.

Whatever had happened, her being unconscious made carrying her here much easier. He hadn't even needed the syringe he'd brought with him. She'd better wake up soon though, or he was screwed. He needed her alert and aware of what was going on so he could extract the information he needed. Just how he extracted it depended entirely on her.

"Well then, let's wake her up," another said, and the men around the table all snickered.

"Not yet."

"When?"

"When I say so." Crossing the room, he dug his phone out of his coat pocket and typed in a text message to the OL. Old bugger probably didn't know how to text back though. So much the better.

Have the mate.

Less than three minutes later, his phone rang. Rick raised a sardonic brow but didn't bother picking it up. It was only five in the morning in Spain, yet the OL was already up. Did the man really think he was going to answer this call? Not likely. Rick wasn't about to give him an opportunity to torture him into changing his mind about this. Or kill him for disobeying a direct order.

He eyed the buzzing phone with derision. Answering it would result in enough pain to make him writhe and scream. To him the noise from the phone seemed frustrated, full of impotent rage. *How's it feel, asshole?* he silently taunted the man on the other end.

Rick was running this operation, not him. And that's

the way it would stay until it was over and he had what he needed to either get his soul back, or blackmail it out of the OL.

Ignoring the ringing phone, he gathered the last of his equipment, stuffing it into his huge duffel in the corner before pulling out the last item from another bag. The others chatted amongst themselves while he pulled it on, but after a moment they all fell silent. He could feel the weight of their stares as he meticulously pulled up the zipper.

"What is that?" one of them asked.

"Exactly what it looks like."

"A ghillie suit? Are you shitting me?"

Rick ignored the man's derisive snicker, re-checking his gear a final time. As a sniper, he had one shot at this. Literally. He intended not to fuck it up. And if that meant covering himself with cedar boughs until he looked like a tree, so be it. One single, tiny mistake and it would all be over. The others could laugh all they wanted. Obviously he was the only one who had a clue about what they were up against. The Empowered had abilities far beyond their comprehension. If he died tonight, it would be because the Leader was a better soldier, not because Rick hadn't been prepared.

One of the others set down his bottle of beer on the piece of plywood suspended between two saw horses. "You sure he'll come for her?"

"I'm sure." Everything depended on it. "And when he does you'd better be ready, or you'll be dead before you realize he's here."

The tallest of the three, a man in his early fifties, made a scoffing sound and folded his arms across his wide chest where the end of his beard brushed his breastbone. "You make it sound like we should be scared of him or something."

"Nope," Rick replied, checking the firing mechanism on his customized rifle one last time. "I'm saying you should be fucking terrified."

The man's eyes narrowed in suspicion. "What for? Even if he is the Coven Leader, he's only one guy."

The man's appalling naiveté only reminded Rick of his dangerous predicament. These Dark Army recruits were new converts who couldn't be relied upon for an operation like this. He could only depend on himself, his instincts and training from here on out. As far as the Leader being only one man, that didn't mean shit. That was why he'd planned the operation this way. As soon as he set everything in motion he had to haul ass to his position, wait there to take the Leader out before he got to them or called in reinforcements. No telling how many more of the Empowered bastards he had waiting in the wings.

"Think whatever you want," he finally answered. "It's your funeral."

The DA member's brows drew together in a menacing scowl. "There are five of us, and you're a trained sniper. He doesn't stand a chance."

Rick clenched his teeth, bit back a retort. During his exhaustive research he hadn't been able to find out much about Daegan Blackwell, but he'd run across a nebulous security contracting business with ties to both the CIA and DIA, whose CEO bore a frighteningly similar profile to the Coven Leader. That was no coincidence. Rick knew in his gut it had to be the same

mysterious man he'd never been able to find. He had
a feeling that was about to change. What he'd seen in
that profile was enough to raise the fine hairs on the
back of his neck.

"Hello? I'm talking to you," the man snapped.

Rick shot him a hard look over his shoulder. "He's
trained and been embedded with the SAS and the
SEALs, asshole. And that was before he started working as a private contractor. He doesn't need any help to
take out this whole place, killing every last one of us
in the process. And if he gets help..." He let his voice
trail off suggestively. "Let's just say we'd better hope
he doesn't."

The man's surly expression changed to one of wary
consideration. Beside him, the informant Rick had met
at the bar finally spoke. "You didn't tell us that when
you called us here."

"Well I'm telling you now. Just be ready and do
what I told you to." Not that it mattered what they did.
These DA members were expendable, and if necessary he could easily call in more reinforcements tomorrow. If he lived that long. Whatever happened, he
could never forget that to the Obsidian Lord, he was
equally expendable. They all were, because he owned
them completely. Every last one of them.

Zipping the canvas bag shut, he stood and retrieved
the sharp kitchen shears he'd placed on the unfinished
island. In the end he'd get what he needed, but he didn't
have much time to get everything ready. If their hostage didn't cooperate, he'd have to leave it to his men
to extract the information.

Crossing to the makeshift table, he handed the scissors to the one in the middle. The quietest one, the one he sensed was the most intelligent. "Go see if Sleeping Beauty is up yet."

MALE VOICES DRIFTED through the haze of pain around her skull. Several of them, speaking low and quietly.

Battling up through the layers of darkness, Liv tried to lick her lips but something covered her mouth. She couldn't move her arms. A memory of the accident surfaced, the man with the cruel eyes and crueler smile as he slapped the tape over her lips.

Slitting her eyes open, she blinked warily and assessed her surroundings. She was on a chair with her hands taped to its arms, her ankles taped to the legs. The room was dim, small, with no windows and what appeared to be a bare concrete floor. The only illumination was the faint light that came in around the edges of the door. All the walls were plain studs covered with plastic.

Was she in some sort of an unfinished house? It wasn't cold but her skin broke out in goose bumps. Shifting in the chair, she tried to twist her hands free or wriggle her fingers around to loosen the tape. It didn't help. A clammy film of sweat covered her as the gravity of her situation hit home. She was trapped, immobilized here, and no one knew she was missing.

Whoever had taken her must be connected to Daegan somehow. There was no other explanation. He must have been suspicious she was under some sort of threat, or he never would have had the alarm system installed. Why had he left her unprotected if he'd thought she might be in danger? The kidnapper was evil incarnate.

She shivered as she recalled the inky black aura surrounding him. All she remembered after that was the fear and that hideous burst of pain before her body whacked out on her and locked her into a series of hard convulsions. She hoped she never had to confront him again, because she wasn't sure she could withstand that kind of agony a second time.

Think, Liv. You have to find a way out. You have to.

But there wasn't one. Whoever had taken her must be on the other side of that door, so she couldn't go that way. The only other exit was the plastic-covered window high up on the wall behind her, and she'd never be able to get out that, even if all her limbs were free. She could move her feet and legs a bit, but the chair she was strapped to was tall. Her struggles to reach the ground with her toes only allowed her to inch the chair backward.

Cringing every time the chair scraped over the concrete, she slowly edged it back toward the far wall. Maybe there'd be a tool or something sharp she could find to cut the tape away from her hands.

Eyes on the door, Liv struggled to get the chair across the floor to the back wall. When it bumped into lumber, she swiveled her head to check for tools. A nail, a sharp edge, something. But she couldn't find anything. A sense of claustrophobia closed in on her, pressing in from all sides until she flailed in her seat, yanking uselessly against her bonds. The tape on her ankles gave slightly, allowing her to slide her legs up a bit.

The door flew open and four rough-looking men strode in. She froze. They all wore black leather vests

over their thick chests, and each of them had dark
orange or red auras, edged in black. Violent, dangerous men. Liv winced as a fresh wave of pain hit her,
but it was nothing compared to when the kidnapper
had taken her. When one of them turned slightly to
shut the door, she caught a glimpse of devil's horns
on his back. Her stomach dropped like a stone. She'd
been abducted by a gang? This didn't make any sense.
They couldn't be connected to Daegan, so why had
they randomly targeted her?

Her heart fluttered like a trapped bird's wings as she
stared at them, bracing for whatever they were about
to do to her.

The tallest one stood in the doorway with a smirk
on his bearded face as he crossed his arms over his
chest and leaned against the jamb. His dark eyes bored
into hers but she was too afraid to look away. "Boo,"
he taunted.

The others laughed.

She shrank back in her chair but got nowhere. The
hard, unyielding wood of the backrest dug into her
spine. Her breaths were rapid and shallow, sounding
loud in the quiet room. When the shortest of the men
came forward every muscle in her body stiffened in
protest, but she couldn't move away. All she could do
was draw up her legs a tiny bit as he approached, gathering her strength. She waited until he was within range
before lashing out with both feet.

He jumped back with a grunt and caught her legs,
but not before she made solid contact to his shins. His
grip on her legs turned cruel, fingers biting deep into
her muscle while she tried to jerk free. Then in a move

too fast for her to counter, he trapped her legs between his knees and squeezed, hard. Liv let out a growl of outrage, twisting as hard as she could, but she couldn't free her legs.

His smile turned mean in his goateed face. "I thought you'd be more powerful than this. I'm almost disappointed."

She shrank back as much as the chair would allow, beginning to tremble. All she could do was turn her head away in a feeble attempt at escape when he reached for her.

His strong hand wound around her jaw, forced her head around. She refused to meet his eyes, staring at the darkened floor while her stomach shriveled.

"Glad to see you're finally awake though," he said, grasping the edge of the tape.

Livdidn't have time to brace before he ripped it off, making it feel like he'd taken her skin with it. She gasped at the sharp sting on her cut lower lip and shut her eyes, trying not to let them see how deeply afraid she was. Something told her they would only feed off it.

The man leaned in closer, placing his hands beside hers on the armrests. Caging her in. She flinched, took deep breaths to combat the violent headache. "So you're the one."

The one? What the hell did he mean by that?

From the corner of her eye she saw the other two coming closer.

"Not very friendly, are you?" the man pinning her said, lifting a hand to trail a finger over her jaw. She swallowed, hating the betraying quiver of fear that ripped through her. "Don't feel like talking, huh? That's going to be real inconvenient for you, but pretty soon I think you'll change your mind."

Get away from me, you sick bastard, she wanted to scream but choked the words back. She refused to give them the satisfaction of breaking her.

"Give me her phone."

Liv shot a sideways glance at the others.

The man eased away a bit to accept the phone the tall one handed him, then turned back to her. "We need you to make a call. You gonna make this easy on yourself, or do we have to get nasty with you? Choice is yours."

She licked her dry lips, but before she could answer the discomfort in her head suddenly increased tenfold. She hissed in a breath, gritting her teeth as the vise tightened around her skull. *Please no, not again...* Beads of sweat dotted her upper lip as her gaze strayed fearfully to the doorway.

The quiet footsteps came closer, closer, almost to the door

A second later another man appeared there, his aura black as the inside of a grave. Liv jerked, the pain in her skull exploding in a fiery burst. She cried out and shut her eyes, trying to block it out. It didn't help. Her stomach pitched sickeningly, sending a hot rush of bile up her throat. She fought it back, forcing unsteady breaths through her clenched teeth.

The man was quiet for a moment. She could almost feel his merciless gaze raking over her. Then to her surprise, his steps retreated. The agony decreased, slowly, just enough for her to open her eyes to slits. Through the blur of tears she found him watching her. He stood well back from her down the dimly lit hallway, arms crossed over his chest while he regarded her, that chilling band of onyx writhing around him like an electrical charge. The pale light from the naked bulb overhead illuminated his harsh features. He raised one eyebrow, those mercurial eyes boring into her. "Better?"

She wasn't about to answer him. She just prayed he stayed where he was before she went into convulsions again.

"Do you know who I am?" His voice was deep, commanding.

"No," she rasped, struggling to clear her mind through the fog of pain.

"Do you know *what* I am?"

Yes, she knew. Shivers rolled through her, uncontrollable and sharp. "Evil."

He laughed, a frightening sound as dark as his aura. "That's right. Know why I've brought you here?"

She managed a tight shake of her head, half afraid to look at him in case it made the pain worse. Was it his proximity that affected the intensity, or making eye contact with him?

"I think you do. Just like I think I cause you pain when I get too close. Am I right?" He took an ominous pace forward.

Her vision was blurred. It was all she could do to keep from screaming.

He eased back. "You see something about me that others can't. What is it?" His tone was hard, but curious.

Clenching her jaw, Liv forced herself to answer him. "Black." *As dark as your heart.*

The others drew in a collective breath as they stared at her.

"And what about them?" he demanded, nodding at the others.

She wanted to throw up. The suffering engulfed her, shooting down her spinal column until her hands and feet went numb. "Red. Orange. Some black."

"Interesting. I'm sure he finds that talent very useful."

At some unseen signal, the man pinning her suddenly grabbed hold of her right wrist and yanked at the tape. Liv made a sound of protest, tugging uselessly against his grip as he unwound it, tearing the sticky surface off her sensitized skin.

"Call him," the man in the hall commanded.

She blinked, dared meet his eyes. The muscles in her neck felt tight enough to snap. "W-who?"

His mouth twisted in a sardonic smile while he stared at her. Holding her gaze, he took two quick, deliberate steps forward.

Liv cried out and twisted away, desperate to escape the hideous pain. "Stop," she begged in a whisper, ready to shatter. After a few seconds, the terrible sensation eased somewhat. When she gathered the nerve to open her tear-filled eyes and look at him again, he'd retreated back to his original position.

His stare was cold enough to burn. "The Coven Leader. Call him to you."

She started to shake her head but the man next to her grabbed her rigid hand and forced her cell phone into it. Her heart slammed in her chest. They wanted Daegan.

But if she called him and he somehow found her, they'd kill him. She knew it in the deepest part of her being.

"Call him to you and we'll let you go. You can go back to your life and put all this behind you. If not…" He let his voice trail off, the unspoken threat speaking for itself. "I've got things to do," he said to his men. "When she calls him, you know how to reach me. Oh, and I should mention that Olivia teaches piano." With a final hard look at her, he turned on his heel and walked away.

His parting words filled her with dread but she sagged in her seat, let out a deep breath when he left, taking the worst of the pain with him. She pulled in a few deep, blessed lungfuls of air, allowed her exhausted eyes to close for a moment. But her relief was short-lived.

A third man in the room walked up with something shiny in his hand. The faint light coming from the hallway glinted on it. A knife? Her fingers clenched around her phone, heavy as lead in her icy cold palm. The short man kept her legs trapped between his knees, squeezing his hand around hers until the edges of the phone dug into her skin. She swallowed a cry of fear, glancing between the two men while her heart raced frantically.

"You like to play the piano, Olivia?" the tall one asked. When he raised his hand she saw the sharp blades of the scissors in his hand. Heavy duty shears, the kind people used in the kitchen to cut through chicken bones.

The blood drained out of her face, a scream building in her lungs. Her captor resisted her futile struggles with heartbreaking ease while the tall man grasped her left index finger.

"No!" she yelled, trying to twist away and curl her fingers into her palm. But he was too strong for her.

He gripped her finger and twisted it up sharply, ignoring her cry of terror and pain. The blades of the scissors made an ominous snipping sound as he opened and closed them. "Call him now, before I lose my patience and start cutting off those pretty fingers one joint at a time."

CHAPTER FOURTEEN

HANDS BURIED IN his hair, Daegan sat on the bottom step near the equipment room, fighting to hold onto his sanity. With his eyes squeezed shut, he focused solely on breathing in and out. His breaths were jerky and shallow, every muscle trembling in an agony of suspense. He didn't give a damn that Vaughn watched him silently from the doorway. All he knew was he'd lost contact with Liv seventeen minutes ago and each passing second crawled by with excruciating slowness. She'd been afraid, and he was certain she'd been in pain too. The inability to do anything devastated him.

Despite his attempts to concentrate on the blank screen he'd erected in his mind, something began to seep into his subconscious.

His head snapped up, eyes flying open. There. He'd felt it again. An awareness. Of dread. And growing fear.

He leaped to his feet and grabbed his loaded M-4, the surge of hope painful in his chest. "*Liv.*" Her name tore out of him like a prayer. The knowledge that she was still alive made his eyes sting. He honed his focus on the fragile link he held with his mate.

"Where is she?"

Vaughn's rough voice barely registered through the haze of emotion but Daegan gave a sharp shake of his head. He wasn't getting anything concrete, but he had a faint impression of darkness. Of trees. Somewhere rural? She couldn't have gone very far in such a short time. Was she on the outskirts of town? Dammit, he couldn't pinpoint the location.

Pushing out a frustrated growl, he shook his head and cleared his mind. Christ. Maybe he was thinking too hard. Maybe he had to let his subconscious do the work for him. Shutting out the static in his head caused by their bond was nearly impossible, but he had to find a way.

Calling an image of her to mind, he held onto it, recalling every last detail about her. The shape of her face, the different shades of green in her eyes. The texture of her skin and the feel of her body wrapped around his. A fierce, protective longing filled him, mixed with fear and despair. Replacing it.

Slowly, everything else faded away until she was absolutely clear in his mind. He could see her, smell her. Almost touch her. Warmth spread throughout his body, long forgotten little tingles that began in his fingertips and traveled up his arms, his torso.

It's working. The rush of relief was so sharp it brought a lump to his throat. *Hang on, Liv, just a little longer. I'm coming.*

It had been nearly a decade since he'd last attempted this, but it was his best and fastest shot at getting to Liv. The tingling in his fingers spread up his arms to his face, down his chest and torso, encompassing his legs. When he dared open his eyes he saw his body was beginning to fade, shimmering around the edges.

"Don't!"

He closed his eyes again to block out the sound of

Vaughn's angry voice, holding that image of Liv. He had to do this now, before it was too late. Couldn't risk losing the connection.

"*Stop.*"

"Can't," he snapped, willing his body to fade. "Only way."

"You'll be too weak to help her."

He shook his head, a tight, angry movement of denial. It didn't matter if he was too weak to do anything when he materialized on the other side. At least he'd know where she was and be able to get help if he needed it. Then he'd do whatever it took to save her, even if he had to crawl every inch of the way to her side.

Vaughn's frustrated sigh was full of resignation. "You call me the *second* you get there so I can follow you. A suicide mission isn't going to save her."

Nodding once without opening his eyes, Daegan embraced the energy flowing through his veins and let his body to fade into nothingness. This was the easy part. Coming out on the other end was going to hurt like a bitch.

The world went black around him, his body sucked through space like an invisible hand pulled him. Each passing second Liv's emotions grew stronger in his mind, so he knew he was going in the right direction.

When the tingling sensation suddenly increased to a burning, like hellish pins and needles pricking him all over, he knew he was close. A few moments later he suddenly materialized at the edge of a road. As his body solidified once again, he fell to his hands and knees while the world spun around him. His skin burned like he'd been dropped into a pool of acid. He bit back a scream. When he tried to get to his feet he all but collapsed.

Jesus. He'd expected to be weakened, but not like this. He could barely hold his head up while he dragged himself to the sandy shoulder and tried to figure out where he was.

It took a moment to get his bearings, but soon enough he recognized the quiet stretch of road along the bluff. Why here? There were no houses nearby, no evidence of Liv. Looking around, he finally spotted the skid marks on the asphalt, veering sharply off the road toward the trees on the downward slope.

Oh, God.

His arms trembled with the effort of pushing his body upright as he slung the rifle around to his back. It felt ten times as heavy as it really was. The Kevlar plates in his vest seemed like they were made of concrete.

Move!

Gritting his teeth, Daegan struggled to his feet, stood there weaving for a moment. The tire tracks seemed to shift and blur as he forced his feet to walk toward them. From what he could tell they'd been made by small, wide tires, the kind found on sports cars. His Porsche had them. So did Liv's BMW.

He followed them down the rise, his heart beating faster with each passing second. When he caught sight of the wreck of Liv's car, he stopped breathing.

"Liv!" Her name was torn out of him. Everything seemed to move in slow motion. Pushing his legs to their limit, he slipped then fell, crashing down to the loamy ground. He lunged upward, racing for the car.

She might still be inside it, too badly hurt to respond. "Liv." No answer.

Reaching it, he approached the open passenger side door. She wasn't in the seat or on the floor. The deployed air bag was deflated, and there was no blood on it that he could see. Had she tried to go for help? He pulled out his flashlight and spun in a circle, looking for clues. When his eyes landed on the smudged footprints in the dirt, his stomach pitched. Bile rose up his throat but he fought it down, fishing out his cell with an unsteady hand.

"Someone's taken her," he said when Vaughn picked up.

"How many?"

"One. A man." He could tell by the size of the print. A dead man walking, if he'd done anything but help her after the crash. Daegan knew in his gut the man hadn't. "Have you got my location yet?"

"Almost."

Daegan gritted his teeth. "How much longer?"

"Few seconds."

Each one dragged past until he thought he'd shatter the phone in his fist, then Vaughn spoke again. "Got you. On my way."

"Alert Cade." He didn't have a clear vision of what would happen, but he had a bad feeling they were going to need all the backup they could find.

Less than a minute later Vaughn suddenly appeared a few yards away from Liv's car, armed to the teeth and shouldering a full rucksack of weapons. He strode toward Daegan with a strong, confident gait, completely unaffected by his journey. Not for the first time, Daegan envied his ability to dematerialize so effortlessly.

"Cade's en route with some gear, twenty minutes out."

Way too long to wait. They'd have to go in without him. "Ready?"

"You look like hell," the Reaper announced with a frown. He glanced at the prints on the ground, then back at him. The frown deepened. "Maybe you should wait here for Cade and I'll follow them."

"Fuck that," he spat. He'd already left her safety in someone else's hands one time too many. Though he trusted Vaughn with his life, he was going after Liv himself. "Let's move."

Every step was an effort, but he struggled forward, eyes pinned to the two sets of prints on the needle-covered ground.

A vivid blast of her fear swept through him, stealing his breath. "Shit." He went down on one knee, wiping the sweat off his upper lip with his sleeve. "She's terrified," he told Vaughn in a low voice when the Reaper looked at him in concern. He was attempting to climb to his feet again when his phone rang. The number in the call display made him suck in his breath. "Liv?" he rasped into it, almost afraid to hope.

"Daegan—" Her voice broke on a choked sound.

He sagged in relief. She was still alive. "Are you all right?"

"I…" Her ragged sob twisted inside him like a knife. His skin prickled. "What?" he demanded.

"They've tied me up."

Oh, fuck. More than one. Had to be Dark Army

members. He couldn't stop the images from forming in his mind. Liv bound and helpless, facing evil beings straight out of a horror movie.

"They're going to…"

Going to what? he wanted to yell, frantic for more information. Whatever it was, he knew it would be slow and painful while they tried to extract his location from her. He fought to keep his voice calm, level. She was scared enough without adding to it. "Where are you?"

"I—I don't know. An unfinished house I think, but I d-don't know where. I can't tell anything else," she whispered brokenly. The stark fear in her voice ate at him.

"Liv, I'm coming. It's going to be okay." She was somewhere close by. He'd find her. His link with her was stronger than he'd initially thought. He'd use it to get her free.

"No, don't! You can't."

The hell he couldn't. All he had to do was follow his instincts and they would lead him to her.

"Listen to me," she continued, a frantic edge to her voice, "it's a trap. They're waiting for you, please don't—" A hair-raising scream ripped through the line.

His heart went berserk. "Liv!" Daegan's blood chilled when she didn't answer. He heard the sound of the phone hitting the floor on the other end. Then her raw, guttural cries of fear that tore him to pieces.

A choked sound."No! Don't! *Don't*!" she cried out. Another anguished scream, then the sound of flesh striking flesh. Liv's whimper of pain made him sick to his stomach. Low male laughter drifted over the line.

Icy cold rage swept through him. Those bastards in

the room with her were breathing their last. When he found them he'd tear them apart. But before he could do or say anything else the line went eerily, completely dead.

Shoving his phone into his pocket, he gripped his rifle tight in his hands then lunged to his feet. His thigh muscles trembled under the strain but he didn't care.

"Wait."

He whirled at Vaughn's protest, opened his mouth to snarl at him, but the Reaper merely handed him a pair of wraparound shades.

"Cover your eyes. They're like spotlights."

He'd been too worked up to even notice the change. Daegan's hand shook as he slid them on. The glare reflecting on the insides of the lenses all but blinded him.

When he looked up, Vaughn's expression remained grim. "If you don't figure out a way to dim them and get control of yourself, we're fucked. They'll see you coming a hundred yards out, easy."

He didn't care as long as he got Liv out safely. They could do whatever they wanted to him after that. "Stay well back from me then."

"Screw that. You die, we will too."

"Isn't that what you've wanted all along?" he shot back, the primal side of him warring with the trained soldier he'd been all his life.

Vaughn's mouth thinned but he didn't respond. It was an asshole thing to say, but Daegan was too lit to take it back. Together, the three of them were a lethal force, but Cade wasn't with them now. He didn't need to explain to Vaughn how dangerous this mission was, though when it came to infiltrating enemy lines,

Vaughn was one of the best he'd ever seen. Whatever booby traps or other nasty surprises awaited ahead, Daegan knew the other warrior could handle it.

Staying in the shadows, he moved silently along the trail on wobbly legs with Vaughn at his back, hugging the edge of the trees. The prints changed a few dozen yards up the slope. Liv's marks disappeared, but the man's changed direction and continued parallel to the bank, cutting through the forest far enough away from the road that no one would have seen him carrying her.

Their slow progress was torture, but checking for trip wires or IEDs was a necessary evil. Even at the sluggish pace, walking the uneven terrain sapped more of his strength. The prints grew fainter and fainter on the trail as the trees thinned out, giving way to newly seeded grass. The kidnapper's bootprints became more visible there, making it easy to follow them through the vacant lots dotting the bluff. He and Vaughn moved like ghosts across the five connecting vacant properties until they reached the first unfinished house.

Daegan stopped with his back pressed against a tall cedar trunk to assess the area. The damn weakness stealing through his body made his thighs tremble.

"That one?" Vaughn whispered over the radio piece in his ear, somewhere behind him in the darkness.

Daegan couldn't see him, but he knew without a doubt Vaughn was in position, covering his back. If something went wrong and he was killed before he got Liv out, Vaughn and Cade would get her to safety. "No." The link with Liv was still strong, but it didn't give him a clear indication of how close she was.

Her fear kept pushing at the edge of his mind no

matter how hard he tried to block it. It fueled the rage, helping him override the weakness, but his eyes were still too bright. "Tracks are gone. We'll have to check each one individually," he answered quietly, careful that his voice didn't carry. Unfortunately there was nothing he could do about his hellishly glowing eyes.

"Copy that."

He eyed the skeletal wooden frames uneasily, wondering if someone had them in their sights already. Perfect place to set up an ambush or hide a remote controlled bomb. Each structure they checked would burn up precious time they didn't have.

No choice.

From his position he studied the edge of forest farther up the bank, toward the road. Another ideal spot for a sniper or spotter to hide. No telling how many men they were up against or how many were waiting for them somewhere in the dark. The amber-embedded rounds he and Vaughn carried would stop a mortal just as well as they would a DA member. They just had to hope the Obsidian Lord wasn't here with them.

Placing his feet with care, Daegan picked his way across the last vacant lot. Once he reached the first house, he pressed his back flat to the bare plywood wall, waiting to search it. With his finger on the M-4's trigger, he listened to the soft footfalls approaching, waited until he felt Vaughn's light tap on his shoulder. When he entered the closest door fast and low, Vaughn stayed on him like a shadow.

They moved from room to room in a well-rehearsed choreography of movements, clearing from bottom to top and back down again. His heart sank when he realized the place was empty. Pushing the dread aside, he picked his line of approach and headed for the next one.

PERCHED IN A crevice near the top of the bluff, Rick consciously slowed his breathing, relaxed his muscles as he set the scope to his eye. His hide wasn't perfect by any means, but with luck it would get the job done. Nestled in the hillside amongst the trees below the road, the cedar boughs he'd used to camouflage his position afforded him adequate protection. For now. Considering the elite training his quarry had, he might have to move to a better position. Initially he'd considered setting up in one of the unfinished houses, but that had seemed too obvious. This provided better concealment and lines of sight, though in some ways it placed him at great risk.

He hadn't been able to wipe out his trail properly, and he hadn't had time to arrange the greenery with much care. If something backlit his position, even for a moment, he'd be in perfect silhouette. Anyone with military training would be able to spot him immediately.

Too late now. Things were already in motion.

A few minutes earlier one of the DA members had alerted him that the call had been made, and ever since he'd fought the spike in anticipation thrumming through his veins. The Coven Leader was on his way, could arrive any time. Question was, when and where?

He had to slow his pulse. Had to regulate his breathing so he could feel each heart beat and be able to fire between them.

His earpiece crackled as someone keyed the radio.

"Ross and Bose are still in there having fun with the

girl," one of the men reported. "They're going to start doing real damage soon because they're getting bored, and I don't know how far you want them to take this. You said you wanted her alive when the Leader gets here. What do you want me to tell them?"

It angered him that he had to break radio silence to deal with something so stupid. "It doesn't take three of you to watch one unarmed woman," he said in as low a voice as possible. "Get your asses in gear and be ready for anything."

"Roger that."

Dumbasses, Rick thought, mentally shaking his head. If any of them survived the night he'd be surprised. As for him, he figured his chances were fifty-fifty. Because when it came down to facing off against the Coven Leader, he knew only one of them would live to see morning.

Trapped between her captors knees with both hands immobilized, Liv choked back a sob when the man raised the shears again. Two men had left a few minutes ago, but two more remained. Their obvious enjoyment of her terror made her want to throw up. Especially the tall one with the goatee. He was loving every freaking moment of this. She'd closed her eyes so she didn't have to look at him. It was her only defense.

He opened and closed the shears with menacing slowness, making sure she could hear the sounds. With each quiet snick the cold metal brushed her fingers held clamped in his vise grip. Sometimes he snipped close enough that she could feel the tiny whoosh of air from the blades closing next to her cringing fingers.

Other times he purposely nicked her, slicing open thin cuts along the back of her hand and fingers that stung like fire.

Every snip of the metal, every fresh blaze of pain magnified her fear until it was all she could do to hold back the scream locked in her chest. But each time she jerked or a muffled cry escaped her they laughed, watching her writhe and tremble, fight not to beg.

Begging wouldn't do any good with these men.

The door squeaked open. She tensed in anticipation of a new threat, but when she dared to slit her tear-blurred eyes open she found another man standing in the opening. One from before.

"Boss says to get a move on. Only one of you stays with her."

"I'll stay," the man tormenting her purred.

The man in the doorway snorted. "He wants her alive, Ross."

"Oh, I won't kill her while you're gone. Later, maybe." His smile was an evil slash that sent a shiver up her spine.

"Want me to tie her back up?" the one next to him asked, still holding her right wrist.

"No," Ross said with a smirk. "I like a challenge. And I think I can handle her." His amused tone made it clear how funny he thought that was. He dragged the point of the scissors down her chin and throat, to the top of her shirt, then snipped. She barely had time to flinch before he reached out to rip the material apart, exposing her bra.

"Whatever, man." The man on her right dropped her hand then left with his friend in the doorway, shutting her in alone with her tormentor.

Liv instinctively grabbed his wrist to still his hand. The sharp point of his weapon dug into the skin over her breastbone, just above her cleavage. "Well, what should we do to amuse ourselves in the meantime, now that we're all alone?"

The cruel intent behind the words was all too clear. She didn't know how she understood, but she knew he was going to mutilate her, starting with her breasts and face, before he raped her. Bile rushed into her tight throat, burning hot. Her shoulders convulsed as she gagged.

He pressed the sharp point harder against her tender skin until the tip punctured it. She covered a gasp, bit back a cry when she felt the warmth of her blood dripping down between her breasts, over her stomach. Compared to the debilitating headache the burn wasn't agonizing, but the pleasure on his face, the hungry way he watched the blood trickle over her skin threatened to destroy the last vestiges of her control. How much more could she take before she lost it?

She had to think of a way to get the shears from him. If she could do that she'd have a shot at wounding him badly enough to attempt escape. If she didn't, he'd slice her up bit by bit until she was screaming and thrashing and pleading for a mercy that would never come. Without a doubt she knew he would kill her. Slowly. Painfully.

A shudder of revulsion ripped through her. Almost as hard as the convulsions when she'd seized earlier.

Wait. The seizure. If she could repeat that and make it convincing, maybe he'd let go or loosen his grip on her free right hand long enough for her to grab the scissors.

If she failed, he'd do a lot worse than cut off her fingers.

Was it better to die fast and violently? Or slowly and painfully?

The answer seemed obvious to her. Daegan wasn't coming for her. No way would he be able to find her.

Reaching deep to gather up every last drop of courage and energy, she drew a hitching breath and sent up a silent prayer. *If I fail, let him kill me fast.*

Liv shook her head once, contorting her face into a grimace. "Don't. No, it's—" She shook it again, hard, fighting past the pain exploding in her temples to mimic what she'd experienced before. "Stop, I'm going to—" With a cry she jerked in the chair and arched up, forcing her limbs into a series of hard contractions. Her whole body spasmed in uncoordinated waves.

"Shit," he muttered, releasing her captive hand to grasp her chin. "Fucking stop that!"

Liv gave a guttural moan and kept up the performance.

"God dammit," he snarled. The pressure around her knees loosened as he moved back. He released his grip on her chin. In her peripheral vision she saw the scissors in his right hand dip. Falling down and away as he lowered his arm.

Liv lunged upward, grabbed for the weapon while she drew her knees up and drove her feet into his stomach. A loud *oof* exploded out of him as he flew back and hit the floor. Wasting no time, she opened the blades and sawed frantically at the rope holding her left hand hostage. The sharp edge gouged her tender flesh but she barely felt the pain as she pulled her hand free.

She leaped to her feet as he rolled to his side with a menacing snarl and started to stand up. In the faint light coming through the window behind her, his dark eyes glittered with the promise of death. He was between her and the door, her only way out. She had to get past him.

Suddenly he sprang, hands outstretched toward her. Liv whirled and struck out blindly with the scissors, putting all her force behind it. The blades plunged into the back of his thigh, sank to the bone with a sickening thud.

His scream all but shattered her eardrums when she jerked the blood-slicked shears free and ran for her life.

She ripped open the door and tore out into the hallway, expecting to be snatched at any moment. Behind her she heard Ross's bellow of rage as he rolled on the floor, trying to get to his feet.

"You fucking bitch, I'll *kill* you!"

Liv swallowed tears and careened around the corner. It was dark. She could barely see but she couldn't let him catch her again. This was her only chance. She clutched the scissors in her slippery hand, ran as fast as she could. When the plywood staircase appeared before her she raced down it but caught her foot on something at the bottom and hit the concrete floor on her belly. The impact slammed her forearms and ribs with bruising force.

"I got you now, bitch!"

No. She scrambled to her feet, lurched onward through the confusing maze of construction equipment. Clear plastic sheets hung from the ceiling like filmy curtains. The smell of sawdust was sharp in the air. Her hip caught the edge of a sawhorse. She bounced off it, stumbled. A cry locked in her throat. At the last second her hands shot out, finding purchase against a bare wooden stud before she crashed headlong into it.

Ross's running footsteps were closer now. Close enough that she could hear his labored panting. Almost feel his hot breath on the back of her neck. Her skin crawled.

Get out, get out...

The muscles in her legs trembled under the strain, on the verge of collapsing. But she couldn't quit. She could finally see some moonlight up ahead, streaming through the gaping doorway.

"Come here!"

She was almost out in the open. Someone would hear her, see her, call help.

Bursting through the empty door, her head jerked back when his fingers snagged the back of her shirt. She ripped free from his grasp, falling forward. A short scream tore out of her as she hurtled toward the ground. She hit hard but managed to roll away when he struck the ground beside her.

Liv lashed out with the scissors. Missed. Struggled to her feet and took off again, running blindly away from him. Slower now, her battered body running out of strength. Her exhausted legs screamed in protest. Her lungs burned. Desperate for air. Behind her she could hear her attacker's angry curses and those heavy footfalls pounding after her. Closing the distance between them again, despite his wounded leg.

She was too slow, she thought with a muffled cry. He was going to catch her.

A gunshot suddenly rang out, shattering the silence.

Liv yelped in terror and instinctively ducked, veering to the left so the shooter wouldn't have a clear shot. She barely heard the thud of a body hitting the ground behind her, didn't dare look over her shoulder to see what had happened. More footsteps pounded. Still coming after her. A scream of denial crowded her throat. She tore over the dewy grass, running down the bank toward the water's edge.

A hard weight suddenly crashed into her back. Her shriek was cut short when she slammed into the ground and lost her grip on the scissors. Before she could move, a pair of strong arms clamped around her ribs, immobilizing her.

Panicked, she lashed out, fighting the iron hold with all her remaining strength. The arms tightened until they cut off her breath.

"Liv. Stop."

When the voice registered in her numb brain she stopped struggling and went dead still. Before she could draw another breath she was flipped over to find herself staring up into a pair of beautiful glowing blue eyes.

CHAPTER FIFTEEN

DAEGAN'S HEART WAS in his throat as he turned Liv over. She was mindless with fear, didn't even realize it was him. Her shirt was covered in bloodstains.

"Baby," he whispered, quickly straddling her hips to take her face between his hands, making her focus on him. He'd lost a decade off his life when he'd seen that asshole chasing her. Now that she was safe he wanted nothing more than to hold her and savor the fact she was alive and whole, but there wasn't time. The open shirt revealed a cut over her sternum, but he couldn't tell how deep it was. Other than that she seemed unhurt from what he could tell.

Her eyes were wide with shock as he stared up at him, but then he caught the quick flare of recognition. She wrenched her head aside to cast a panicked glance behind him.

"He's dead," he said quietly.

Meeting his gaze once more, her face crumpled. With a ragged sob, she reared up to bury her face in his neck.

Daegan swore and held her close for a moment. "I've got you."

Both her hands dug into his back like she was afraid someone would tear her from his arms. He'd die before he let that happen.

He allowed himself to comfort her for another few seconds, but the prickling sensation between his shoulder blades told him they had to move. They were completely exposed out here, and that gunshot would have alerted any other DA members of their position. At least his eyes had dimmed once he'd known she was all right. Without the glow making them an easy target, they still had a chance of getting out of this alive.

"Come on," he ordered, dragging her up with him. "We have to go."

She didn't say anything, didn't utter a single protest as he pulled her to feet and made for a clump of cedars a few dozen meters away. Her silence alarmed him but he understood she was in shock. She simply clutched the back of his vest, following at a stumbling run.

Once he had them behind cover he hunkered down, placing her between him and the largest tree trunk. His muscles quivered with exhaustion. When he'd seen her come tearing out of that house the rush of adrenaline had allowed him the burst of strength necessary to reach her, but now the crash was taking its toll. "Vaughn, you copy?" he whispered.

"I've got you covered. Be advised, there are three enemy contacts moving toward you from the south."

Then they'd have to go north. Only he didn't know if he had the strength to get Liv up the bank and to the road for pickup. "We'll move toward you—"

"I'm up and in position." Cade's voice surprised him when it came over the radio.

Finally, he thought in relief. "Copy that. Any contacts in your area?"

"Negative. I've got the truck waiting four hundred meters to your northwest, at the end of an access trail."

"We're on our way." Cade could get her the hell out of there, treat any injuries, while Daegan and Vaughn hunted down every last one of the animals that had taken her.

Keeping his eyes trained on the open ground between them and the edge of the tree line farther up, he reached back to set one hand on Liv's shoulder. She vibrated beneath his touch, her fear and shock palpable. "Almost there, love. We're going to get you out of here."

She didn't respond, but her fingers closed around his in a tight grip.

Reluctantly he withdrew his hand, raising his rifle. "Stay close."

He'd only taken a few steps when Liv let out a sharp gasp and grabbed his shoulder. "*Stop.*"

"What?" When he glanced back her face was pinched, her eyes narrowed into asquint. As though she was in a great deal of pain. His skin prickled.

"He's out there," she whispered, staring out at the dark slope before them.

RICK TENSED AND raised his head slightly when he heard the gunshot ring out. He hadn't seen anyone approach.

A second later the radio crackled. "Shit! Ross is down," one of his men said. "Bastard got him in the head."

A clean head shot. Was it the Coven Leader? "Move in," he said quietly, tightening his focus. The rifle's scope gave him a perfect view of the open ground below. In a few seconds he'd know whether it was the man he'd been waiting for.

He fought the instinctive leap of his heart when his quarry finally came into view. Olivia had somehow escaped, but that didn't matter. She wasn't his real target anymore.

The man leading her raised his head. Rick's heart leaped.

It was him. The Coven Leader. He recognized him instantly from that old British Army photograph he'd been shown.

Rick adjusted his aim, but the Leader and Olivia disappeared behind a stand of cedars before he could take a shot.

Didn't matter. The instant they cleared those trees he would put a bullet through the man's head. Then he'd finally get his soul back.

"WHO'S OUT THERE?" Daegan frowned as he whispered it.

Liv swallowed and reached for his hand. She needed his touch. The instant his fingers closed around hers the pain in her head lessened. She pulled in a relieved breath before answering. "I think it's him. The one who took me. His aura was completely black, not just edged with it like the others. He made my head hurt the worst."

"All of them had black in their auras?"

She nodded.

"Dark Army members," he muttered, then relayed the information to the others via the radio.

It made sense. But it also had to mean the war had begun. That scared her even more. "He's the most powerful," she added. "The leader. He was giving the rest of them orders."

Daegan keyed his radio. "Any enemy contacts visible on the ridge?" After a second he spoke again. "Copy that."

"Do they see him?"

"No. Where do you think he is?"

"I can't pinpoint the location. Somewhere over there I think." She waved a hand toward the left side of the bluff.

Daegan's jaw tensed as he studied the terrain ahead of them. "We can't go back because three more are coming this way."

A frantic glance behind her assured her nothing moved in the moonlight. It was impossible to tell if the sudden increase in pain she'd experienced was from them, or the man she sensed waiting for them up ahead in the darkness.

Daegan squeezed her hand to bring her attention back to him. His eyes had stopped glowing, but the deadly serious expression in them did nothing to dispel her fear. "Once we clear these trees we have to make a run for it. No matter what happens, don't stop. You keep running, straight up there." He pointed in a diagonal direction that cut across some vacant lots toward the right side of the bank. "Vaughn's got us covered, and Cade will too. He's got a truck waiting up there." His voice barely carried over the still night air.

She nodded, too afraid to speak. Her fingers stayed locked around his.

"Can you run if I let go? Or will the pain be too bad?"

She didn't know, but she'd just have to suffer through it. If this was their only chance of making it to safety, she'd do whatever it took to not jeopardize his wellbeing. "I'll be okay."

He studied her for a moment, holding her gaze. "I go first. Stay right behind me, and when I stop to cover you, keep running as fast as you can. Understand?"

"Yes."

"All right. Let's move." He keyed the radio again. "We're moving out." He dropped her hand, raised his rifle and ran.

Fresh pain sliced into her skull with every step without Daegan's touch to shield her. Sharper. Until her vision blurred and her stomach rolled. They were heading right toward the leader, she realized with a sickening rush. She followed Daegan blindly, but within a few seconds the pain buckled her knees. "No," she cried as she fell, desperate to make Daegan stop.

Daegan whirled. "Liv."

"Not this way," she gasped out, struggling to her knees. "Heading right to—"

He took a step toward her.

The thin tree trunk next to him exploded in a shower of bark.

"Down!" he yelled. He tackled her flat to the ground, covering her body with his.

The pain in her head vanished the instant he touched her but her fear spiked when she heard him snarl the word *sniper* over the radio.

"Move," he commanded, shoving her toward a nearby tree trunk.

Liv scrambled to her knees and crawled for it. She

was only a few feet from it when Daegan suddenly grunted and fell. Liv whipped her head around.

He lay on his side, struggling up onto one elbow. His face was a mask of agony, blood dribbling down his arm. *No.* She reached for him. Had to help him. "Daegan—"

"No! Don't move!" He flipped onto his stomach and dove for her as another round hit where he'd just been. Dirt sprayed up.

Liv bit back a scream and grasped the back of his uniform when he reached her, frantic to drag him to safety. He merely jerked backward again, and this time she saw the glistening hole the bullet had made in his shoulder. His animalistic growl of agony made the hair on her arms stand up. Ignoring his protests, she lunged over, grabbing the strap of his bulletproof vest to drag him behind cover. A low snarl erupted from her as she strained to pull him with her, but he refused to cooperate. Before she'd moved him more than a few paces, he shoved her flat and crawled on top of her.

She pushed up, tried to turn over, hating that he was exposing himself to more fire. "Let me—"

"Stay...down," he rasped, his voice thick with torment while he covered her, surrounding her head with his arms. Shielding her with his body.

An enraged roar came from the left. Liv jerked her head around in time to see a man running at them, pistol aimed. The sniper hadn't been the only one shooting at them. She opened her mouth to scream a warning but Daegan had already raised his rifle and fired. The bullet hit the man dead center in his chest. He crumpled to the ground with a shocked expression on his face.

"Move," Daegan growled near her ear.

Terrified, Liv slithered forward until she'd reached the tree, pressing flat into the dirt at its base.

"Cade," Daegan panted as he came down beside her. She laid a hand on his back. To offer comfort, but also because touching him reduced her headache enough to clear her vision. "Did you see the muzzle flash?"

She risked a quick glance toward the ridge. The distant roar of an engine broke the stillness. A second later Cade's Range Rover's headlights cut a swath through the darkness as it barreled toward them.

"Stop!" Daegan commanded.

The vehicle skidded to a halt.

"Turn to your right. Two o'clock."

Dirt and gravel hissed under the truck's tires when it turned.

"Right there," Daegan murmured, and the vehicle stopped.

Liv stared at Daegan. What was he doing? He'd obviously spotted something on the ridge, but she didn't see anyone up there. Just some brush and a mound of cedar branches illuminated by the headlights.

Daegan stilled, curling his finger around the trigger. "Got him." He fired. Two carefully placed shots. Then, "Sniper down. Move in." His arms trembled as he lowered the muzzle of the rifle. The instant it touched the ground he all but collapsed onto his side.

"Shit," she breathed, finally seeing all the blood covering him. Liv grabbed his shoulder but yanked her hand back when he growled. Her palm came away covered with his blood. "Oh God, Daegan," she whispered, helping him onto his back.

The headlights shut off. She dimly heard the sound of the Rover's door open then slam shut.

"Stay down," he whispered between gritted teeth.

She heard the running footsteps. Instinctively she ducked down low. Cade pounded toward them, carrying a rucksack. He dropped to his knees beside them.

"Vaughn's gone after the sniper. Where are you hit?" he asked, sweeping his gaze over him.

"Few shots in the arm," Daegan bit out. "Not too bad."

Cade met her stare and opened the bag. "What about you?"

"I'm fine." Her cuts were nothing, but she couldn't stop shaking. Was Daegan really all right?

Cade took out a dressing but Daegan shook his head and tried to sit up. "Get me up."

"Vaughn's taking care of it."

"I said, get me *up*." He practically barked the words.

Cade raised his eyebrows but didn't say anything while he looped an arm under Daegan then helped him to his feet. Liv slid her arm around his waist to steady him, alarmed by the obvious anguish on his face, the amount of blood soaking him. "You have to lie down."

He shook his head, a muscle working in his jaw. "I want the sniper. If he's the leader we need to know how many men he has."

"There were four of them plus him in the house," Liv said, wishing he'd lie down and let Cade treat his wounds. The coppery smell of his blood was strong in the warm night air. It dripped down his arm off his fingers in a thin rivulet. "We have to get the bleeding stopped."

"Listen to your mate," Cade advised.

"Fine, wrap it quick then," he snapped.

Cade quickly bandaged his wounded limb. Liv winced when Daegan hissed through his teeth.

"Stay with her," he ordered Cade, then started to pull away from her.

Bracing for the pain, Liv loosened her hold but before she'd let go he and Cade both stilled and swiveled their heads toward the rise. Had they heard something over the radio?

A sharp, short scream rent the air in the distance.

Her heart leaped, thudding hard against her ribs. "What was that?"

"The sniper just met our grim reaper," Daegan answered coldly.

HE WAS FUCKING dying.

Rick's heart pounded out of control while he struggled up onto his elbows. His ruined lung made it almost impossible to breathe. Every inhalation was its own separate torment, sending shards of agony through his left side.

He'd known he was fucked when those headlights swept over him. Just hadn't thought the bastard would be quick enough to take a shot before he could squeeze the trigger a second time. And there was amber in the round that hit him. He could feel its poison spreading through him already. Burning like lava beneath his skin.

You're not dead. Get up. Finish this.

The words reverberated in his skull. He was down, but not out. Not yet. If he could get back up to his gun he still had time to get one well-aimed shot in before shock shut down his body.

His trembling fingers reached for the stock. So close, just out of reach.

"Freeze."

His heart jumped into his throat but he did as he was told. He had no other weapons on him and the man was already practically on top of him.

Hard hands grabbed him by the shoulders then flipped him over, none too gently. He screamed as his ruined ribs compressed.

"Get up." A big fist seized the front of his suit, yanked him off the ground.

Gasping, dizzy, Rick looked up into the shadowed face. When the man turned his head slightly and the moonlight struck him, Rick's blood turned cold. The eyes were unnatural. Pure yellow shards embedded in onyx.

"You don't get to die yet," the man snarled in a chilling voice, dragging him down the slope.

Rick grabbed the meaty fist holding him prisoner, but it was no use. Already his strength was failing. The treetops spun above him as his vision blurred, going hazy and dark. Blackness took him.

When he came to, he was face-to-face with the injured Coven Leader and still dangling off the ground, trapped in an unbreakable grip. A pair of pale eyes bored into his, steady and alert despite the man's heavily bleeding wounds. But the yellow ring around the irises told a different story. Soon the blood loss from those bullet holes would be the least of his problems.

"How many men did you have here?" the Leader growled.

A bitter laugh rumbled up from deep inside him. He choked on his own blood as it streamed up his throat, out his mouth. He felt it dribble off his chin. "Not enough," he wheezed.

"How *many*?"

The icy rage in the other man's eyes didn't scare him. He was dying anyway. The knowledge brought a sardonic smile to his lips. The Obsidian Lord had led him to this, but in the end that monster wouldn't be the one to kill him. He'd also lose a soul, and some of his terrible power with it. "F-four."

"Where is the Obsidian Lord?"

"You're...dying too." He grinned at the thought.

Those icy eyes narrowed to slits. "What?"

"Amber in...bullets."

The man holding Rick up whipped him around to face him. Rick blinked in surprise as those strange eyes began to swirl. Almost as if they were heated from within. His body felt lighter all of a sudden. The pain began to fade away. The hellish burn from the amber disappeared. Was he dying already?

Not yet. The deep rasp was loud in his head.

He stared into the man's eyes, unable to look away. *You're evil.*

And in that moment he finally realized what the man was.

A Reaper.

The irony of it dragged a garbled laugh up from the depths where his soul had once lain, making the blood

in his mouth and lung froth. This would be a far better death than he deserved.

HIDDEN BEHIND THE tree with Cade, Liv gritted her teeth
and breathed through the pain pounding through her
skull. Without Daegan's touch to shield her, at this close
range the man's malevolence threatened to make her
lose consciousness. Vaughn was having some sort of
weird staring contest with the Dark Army leader. The
prisoner was drenched in blood, choking on it, but his
aura remained black as night. His smile was defiant,
even though his teeth and lips were coated with his own
blood. The sight made her stomach roll.

She must have made a sound because Cade slid his
arm around her shoulders and pulled tight her into his
body. His touch didn't take the pain away like Daegan's did, though she was glad for the comfort. The DA
leader was pure evil, but she'd never condemned anyone to die before. And that's exactly what she'd done
when she'd confirmed his identity and aura to Daegan.
She knew without a doubt they'd never let the man go.

Suddenly the man laughed, breaking the tense silence. A hideous, gurgling sound tinged faintly with
madness. The flesh on her arms prickled.

Cade's muscles tensed against her. "Close your
eyes," he whispered.

She shook her head, unable to look away from the
awful spectacle before her, afraid Daegan might be in
danger.

"Well?" Daegan said to Vaughn.

Vaughn shook his head once.

"Do it," Daegan said in a hard voice.

As she watched, Vaughn raised his free hand and touched the man's neck. A flash of blue light exploded from his fingertips with a sharp zapping sound. Liv jumped. The DA leader jerked once, hard, then went limp. In an instant her blinding headache vanished. Completely. As though it had never been.

Vaughn lowered him to the ground and stepped back.

Liv stared at the body in shock, trying to comprehend what she'd just seen. "Is he…"

"Dead," Cade confirmed, drawing her closer.

A cold numbness began to take hold in place of the pain. What had just happened?

When Daegan turned and took a stumbling step toward her, Liv snapped out of her daze, leaping up to grab him. His face was pale as snow, his mouth pinched. Blood soaked the bandages on his left arm, continued to drip off his fingertips. Why wouldn't he just let them dress his wounds properly?

"Lie down," she begged, steadying him around the waist.

"No time," he rasped. She could feel him trembling with fatigue and shock, his weight increasing on her as his legs began to give way.

"I can't hold him," she cried out in alarm.

"I've got him," Cade said, brushing past her to lift Daegan over his shoulder.

She ran around him to the waiting Rover while Vaughn tossed the DA leader's body into the back. He slammed the trunk closed then came around to slide behind the wheel. The engine roared to life as Cade slid Daegan onto the backseat. Liv clambered up beside him to cradle his head in her lap. His eyes were closed, but the memory of his last words frightened her.

What did he mean, *no time*?

Cade slammed his door shut, started ripping medical supplies out of his rucksack.

"How bad is he?" she whispered, stroking the hair back from Daegan's forehead.

"He's lost a lot of blood," Cade replied, ripping the Velcro straps off the bulletproof vest Daegan wore, removing it with her help. "But that's not what worries me most."

When he cut away the shirt beneath it, Liv gasped. Three dark bruises were already forming across his chest from where the bullets had impacted the vest. Without it, any one of them would have killed him. Judging by the tense expression on Cade's face, the bullet wounds marring his left arm and shoulder still threatened Daegan's life.

"Hold on," she told him. "We'll get you to the hospital."

"No hospital. Just home."

He was in shock. Couldn't seriously mean that. "We have to get you to the hospital. You need x-rays, maybe surgery."

"I've got everything he needs at the mansion," Cade said, pressing some sort of gauzy pads to the bullet wounds.

Anger rose sharp and hot, mixing with the fear. "No. He needs a damn hospital." Her voice cracked on the last word. She was ready to lunge at Cade. "Vaughn, you have to take him!"

"It's okay, Liv."

She jerked her head around to stare at Daegan. It shocked her to see his eyes open, watching her. "You need—"

"Shhh. C'mere." He reached up his good arm for her.

Liv slid out from beneath him to kneel on the floor to make it easier. When he wrapped his fingers around her nape and pulled she bent toward him without resistance. But he didn't kiss her. The angle was wrong. His hand pulled her up past his mouth, past his head until she had to brace a hand on the edge of the seat to keep from falling.

"Daegan, what—" She sucked in a quick breath when she felt him nuzzling the valley between her breasts. What the hell? He could be dying, yet this is how he responded? And right in front of Cade and Vaughn?

The shock of it held her immobile for a second but when she began to pull away his tongue stole out to lick over her breastbone. Her heart clenched when she realized what he was doing. He was trying to heal her. To seal the cut closed with the clotting agent in his saliva.

Liv closed her eyes against a rush of tears and bent over him, cradling his head to her. When he was done he eased back. She could see the exhaustion in his face. That final act for her comfort had sapped the last of his energy reserves. The knowledge broke her heart. She choked back her tears.

The truck's wheels squealed as it turned a sharp corner. Liv tried to brace Daegan with her body to keep him from sliding on the seat, but the sudden movement made him jerk and cry out. The backseat was littered with bloody bandages while Cade continued working on him.

She glanced up nervously. Daegan seemed to be fading right before her eyes. "Cade?"

"Drive faster," he snapped at Vaughn, then jerked his chin at her. "Put your hands right here." He grabbed them, pressing them down over the largest wound in Daegan's upper arm.

He shook his head in protest and growled, but she bit down on her lower lip and maintained the hard pressure. Blood continued to seep out beneath her white-knuckled fingers, soaking the leg of her jeans beneath.

"Can I seal his wounds too?"

Cade shook his head. "Not until I get this stuff out of him and stitch him up."

"What stuff?"

"What's left of the bullets."

Her heart plummeted. "It's going to be okay," she murmured to Daegan, hoping he could still hear her. His skin already seemed unnaturally warm. How much longer until they reached the compound?

The vehicle raced through the darkness. Streetlights flashed by overhead, painting Daegan's contorted features in a ghastly pallor. Tears clogged her throat, making it hard to breathe. He was in so much pain, losing too much blood. The grim look on Cade's face turned her insides to ice. He didn't have to tell her that her mate was fighting for his life. The thought of losing him was more than she could take.

A tear dropped onto Daegan's pale cheek. His eyes flickered open briefly to find hers. He tried to raise his good hand to her face.

Liv grabbed it, brought it to her cheek.

"Don't cry, *mo ghrá*," he whispered weakly. Then his eyes closed, his hand going slack in hers.

A ragged sound tore from her chest.

"Stop," Cade hissed.

She jerked, lifted her chin to meet his eyes.

His glare was like a slap. "Either hold it together or get the hell away from him before you make it worse."

Shaken, Liv ducked her head and closed her eyes, struggling to keep the tears at bay. Fear and grief battled inside her, clawing through her chest. But Cade was right. Crying would only make things worse. Daegan needed them all calm so they could focus on him.

The drive to the compound seemed to take forever, but finally the Rover sped through the gates. When she glanced out the rear window she saw the blue electrical charge that sparkled over the intricate wrought-iron gate. She hoped it was sealing them in, and anyone who could harm them out.

Vaughn pulled the truck to a sudden stop at the far door that led into the kitchen and jumped out. The men carried Daegan inside, down to the equipment room, keeping pressure on his wounds the whole time. They placed him on the steel gurney in the center of the room. Cade quickly cut the tattered shirt off to reveal the true damage beneath. Liv flinched when she finally saw all the raw holes in her mate's flesh. Five of them, the edges already turning from purple and blue to black.

"Shit," Cade muttered as he pulled on some latex gloves.

"What?"

"They're already infected."

That fast? "From something in the dirt?"

"No." He looked up and shared a look with Vaughn. "Amber."

She looked between them, their grave expressions making her want to scream. Amber. The DA leader had said his bullets had it in them. "Is it dangerous?"

"Yeah. It's poisonous to us if it's absorbed into the bloodstream. Have to get it out of him, fast."

Without a word, Vaughn got onto the table and straddled Daegan's thighs, pinning them tight with his knees while he did the same to his wrists. "Hold his hands tight," he said to her roughly.

She did as he said, reaching around Vaughn to grip them tightly in her own. His skin was already hot to the touch.

Cade looked across the table at Vaughn. "Got him?"

He nodded once.

Without administering any pain medication, Cade took a scalpel and a pair of tweezers to the wounds. Liv's eyes widened in horror.

Daegan's eyes flew open on a guttural growl, his whole body cording against the pain.

"Cade, give him something," Liv begged.

"Can't. No time. Later." His brow furrowed in intense concentration.

Daegan tossed his head from side to side as he arched up, like his body was trying to escape the pain. Liv didn't know how she'd bear it.

"Talk to him," Vaughn rasped.

She met his cold stare for a moment before leaning around him to look down into Daegan's tortured face.

Her fingers squeezed around his, and she prayed he knew she was there. "Focus on me, Daegan. I'm right here, holding your hands. Can you feel me?"

His head torqued back but the awful sounds lessened, restrained by sheer force of will as he gritted his teeth.

Cade pulled something from one of the bullet holes, cursed when he held it up to the light. "Pure amber," he said, tossing it with a clunk into a metal pan beside him. Time after time he extracted slivers from the wounds, dumped them into the dish. The pile of dark yellow shards glistened with Daegan's blood.

Without warning, Daegan began to shiver uncontrollably.

Cade gripped the injured shoulder tighter. "Hold him down," he ordered Vaughn. When he was finally through he stripped off the gloves then placed a thermometer under Daegan's tongue. "Shit," he said again, and Liv's heart dropped. He looked up at Vaughn. "We've got to get him into the water."

"What?" she blurted. "A bath?"

Cade wrapped a hasty dressing around the arm. "Let's go." He hauled Daegan's torso up by the armpits as Vaughn took his legs.

"Where are you taking him?" Liv demanded, trailing after them.

"Downstairs. Hurry."

Heart in her throat, she followed them through the medical area to what looked like a mechanical room of some sort. A thin stream of blood covered the floor as it dripped over Daegan's arm and ribs. Cade and Vaughn completely ignored her, all but running toward a control panel against the far wall. She stared in amazement when Cade entered a code into the keypad next to it. The door slowly swung open to reveal a darkened corridor. He hit another button, started inside as some sort of emergency lighting came to life, illuminating the narrow stairway.

Inside it was cold and damp. She barely noticed as she hurried in their wake, descending the hundreds of stairs until they reached another steel door at the bottom. "Ready?" Cade asked.

She and Vaughn both nodded, although what she was agreeing to she didn't know. But whatever she needed to do, she would.

"Keep him in until the wounds change color."

In where? she wanted to yell. He entered another code and the door squealed as it opened with a deep groan.

The salty scent of the water hit her. She stepped out onto a set of cement steps, found herself standing less than a hundred feet from the water's edge. The tide was in, the water still as glass with the waning moon shining brightly on its surface. Vaughn and Cade rushed ahead, carrying Daegan straight into the water until it was up to their waists.

"Stop! What are you *doing*?" Liv kicked her shoes off and followed, thinking they'd gone mad. God only knew how many contaminants were in the water. Why the hell would they risk exposing Daegan to that? And the salt would be agony in his wounds. The cuts on her left hand burned like fire in the water.

Even as she thought it she flinched, but then they submerged Daegan's upper body. His eyes flew open when he let out an agonized scream that made her flesh prickle. Liv plunged in after him, wading fast through the cold dark water. The chill of it stole her breath but she struggled toward them, keeping her eyes locked on her mate.

"You're hurting him!" Why were they doing this?

Every muscle in his chest and arms stood out in sharp relief as he bucked and strained against the arms imprisoning him. She grabbed hold of Vaughn's muscular arm, trying to wrench it away. "Stop it! Stop it, you're hurting him!" Her voice cracked.

He shrugged off her attempts to dislodge his grip like she was an annoying mosquito buzzing around him. She shoved him, but it was like trying to move a brick wall.

"The water will clean out the poison," Cade said in a strained voice, fighting to subdue Daegan. "We have to do this."

Her heart slammed in her ears."Why this way?"

"Our kind draws strength from the ocean. The salt and its energy will help heal him."

She fought the urge to rip them off Daegan and cradle him to her. His cries had turned ragged, like his throat was too raw to keep screaming. It made her sick to her stomach.

"How much longer?" Vaughn bit out. He kept glancing behind them, searching the shore for something. Or someone. Was he checking for threats? Here?

"Another minute or two. Christ, let's hope this flushes out the wounds well enough." Then Cade turned his gaze on her. "Come here and touch him. Talk to him. Help him breathe through it."

Without a second thought she waded forward to take Daegan's pale face between her palms. She might not like their methods, but these men were his friends and were doing their best to help him. Right now she had no choice but to trust them. But God, watching him suffer was like taking an arrow to the heart.

She fought to keep the fear out of her voice. "Daegan, listen to me. I know it hurts, but the water will help you. Just listen to my voice and breathe nice and slow."

He stopped thrashing. He trembled in the men's grip, and when he opened his eyes they were glassy, unfocused. Blind with pain and fever. It scared her.

"That's right," she coaxed, stroking her thumbs over his cheeks. "Just breathe. In and out, nice and slow. It'll be over soon, I promise."

His eyes closed but he appeared calmer, his jaw tensed against the pain that must still be raging through him.

She looked up at Cade beseechingly. "Now?"

He nodded. "Yeah."

Without another word he and Vaughn hustled Daegan out of the water, running back to shore. Liv's wet feet slipped on the sand as she followed, the sharp rocks hurting her feet. Her body was chilled by the night breeze blowing off the water. By the time they reached the concrete steps she was shivering, then in the middle of the secret tunnel her teeth began chattering. She didn't care how cold she was. All that mattered was Daegan and stopping the spread of the poison.

In the relative warmth of the medical room they placed Daegan back on the metal exam table. Liv flinched at the sight of him. He was almost blue with cold, his lips pinched and turning purple around the edges. She helped strip off his wet pants and underwear, covered him with a thick blanket from the desk across the room. When Cade unwound the bandages to expose the bullet wounds in Daegan's arm, she pressed a hand to her mouth to keep from crying out. They were brilliant red and swollen, as though they'd been cauterized by the salt in the water. She took up position at his side, cradling his hand between hers while Cade started an IV in Daegan's arm and Vaughn disappeared through the steel door to the secret passageway.

Cade was just injecting some sort of medication into the line when Vaughn came back in. "Perimeter's still clear. No one followed us out there."

Cade nodded and set the drip running. "This will make him feel a whole hell of a lot better."

"What is it"?" she asked.

"Propofol. A very powerful anaesthetic. Trust me, he's not in any pain now."

It seemed true enough. Daegan's eyes were closed but not squeezed shut, and his body appeared to have sagged in relief. He looked like he was sleeping peacefully.

She rubbed his good arm in an effort to warm him. "He's freezing."

"Go ahead and find something to warm him up with while I check these," Cade answered, bending to dig at the holes again. Liv hurried to the cabinets and dug through them to find some more blankets, then wrapped him up tight.

Cade grunted in satisfaction, picked up a suturing

kit to close the wounds. "Looks better, but we'll have to wait and see now."

She dried Daegan's damp hair then rubbed his feet briskly to get his blood flowing again.

When Cade finished he stripped off his gloves, flicked a glance at her. "Better get out of those wet clothes and dry off before you get sick."

Realizing she was still shivering, she nodded. "What happens now?"

"There's nothing more I can do for him now. The rest is up to him. And you."

She raised her head, stared at him in astonishment. "Me? What can I do?"

Cade met her eyes as he finished securing the final dressing. "You need to stay with him."

"Of course I will." How could he think otherwise?

"No, I mean *right next* to him. He needs you to be close to him, to touch him."

She squeezed Daegan's hand, smoothed a damp lock of hair away from his pale forehead. Despite his color and dip in the cold water, the fever raged inside him. "He's still so hot."

"It's the amber. I think I got all of it, but I don't know how much was already absorbed into his bloodstream. It'll be awhile until we know how severe the damage is."

Liv swallowed hard. "But he'll be all right, won't he?"

"He's strong," Cade answered without looking up. "We should know by morning if he's turned the corner."

Morning seemed like an eternity from now.

"We'll move him upstairs now. I'll unhook the IV in a bit so he'll be more comfortable when he wakes up."

"Okay." She prayed he'd wake up.

Once they'd settled him in the king-sized sleigh bed, Cade handed her a bottle of pills. "Give him two of these if he wakes up in a lot of pain. If I got most of the amber out fast enough, he should rebound fairly quickly. Our kind heals faster than mortals, and I think he'll surprise you."

She felt so helpless. "Isn't there something else we should be doing? An x-ray at least?"

"Nope. The fracture in his humerus was incomplete and it's already in position to set. What he needs most right now is a deep sleep and your touch." Before she could ask him anything else he shocked her by lifting a hand to her face to cradle her cheek in his palm. She stilled at the unexpected contact, staring up into his clear green eyes as he brushed his thumb over her bruised cheekbone. "You all right?"

"Yes," she managed in a whisper. In that moment she understood exactly why he'd developed the sexual reputation he had. His touch didn't arouse her, but it held an undeniable power all its own. There wasn't a woman alive who wouldn't respond to that kind of animal magnetism on some level.

He assessed her for another few seconds before dropping his hand and stepping back. "Go change and try to get some sleep. I'll be downstairs if he needs me."

She cast a hesitant glance at Daegan. The last thing she wanted to do was leave him, even just to go to the bathroom.

"One more thing," Cade said when she finally turned away toward the ensuite.

"What?"

"Remember he's linked to you, so he can feel any strong emotions you emit. If you can't hold it together he'll sense it and waste precious energy he needs to heal worrying about you. You have to be strong for him through this."

She nodded, glanced at Daegan while a fierce protectiveness rose within her. "I will be."

Liv took the pills into the bathroom to set them on the granite vanity, then stripped off her wet clothes and put on the black terrycloth robe hanging on the back of the door. It smelled faintly of Daegan and that clean, spicy scent brought a lump to her throat. When she came out, Cade was gone and Vaughn stood next to the bed, staring down at Daegan's still form with an unreadable expression.

She walked around to the other side, crawled up to kneel next to her mate, took his limp hand. It was large and strong compared to hers, but he'd always touched her with such gentleness and care. He'd willingly taken those bullets to protect her. She blinked fast to stem the burn of tears, reaching out to smooth his dark hair away from his forehead. Unconsciously he turned his head toward her, as though he truly did crave her touch.

She bit her lip, fighting the torrent of emotion. Strong. She had to be strong and not sap his energy, and she wouldn't embarrass herself by losing it in front of icy-cold Vaughn. But God, what would she do if she lost Daegan?

Vaughn remained at the bedside, unmoving, as

though he felt obligated to stand watch over his leader. Or was it because he didn't trust her to take care of him?

Once she had control, she thought about what to say that might break the growing tension in the room. She searched her memory for a happy time in her childhood, focused on that as she stroked Daegan's hair.

"I had a dog once," she said to Vaughn, impatiently swiping a stray tear away with the heel of her free hand. Stupid to cry. It didn't help anything and it made her look weak. "A chocolate lab named Hershey when I was a little girl. He was my best friend. My only friend. After I lost my parents, he was the one I talked to all the time, and I know he understood. No matter what, I knew he loved me, completely and unconditionally." She was babbling and probably making Vaughn uncomfortable, but she couldn't stop the words. "When he died I felt like I had nothing, and I was too devastated to get another dog because I knew I could never replace him. That probably sounds crazy to you. Did you ever have a pet?"

Vaughn met her gaze almost reluctantly then shook his head, but she could see an echo of pain in his strangely colored eyes. The yellow shards should have disturbed her but they didn't. Unless she did something to jeopardize Daegan, Vaughn was no threat to her.

She sniffed, wiped away more tears with the back of one hand. "Just in the last few months I was starting to feel really lonely and thinking about getting another dog. But then I met Daegan, and in the space of a few days everything's changed for me. I realize I barely know him, but I feel like I'll shrivel up and

die if he doesn't make it through this. Like my whole
world will end, even though I only just met him. That
doesn't make any sense, does it?"

"Yes, it does."

Surprised that he'd spoken, she looked up into the
Reaper's scarred face. The unguarded moment of raw
grief she read in his expression made her heart clench.
Swallowing, she turned her attention back to Daegan.
All she wanted was for him to open his eyes and look
at her, smile or somehow acknowledge that he knew she
was there next to him. Some sign that he recognized
her, that he'd be okay. She wanted to hear his deep
voice again, saying that lovely endearment she still
didn't know the meaning of. She stroked his hair helplessly, wishing there was something more she could do.

Vaughn stayed next to the bed for another minute,
then turned to leave.

"Wait." She shifted on the bed so she could see him
better.

He stopped, looked over his broad shoulder at her.

"He said something to me earlier. In the car, and a
couple times before. In another language I didn't understand."

Vaughn raised an onyx brow, waited.

It felt right to ask him. "He called me *mo ghrá*, but
I don't know what it means. Do you?"

He held her questioning stare for a moment, his eyes
flashing a stark sadness before turning ice cold. He
looked at the floor before responding. "It's Gaelic," he
answered quietly. "And it means 'my love.'"

My love. The words echoed deep inside her.

He might have meant it only in an affectionate way,

but she didn't think so. Not the night he'd made love to her, anyway. The context when he'd used it, the tender way he'd said it told her otherwise. She *was* his love, or would be eventually. In the short time they'd known each other, he already believed and accepted that.

The lump in her throat swelled even more until she thought it might choke her. Holding back a ragged cry, she buried her face into Daegan's hot throat and carefully wrapped her arms around him, battling to hold her fear and worry at bay. She hardly noticed when Vaughn left, closing the door quietly behind him.

CHAPTER SIXTEEN

WHEN SHE WOKE in the middle of the night, Liv pried bleary eyes open to check the bedside clock. The blue digital display read just after four. Almost dawn. She'd been sleeping for a little over an hour. Soon the birds would start singing and the sky outside the tall master bedroom windows would lighten.

Fighting a yawn, she carefully turned onto her side to look at Daegan. He was sprawled on his back with his head turned toward her, his injured right arm bound up against his bruised chest. Her throat tightened as she watched him sleep. The man was so beautiful, so brave and selfless. It might have partially been instinct or his military training that made him throw himself over her when the bullets started flying, but she knew without a doubt there was more to it. He'd been acting as her mate.

And as far as her feelings for him went…

She was inextricably bound to him already, even without marking him. Because he'd already managed to steal her heart, even before he'd taken those bullets for her.

Careful not to wake him, she laid her palm ever so gently on his forehead, bit her lip when she felt how hot he was. Maybe a bit cooler than a few hours ago, but still far too warm. The unnatural heat emanating from his skin alarmed her. She tried to fight the negative emotion back, but the fear of losing him took root, sending its tendrils snaking through her mind. Knowing her thoughts might project to him, she slid out of the bed and headed to the bathroom to get him a cool cloth while she got hold of her emotions.

"Liv?"

She whirled at the sound of his groggy voice. Before she could find her own he was already trying to prop himself up on his uninjured arm, searching the room for her. Her heart swelled with hope.

"Here," she whispered hoarsely, covering the few steps back to the bed to cradle his hair-roughened cheek in her palm. The relief flooding her made her dizzy. Her thumb stroked over his hot, whisker-stubbled skin. "Hi." Her voice was thick with emotion. "How do you feel?"

"Cold," he whispered, making her heart clench.

When she climbed in next to him and pulled the covers over them both, he immediately turned toward her to wrap his good arm around her back, bringing her flush up against his naked body. Careful of his bandages, she snuggled in close and cradled his head to her breast, kissed the top of it. Daegan sighed deeply, closed his eyes.

She kept her touch gentle as she caressed the back of his head, his neck. Just so damn grateful he was awake and coherent. "Are you in pain?"

"Not too bad."

Liar. She stroked his hair, aching to soothe him. Her heart squeezed when he moved closer into her embrace. "The bullets had amber in them. Cade took all the fragments out and checked the fracture in your upper arm, but the poison was already in your bloodstream. He and Vaughn had to take you into the water."

"I remember."

It didn't surprise her. Even raging with fever it would be kind of hard to forget the sort of pain that had made him scream like that. Thank God he'd been out cold since Cade had given him that medication. Maybe her worrying had finally disturbed him. "Did I wake you up?"

"No," he mumbled. "Thought you'd left."

Her hand paused in his hair. "I wouldn't leave you." She hated that he thought she might have.

His only response was a sleepy rumble as he rubbed his rough cheek against the sensitive skin of her breast. Instant heat blossomed under his touch, spreading out to every place they made contact. Her upper gums had been tender for the past few hours, but now they throbbed and ached. When she ran her tongue over her upper teeth, both her incisors were sharper than normal along the bottom edge. At least now she understood what it meant.

His scent reached out to her, a seductive temptation she had to ignore. He was in no condition to have sex right now, even with her doing all the work. But the idea of claiming him, bringing him pleasure, sent a frisson of need between her thighs. She imagined cradling his dark head between her hands as she nuzzled and nibbled along his neck. He'd moan and grip the back of her neck with his palm, but she'd tease him with her tongue, moving lower, across the hard planes of his body until she reached the rigid length of his erection—

"Liv." The syllable was an erotic purr.

When she met his gaze she wasn't surprised to find his eyes beginning to glow a bright blue in the darkness. But that ring of yellow around his pupils remained. She alone had the power to heal that part of him.

He must have somehow sensed the erotic turn her thoughts had taken, because she felt the growing erection against her hip. His lips brushed her jaw. "Come up on top of me."

The answering pulse between her thighs grew stronger, eroding her resolve. "We shouldn't."

He pressed closer. "Need you."

She shivered at the stark desire in his voice, his beautiful glowing eyes. He was still so ill, but if her touch alone eased him maybe this would help him heal even faster. She started to get to her knees so she could straddle him, but when he shifted he suddenly sucked in a sharp breath and went rigid.

"What?" she whispered, leaping back.

Daegan pulled in a breath between his gritted teeth, his eyes shut tight, every line of his body drawn stiff.

She jerked her gaze to the bandages covering his arm. She didn't see any blood, but maybe he'd opened the incisions. Damn, she'd known it was too soon—

"I'm okay," he said in a raspy voice. "Just moved too fast."

She searched his face for a moment. He was still in a great deal of pain; she could read it in the tension around his eyes and lips. "Just lie still and don't move," she ordered, then hopped off the bed and rushed to the bathroom. When she came back with a glass of water and two T3s he silently watched her from the bed. "Here." She eased his head into the crook of her arm to prop him up, bringing the rim of the glass toward his lips. But he grasped her wrist, halting the glass a few inches from his mouth.

"I'd rather be inside of you instead." His voice was weak, the soft Irish lilt more pronounced than usual.

God, she wanted that. "Do me a favor and just take them," she said in exasperation. Didn't he realize she couldn't stand to see him hurting?

The hand on her wrist tightened slightly, bringing her gaze to his. Then his thumb brushed over her inner wrist in a tender caress. "I'm fine."

She ruthlessly ignored the tingles his touch sent along her skin. He wasn't fine. Not by a long shot. "Just take them. For me. We'll get to the rest of it once you're feeling better. I'm not going anywhere."

He held her stare for another moment, then relented and raised his head slightly to take the tablets with a few swallows of water. Liv placed the glass on the night table and started to climb off the mattress, but he grabbed her hand.

"Where are you going?"

"I was just going to pull the chair over and sleep there so I don't—"

He tugged on her hand, making her stumble toward the bed.

She resisted. "Daegan, you need to sleep and I don't want to hurt you." And she wasn't sure she could keep her libido in check if he kept seducing her like this.

"You won't." He pulled again, harder this time, until she gave in and got in beside him. His strong arm curled around her waist, bringing her flush against his rock hard body. Sick and weak as he was, he still exuded raw power and authority. As well as a bone-deep sensuality that made every inch of her tingle in heightened awareness. "Pain's better with you next to me like this," he mumbled. Her eyes misted over when he kissed the top of her head.

"I should get Cade."

"Later. Tired. Just need you."

His words choked her up. Damn, she had to put a lid on her emotions. They'd already woken him once—she knew it, despite what he'd said. He needed to rest. She had to stay calm and in control, for his sake.

Clearing her mind of everything but the feel of Daegan's overly warm body nestled against her, Liv took a deep slow breath before cradling the back of his head with one hand and running the other over the length of his spine.

Sleep, she willed him, filling her touch with all the love and comfort she ached to give him. It might have been wishful thinking, but she thought she heard a soft groan of contentment from him as he drifted off in her arms.

CHAPTER SEVENTEEN

THE MOMENT LIV stepped back into the master bedroom she smelled him. Spice and musk and the indefinable scent that was Daegan's alone. The king-size bed was empty, that delectable scent coming from the ensuite. Liquid heat pooled between her legs, her nipples tightening in anticipation of finding him in there naked.

In the steam-filled bathroom, she found him at the sink rinsing the last of the shaving cream from his freshly shaven face. He caught sight of her in the mirror, raised his head. A sexy smile formed on his lips as he wiped his skin dry, turning toward her.

The sight of him standing there shirtless made her heart rate skyrocket. Her gaze ran hungrily over his sculpted torso. "You look…good," was all she could manage, astounded at the rate of his recovery. Good wasn't even close. Cade hadn't been kidding when he'd said Empowered healed faster than mortals. Only three days after being shot, Daegan looked nearly well again.

He lifted his good shoulder in a negligent shrug, making the muscles bunch and ripple beneath his smooth skin. Muscles she desperately wanted to slide her hands all over. Then her mouth. "Feeling better. Where'd you go? I woke up and you were gone."

Her heart pounded so hard she was sure he could hear it. God, he was sexy. "To see Cade. He's coming up shortly to check you out. Are you sure you're ready to be up and about so soon?"

One side of his mouth titled upward, his eyes heating. "I'm feeling stronger by the second."

Before she could stop herself she glanced down at the white towel wrapped around his lean hips. The knotted edge rode low beneath his navel, framing his defined abs. The unmistakable hard ridge of his erection pressed against the cloth. With effort, she tore her eyes away and met his seductive gaze.

"C'mere and see for yourself how good I'm feeling."

He was far too tempting standing there in nothing but a white terrycloth rectangle. "I shouldn't." She edged backward.

He took a predatory step toward her, that knowing smile doing wicked things to her insides. "You're backing away but I can smell how much you want me."

Heat crept up her cheeks. "It's too soon, and Cade is coming up." She deserved a freaking medal for keeping her hands off him this long when every cell in her body screamed at her to walk over there and take what was hers.

He's mine.

"Cade won't interrupt if that's what you're worried about." His eyes held hers. Hypnotic. "You want me. And I promise, I'm more than willing to let you have me."

She swallowed, studying the barely healed-over wounds in his left arm and shoulder, doing her best to ignore the pounding need in her body. All on its own her tongue stroked over her sharpened teeth. His eyes dropped to her mouth, tracking the movement of her

tongue beneath her upper lip, without a doubt understanding what it meant. When he met her gaze the stark
lust there made her suck in a breath.

"Come here," he said softly, the erotic timbre of his
voice making it both a command and a promise.

As though his words cast a spell on her, she closed
the distance between them without even being aware
of moving. She took his face between her hands at the
same time his slid into her hair, then leaned up on tip-
toe to kiss him. It wasn't gentle. It was hungry and possessive, full of everything she felt for him. Telling him
without words how much she wanted him. Needed him.

Daegan moaned into her mouth, shuddered lightly
when her tongue caressed his and her aching breasts
pressed into his chest. She kissed him hard and deep
while she maneuvered him backwards to the uphol-
stered bench set against the far wall. Daegan moved
willingly, letting her guide him there until the backs of
his knees hit the bench and he sank down on it. With
a hungry growl Liv undid the sash of her robe then
straddled him.

He groaned, releasing her hair to cup her naked
breasts while his hips lifted between her open thighs.
The hard ridge of his erection pressed insistently
against the towel covering him as she settled her throbbing sex over it. Her spine arched when his skilled fingers rubbed and pinched her sensitive nipples.

She slid her hands up into his hair, dragging his
mouth down to the aching points, then cried out in
pleasure as he slid his warm, moist tongue over them.
Liv let her head fall back, loving the feel of his mouth
on her and the proof of his arousal pressed against

her folds. He licked and sucked her nipples, cradling her breasts tenderly in his palms while he made a low sound against her skin, moving his hips in time to her slow rhythm. But when he slid one hand down her belly toward her damp folds, she stopped him and climbed off his lap.

"Liv—"

"Shhh." The hunger inside her was so intense she could barely breathe, but the need to make him writhe was stronger. She wanted to make him drown in pleasure, give him enough to make up for everything he'd suffered since meeting her. Give him something he'd never forget. "You're mine," she breathed against his lips.

His glowing eyes turned molten. "I'm yours."

Emboldened by the heat in his stare, she reached down and pulled the towel away. The swollen length of his erection sprang up, the sight of it making her mouth water. She licked her lips, wrapping both hands around his swollen cock.

"Oh, God, baby…"

Thick. Hard. Hot. She stroked him slowly from base to tip, loving the way his eyes closed in rapture. The marble tile was cold against her bare knees when she knelt on it.

Daegan opened his eyes to stare down at her. The yearning on his face made her smile as she leaned down and delicately licked the tip of his cock. The breath hissed between his teeth. He slid one hand into her hair, holding her there firmly. Waiting. His fingers tightened in the strands.

She parted her lips, took him in her mouth. He gasped

and widened his thighs, watching her with that erotic stare. Her tongue slid around the head as she sucked him, savoring his masculine taste, the knowledge that he loved what she was doing. He was hot and salty against her tongue, the skin stretched taut over the swollen head. God, she was starving for him. Losing herself in the experience, she sucked, caressed him until he protested and tugged on her hair.

"Stop or I'll come," he panted.

She hesitated, but eventually released him slowly, then stood. "Condoms?"

His eye glittered with raw lust, that magnificent chest rising and falling with his ragged breaths. "Drawer under the sink."

She found one then came back to smooth it over the length of his swollen cock. A muscle jerked in his jaw when she straddled him once again. Settling in place, Liv bent to tease his lower lip with her tongue, bringing her slick sex over him. She sank down on him. Slowly. So slowly she wanted to die from the pleasure, letting her tender flesh stretch around his thick shaft. Daegan made a rough sound and palmed her hips, holding her tight as his tongue played with hers. The kiss was hot. Dreamy. So erotic she could barely breathe, each slow stroke of his velvety tongue pushing her need higher.

Liv whimpered, trembling all over. He was so thick and hot inside her. Filling her so perfectly. Setting all her inner nerve endings on fire.

She rose up then slid down again, her slickness easing his way. The stretching fullness ignited the glow hidden inside her body. They both moaned when she pushed down fully, taking his whole length inside her.

Ripples of sensation spread across her nerve endings. "Daegan..." Pleasure streaked through her, so intense it stole her breath.

"Yes," he breathed against her lips. "Take more."

Suppressing a territorial growl, she took his head in her hands to give him a quick, hard nip on the lower lip. Daegan jerked in surprise and tightened his hold in her hair. With a low laugh, Liv tipped his head back, trailing a string of kisses along his jaw, down the side of his throat. His fingers bunched in her hair, pulling the strands with a delicious pressure that spoke of his unquenched hunger for her. The desperate need only she could sate.

Her tongue slid over his smooth skin, right where his pulse beat so frantically. Just to drive her point home.

"God, Liv," he groaned, arching into her mouth, that thick cock buried deep inside her.

She wanted to mark him. Needed to with a power that eclipsed everything else, even the raging sexual hunger between them. Her tongue moved slow and tender against his skin, in time with her hips, lapping at the place she longed to bite. She scraped her teeth against him, reveled in his low moan and the taut, quivering muscles pressed against her body. In that moment she knew if he hadn't been recovering she would have been on her back, pinned flat underneath his weight while he pumped in and out of her core. She shuddered, barely heard his raw curse as he neared the end of his control.

But then he tried to draw her away. She instinctively resisted, burying her face harder against his neck.

The hands in her hair tightened. Tugged, hard. "Stop."

Reluctantly, she raised her head. His eyes were a

beautiful, brilliant blue ringed with gold, half blind with pleasure. So why was he trying to stop her? "What's wrong?"

He stared at her, panting. Then he shook his head. "Don't do this. Not unless you're sure."

Still trying to protect her from herself. But she knew what she wanted. "Daegan, can you see yourself falling in love with me?"

His hand caressed her nape, so tender despite his obvious need that it made her heart turn over. "Yes." The conviction in his stare filled her with desperate longing.

"Then I'm sure. I want you for my mate, and I want my mark on you so the whole world knows you're taken."

His blue eyes flared like the leap of a flame as he leaned up to kiss her. "Then take me," he whispered against her mouth. An erotic invitation she couldn't ignore.

Take him. *Yes.* Her body throbbed with unrelieved tension at the thought. This was what she wanted. *He* was what she wanted.

With a soft sigh she bent and sucked the spot she'd nibbled at on the side of his throat.

His reaction was immediate. Those strong fingers tightened around the back of her neck, pressing deep into the muscles there while his other hand bit into her hip. Drawing him to her in silent command, demanding she mark him. It made her want to purr, to draw out this moment forever.

"Oh yeah, right there," he urged breathlessly when she rolled her hips and nuzzled him again. "Please, *mo ghrá. Take* me."

Liv closed her eyes at the stark plea in his voice. She

did this to him. She'd made this strong, powerful man tremble and beg her to mark him.

Moving at an unhurried pace, she raised up one last time then slowly sank down on his rigid length, taking him all the way to the hilt. Clenched her inner muscles around him. Daegan growled low in his throat and squeezed his eyes shut, his muscles bunching, twitching in an agony of suspense. *Yes*, she thought. *More*. She cradled his head, parting her lips wider to set the points of her teeth against his skin. Bit down hesitantly.

He cried out and arched in her arms, his hold almost bruising. "Harder." The word was a ragged plea, his body tensed in anticipation. Right on the edge.

Forcing her body to relax, Liv closed her eyes and added more pressure. She wanted this so badly but she was afraid of doing it too hard, too rough. Too deep. He was hurting for release, the same as she'd been before he'd marked her, but she couldn't take that final step and punch her teeth through his skin. He'd suffered enough. She wanted this to be nothing but pure pleasure for him. What if she did it wrong?

His hand stayed locked around her nape, urging her on along with his hoarse whisper. "Baby, you won't hurt me. Do it harder." He arched his neck, rubbing his throat against her open mouth. His pulse throbbed beneath her lips. She could feel her heart pounding against her ribs, ready to explode.

Her tongue stole out to caress him, tasting the salt of him.

"Ah God, *harder*."

As tenderly as she could, she bit down, increasing the pressure until she finally felt his skin give way.

She stiffened. The tang of his blood hit her tongue instantly. A jagged bolt of fear ripped through her that she'd gone too deep and punctured a vein.

But Daegan let out a roar that echoed throughout the humid bathroom, holding her tight. He arched wildly in her arms, his hips pounding repeatedly up into her slick sex, lost in his response to her bite.

God. It was so good she would have thrown back her head and yelled with him except she didn't want to end this primal link between them. Unable to make herself release his neck, she sucked at him, letting the powerful tide of orgasm build deep in her core with each roll of her hips. The rapture in his ragged cries while he came filled her with relief and a growing sense of power. She rocked against his hard length, seeking an end to her torment. As he finally settled he leaned his head back against the wall with a satisfied groan. The hard hand clamped around her nape gentled, caressing and cradling. She shook with the need for release.

"Don't stop," he whispered. Shivers passed through him while she drew gently on his skin, lost in his taste, his scent, the knowledge he was now safe from the threat of turning to the darkness, that they were linked forever. His fingertips drifted over her neck, her back. "Mmm, more. Feels so good, *mo ghrá*." To her amazement she felt him lengthen and thicken inside her once again, intensifying the building sensations.

Liv trembled and yielded in his hold, undone by the tenderness in his touch and voice, the growing pleasure that filled her body until she wanted to weep.

"I'm already falling in love with you," he whispered

as she rode him, getting closer to the peak with each gliding thrust.

He slid one hand between them to find then caress her slick nub, and she whimpered against his throat. It was exquisite, perfect. Exactly what she needed. Three more long, luxurious strokes on his hard length and she came with a soft cry. Her spine arched tight. The pulses went on endlessly until she was limp and boneless against him. She was barely aware of him joining her, his erection kicking deep inside her as he found release a second time.

Tired, dazed by the pleasure, Liv reluctantly released her hold on his neck, lapping tenderly at the puncture wounds. The action was purely instinctive, even as she was aware it would seal the marks and soothe the sting of her bite. Daegan chuckled in response, sliding his hands into her hair, stroking the waves gently. She licked across his skin softly, slowly, unable to make herself stop. She was drunk on the taste of him, couldn't get enough of him or the blissful lassitude stealing through her veins.

But after a few moments he gently drew her head away, tilting it up until she met his eyes. They were a gorgeous pale blue, without any trace of gold or the unearthly glow they'd held while he'd suffered for her mark. When she glanced down to examine her handiwork, she saw the tiny wounds on his neck were already closed, the elaborate Celtic knot design already forming on his skin. The stylized O stood out clearly amongst the intricate swirls.

A slow, satisfied smile curved her lips as she looked down into his face. "You're really mine."

His eyes crinkled at the corners. "I'm damn glad you love that so much."

Her smile widened. Daegan grinned, leaned up to kiss her. Liv made a purring sound, meeting the lazy caress of his tongue while she ran her hands over the powerful muscles in his chest and arms. "I'm falling in love with you too," she told him when she pulled back. She'd never meant anything more. His eyes held a thoroughly satisfied gleam. It pleased her immensely. "Did I hurt you?"

"Not at all." He nodded toward his healing arm. "In a few days I'll be good as new."

The wounds looked sore, but none the worse for wear. She switched her attention back to the forming mark on his neck. "So...can we do this again sometime, or is it a one-time deal?"

He grinned again. "Sorry, it's a one-time only thing. But I'll let you nibble on my neck anytime you like. When your mate puts their mouth on the mark they made, it feels really good. C'mere and I'll show you." His hand settled around her nape, tugged gently.

Smiling, Liv bent so he could nuzzle the spot. A shiver cascaded through her at the feel of his lips brushing her skin. He kissed the mark, sending a jolt of pleasure straight to her breasts, her swelling sex. When his tongue stroked across it, she moaned aloud at the sensual rush it created.

Daegan eased back, a smug smile on his face. "Told you."

She pressed a tender kiss to his lips before summoning the energy to lift off him. "Come back to bed with me."

"Thought you'd never ask." He got up and disposed of the condom, but as he followed her she caught him checking out his newly marked neck in the mirror.

"It looks good on you." And she was supremely proud it was right out in the open where everyone would see it.

His eyes met hers in the mirror. Crinkled when he smiled. "That it does."

Daegan slid into bed with her, pulling her up tight into his body. There was no fever, no sign of pain in his expression, just a drowsy, contented sigh from him that made her smile. They still had a lot of things to work out between them, but compared to what they'd already overcome, the rest was manageable.

One thing she was absolutely sure of—together, they could handle anything.

XAVIER WOKE IN the darkness with a strangled scream tearing from his throat.

Marie. For a moment he'd thought she'd been there, right in front of him. She'd been close enough for him to smell her sweet rose scent, feel her warmth.

But he was alone. As always.

He collapsed back against his clammy pillow. The dream. It had been so vivid. His heart knocked against his ribs like a terrified animal trying to fight its way out of a cage.

They'd sealed their bond. He was too late.

"It can't be true," he whispered, fighting the fear smothering him. The dark prophecy, the blind boy had both told him the woman was the key.

His throat was so dry he could hardly swallow. Tangled amongst the damp sheets, he reached out a hand to switch on the bedside lamp and froze. The room seemed to be lit with a faint glow already, but he never slept with the lights on.

He sucked in a harsh breath as realization dawned. Raised his trembling hands toward his face. Warm, yellow light stained his palms and fingers.

My eyes.

Xavier rolled out of the bed and stumbled toward the bathroom. The instant he stepped inside he caught a glimpse of his reflection in the mirror. His eyes glowed an unearthly gold, shining back at him in the glass. The irises were completely yellow, all hints of brown swallowed up. Eaten away by all the souls he'd claimed. He raised a trembling hand to his face. Touched his fingers to one gaunt cheek.

He was finally ready.

The enormity of the affirmation settled in, chasing away the chill in his bones with a flowing warmth that filled his sunken chest like a balloon.

"How..." he whispered, battling to understand why this would happen now. It made no sense that he'd attain his full power when there was no chance of exploiting it. Unless there was another way...

Did he still have a chance to kill the Coven Leader? Could he somehow still get to his mate?

Rushing back into the bedroom, he found his phone and called the last Dark Army member he'd spoken to. He'd lost Iceberg and three others a few days ago, but one had survived to contact him. Plus he had another lead to follow up on.

"Is she still there?" he asked in Russian when Vasilli finally answered.

"It's two in the morning," he grumbled sleepily. "Who are you talking about?"

"The woman asking about the Empowered. Is she still in Nida?" he demanded.

"Yeah. I've been following her, just like you said."

"Get her."

A startled pause answered him. "You mean kill her?"

"No," he growled, impatient to find answers. "I can't get information from her when she's dead, can I? You can kill her after I'm finished with her." *If she survives the interrogation.*

"Now? Today?"

"Today." He used his telepathy skills to project an image into Vasilli's mind. Of him chained to a wall in a dark room, his chest bleeding heavily from the strips of skin Xavier would peel off him should he fail to kidnap the woman.

"Jesus, okay! I'll take care of it today. She's supposed to meet my grandmother later."

"That should make it easy for you then. I'll meet you in two days at the place we discussed."

Until then, his only other hope of finding what he needed was the surviving DA member in Vancouver.

CHAPTER EIGHTEEN

CADE KNOCKED SOFTLY on the master suite door and waited stiffly, half afraid of what he'd find on the other side when it opened.

A moment later Liv appeared in the opening, smiling in welcome. "I just got him to finally lie down again."

The lack of concern in her expression reassured him Daegan was on the mend, but the instant he set foot inside the room he caught the lingering scent of sex. Subtle, but obvious nonetheless. It made his guts knot with something close to dread.

Steeling himself, he walked in, closing the door behind him. Daegan was fully dressed, propped against the leather headboard while Liv took a seat in an overstuffed chair next to the bed. He met his cousin's eyes briefly, relieved to find the clear irises devoid of the gold that had tainted them. So they'd completed their bond. God knew those yellow rings had kept Cade awake these past few nights, but the violet shadows beneath Daegan's eyes, his lingering pallor told Cade his Leader was far from back to normal.

Approaching the bed, his morbid sense of curiosity got the better of him. Of their own volition, his eyes tracked down Daegan's face to his neck, exposed by the unbuttoned shirt. When he saw the fresh mating mark on the left side, a strange prickling sensation raced over his body. A kind of foreboding. Doing his best to ignore his reaction and the reasons behind it, he found his voice. "You look like you're on the mend."

"Feeling much better." His voice was clear, alert, if still a bit weak.

Cade strode to the bed wearing his best physician's expression, shoving aside his unexpected discomfort. All he wanted to think about right now was Daegan's recovery. Getting him up and operational was paramount. He took the digital thermometer from his pocket. "Open up, big guy."

Daegan arched a brow but took the device from him, placing it under his tongue.

When it beeped Cade removed it to read the display. "Still not normal," he mused, "but down enough that at least we know the worst of the poison's flushed out." He glanced up into his face. "All your plumbing working okay?"

Daegan turned his head and grinned at Liv. "Yep."

That prickling heat spread across his skin again and he had to clear his suddenly dry throat. He hadn't meant *that* kind of plumbing—like it wasn't freaking obvious enough by the mark on his neck and their intertwined scents all but choking him? All business, he pulled the left side of the open button-down shirt aside to expose the affected arm. The wounds were healing nicely, with no suspicious red streaks radiating from any of them. "How much can you move your arm without pain?"

Daegan raised his left hand up and rotated it, proving he had full range of motion in his forearm. But when he started to lift his upper arm he only got a few inches before he slowed, tensing his jaw.

"Stop," Cade ordered with a grudging chuckle. "I said without pain, dumbass."

Daegan cracked a grin. It managed to dispel some of the tension inside him, but Cade remained vividly aware of the heightened connection and attraction between Liv and his cousin. It made him feel awkward, like his skin was too tight. The implication wasn't lost on him. After nearly two centuries together, Daegan was now officially a mated, bonded male. Everything would be different now, and without being able to hang with him…

Well shit, he wasn't going to be able to hang out with Vaughn, was he? He'd get better conversation out of the nude male marble statue in the fountain out in the front yard.

The morose thought gave him pause. Jesus, what the hell was wrong with him? He was glad for Daegan. His Leader deserved to be happy, and so far Liv seemed to be worthy of him. She was smart and independent. Surprisingly strong, considering all that had happened. She'd stayed by Daegan's side ever since he'd been wounded, so she obviously cared about him.

Her fresh mark in his skin had saved him from a fate worse than death. Had saved them *all*. And there was nothing missing between them in the lust department either. It was a good match. Hell, a great one, considering how fast this had all happened.

He kept telling himself that as he palpated Daegan's injured arm a bit more. Fracture didn't seem to be bothering him much, which was a good sign. He tested all the joints for range of motion, checked for swelling a few moments longer than necessary. Some edema at the elbow and wrist, around the finger joints, but that was to be expected.

"Spill it."

He met his cousin's forceful stare, blinked. "Spill what?"

"Don't insult my intelligence. I'm well out of the danger zone and halfway down the road to recovery, so how about you cut the bullshit? You're sitting here stalling while you figure out how to tell me what's bothering you."

Cade hid a grin. Daegan had always been able to read him. "Nothing. But I, uh, finally got those results from your DNA sample," he said to Liv. Was he stalling? Shit, yeah. With good reason.

"Oh." She sat forward in her chair, eyeing him curiously. "And?"

"You're definitely one of us. More closely related to Vaughn through your maternal lineage than Dae and me, though." When he looked over at her she shared a private grin with Daegan. "You don't seem surprised."

"I'm not. But thanks for telling me."

He nodded. At least he was useful for something else around here other than patching up his buddies' war wounds.

"Any new intel on the missing DA member?" Daegan asked.

"Nope. And no word on the OL, either."

Daegan shifted stiffly, his restricted movements a clear indication of his pain level and fatigue. He reached for Liv's hand, his body seeming to ease when she touched him. Exactly the way it was supposed to be between mates. "He's out there. Makes me insane not to know who or where he is though. But first we need to find that missing DA member. He'll know something."

"Yeah." He stood, rubbed the back of his neck. The growing sexual pull in the room between Daegan and Liv was beginning to wear on his nerves. It made him feel twitchy, restless.

That's because you want it too.

He almost snorted. The sex? That went without saying. It fuelled him. Eased him when nothing else could. But the mating and bonding? Not fucking likely. He wasn't exactly mate material. Not with his lifestyle and rough-edged…predilections.

"You make sure there's no remaining evidence of our location anywhere on the web?"

Daegan's words brought him out of his head. "I took the property listing offline and put in a false one the other day. Did another check and found nothing." Shit, he couldn't keep it from him any longer. "It's uh…it's our identities I'm starting to worry about."

Daegan's tired gaze sharpened. "Why, what's going on?"

How did he say this? He wouldn't bring something like this up while Daegan was recovering from amber poisoning and multiple gunshot wounds, but he had a gut-deep certainty this was important. "The woman who's been doing our recent DNA analysis. I feel like she knows too much." Only he didn't have solid proof.

"Meaning?"

"I dunno yet, but I'm looking into it. I'll get back to you once I talk to her." The idea of speaking to her filled him with trepidation. Something told him he wasn't going to like what she had to say. Not at all.

His cousin's black brows came together. "Sounds important."

Yeah, he was afraid it was. But it was after midnight in Lithuania, so the call would have to wait. He turned to Liv. "Make sure he gets more sleep."

"Will do." She rose from the chair to climb in next to Daegan, snuggled up into him. The smile they shared made him feel invisible, like he'd already left the room. And there was no doubt as to how she planned to tire Daegan out enough to send him off to dreamland.

It wasn't envy he felt, Cade told himself as he pulled the door shut behind him. Not at all.

DAEGAN WAS CURLED around her protectively when Liv woke next morning. Stretching in contentment, she savored the feel of his warmth and strength against her for a few minutes. When she got up she was careful not to wake him while she climbed out of bed. Drawing her robe around her, she studied the most serious wound in his shoulder. Cade had come back after dinner to remove the stitches, and the purple edges were slightly puckered. Hard to believe it would be all but invisible in another few days.

A sappy smile spread across her face while her gaze traversed the naked length of him. Just over two hundred years old. That was still so hard to comprehend. It made her shake her head to think of the things he must have seen over the centuries. The unimaginable changes he'd adapted to. He looked like he was in his mid-thirties, and his body was in incredible shape. The way he treated her, with such courtesy and respect on top of all that protectiveness and heat… She was so attached to him already she ached with it.

Wandering downstairs toward the kitchen to find them something to eat, she paused. Was she hearing things? It sounded like the scrambling of little feet, then a high-pitched whine coming from the other side of the closed pocket door. It wasn't usually kept closed.

Frowning, she hurried over. Another whine, then a soft scratching against the heavy wood. It sounded like—

Liv gasped when she pulled the door open. A medium-sized black dog crouched between her and the island. Its ears were flat against its head as it crept back from her. Those wide brown eyes were full of uncertainty, staring up at her. Wary. Watching her closely, ready to bolt if she made a wrong move. It pulled at her heartstrings.

Folding her robe around her legs, she crouched down and held one hand out, palm up. "What are you doing here?" she asked.

The dog's nostrils flared a few times, sniffing the air between them, then it lowered its head and meekly wagged its long tail.

"Come on, I won't hurt you." She edged a few inches closer, noticing a piece of paper attached to the tiny red bow on the dog's collar. A note? "It's okay, come on." Its fur looked so soft. She wanted to stroke it, reassure the animal.

The black ears went down. Then it shyly inched forward on its belly. God, had someone abused this beautiful dog? When Liv reached out farther, a wet pink tongue darted out to meekly lick her fingers while that silky tail swished across the hardwood floor.

"Oh, you gorgeous thing," Liv crooned, gently stroking the dog's head and chin. Just touching it made her throat clench. The urge to wrap her arms around it and hug it close was almost overwhelming.

After deciding she was safe enough, the dog crawled forward, almost into her lap. Liv bowed her head and wrapped her arms around its neck. The fur was just as soft as it looked, the dog's eagerly swishing tail making its whole body wriggle. With a laugh, she hugged it and plucked the note from the bow.

> *Her name is Ebony. The shelter didn't have any Labradors, but she's a Golden Retriever/Border Collie cross. Thought that would be okay.*
> *V*

The words made her throat tighten further. She couldn't believe that Vaughn—the hard, remote warrior—had done this for her. He still frightened her to some extent, but obviously there was much more to him than a cold-hearted assassin. Shame on her for believing otherwise.

She sat on the floor battling tears while she cuddled her new pet and received grateful, sloppy kisses in return. Ebony's fur was silky and warm, smelled clean when she buried her face against the dog's neck. Raising her head, she spotted the matching pink and white food and water dishes placed next to the island, the few dog toys scattered around the room, the sparkly pink leash sitting on the counter. Looked like Vaughn had thought of everything. The gifts touched her deeply, but their implication weighed heavy on her heart.

No one had to tell her that her old life was gone. Her place was with Daegan, so the mansion was her home now, from this day onward. She couldn't go back now. Ever. Not to her house or her career. Something as simple as leaving the property would put her at risk. Put them all at risk. Even now at least one threat existed somewhere outside the gates, sealed with some sort of spell. The remaining DA member still hunted them. But she couldn't live out the rest of her days holed up in this big house, lovely as it was.

The threat was reason enough to not bother Daegan with all of her troubles now. He had enough to worry about at the moment.

It was obvious Ebony wasn't a watch dog, but Liv thought she understood the purpose behind Vaughn's gift. Ebony was meant to remind her of a happy time in her childhood, to help ease the sudden transition into her new role. At least now she had something to keep her company when Daegan couldn't be with her. She wasn't sure how everything would affect the relationships she had with her friends, namely Catherine. Over the past two days Liv had texted her a couple times to say she was okay, but hadn't found the nerve to talk to her about everything yet.

She smiled at the dog. After being cooped up inside for the past few days, she craved a taste of the fresh sea air. "Want to go for a walk?"

Ebony's ears perked up, her head tilting in an adorable expression.

Liv laughed. "Come on, let's go."

The dog surged to her feet and pranced in place, tail wagging so hard it lifted the hem of Liv's robe. With the animal following at her heels, Liv pulled on a pair of boots then opened the front door. Ebony raced out ahead, running around her in excited circles as Liv walked across the cobblestone driveway, up the flagstone path that lead to the caretaker's house.

There was no real fear in her this time at the thought of facing Vaughn alone, just a few nerves. He wasn't the easiest person to have a conversation with, but she hoped he'd let her thank him properly for his thoughtful and unexpected gift. She knew he'd block whatever it was that made his aura so dangerous, to spare her any pain.

The house was dark inside, no lights on that she could see through the windows. Smoothing her hands down her robe, she knocked firmly on the door, waited. Ebony trotted over to sniff around the place, then came over to lean against her leg, gazing up at her with adoring brown eyes.

"You're killing me," Liv told her and knocked again. Was he still sleeping? She doubted it, and didn't think he'd avoid her. He might be antisocial, but he wasn't the sort of man who hid from anyone. Or anything.

Ebony sat staring at the door with her ears perked, as though she expected it to open at any moment. But after another minute when Liv didn't hear him coming to the door, she gave up. "C'mon," she said to the dog, bending to scratch her fluffy ears. "Back to the house."

In the kitchen she started the coffee and sliced some strawberries into bowls while the toast browned. She was just loading everything onto a tray to take upstairs when she heard someone coming. She caught his rich, spicy scent and smiled as warmth chased along her skin.

Daegan stepped into the kitchen, stopping short when he saw the dog. "Who's this?"

"Ebony. Vaughn gave her to me," she explained, handing Daegan the note. He looked great, considering he'd nearly died just a few nights ago.

His mouth quirked as he read the slip of paper. "Isn't he just full of surprises."

Stroking Ebony's head, she chewed at her bottom lip. "Is it all right? I mean, are you okay with a dog living here? She's super friendly." The words blurted out before she could stop them.

He raised a brow. "Why, you think I'd make you take her back?"

"So it's okay?"

His chuckle warmed her to her toes. "If she makes you happy, *mo ghrá*, then of course we'll keep her."

Her heart swelled at the love in his eyes. "Thank you." She bent to scratch Ebony's ear. "I think we're already attached to each other."

"I hadn't noticed," he said dryly.

Liv shook her head. "I can't believe he did this for me. I went to thank him, but he's not home. Think he'll be back soon?"

"Maybe."

His tone seemed doubtful. She cast him a funny look. "What does that mean?"

"Nothing. Just sometimes he goes away for awhile."

Now? It didn't seem like the right time for him to take off. With Daegan still recovering and the DA member on the loose, they needed all the manpower they could get. "Away where? Where else would he go?"

Daegan exhaled, coming over to draw her into his arms. His movements were almost normal, didn't seem to cause him any discomfort. While she loved the show of affection, his avoidance of the question alarmed her. "Is he all right?"

"As all right as Vaughn will ever be again." He stroked one hand over the length of her spine, pulled her tighter against him.

She raised her head. "What do you mean?"

Daegan smoothed a lock of hair away from her cheek with the side of his hand. "He just needs some time to himself."

"Why?"

"To visit his mate."

Her eyes widened. "He's mated?" She couldn't imagine him being mated to anyone, but if he was, how come he lived alone if mates couldn't stand to be apart?

"He was."

The words filled her with an awful sense of dread. "What happened?" But she was afraid she already knew the answer.

For a moment, Daegan only stared at her. When he finally responded, his eyes were shadowed with distant memories. "She was murdered back in World War Two."

CHAPTER NINETEEN

THE FAINT CRY of gulls followed Nairne as she moved deeper into the thin band of forest edging the village. Shadow and light played across the ground in changing patterns, the leaves overhead sighing and rustling in the evening breeze. Adjusting her grip on her camera, she approached her quarry, a two-hundred-year-old cemetery at the edge of the forest she'd spotted the day before during her walk.

When she cleared the trees, she saw the man standing there with his back to her. Nairne faltered. He was huge. His wide shoulders blocked the sunlight beating down on his black leather jacket as he stared down at the weathered grave marker. Something about his posture, the way he bowed his head, made her think he was no ordinary tourist. It almost looked like he was grieving.

Backing up a step, her foot landed on a twig. She drew up short, wincing at the quiet crack it made.

The man whipped his head around, his gaze freezing her. The breath caught in her throat. He was young, maybe in his early thirties, and terribly scarred down one side of his face and neck. But that wasn't what gave her pause. Just before he'd masked it, she'd seen an aching, terrible loneliness in his expression that twisted her heart.

She quickly broke eye contact and looked down, feeling awful for intruding on his privacy. He'd obviously come here to visit someone, but she didn't understand how that could be. He wasn't old enough to have known someone in here. The people buried in this woodland cemetery had died over a century ago. Unless they'd allowed someone to be buried here recently?

Nairne took another step backward, risked a quick glance up to see the man again.

He was gone.

Like he'd just disappeared into thin air.

She blinked.

Nairne looked left, right. Walked forward to get a better look around. No sign of him. When she approached the grave, there wasn't so much as a single track in the sandy soil, other than the two big footprints he'd left at the marker.

Jesus. That was impossible.

Nairne put a hand to her suddenly drumming heart, turned in a slow circle. She felt like she'd just seen a damn ghost. Had she? Granted, some odd and inexplicable things had happened to her over the years, but she'd never suffered a hallucination before. God, maybe she was going crazy. Maybe her obsessive research about the Empowered was making her see things that weren't really there.

After a moment, her curiosity got the better of her. She had to see for herself if there was anything on the marker.

Drawn toward it by some invisible force, she neared the old, silent grave. A warning tingle slid down her spine. The weathered gray wooden marker sat tilted in the soft ground. Like all the others here it bore no name, no date of birth or death. Just the carved bird at the top, marking the grave as a woman's.

But when she got close enough, she saw it.

Resting against its base lay an oval cameo brooch. Its rose quartz backing gleamed in the sunlight, making the intricately carved ivory woman's head and shoulders glow with an unearthly light. Beautiful. And obviously of great sentimental value. Had the man left it there?

Idiot. There was no man. You were imagining him.

Well she sure as hell wasn't imagining the large footprints in the soil, or the brooch. How did she explain that?

It looked like a vintage piece, maybe from the twenties or thirties. Her grandmother had owned something similar, had sometimes let Nairne pin it on to play dress-up when she'd gone to Edinburgh for a visit.

Taking a final glance around to make sure no one was watching, Nairne bent and tentatively picked up the delicate piece.

Instant fear crashed through her. Frantic and sharp. Horrific. Her lungs constricted as she felt the former owner's terror and despair. It twisted hard inside her, turning into pure, blind panic. So vivid she could almost see it, like an image on a movie screen.

They're going to kill me. Oh God, Vaughn, they're going to kill me.

Liv dropped it with a gasp and jerked back, shaking all over. Dear God. A dying woman, facing an end so hideous it had left an echo imprinted on the jewelry. She couldn't get that woman's panic out of her mind,

off her crawling skin. It had been so real, so fresh. Like
it had just happened.

She backed away from the grave, nearly stumbled
on a tree root in her haste to put some distance between
herself and the marker. Her arms were covered in goose
bumps despite the warm summer air. She wanted to
clap her hands over her ears, somehow block or better
yet, erase the memory of what she'd just felt. It reverberated through her while it faded away, but she knew
she'd never be free of it. Not entirely. That poor woman's death, her dying thoughts, would forever haunt her
now. She didn't know who Vaughn was, but she knew
he hadn't been able to save the woman.

The brooch lay on the sparse blades of grass pok-
ing up from the sand. Looking completely harmless.
Jesus, she wished she'd never picked the bloody thing
up. Why did she always let her curiosity get the better
of her? She'd pay for it this time.

Using a stick, she gingerly lifted the fragile piece
and put it back against the marker. Trying to shake off
the shivers skating down her spine, Nairne hurried back
the way she'd come, through the forest, up the slope
toward the paved road. Halfway to it her phone rang.
She checked the call display, frowned.

The number had a Vancouver area code, but it wasn't
her lab. Her phone rang for the third time and she almost let it go to voicemail, then a faint stirring of excitement made her change her mind. It could be Dr.
Mackintosh returning her call about the DNA results.

What he didn't know was that she had a lot of questions for him. Ones she'd bet he knew the answers to.
Right, then. Drawing a steadying breath, she an-

swered it. "Hello?" She waited a second to account for any delay in the line, but no one replied. Her frown turned into a scowl. Hell, if someone was trying to scare her, they'd picked a good time. That's all she needed right now—a prank call after what she'd just experienced in the cemetery.

"Hello?" She didn't bother to disguise her annoyance. "Bloody well say something or I'm hanging up."

Then a smooth, rich baritone voice came over the line. "Dr. Roberts? This is Cade Mackintosh."

CADE ALMOST STRANGLED on the words.

Holy shit.

His hand grew damp, his fingers clenching around his phone. He almost hadn't responded when she'd answered. Because he'd damn near swallowed his tongue.

Her voice. It did something to him. Deep inside him there'd been a leap of primal recognition. Which was insane. Worse, the moment her Scottish burr had registered in his brain he'd gone rock-hard in his jeans.

A first for him. He'd never gotten hard just at the sound of a woman's voice before.

It scared the living shit out of him.

"Dr. Mackintosh, hi. I've been expecting your call."

Well he sure as hell hadn't expected this reaction to her. He shoved aside the niggling worry, got down to business. "I received your report on the latest DNA samples I sent you. They were very thorough."

"Thank you. I trust it gave you what you needed?"

"Yes, thank you."

"The individual is from the same haplogroup as the others in your sample group. The lab ran the standard mitochondrial DNA sequencing, but I also ordered an SNP Backbone Panel—that means single nucleotide polymorphism—"

"I know what it means," he growled, pinching the bridge of his nose between his fingers. While he appreciated the woman's enthusiasm for her work, he wished she'd just get to the damn point so he could find out what he needed to know and end the conversation.

"Aye, well, the mutations I found revealed some fascinating evidence. All your individuals belong to haplogroup H, and more importantly, subclade H-one. That group originated in Egypt, spread out over the Caucasus then up to Eastern Europe, eventually settling there and further north. Including the Baltic region and even the UK."

His scalp prickled. Something in her tone sent off warning bells. An emphasis she'd placed on the last sentence. "I'm guessing that's an important detail for you."

"Aye, I've been working on a special project for several years, Doctor."

Special project. His free hand balled into a fist. Exactly what sort of project? Linking his subject's DNA to the haplogroup settling in the Baltics and UK was a pretty goddamn narrow field of interest.

Easy. It might be nothing.

His gut said otherwise. "And?"

"And I found it most interesting that this latest sample was so closely linked to several others I've analyzed in the past. Including yours."

Cade bit back a curse. He hadn't known she'd been the one to analyze his sample, and it seemed like she'd looked into his files. It wasn't illegal or unethical, but she must have had a reason for doing it. Now she seemed to know too much. Way too much for his peace of mind.

"And I also find it remarkable that you're so keen on researching the Baltic-Celtic connections, as I am. What's your interest in it?"

"Just a hobby." His ears began to ring.

"For me too. Well, people tell me it's more of an obsession," she said with a laugh. "Even your company's name—Trident Group—I assume it's in reference to Neringa's Trident? And the legend of the Empowered?"

Cade blanched. Actually felt the blood drain from his face. He swallowed once, leaning back in his chair for support while his pulse pounded dully in his ears. "What?" The word was guttural, almost strangled.

"The ancient Lithuanian legend of Neringa, the giantess born of the sea. Do you not know of it? I only recently found evidence linking the legend of the Empowered to her, with the mention of Neringa's Trident. Supposedly they're a triad of male Empowered warriors. According to prophecy, anyway."

Cade rose from his chair very slowly, fighting back the fear beginning to eat at him. Every muscle in his body was pulled tight, ready to snap. Her pleasant voice continued to float over the line, but he didn't hear a word she said. Holy fuck. No way should she know all this. How the hell could she know? Either she'd managed to somehow unearth the secrets they'd all thought were long since destroyed...

Or she was somehow linked to the Dark Army and the Obsidian Lord.

Either way, she was a threat to their very existence. *Scrub her. Scrub her* now.

"Are you still there?" The impatience in her voice was unmistakable.

"Yes," he managed. Gripping the edge of the desk, he called all his considerable mental concentration to bear. He'd scrubbed the memory of countless people over the decades, scores of them women over the phone. He projected the mental commands to her, focusing with all the force of his will.

Hang up. You've never heard of me or anything about the Empowered. This conversation never happened. You won't remember anything about it, or anything about the DNA samples I sent you. He'd worry about the possibility of her rediscovering everything in her research later.

He forced the thoughts into her brain, straining with all his might until sweat beaded his forehead and upper lip.

Hang up now and go back to your hotel. Fly back to Vancouver, go back to your lab and forget all about your research. Go home and start a new project.

It was a tall order, but he was confident the gist of it would register with her.

Hang up and go home.

An indelicate snort shattered his concentration. "Dr. Mackintosh, are you there or not?"

Cade jerked upright, blinking in surprise, his thoughts splintered like a pane of glass shattered by a rock. "I'm here."

"If this is the kind of awkward conversation you normally conduct, then I'd prefer not to speak with you over the phone from now on. I have work to do, and can't afford to waste my time filling in the gaps while you decide whether to answer me or not. If you want to contact me in the future, send me a bloody e-mail."

Click.

Cade jerked the phone from his ear, staring at it in a kind of detached horror. His efforts to scrub her hadn't worked. Not even a little. And now she was well and truly pissed at him. Might not answer again if he called to make another attempt at erasing her memory. He couldn't understand it. What the hell had gone wrong?

He ran an unsteady hand through his hair, trying to figure out what the fuck to do next. Was it possible it hadn't worked because she was too far away?

Because there was only one other reason he knew of why scrubbing her memory wouldn't work.

Dr. Roberts wasn't a mere mortal.

And if she wasn't a mortal, plus the way his body had reacted to the sound of her voice like that...

No. No fucking way.

Chilled to the bone at the implications of it all, he threw open his office door and tore up the stairs to find his cousin.

CHAPTER TWENTY

"I CAN'T BELIEVE how fast you're healing."

Daegan smiled at Liv as she passed him a mug of fresh, hot coffee, absently rubbing Ebony's ears. The mutt had her chin propped on his thigh, staring up at him in anticipation, as though she hoped he might accidentally drop a piece of his toast. It was obvious how much Vaughn's gift meant to his mate. That rare glimpse of thoughtfulness gave him hope they'd somehow be able to bring Vaughn back from the brink of destruction. "Fast healing's one of the perks of being our kind." God knew there were enough negatives that came with it.

A door slammed shut downstairs. Then running footsteps came up the steps. He glanced at the head of the stairs in mild interest at what the rush was about, but tensed when he saw Cade. The naked alarm on his cousin's face made Daegan come out of his chair so fast it crashed to the floor behind him.

"What?" Daegan demanded, reaching his good arm toward Liv. Cade's expression screamed threat, and he didn't want her facing another one.

Cade ran a hand over his mouth. "The DNA specialist knows too much. I tried to scrub her but it didn't work. Not even a little."

He didn't like the sound of that. "What do you mean, she knows too much?"

"She knows about our lineage, about the Empowered. She even found out about the goddamn prophecy."

"What?" He couldn't hide the alarm in his voice.

Liv moved closer, pressing against his side. She glanced between them uncertainly, but didn't interrupt.

Cade nodded. "She even figured out Trident Group is a reference to Neringa's Trident, and the three Empowered warriors mentioned in the prophecy."

Daegan's stomach clenched. "That's impossible."

Cade's hard stare said it wasn't.

"How could she know all that?" he demanded, pulling free of Liv. They had to find this woman, fast.

"She's a scientist. A geneticist. I guess she's good at research."

"No one's that good. She has to be getting help. Do a background search on her."

"I already did. Came up with less than zero. Not even a decent picture of her so I can tell what she looks like. All I know is, she's in Nida right now."

"Hell. Then get over there and scrub her in person."

Something flickered in Cade's eyes. A flash of dread, then it was gone, back behind the calm mask. "What if it doesn't work?"

"It'll work." It had to.

His cousin swallowed, his Adam's apple moving visibly. "No, I mean—what if it doesn't work because she's not...mortal?"

Daegan's jaw almost fell open. Holy shit. "Are you serious?"

"I don't know. I don't know what to think right now."

"Then get your ass on a plane and find her A-fuck-ing-SAP so we *do* know what's going on." This unknown threat might put them all at risk. She could be one of the Lost, or a DA member posing as a scientist. Who knew how far the Obsidian Lord's network stretched?

Cade shoved a hand through his mussed blond hair and nodded, but he didn't look happy about the order. "Okay. Okay, I'll get on the first flight out—"

"*Daegan.*"

He whipped around at Liv's sharp voice. She'd risen from her chair. Her fingers were pressed to her temples, her face drawn into lines of pain as she gazed past him at the kitchen door.

"Liv?" He reached out an arm toward her but she rushed past him to stare out the window set into the bronze door.

Her sharply indrawn breath was loud in the quiet room.

Cade was right behind him when he stalked over to join her. When Daegan put a hand on her shoulder she exhaled in relief, her pinched expression easing. He knew what the sudden headache meant, but he couldn't quite believe it. No one could've gotten into the compound. Not with the masking spell still holding.

Before he could ask her anything more, Liv unlocked the door and stepped outside. The yard was quiet. Empty, except for their cars parked under the porte-cochère.

"Liv, what—"

She stopped him with a brusque shake of her head,

staring up the long, curving driveway. "Someone's coming."

Daegan's nape prickled. Cade cursed under his breath, sharing a long look with him.

He needed a weapon. "I'll—"

"No. You stay with Liv," his cousin replied, then jogged off in the direction of the front gate.

Daegan grabbed her arm to tow her back inside while he got a gun, but she resisted his hold and pulled away.

"Look," she said shakily.

He turned his head in time to see Cade skid to a stop in the middle of the cobblestones. An instant later, Vaughn appeared in the center of the driveway, towing a man in front of him.

Liv gasped. Daegan immediately took her hand, relieved when her eyes cleared, the lines of pain disappearing from her face. "It's one of them," she said softly.

"One of whom?"

"The Dark Army."

He tensed. "Are you sure?"

She nodded, never taking her eyes off the man Vaughn held. He looked average enough. Clean-cut. Medium height, average build, dressed in jeans and a dark hoodie. But Liv seemed adamant. "His aura is red, edged in black. He's Dark Army."

Daegan swallowed the territorial growl trying to work its way up his throat and gripped her arm tightly. "Inside. Now."

"No," she said, squeezing his hand harder, resisting his pull. "I need to know."

He narrowed his eyes, making it clear he was not to be messed with. Opening his mouth to order her to stay put, he realized he couldn't leave her. She needed his touch to anchor her through the pain of the DA member's presence.

Shit. "Stay behind me."

He walked out to meet Vaughn partway. The Reaper frog-marched the struggling man toward them, but stopped when Daegan did. He didn't want Liv any closer to this asshole than necessary. And if the bastard so much as made a move in her direction, Daegan would kill him with his bare hands. Not that it would be necessary. Vaughn or Cade were closer and would take care of it before he ever reached the man.

"Found him wandering around outside the gates," Vaughn said with a lethal edge to his rough voice. "Perimeter's still solid. He never found a way through."

So their spell was still holding. "How did you find us?" he demanded in a cold, hard voice.

The DA member glared up at him out of his swelling right eye. "Screw you."

Liv edged closer to him and Daegan could sense her unease. He pulled her up tight against his back to reassure her, protect her. This piece of shit was no threat to her anymore. They'd make sure of that.

He clenched his hands into fists, staring the DA member down. *"How?"*

When he didn't answer Vaughn yanked up on his immobilized arms, sending him up on his toes with a muffled howl.

"The listing," he finally gritted out. "I found it in Rick's bags."

He looked at Cade. "Who's Rick?"

"The sniper. Found his ID in a duffel hidden on the property where Liv was taken."

"And this clown had this in his hand when I found him," Vaughn said, passing something to Cade.

Daegan took the photograph from his cousin, stared in disbelief at his WWII British Army picture. "What the hell?" He couldn't believe it. He'd been thorough at erasing all of his records. Anything that could be traced back to him or the others. On paper he barely existed, and only as a faceless businessman. Yet someone had found him anyway. He glared at Cade. "You knew they had our address and you didn't tell me about it?"

Cade looked uncomfortable. "We thought we should wait until you'd recovered more."

Bullshit. Fucking bullshit. Reining in his temper, he nodded to Cade. "Search him."

Cade moved forward to pat the DA member down while Vaughn maintained his hold. At last his cousin turned around, holding up an unfolded piece of paper. "It's the listing."

Daegan set his jaw. He didn't want Liv hearing or seeing any of this, but what choice did he have? "Who else had access to this?" he said coldly.

No answer, until another hard jolt from Vaughn ripped a cry of rage and pain out of the prisoner. "I dunno! Me and the others, I guess."

He *guessed.* "How many?" A demand, not a question.

He twisted and strained in Vaughn's grip. "You're gonna break my fucking arm!"

"He'll do worse than that if you don't tell me what I need to know."

"The four of us and Rick," he panted, his face glistening with sweat.

Five of them. They'd killed four the night Liv was taken, so if he was telling the truth this asshole was the last of them. "Who recruited you?"

He stilled. His lips curled in a bitter sneer. "*Recruited*?" His eerie laugh sent chills down Daegan's spine. "The Obsidian Lord doesn't recruit. He fucking *owns* us."

Yeah, he was well aware how it worked. An invisible hand squeezed his stomach. "Who is he?"

"Xavier. His name's Xavier. That's all I know. C'mon man, ease up."

"Where is he?" Daegan pressed.

"Was in Spain." He twisted again, fighting against the hands wrenching his arms behind him, but soon stopped with a muffled groan of discomfort. "Gone now."

"Gone where?" His patience was running thin. In another second he'd tear the asshole from Vaughn and dole out some physical punishment of his own. He wanted to. His muscles trembled with the need, despite the lingering ache in his wounded arm. The only thing that held him in check was Liv's weight pressed up against his back. He had to stay calm, shield her.

"Lithuania," the man muttered.

Oh shit. He looked at Cade. His cousin's face drained of color. Seemed they had one more reason to be concerned about the geneticist. "Why is he going there?"

"I dunno—to see someone named Vasilli. That's all I know!"

Daegan had a bad feeling that Doctor Roberts was somehow connected to all this.

The DA member kicked out at Vaughn. "I've told you everything I know. If you're gonna kill me do it now, or fucking let go and take me on like a man," he spat.

Liv suddenly shifted away from Daegan, stepped up to his side without releasing his hand. He glanced down at her, assessing her expression as he stroked his thumb over her fingers in silent comfort. This had to be hard on her. Hearing all of it probably scared her to death but she refused to show it. Her quiet strength amazed him. He loved that she had chosen to stand by his side through this. She seemed to be studying the man, but for what he couldn't be sure. "What do you see?" he asked her softly.

"Rage. Bitterness. He wants to kill us all." Her voice was calm, firm, without a trace of fear.

"Vaughn?" he asked.

The Reaper nodded. "She's right."

"Can you turn him?"

"No," Liv said quickly. "His aura's too dark. He's too far gone, he'll never change."

Daegan glanced at Vaughn, who nodded in assent. *So be it*, he thought with a sigh. "Wait until I've got her back in the house."

But Liv surprised him again by holding her ground. "No, you don't need to shield me from this. I've already seen it once."

"I don't want you seeing it again. You've been

through enough." More than enough. He wished he could erase her memory of all the ugliness she'd seen since coming into his life.

Her gaze strayed back to the DA member hanging in Vaughn's unbreakable grip. "I need to see it so I know for sure it's over."

Fuck. The last thing he wanted was for her to have to witness any more violence and death, but if it would give her comfort he couldn't refuse. "Are you sure? You don't have to prove yourself to any of us."

She gave a firm nod. "That's not why. And I'm sure." He thought he caught a flare of vengeance in her eyes, and he understood completely. This bastard was one of the men who'd held her prisoner, had been about to torture her. And worse if she hadn't managed to escape.

If he couldn't be turned he deserved to die, just as Liv deserved the chance to see it happen if she chose. Closure. It was the least he could give her.

At his signal, Vaughn let go of the man and stepped in front of him before he could even attempt to run. The man's head snapped back in surprise as he met Vaughn's deadly stare. He held it without blinking for a few moments, as though mesmerized, and Daegan knew the Reaper was giving him one last chance to repent. But that must have been an exercise in futility because Vaughn at last raised his right hand, touching the side of the victim's neck.

A quick flash of blue, like an electrical impulse, and the man dropped to the ground. His mouth was open, eyes wide as he attempted to grab his chest, right over his stopped heart. Another second and it was over.

Daegan pushed down the rage building within him,

nodded to Vaughn. "Take care of the body." A sick feeling took root. This entire incident with the new group of DA members was only the start of it, and he was powerless to stop what was coming. The best he could do was protect his mate and his Brethren, and hope the hell he had what it took to be worthy of the title Coven Leader in the battle ahead.

Beside him, Liv took a deep breath, let it out slowly. A frown pulled at her forehead as she stared at the body. Enough. He turned her away from the sight, pulling her into a tight hug. Tucking her head under his chin, he ignored the flare of pain in his left arm and shoulder. Behind him he could hear Cade and Vaughn walking toward the vehicles. Getting ready to drive out and dispose of the body.

"It doesn't seem fair, does it?" she murmured as she burrowed closer.

"What doesn't?" He eased his right hand beneath the soft tumble of honey and caramel waves to find her nape, squeezing gently, hoping to take away the tension there. Soothe her.

She tilted her head back, stared up at him with tormented hazel eyes. "The way he died. So fast. No suffering after all he's done." She shook her head. "Does that make me as evil too?"

"No." He could all but smell the guilt coming off her as he kissed her gently, sliding an arm around her shoulders to guide her back to the house. "But you know we couldn't let him go."

"I know. When you asked Vaughn if he could turn him…he did that with Aaron, didn't he?"

"Yes."

She nodded, reached down to pet Ebony's ears when the dog came running over to lean against her. "It's just the start, isn't it?"

The burden he carried weighed heavy on his shoulders, but he wouldn't lie to her. "Yes."

She drew a deep breath while she stroked the dog's head. "And I'm the weak link right now."

"You're not weak." He didn't ever want her thinking that. "You're stronger than any woman I've ever known, and you have no idea how proud I am of you."

A small smile curved her lips, but when she lifted her chin he saw the blaze of determination in her eyes. "But I'm going to be even stronger. I want to learn how to defend myself. And I want to learn how to handle a gun."

He'd already planned on teaching her all that, but it made his life easier if she was already on board. "I'll teach you everything you need to know."

Those big eyes met his again. "We're in this together now."

"Yeah, we are." Though he wished like hell he could shield her from this as easily as he could take away the headaches brought on by her gift. "I'm so sorry, Liv."

She shook her head. "Don't be sorry. None of this is your fault. Besides, I got you out of the deal, so that more than makes up for all the scary stuff."

Her inner strength amazed him. If he spent the rest of his life earning the right to be worthy of her, he could die in peace. He ran the pad of his thumb across her soft lower lip. "I'll do whatever it takes to protect you, Liv. I want to make you happy."

With a sad smile she reached up to cup his cheek in one slender hand. "Will you do something for me?"

He turned his head to kiss her palm. "Anything, *mo ghrá.*"

"Take me upstairs and make me forget about all this for a while."

Daegan closed his eyes and pulled her into his arms, so grateful for her that he feared his heart might burst. "I'd love to."

CADE COULDN'T SLOW his heart rate down as he pulled his phone out of his pocket and sat down at his computer. Daegan and Liv were upstairs. The perimeter was secure. Vaughn had already put the DA member's body in the trunk of his Mustang and driven out to dispose of it where it wouldn't arouse any suspicion or lead the authorities to the mansion. But that asshole's words about the Obsidian Lord kept ringing in his head.

He was out there right now, on his way to Lithuania to see someone named Vasilli. The anxiety scraped at his insides until he could barely stand it.

Either Dr. Roberts was the greatest threat to their existence since WWII, or she was in a shitload of trouble and didn't even realize it. Both possibilities had his stomach in knots, but that's not what made his hand shake as he hit the redial button and called her.

What if she was one of them? What if she was—

"You've reached Dr. Nairne Roberts," her voice said on the pre-recorded message. "Please leave a message and I'll get back to you as soon as I can. Have a nice day."

Not so much, sweetheart.

The beep that followed seemed overly loud to his roaring ears. It was only early evening over there and he'd talked to her not half an hour ago. She'd obviously meant what she'd said about communicating solely via e-mail from now on.

But Christ, so much had happened since that phone call. He had to speak with her.

"This is Cade Mackintosh again. Listen, something important has suddenly come up, and I'm heading to Lithuania tonight. I should be in Nida by tomorrow evening your time and if you're willing, I have some new research to show you. Maybe we can meet for dinner." She might not be happy with his phone etiquette, but he was willing to bet she wouldn't pass up the opportunity to find out what sort of research he had. "Call or e-mail me and I'll get in touch with you when I arrive."

His voice had sounded normal enough, he decided as he hung up. No sign of the strain inside him that made his skin clammy. He didn't really want to go there to meet her face to face. But he had no choice.

The tension inside him continued to build. A growing dread at what was coming. A knowledge that he was on a collision course with disaster but couldn't do a damn thing to stop it.

His gaze strayed to his keys, lying on the edge of the desk. He had to get out for a while. There was no immediate threat to any of them here; the mansion was safe. If he didn't leave he'd lose it completely. It was only ten in the morning, but he could still find what he needed.

Addict.

The increasingly familiar voice in his head sneered the word in derision.

"I'm not an *addict*," he snarled under his breath. Addicts were weak. He wasn't. He could stop if he wanted to. But he didn't. Because this was the only thing that worked. God knew he'd tried everything else over the centuries, but this one thing eased him. In deep and inexplicable ways nothing else ever had or could. And besides, it was always consensual. He made good and sure his partners more than enjoyed their time with him. Otherwise, what would be the point? The control he held over them, the helpless pleasure on their faces were what helped him. Then he scrubbed them and walked away.

Before that censuring inner voice could say anything else to make him hesitate, he snatched up the keys and headed for his truck.

CHAPTER TWENTY-ONE

THE SOFT GLOW of the sunset streaming through the tall master bedroom windows bathed Daegan's face as he bent to kiss her lips tenderly. Liv sighed and shifted beneath him, smoothed her hands down the length of his back.

"How's your arm?" she asked drowsily.

"What arm?" he whispered, still buried deep inside her. His eyes held that sated, slightly sleepy look she was coming to love.

With a smile she pulled him down to rest fully against her, glorying in his weight and the feel of him pressed along the length of her body. When he gently disengaged from her embrace she made a sound of protest, but he rolled them over to cradle her against his chest. She laid her cheek over the pad of his pec, listening to the strong, steady beat of his heart.

"You okay?" he asked, playing with a lock of her hair.

"Yeah." All things considered, she felt rather peaceful. Odd, when she took into account all that had happened and what might await them outside the main gate. "I wish we could just hole up in here forever."

Daegan kissed the top of her head but didn't reply.

She raised up on an elbow. "Do you think the woman in Lithuania is a danger to us?"

"We won't know until Cade meets with her."

It bothered her that he was making the trip alone. "Shouldn't Vaughn go with him?"

"He'll be fine. Believe me, despite his movie star looks he's more than capable of protecting himself. He's done almost as much time in the military as I have. And if he needs backup, Vaughn can be there in a matter of seconds."

Right. He could just poof his way there. How amazing was that? The next words were difficult for her, but they needed to be said. "You should go with him."

Daegan arched a brow in surprise.

"I'm serious. I can handle being here on my own if you need to go. I don't want to hold you back from what needs to be done, and I have to adjust to staying here by myself anyhow."

A strong finger beneath her chin titled her head up until she met his crystalline eyes. "I'm not leaving you here alone. And this isn't a prison, Liv, it's your home. You can still come and go as long as you have one of us with you. We just have to be careful, that's all."

His words surprised her. "You mean I can still go to my place? All my stuff is there." Including her grandparents' piano, the one possession she truly held dear.

"Sure. I can take you over now if you want."

Only because the immediate threat was over for the moment."Are you up to that?"

"You'd be surprised what I'm up for," he murmured, pressing his hips against her.

She smothered a laugh when she felt his hardening erection against her belly. "You're insatiable."

"For you? Hell, yes." He kissed her once, gently,

before rolling over and climbing out of bed. "Come on, let's go. I'm sure Ebony would love a ride in your Beemer."

"It's fixed already?"

"Cade took care of it while you were spoiling me with tender loving care."

Why was she not surprised? "She can't go in the Porsche?" she asked, tongue in cheek.

He snorted. "Not in this lifetime."

"Fine, we'll take my car. But I need to make a call first."

"To who?" His tone wasn't suspicious, just curious.

"My best friend, Catherine. I won't tell her everything, but I need to at least tell her about you. I'll keep the parts about the magic to myself, though."

"Of course. Go ahead."

Sitting on the edge of the bed, she retrieved her phone and dialed. "Hey, it's me," she said when Catherine answered.

"Hi, are you okay?"

Liv's eyes misted over at the worry in her friend's voice. "Yeah, I'm fine. Listen, I've got so much to tell you and I don't know where to start."

A cautious pause. "Okay. Give it to me from the top."

She exhaled. "Remember the man I told you about the other day?"

"Oh my God, the sexy one? Did he buy the house and then you hooked up? Is that why you've been too busy to talk to me?"

"He bought the house," Liv answered with a laugh, "and we're um, together now."

A shocked silence met her words. "This is so unlike you."

"I know. But he's the one for me." She smiled at Daegan.

"Wait, you mean *the* one? Honey, I don't want to put a damper on things, but you've only known him a few days."

"Everything's happened really fast, I admit, but I know this is the real thing."

Catherine paused, blew out a long breath. "Well when do I get to meet this rich, sexy man of yours?"

Liv held the phone to her chest, looked at Daegan. "She wants to meet you."

An amused smile curved his lips. "Does she? Tell her we'll set something up for tomorrow night."

Her eyes widened. "That soon?"

He nodded, gestured for her to carry on with the conversation.

Liv swallowed a laugh, put the phone back to her ear. "How does tomorrow night work?"

"Works just fine. I can't wait to meet him. What's his name?"

"Daegan. You're going to grill him for me, aren't you?"

"Bet your ass I will."

Livchuckled, feeling like a weight had been lifted from her shoulders."I'll call you tomorrow, hon." She paused, swallowed the lump in her throat. "Love you."

"Back atcha, babe. And if Daegan winds up breaking your heart, I'll kill him for you and dispose of the body for free. No payment of wine necessary."

"I love knowing you always have my back," Liv answered with a laugh. Ten minutes later, Daegan drove while Ebony sat in the backseat with her chin resting on Liv's shoulder, her muzzle stuck partway out the open window. It made Liv smile, but she couldn't forget the gravity of leaving the mansion's grounds. The black pistol she'd seen Daegan tuck into his waistband was yet another reminder of the constant threat of danger they all faced.

All four of them, she thought with a sinking feeling.

At her house, Liv let the dog in then disarmed the alarm system before heading to her bedroom. Daegan's scent still remained there, faint but unmistakable. She gazed at the bed where they'd first made love, a flare of heat rippling through her abdomen, between her thighs.

As though he sensed her thoughts, Daegan stepped up close behind her to wrap his arms around her waist. She sighed at the feel of him, at the knowledge that she'd have him in her corner for the rest of her life. Her life that would hopefully last for another few centuries.

"We can keep the house if you want," he whispered against her bonding mark. A quick shiver rolled through her when his lips brushed her skin.

"What for?"

"We could rent it out, or work out something so you can still teach piano lessons if you wanted."

She turned her head to look up into his eyes. "Really?"

"Really. I'll figure something out. But working in real estate…"

"I know. I already realized I'll have to quit." That wasn't what bothered her. The job had been satisfying, but it wasn't necessary to her happiness. Like the house, she wasn't attached to either of those things. It was the loss of control and independence that sucked. Still being able to teach music would help ease that, though she wasn't sure it would be enough to fulfill her in the years ahead.

Daegan tightened his arms. "You know, the whole reason I contacted you about the property listing was because you came so highly recommended. Your boss couldn't say enough good things about your work. I could use a hand with running Trident Group and all its investments."

That piqued her interest. "Doing what?"

"Bookkeeping, accounting, management. Keeping me from drowning in paperwork. Whatever you want to help with. You interested?"

"Very." A smile spread across her lips. "I'd like that very much."

He kissed the mark on her neck, soft and slow, distracting her with a flood of sexual need. "Want a hand packing your things?"

She pulled free of his embrace before she lost her head and tore his clothes off. They were vulnerable here, and she couldn't forget that. "No, I can do it. Go relax on the couch and I'll be done shortly." Feeling immensely better about her situation, she went to her closet and packed all her suitcases full.

When she came out of the bedroom she found Daegan standing next to the piano, Ebony lying at his feet. His slow smile when he met her gaze was so beautiful it made her ache.

"Play for me. I've never heard you."

He seemed so sincere, so interested that she couldn't

deny him that small request. Liv skirted the cherry wood bench and sat, then lifted the cover to reveal the keys. Her fingers settled over their cool surfaces, stroking lovingly while she chose a piece of music. She began it slowly, caressing the ivory keys as the music flowed from somewhere deep inside her. Another old Gaelic love song.

The haunting melody filled the air and she was surprised when she realized Daegan was humming along. His strong hands settled lightly on his shoulders as she played. Sharing his warmth. His solid presence. Linking them irrevocably.

When the last notes drifted off into silence, she swiveled on the bench, smiled up at him. "Why am I not surprised you know that piece?"

That sexy smile was as mysterious as the man himself. "I've heard it sung a time or two in the pubs back home." He bent, kissed her softly on the mouth. "I'll have the piano brought over to the house as soon as possible."

"Thank you." It meant a lot to her. She stood and wrapped her arms around his back, marveling at the transformation in her life in just a few short days. "I never thought I'd have a man like you for my own."

"You mean one with ancient magical powers plus incredible stamina and skill in bed?"

"No," she said with a laugh. "Loving. Strong and brave. Protective. So damn sexy I keep wanting to pinch myself."

His delighted chuckle warmed her to her toes. "I never thought I'd find you either. I spent more than two centuries alone. You're like a miracle to me, Liv."

The words filled her with joy.

His lips nuzzled her temple, his murmur soft as a breath. "Think you'd want to marry me someday?"

She glanced up at him, startled. "I thought…I thought the bonding thing made it kind of irrelevant."

"No, not if it's important to you."

For a moment she wasn't sure how to answer. "But what about keeping a low profile? There'd be all kinds of people there you'd have to scrub afterward, not to mention a paper trail."

"We could keep it low-key. Just us, Vaughn and Cade, maybe a close friend or two of yours and a justice of the peace."

She could see it. Could see them standing under the arbor in the rose garden while the sun set over the ocean in the background. Not yet, though. The few friends she had would have heart attacks. Especially Catherine. As it was she didn't know how she was going to explain the mark on her neck. "I think I would."

Relief flickered in his eyes. It stunned her. How could he not know how much she loved him? "Then we will. When we're ready."

"I'm falling hard for you," she told him, wanting him to see the sincerity in her eyes. In her heart. "I know things aren't always going to be easy and part of me is still scared to death, but no matter what happens I'll *never* regret being your mate. Showing you that house was the best thing that ever happened to me."

Daegan made a low sound and gathered her tight up against his chest. "For me, too, *mo ghrá*. You ready to go home now?"

Liv gently pulled out of his embrace to look around

her house. Her tastefully decorated bedroom. The cozy family room she'd filled with carefully chosen furniture. The tidy patio outside the French doors that led from the brightly lit kitchen. Her favorite room in the house. This had been her haven, her sanctuary for more than four years, but it didn't feel like home anymore.

Now home was wherever Daegan was.

Linking her fingers through his, Liv smiled up at him and gave a firm nod. "I'm ready."

* * * * *